Bigtime

Marc Blake

flame

FLAME
Hodder & Stoughton

First published in Great Britain in 1999
by Hodder and Stoughton
First published in paperback in 2000
by Hodder and Stoughton
A division of Hodder Headline

A Flame Paperback

10 9 8

A CIP catalogue record for this title is available
from the British Library.

ISBN 0 340 71774 2

Printed and bound in Great Britain by
Mackays of Chatham PLC, Chatham, Kent

Hodder and Stoughton
A division of Hodder Headline
338 Euston Road
London NW1 3BH

For Paul

ACKNOWLEDGEMENTS

Firstly, a million thanks to Claire.

Then: Carolyn, Jon and Alexandra at Hodder. Chubbs. Pete Graham and Huw Thomas, all at the Banana and any other venues where I had the opportunity of being 'King for the night.' Malcolm Hay, Jasmine, Milly ('*Evil Norman*' lives), WPC Sarah Masters, Rod and Clare, Tony Thompson (whose book 'Gangland Britain' is a great primer on Yardies, Asian gangs and guns), Ben Ward and Zed.

AUTHOR'S NOTE

Since this book was written, Corley services has under-gone a thorough re-fit although the Carmody module remains in place. The use and abuse of pheromones and/or steroids is not recommended to children of any age, nor is the performance of stand-up comedy.

'Nothing in the world can take the place of perseverance. Talent will not; nothing in the world is more common than men with talent. Genius will not; unrewarded genius is almost a proverb. Education will not: the world is full of educated derelicts. Perseverance and determination alone are omnipotent. The slogan "press on" has solved and always will solve the problems of the human race.'

Calvin Coolidge

'Never trust a book that starts with a quotation.'

Marc Blake

CHAPTER ONE

Rescue, Recovery, Wreck

———◆———

Andy Crowe pulled to a halt beside the North Circular Road. Steam was billowing from the heating vents and a pool of viscous liquid had oozed out into the footwells. He swatted on the hazard lights, killed the ignition and rolled down the windows. The vapour funnelled away and the temperature inside the car plummeted to that of a Siberian summer. Zipping up his leather jacket, he tugged the door open. The vacuum from passing lorries almost tore it from his hand.

Hoisting up the bonnet of the elderly Polo, he glared at the engine like a schoolteacher entering a rowdy classroom. The greasy components sat smug and silent in their casings, daring him to tamper with them. The only thing he knew about mechanics was how to unsheathe the dipstick. He did so and a nasal drip of oil fell on to the engine block. Replacing it, he noted that the opaque orb which usually contained the coolant was empty.

That's not a good sign, he thought.

It was barely noon and the spitting sky was the colour of an Etch-A-Sketch. Across the busy carriageway were a Chinese supermarket and the Universe of Leather. In the knowledge that his vehicle consisted of no components made of noodle or hide, he decided to look elsewhere for help. In front of him, the road rose to Hanger Lane and the risibly named gyratory system. Stuffing his hands into his pockets, he strode off towards it.

Andy had been up for three hours, something of a major feat for a stand-up comedian. Not that it was intentional: he had woken when the front door slammed and, on thrusting out an arm to find carpet instead of duvet, he'd guessed that there was a problem.

It was then he remembered he was on the sofa bed in the living room.

And something else.

Michelle had dumped him.

Well, not technically dumped – but after intense negotiations she'd demanded a trial separation, which was the same thing.

His first task that morning had been to chain three Marlboro Lites in quick succession while he formulated a way of winning her back. The plan was unoriginal but had the benefit of getting him out of the flat. He would purchase a conciliatory present, then phone her at work to arrange lunch. He went to the florist's in the high street where the surly teenage assistant showed him a number of laminated pictures of flowers in woven baskets. He felt his interest wane. This was like Michelle asking him to choose a cushion.

'What I really want,' he said, 'is something that symbolises love and respect for my partner . . . along with a measure of guilt and resentment.'

She pointed to the thirty-six-pound bouquet.

Back in the flat, he found that Michelle wasn't taking his calls. Apparently, like the entire population of London, she was 'in a meeting'. He tried again several times but her PA had the fielding skills of a West Indian cricketer. Refusing to be discouraged, he decided to drive into town to confront her in her office. After an hour spent teasing his quasi-scrapheap into life, he nosed the vehicle on to the A406.

Five minutes later he was marooned under the bruised February sky.

'Can you describe the fault, please?'

He had located a phone box with a dial tone and enough glass in it to deflect the noise of the traffic and wind. 'It's bleeding to death.'

'Could you be more specific?'

'That would be why I'm calling you.'

The incident manager, who had clearly come top in a one-day training seminar for public speaking in a patronising tone, fired more questions and then assured him that the breakdown service would be 'on-scene' within an hour.

'Are you sure that's an hour?' Andy queried. 'Not a railway hour? Or a pizza half-hour, which is a movable feast – or rather it isn't.'

A long, uncomprehending pause.

'Hello?'

'We're very busy at the moment, sir. Just call us back if there's any problem.'

He hung up and returned to his injured vehicle, thinking of how he hated technology and telephones and of the many hassles they caused him. Case in point – the call at seven the previous evening that had precipitated the bust-up with Michelle.

'Andy?' The voice was marinated in whisky with a gravel chaser.

He fumbled with the tagliatelle of flex by the answering machine.

'Yup.'

'It's the Agency.'

He almost dropped the phone. Despite never having had any direct dealings with them, the Agency ruled Andy's life. What was this? A friendly call to assure him that they'd be ignoring him for *another* three years? He had become convinced of late that when he began his career in comedy he had unknowingly ticked the box marked 'No Publicity'.

'Wanna do Birmin'ham tomorrow night?'

He agreed nonchalantly as he skipped round, gleefully punching the air.

Andy had always hoped they were studying his progress. He and his colleagues spoke of the Agency in reverential tones, knowing that if a blessing were bestowed then success would surely follow. Initiates were like deflowered virgins, half bashful at first but soon boasting of their exploits with a new-found confidence. As soon as they were accepted into the fold, they became like concubines to these mysterious men in big suits and small offices. They were pampered and showered with trinkets: the warm-up work, the TV game-show guest slots and the criminally underpaid radio series. Andy wanted it: they all wanted it. And when one of them got it, there was an abundance of fresh envy, bitterness and bitchery to fill their absence on the comedy circuit.

Only a handful of comics dared to criticise the Agency; warning of the strip mining of talent, hidden financial responsibilities and contracts so inescapable that even Houdini would have tutted and stormed off in a huff. These views were discredited, and anyone allying themselves with the dissidents achieved refugee status quicker than a Bosnian in a blanket.

Andy reckoned his chances of becoming one of the Agency's golden boys to be slim. To gain entry there were no required qualifications, no interview board and no need to pump your CV with imaginary sporting prowess: it was simply understood that when your time came, you would be called. He never had been – until now.

'One-fifty on the night. You driving?'

'I'll be wrestling my car, yeah.'

'Gillen's going up with you. He's got the details. You can give him a lift.'

'I, er . . . haven't got his number,' Andy said, warily.

The voice was replaced by the sound of a keyboard being pummelled into submission. Andy flashed on images of fame: the adoring crowds; Gag-hags; his own Channel 4 series; appearing with balding chat-show hosts; forcing a corkscrew into the eye of balding chat-show hosts. The baritone returned, read out a mobile number and rang off. Andy scrawled it on a bit of paper and hurried into the front room.

Michelle was spread out on the sofa in her trakky bottoms and an old charity T-shirt. She was watching telly.

'Guess who phoned?'

'Your parents? No, you wouldn't be smiling.'

'The Agency.'

'Really?'

'Really.'

'That's brilliant.'

She sprang to her feet and hugged him. He slipped a hand round her waist to the small of her back and threaded the other through her short black hair. They kissed hard until their teeth bumped together. She pulled away, planting a final peck on his cheek.

'So what did they want?'

'It's an out-of-towner. With Rob Gillen.'

'You hate Rob Gillen.'

'Yeah, well . . .'

'But you're always going on about him.'

'It's a hundred and fifty quid,' he offered.

She paused for a moment. 'Would you pretend to like my dad for a hundred and fifty quid?'

'Come on. I haven't seen Rob in a year. Maybe he's changed.'

She hooked her thumbs over the elasticated waistband of her track suit. 'I remember you saying he was cruel to audiences and bitchy about the other acts.'

'If you're going to quote me, can you do the funny stuff?'

She failed to suppress the smile. 'I hope this makes the difference, Andy.'

'It will.'

He fished out a cigarette while she hunted for the remote amidst a pile of magazines on the packing crate that they used for a coffee table. Perching on the arm of the sofa, she jabbed a button and turned the screen into a static crackle.

'So when's the gig?'

'Tomorrow night.'

Her eyebrows jostled towards a frown.

Andy scanned for reasons until he got there. The card was on his desk.

'I hadn't forgotten.'

'Can't you call back and reschedule?'

He held up his palms.

'Never mind,' she said, brightening. 'We'll go out on Saturday night.'

He winced. 'I've got a gig Saturday.'

'Friday, then.'

'And Friday.'

'Where?'

'The Crypt.'

Now there was an edge. 'That's an absolute shithole and you're on a door split. You won't get more than a tenner.' Nothing from him. 'Oh, come on, Andy. You can blow that one out.'

6

He went to the kitchen to get a beer, but by the time he had returned she had stormed off to the bedroom.

'Sod it,' he said, sucking on the can. 'Bloody Valentine's Day.'

He went over to his desk, on which was balanced the computer he'd bought second-hand from a shop in Notting Hill. Tilting it, he slid the envelope out from under the hard drive. It's not that I don't love her, he thought. Just that Valentine's is only any good when you're sixteen. Mentally halving his age, he remembered an anonymous card that had been put in his locker at school. Unfortunately, the billet-doux turned out not to be from Samantha Turner (who at that time he loved more than anything else in the world except Debbie Harry) but from her mate Bev. Big Bev. This became apparent at the disco that weekend when she jumped him for a snog and he came away looking like Mick Jagger pressed up against a pane of glass.

He went through to the bedroom. Michelle was lying on the bed pretending to read. He dropped the card in front of her.

'Miche, I'll make it up to you.'

She flipped over the paperback. 'Andy, this isn't about Valentine's.'

'It isn't? But last year . . .' He paused, recalling a long evening when he had failed to find a restaurant not stuffed to the gills with doe-eyed simpletons. They had ended up at the local Indian and there were tears before biriyani.

'No, this is about you dropping one shitty little gig so we can go out together.'

'Well, I can't *not* do tomorrow night . . .'

'Friday, then.'

Andy adhered to the long-held and immutable showbiz principle that you never cancelled a show as someone else might get the work. 'Let's go out next week,' he suggested.

'When next week?'

They volleyed dates until she had her arms folded and was glowering at him.

'Don't you realise how *important* tomorrow night is?'

That got a nod.

'Then why are you being like this?'

'I'm not being "like this".'

'You are.'

'I'm not.'

They knocked this semantic ball of tension back and forth until he was pumping cracks in his empty beer can. They fell to silence. When she spoke again there was flint in her voice.

'You know I support you, Andy. I was a performer too, remember?'

He snorted. 'But you're Mrs Media now, aren't you?'

'It was lucky I met Charlotte, that's all.'

'*Lucky?*'

Michelle had met her while she was temping. Charlotte was her old boss at the advertising company and had for a long time been thinking of going solo and starting up a castings agency. When she did so, she took Michelle along with her as a business partner. Pay was non-existent at first, but their combined flair ensured that they had broken even in a little over eighteen months.

Andy beefed up the sarcasm. 'Lucky! That's what they all say . . . I was *lucky*. I just fell into it. Where are these sodding careers? Lying about in the street like open manholes? Whoops! You want me to become a TV producer on thirty grand a year? Oh, what a surprise . . . Isn't it ever *hard* for anybody?'

'No. Just you.'

'That's not fair.'

'Well, you ask for it sometimes. There's no monopoly on the tears-of-a-clown stuff.'

'There isn't? I thought I had a hotel on it.'

She pounded a fist into the duvet. 'Sod it, Andy. I love you and I hate seeing you go through all this crap. I just want you to get some distance, sort out your head now, before—'

'Before what?'

'Look, from what I've seen it only gets worse once you do succeed.'

He raised a superior finger. 'Aha. So you acknowledge that I *will* be famous.'

'Stop fishing.'

His lips formed a smile. She couldn't prevent herself from returning it.

'Come on. Gimme a hug.'

She held out her arms and he snuggled up to her on the bed. He sharked up to nibble at her earlobe and ran a hand over her thigh towards her crotch.

'The thing is,' he said to her neck, 'word's got through at last. This could be the end of three years of sod-all money and telling jokes in crappy pubs.'

'Where's this gig, then?'

'Birmingham.'

'That's not what I'm asking.'

A pause.

'OK, so it's probably another crappy pub – but it'll be a big one.' He rotated his fingers between her thighs. 'We could have sex and go out tonight.'

'I'm not exactly in the mood.'

'For sex or for going out?'

'Let's make a thing of it for Friday.'

'But—'

'You're not still going to do it, are you? It pays sod-all and it's bound to be cancelled anyway.'

'Tell you what. If I storm tomorrow night then I'll blow it out.'

She pulled away and swung her legs off the bed. 'Think about what you're saying. If a couple of hundred drunken blokes decide *not* to throw bottles at you, then you'll deign to go out with me.'

'*Deign*? You never say "deign".'

'Oh, forget it.'

'Great Dane?'

She pushed his head into the pillow. Andy stayed there, giving himself time to collate a suitable response, but when he rolled back over, she was gone. On the bedside table, the dented beer-can blazed like an aluminium sun.

Later, when she returned from a walk, her mood had worsened and they entered serious-talk territory, mostly shouted recriminations, sulking and crying.

'I don't want us to grow apart,' sobbed Michelle. 'Not with all we've been through.' She was hunched on the sofa clutching her security cushion. 'We're living so separately and sometimes . . . well, well, sometimes I think I don't get through to you at all.'

'Sorry. What?'

Andy was by the bookcase, picking at the price label on his tin of industrial-strength lager.

'God, you're not even *listening*.'

'It's a really important gig,' he murmured.

'I'm not trying to *stop* you. I'm not the enemy.'

Beyond the bay window, the streetlights made butterscotch pools on the wet tarmac. Andy was entrenched in his position. Career versus relationship was the commonest dish on their argument menu and, like nervous tourists in a strange hotel, they chose it regularly. Tonight they were sick of the taste.

'I'm going to bed,' he said.

'Not with me.'

'It's my bed.'

'It's not your bed. The flat's rented.'

'I pay rent.'

'Occasionally.'

They then proceeded to pull out and air all their petty grievances. It did not encourage them to patch things up and have frenzied make-up sex but instead led to her demand that he move out so as to allow them some space. Andy nodded his assent, furious that she'd nabbed an exclusively male excuse for non-commitment.

Blowing on his hands, Andy stared through the windscreen and prayed for the arrival of the recovery vehicle. The wind was freezing and he didn't want to miss the RAC by going back to the phone box. He eased another cigarette into his mouth and tugged at the ashtray. It slid off its runner and tipped a garnish of crumpled butts into the oily soup at his feet.

In front of him, a grey Ford Cabriolet slowed with its warning lights flashing. It parked up and the driver hoisted a mobile to his ear. When he had finished the call, he lit up a small cigar. Looks nice and warm in there, Andy thought. Maybe I could go and join a fellow castaway? He raised a hand and gave a sympathetic wave. It provoked no reaction.

Five minutes later, when he had definitely decided to ask the driver if he could borrow his mobile, strobing orange lights appeared in the rear-view mirror. To his annoyance, it wasn't the RAC but the yellow-and-black chequered van of the AA. It pulled over in front of the Cabriolet and a uniformed man emerged.

Andy watched impotently as the driver clambered out and chatted amiably to the AA man. After a few moments, the mechanic bent to the engine, gave a diagnosis, tweaked something inside and called out to the driver. He gunned the engine successfully and, with a friendly toot of his horn, sailed away.

'This is not my century,' said Andy.

'Scuse me, but I've been waiting here for well over an hour.'

The AA man turned from the racks of plastic tool-holders and studied Andy's pallid face.

Andy cracked a hopeful smile. 'I was wondering if you could you take a look?'

'Are you a member, sir?'

'Yes,' Andy lied. 'But I haven't got my card with me. I had to get the emergency number out of the book.'

The man gazed at him with the languid superiority of a passport official. Eventually, he broke away to check a clipboard in the rear of the van.

'Looks like I've got a couple of minutes. What's the problem?'

Andy explained about his owning the *Marie Celeste* of cars.

With a quiet nod, the AA man propped up the bonnet and dug about in the vehicle's intestines.

'Your heater matrix is leaking. You've lost about three pints. Was the engine overheating?'

'Sorry, I don't speak car.'

'Was the temperature dial in the red?'

'I wouldn't know. It doesn't work.'

'I can bypass it. Going far?'

'Back to Willesden – but I've got to get to Birmingham tonight.'

The man severed a pipe and tied it off. 'Should be safe to drive. But you don't want to go to Birmingham this time of year. Not without any heating.'

Andy nodded dumbly as the man sutured the pipes with metal clips. The mechanic then wadded up a bunch of paper towels and handed them to Andy so he could mop up the mess in the footwells.

'Shouldn't be any more trouble. Ought to get it to a garage, though.'

He was about to offer him something for his trouble when the RAC van drew up.

'Mr Crowe?' enquired the burly driver. Although he was speaking to Andy, he was staring at his rival with a brow as furrowed as a recently tilled field.

Andy's throat had silted up. 'Yes,' he croaked.

'What's all this, then?'

'I can explain.'

'I think you better had.'

'It's not what you think.'

'Isn't it?'

'All right, it *is* what you think. You weren't here so I had to go to him.'

'Had to?' There was petulance as the RAC man studied his fingernails.

Andy turned to the AA man. 'Go on. You tell him.'

The AA man rubbed his hands on his trousers. 'Since you're clearly *not* a member, sir, I'll be on my way.'

'No, don't go,' barked Andy. 'You helped me out. I could've waited for ever for him to turn up.'

'Perhaps you'd like to join *our* organisation?' said the AA man.

The RAC man took a step forward. 'This is *my* member, mate.'

'Well, you want to look after him a bit better.'

'And what's *that* supposed to mean?'

The two men were within a foot of one another. Andy stepped in between them.

'Look, I'm sure we can sort this out reasonably. Like adults.'

Both men glowered at him.

'This has never happened before.'

'Only got your word for that,' sniffed RAC.

Andy moved towards his car.

The RAC man: 'Where are you off to?'

'Well, the car's fixed, so I thought I'd leave you to it.'

'Punters,' snorted AA.

'I don't know why we bother sometimes,' said RAC.

'You're telling me.'

The AA mechanic went back to his van and the RAC man approached Andy.

'Might I see your membership card, please, sir?'

Andy took it from his wallet and handed it over for inspection. The RAC man tapped the hard plastic with a callused finger.

'Member for four years. You ought to know better, pulling a stunt like that.'

'Sorry.'

'We have to build a relationship on trust now, don't we, Mr Crowe?'

'Yes,' mumbled Andy.

Without another word, the RAC man spun the card into the middle of the busy carriageway.

CHAPTER TWO

Business in Birmingham

Danny arrived at Doug Mahoney's bed-sit at 7.15 that morning. Up in his room they changed into paint-spattered overalls: Doug's were loose on his scrawny frame, Danny's stretched taut with the cotton seams screaming. They corralled several cans of paint and rustled a large dustsheet out of the cupboard under the stairs. Then, after tossing the gear into the back of a van, they set off up Soho Hill Road for Handsworth.

Half an hour later they ambled into the redbrick entrance of Thornhill Road police station. Danny stood mutely with the dustsheet as Doug dumped one of the tins of paint on the counter. The desk sergeant, a middle-aged man with cropped hair and ambitions, scrutinised them. Doug was thin, of above average height and possessing a lined smoker's face and a shaven skull gone to stubble. The sergeant put him in his late twenties, perhaps older. His co-worker was more unusual. Danny had a coffee complexion, hooded, almost slanted eyes, a broad, flat nose, wiry hair, an earring and a goatee beard. Not black – half-caste? The giant must have weighed in at a good eighteen stone, and in dungarees he resembled the Michelin Man in negative.

'Where d'you want us to start, then?' asked the stubble-headed one. London accent, touch of Irish about it.

'Start what?'

Doug raised the can. 'We're doing the Sistine Chapel ceiling in here. In Peach Mist.'

The sergeant rolled his eyes and turned away.

Doug counted out four seconds. 'Far as we know, we're doing the corridors and your canteen. Job's booked for today. Thursday the fourteenth.'

'Don't know nothing about it.'

Doug gazed at the CCTV video screen in the corner. The image was carved into four views of the outside of the building. 'Anything good on telly?' he asked.

The desk sergeant didn't dignify this with an answer.

Doug Mahoney slipped a Golden Virginia tin from a side pocket and patted tobacco on to a Rizla.

'Can't smoke in here.'

'Usual story, is it? They never tell you anything, right?'

'Who's your contact?'

Doug put the tin away. 'The boss sent us along to start the prep. He'll be along about nine.'

'Who's he, when he's at home?'

'Joey Fisher. And you're right there. That's where he is most of the time.'

The desk sergeant made a long tutting sound like a woodpecker drilling at a tree. A pair of uniformed officers strolled past and went out. Then, mustering a sneer, the sergeant reached for a plastic folder.

'I reckon this is all down to Accounts. Bloody mess, they are.' He flicked pages, located an extension number and punched buttons. There was no reply. 'You'd better come back at nine.' The ropes of muscle in Danny's neck twitched like a ship straining against its moorings.

Doug studied the cold entrance hall. 'We can't leave the stuff here. And there's no point lugging it back to the van. You got somewhere we can bung it while we go off and find a caff?'

The desk sergeant gazed heavenward as if for confirmation that his sainthood was imminent. Seeing only cracked plaster, he sighed, turned, straightened his tie and left the room.

Beneath the counter on his side was a bright blue plastic amnesty bin. This had been placed there as part of a nation-wide scheme to encourage criminals to turn in their arms. In practice, they only ever filled it with weapons stolen from other criminals.

In seconds, Doug and Danny were up and over the counter. As Doug ejected the videotape and inserted a replacement, Dan got to work with the bolt-cutters he had hidden in the folds of the sheet. With a metallic snap, he severed the chain linking the bin to the radiator. He hauled the amnesty bin over the counter and wrapped it in the dustsheet. Doug vaulted back over and held the doors as Danny carried it out into the street.

Then they legged it back to their stolen van.

Moments later the desk sergeant returned to find them gone and the CCTV screen playing a pirated copy of *Babe*.

'Bostin', guy, you're a genius,' said Danny One-Slice as he stared in awe at the arsenal of weapons. They were back in Doug's bed-sit and had changed into their normal clothes. Scattered on the bedspread were daggers, choppers, a serrated-edge Bowie knife and a machete. Among the guns were a Glock, a pair of old Browning service revolvers, a Webley, two double-barrelled shotguns (one sawn-off), an airgun, and an old Lee Enfield rifle. They were sprinkled with shells and bullets of all calibres.

'Looks like a car boot sale for serial killers,' noted Doug.

Grinning, Danny plucked out the sawn-off shotgun and cracked it open. The twin chambers had recently been oiled. 'Who'd wanna dump a beauty like this?'

'Beats me.'

'Genius guy.'

'Yeah, you said.'

Danny set about weeding the crop for matching shells. Suddenly his face crumpled and his hand shot to the breast pocket of his sleeveless camouflage jacket. Extracting a wad of tissues, he blew his nose so loudly that the window frames rattled. He wiped off, eased a couple of yellow tablets from another pocket and necked them.

'What's that? Speed?' queried Doug, wondering why Dan would want a chemical high when they were still buzzing from the adrenalin rush of the robbery.

'Anabolics. Gotta shift this cold somehow.' He burped and thumped his chest. 'Need a chaser.'

He slid an evil-looking luminous green bottle out of his other breast pocket.

'Jesus. What's *that* stuff?'

'Day Nurse,' muttered the giant, struggling with the childproof cap.

Over the years Doug had learned that his best friend was omnivorous in his choice of pharmaceuticals. Speed, skank, coke, amyl nitrate, grass and copious amounts of rum 'n' Coke were all consumed on a regular basis: the only visible signs of intoxication being Danny's glazed grin, a high-pitched maniacal laugh and a demand for more.

The steroids were a recent addition.

Danny always kept in shape: it was a large shape often seen planted outside the 23 Skidoo nightclub or bench-pressing at the local gym. Doug, watching as Danny sank the bottle in one, was grateful that the mammoth flu-ridden, steroid-enhanced Filipino was on his side.

'Bostin'. Genius man!' said Danny, wiping green syrup from his Brillo beard.

'So you keep saying.'

'What're we gonna do with these guns, then?'

A Rizla puckered as Doug sparked his roll-up. 'Can you sort out the van first? Go dump it somewhere?'

Danny brushed his temple with a two-finger salute. 'I'll stick it in the canal on me way down the gym. So, come on. What's occurring?'

'Got a busy day, so I'll fill you in later. What I can say is that by this time tomorrow we're gonna be quids in.' He rubbed his hands together. 'We're hitting the bigtime, boy.'

'So this is all for tonight?'

'That's right.'

'Genius.'

'Stop it now.'

'But you are.'

'Dan, I don't want to be pedantic but they don't give out Nobel Prizes for doing over police stations.'

Dan rustled a hand through the coarse wire of his goatee. 'Well, they should.'

'Maybe in Mexico. Not Smethwick.'

A grin from Dan as a shiver of anticipation skittered down his spine. The last few weeks had seen a change in his old friend, a return to the sense of purpose he had so admired in him when they had met in Wandsworth over a decade ago.

At that time, Danny was flaunting his twin Section 18 wounding charges as a badge of courage. They gave him a status among the inmates that, combined with his physical stature, made him virtually an untouchable. Trouble was, being British-born yet half Filipino, he was a misfit and had been abandoned by black and white gangs alike.

Doug arrived one chilly May morning, a bony youth with lank, dark hair and darting nervous eyes. Clocking him, inmates and screws alike saw a white kid too young to be a face: another mug, easy pickings. Before he could talk to anyone he was given his food tray, told to collect his meal and marched off to his cell.

During association that evening, he entered the games room to the staccato sound of ping-pong. As he clearly did not not know where to sit, one of the ponces devilishly gave him Dan's chair near the telly. As might be expected, a hush greeted Dan's arrival. He crossed his arms and towered over the boy, who wondered if there had been a sudden eclipse.

'You win the prize,' said Doug.

'What prize?'

'For being the biggest fucker I've ever seen.'

Danny, whose temper took its time grinding up through the gears, considered the statement. On the one hand it was true. No doubt he was the biggest fucker this kid had ever seen. On the other, the sheer effrontery of mentioning it demanded either swift retribution or acquiescence. In the end he punched Doug to the ground – but his heart wasn't in it.

The boy soon demonstrated a knack for obtaining weed and cigarettes and they become firm friends. Danny once even offered him the option of a return blow, but Doug refused on the grounds that he didn't want to break a knuckle. He was in for three years for dealing, which he intended to boil down to his third with remission. He'd already been through the system, from probation to reform school to the detention centre at Feltham. Wandsworth was to be his Oxbridge: an august institution where he might study without the inter-ference of rag week or the nonsense of people his own age pretending to be socialists.

He obtained his release eighteen months before Danny and promised him faithfully he'd keep in touch. This he did with postcards, the last few showing views of the Kiezergracht or landscapes from the Van Gogh collection: Dan figured he'd made his home in Amsterdam and – judging by the hand-writing – he had managed to locate some blow.

Danny One-Slice returned to Birmingham in the early nineties and was reunited with his mother. There, he became engrossed in his own problems of readjustment and thoughts of his old cellmate soon disappeared. So when a grinning hippie turned up at the flat one blazing summer's afternoon, he was overjoyed.

'Got you a present from Holland,' said Doug, his shrewd smile slewed by the crystal skunk they had already consumed.

'I thought this was it,' queried Dan, rolling the reefer between his myriad fingers and thumbs.

'Nah, that's for now. Something to bring in a bit of cash.'

'Cool,' said Dan, who never normally used the word but had picked up the verbal tic from Doug.

'Trouble is it's caught up in a logjam.'

Dan flashed on an image of lumberjacks rolling a herd of giant spliffs along a river in British Columbia. 'Huh?'

'Can't drop the pay-load.'

'Not with you.'

'Unable to build the log cabin.'

A blissed-out stare.

'Constipation, Dan. I've got a hundred microdots of acid stashed up my arse.'

'No shit.'

'Exactly.'

'How about black coffee?'

'I tried coffee *and* fags and I even done a Balti last night. Nothing's shifting it. I've been back here for three days and I can't crimp a fucking length.'

'I hope it's bagged up,' muttered Dan, 'or your arse is gonna be tripping for a month.'

Doug pulled a mournful expression.

Danny saw the funny side and collapsed on to the carpet, where he wept fat tears and rolled about like a lion basking in the sun. Once his laughter had subsided, he sat back on his haunches and caged his face in his hands.

'All right. C'mon. What you gonna do?'

'Wait for nature. What can I do?'

The Filipino's eyes flared briefly, and in an instant he was on his feet. He pinned Doug to the wall by his throat.

'You think I wanna go near something that's been up your arse?' he bellowed. 'What's up with you – prison turned you into a Mary?'

Doug paled.

'This what you call looking after me, is it?' Dragging Doug into the kitchen, Dan rattled open a drawer and extracted a scratched tablespoon. He pressed the convex side to Doug's nose. 'Maybe I ought to dig it out of you with this?'

'Leave it out, Dan,' croaked Doug.

Danny loosened his grip a notch. Outside, children were playing on the baking asphalt and darting in and out of the bright washing on the clothes-lines. Doug released a small, noxious smell. Danny held his nose with two plump fingers.

'Yich. Feel like a dump now?' he asked, releasing him.

'Bastard,' called Doug, as he bolted for the smallest room.

'You take the shotgun. I'll use the Glock.'

Doug had pulled a baton of black bin-liners from the wardrobe and was snapping them off the roll. Plastic fluttered to the floor. 'I'm gonna stash the rest of the guns in the garden and we'll flog them in a few months.'

'Do I need to get someone to fill in for me at the club?' enquired Dan.

'Nah. You'll only need cover from eleven until one. We'll do the job in a couple of hours.' He laid black sheets over the weapons. 'One more thing. We're gonna need a Transit and some cutting equipment. Oxyacetylene. And you want to keep hold of them bolt-cutters.'

Danny clenched his fists in excitement.

'Know that kid?' continued Doug. 'Handy with motors? Always in the club?'

'Jason?'

'Yeah. Works in a lot over at Perry Bar, doesn't he?'

'He's a twat.'

Doug waved aside the objection. 'Go have a word, will you? Tell him we need a van.'

Danny's hands were hanging at his sides like two glazed hams. He folded them across his chest and flexed his biceps. The muscles jumped like twin pulsating hearts.

Jason was the teenage nephew of the club-owner and took every liberty with his free pass and bar privileges. Night after night he would arrive with a giggle of under-aged girls in tow. Danny always demanded proof of their ages, then greeted their excuses with a deadpan stare and watched ruefully as they clopped inside anyway. Other times, Jase brought his drunken friends. Danny had lost count of the number of times he'd had to escort the brawling, vomiting nuisances from the premises. What got him more than anything was that no matter how many suitable cooling-off periods went by, Jason always scuttled back like a dose of crabs.

'Well?'

Doug was matching weapons to ammunition. The bed was like a Fisher-Price activity centre for psychos.

'All right,' murmured Danny, turning to the door. He released another enormous sneeze. Spittle flecked the crumbling, blistered paint. His brain seemed to be stuffed with cotton wool.

'Danny?'

'Yeah?'

'Leave the sawn-off shotgun.'

Danny looked at the object in his hand. 'What? This one?'

'Yes, Dan.'

With an exaggerated slump of the shoulders, Dan tossed it on to a chair and stomped out into the cold.

'Stolen?' Jason barked a quick laugh and threw back his head. His long blond hair billowed out over his shoulders. 'Who d'you think I am, mate?'

He and his customer were standing in the forecourt of the used-car lot owned by his father. Dad was away at a car auction and had entrusted his only son with running the business for the morning.

'Sorry, but I thought I'd ask,' said the punter, shuffling from foot to foot in a puddle.

Jason had sussed him the moment he crept in round the chain-link fence. An obvious first-time buyer, he was clutching a copy of Parker's *Price Guide* and a ring-bound notebook. No doubt in his pocket there would be a magnet for detecting filler. Sure enough, after he had finished peering through the windscreen (on which Jason had artfully placed cardboard price tags to obscure the dodgy speedo readings), Mugsy selected an E-reg Fiesta and bent to the bodywork. Duuuh, Jason thought as he straightened his tie. Doesn't he *know* I used a layer of tinfoil underneath so that a magnet will stick to it?

'Let me tell you something about ringing motors,' he began. 'They never bother respraying or mucking about with it. They just nick another car. Same type, same colour, same year. Swap the VIN number and the plates, cut off the chassis number, and weld in the number of the write-off. Bob's your uncle. Got yourself a clean motor with everything but the legit logbook.'

The punter was thrilled to have been let in on a trade secret and looked even more gullible. Jason had already ferreted out his occupation: trainee teacher. In his view teachers were about the most stupid people on the planet.

'So . . . how much would this be for cash?' the punter asked.

Jason drummed his fingers on the bonnet and juggled numbers. 'I could let you have it for six.'

Love that, he thought. Like I'm doing him a favour. Ha.

'And as you say – it's got all the documents?'

'All except the logbook.'

As the man's face fell, Jason emitted another huge guffaw. 'No, you're all right, mate. I'm having you on. It's in the office . . . somewhere.'

While the teacher pissed around with the wipers and over-revved the engine, Jason went back into the Portakabin to root around for a good excuse.

'Think me dad must have it,' he said on his return. 'He'll be back next week. You could pop over, see us then.'

The teacher was torn. The car was so right. A touch of wear and tear but, as the salesman had said, it was nothing to worry about. The brakes were a bit spongy but that was quite normal in a second-hand car, wasn't it?

'All right, then,' he said briskly. 'What about the radio?'

In the centre of the dashboard was a deep oblong hole stuffed with dangling wires.

Jason thought for a moment.

'You got the cash on you?'

'Yes.'

'Give us five minutes.'

Jason took off down the road and, among the parked cars, found what he was looking for. Removing a thin-bladed screwdriver from an inside pocket, he rammed it deep into the lock of a Vauxhall Nova. He went left and right and up and it sprang open. In moments he had liberated the car stereo from the console and was ambling back towards the lot.

*   *   *

'I don't know anything about the job yet and if I did I wouldn't tell you,' growled the giant.

Jason's voice was the wrong side of nervous. 'All right, Dan.'

'You little scrote.'

'Let us go. Please?'

Danny One-Slice grinned and loosened his grip. The boy clung to his arm, his legs flailing over the inspection pit.

'Listen, Muppet, I want you to get everything ready for four and bring the van over to my place, right?'

The boy nodded furiously.

Danny reeled him in, dropped him to the floor and strode off.

It was now nearing lunch-time. Danny's plan was to dump the stolen van, walk to the gym and get home for half two. He cut the engine, blew his nose and worried his knuckles into his eyes. He hated going home, and ascribed his constant sniffles to the damp flat. It was an eleventh-floor breeze-block cell with mildewing walls and a biting wind that snuck in round the window frames. The reputation of the estate was such that its needle-strewn walkways featured in the Sunday supplements almost as often as the spindly African children.

Danny forced open a fresh bottle of Day Nurse. It was having less effect. He wondered if Night Nurse mightn't override his high pharmaceutical tolerance level? He took a swig. Or maybe there was an in-between. Afternoon Nurse? He examined his tongue in the rear-view mirror. Astroturf.

He was parked opposite an expanse of flattened land. The crumbled black earth was striated from the attentions of bulldozers, and piles of rubble were dotted about like over-sized molehills. Attached to one low wedge of wall was a bright daub of old, flowered wallpaper. A continuous metal-link fence ringed the site.

This was new.

Danny clambered out of the car and threaded his fingers through the wire. Three men in yellow hard hats were huddled in the distance, poring over a set of blueprints. Dan tugged at the gold ring in his left earlobe as he tried to make out their faces.

Stepping back, he saw that a sign had been attached to the fence. He read it out aloud, taking in the name of the construction company and the information that the new erection was to be a 'Business Park'.

He frowned. What's a business park? You don't do business in a park. You walk the kids and the dogs or score weed if you're desperate. Mind you, I suppose that is a business. Don't wanna advertise it like that, though.

Plucking a vial from his top pocket, he popped a capsule of amphetamine and crunched it thoughtfully. Then he tore the sign from its housing and stomped it into the gutter.

CHAPTER THREE

Our Father, Who Art in Heston

At 7 a.m. that morning, the Hitchhiker enjoyed a continental breakfast at Leigh Delamere services. Performing his daily ablutions in the rest room, he loosened his bandana, shook out his shoulder-length grey hair, and ran a comb through it to untangle the knots. He tied it up with an elastic band, then went into one of the cubicles and removed the top of the cistern. He carried it out to the sink and balanced the porcelain slab on the heads of the two automatic taps. He knew from experience that this was the only way of ensuring a steady stream of water. He then used the soap from the dispenser to wash his liver-spotted hands and weather-beaten face. Finally, he angled two of the hand driers so that the twin jets of warm air dried him off.

He did not need to wipe his hands on the seat of his trousers.

He emerged on to the white-tiled concourse.

'Goodbye, Father,' said a diminutive Irish woman as she raised the white metal grille in front of the shop.

He smiled benevolently. Two steps away from the automatic doors he flung his arms in the air and they shushed open. How do they clean these things? he wondered, making a mental note to put it in his diary.

Outside, he took a deep breath, drawing in frosty air with a hint of petrol vapour. The sky was a flat ash-toned canvas, but as yet held no threat of rain. He checked the pockets of his jacket and realigned the straps of his knapsack against his shoulders.

'Father. For your journey?'

The woman had followed him outside and was proffering a paper bag. He peered inside it. It contained a jumble of multicoloured confectionery, including his favourite. Jelly-beans.

'Bless you,' he said as she shrank away.

Pocketing them, he walked across the forecourt and over to the petrol station. Several cars were already filling up, and he reckoned he stood a good chance of finding a ride donor. Knowing better than to pester them here, he crossed the asphalt apron to the slip road, making sure that he was in full view of the cars leaving the service area. The traffic was sparse on the motorway.

He decided not to use his set of number plates or his selection of destination boards: instead, he would rely on the driver's innate sense of altruism. This added a good half an hour to his waiting time. Golfs, estates, Citroëns and Cavaliers drove past, accelerating away from him. Finally, a Ford Orion drew to a halt and the glass drawbridge of the passenger window slid down. He stole a glimpse through the rear windscreen. Male, suit hanging above the rear seat. Sales rep. The man was in his late thirties with receding hair. Male-pattern baldness is not an attractive pattern, thought the Hitcher. The driver had appended a moustache to his upper lip to atone for the hair loss.

'Where are you headed?'

'London.'

'Don't hang about, then.'

The Hitcher removed his knapsack and sank into the

passenger seat. The vehicle was new, either a company car or a prize for achievement. The driver was comfortable with the machine and passed the wheel easily through his hands as he wove into the fast lane.

'Where do you want in town?'

A Bristolian twang. Plus, no native of London would ever refer to the capital as 'town'.

'The North Circular Road if possible?'

'I'm coming off before then. Hounslow?'

'That'll be fine. I can walk to Heston from Junction Three and get another ride.'

'You know your way around.'

'I do, yes.'

The driver toasted a Dunhill. 'Toner.'

'Hello, Tony.'

'No, Toner. Do you know much about photocopiers?'

The hitchhiker sensed that the driver was going to be typical of people who give rides in that he'd want payment in the form of supplication to his opinions. These, it transpired, ranged from a naïve economic strategy to the kind of racial views often associated with men in black shirts. As luck would have it, he then moved on to his favourite subject – the sale and maintenance requirements of the photocopying machine.

Throughout the lecture, the Hitcher muttered agreeable vowel sounds as the motorway undulated through Wiltshire. Outside, the sky was a solid blanket of grey cloud. The traffic grew heavy as they passed into Berkshire, and the man's conversation began to drift to the personal.

'Off home to the wife, then, are you?'

'No.'

'Lucky bugger.'

'I've never been married so I wouldn't know if I was lucky or not.'

A grunt. 'Trust me, you're lucky, old son.' A pause. 'I'll tell you this for nothing. No names, no pack-drill—' He tapped his nose conspiratorially.

The Hitcher found it hard to believe that people still tapped their noses to indicate a secret.

'But with this job, there's plenty of time to play away from home, if you catch my drift?'

'I see.'

'Asian girl. Indrani. Tucked away in a flat in Isleworth. Very accommodating. See her a couple of afternoons a week.'

'Really?'

The driver warmed to his theme. 'We all need a bit on the side, don't we? Come on, we're men of the world—'

The Hitcher found it hard to believe that people still said they were 'men of the world.'

'But you should see what she gets up to. Versatile little thing.'

'You mean she juggles several careers?'

The driver stubbed out his Dunhill.

'So what about you?' he asked, frost creeping into the voice. 'Are you working?'

'No.'

'Not one of those dole scroungers, I hope?'

'I take nothing from the government.'

'Well, how d'you live, then?'

'People feed me at service stations. And some of the lorry drivers are very kind.'

The driver's turn for disbelief. 'Bloody hell. People give you things just like that?'

'Yes.'

'Who do you think you are — God?'

'That's what people tell me, yes.'

With his neck reddening, the driver reached for the radio and drowned them in the cheery sound of Chiltern FM.

* * *

The two diners in the central Birmingham hotel restaurant showed no signs of leaving. They were marooned on an island of detritus amidst a sea of crisp linen tablecloths which had pointedly been set for the evening session. Each time they sent out smoke signals with their cigars, the waitress sailed over and paddled back to the kitchens for fresh supplies. These included Havana cigars and a bottle of vintage port.

All this came on top of a three-course lunch. They were not, the waitress noted, the fashionable kind of customers who diluted their alcohol intake with mineral water. In frustration, Chef had brewed up a pot of best Colombian roast and she'd ridden it round on the sweet trolley in the hope that the smell would entice them to sobriety. It hadn't.

'So you'll have words with the Rotarians?' asked Stephen McCreary. He was a red-faced Yorkshireman with a gut that had long since given up the battle of the belt.

'I shall, yes.'

'I've given up trying to get anywhere with them bastards.'

'It would help if you didn't refer to them as bastards,' offered his guest.

Neil Jacobs was a Birmingham city councillor who enjoyed the cut and thrust of local politics, with emphasis on the cutting and thrusting. His hair had thinned to strands as a result. A tiny man, he had a long beak of a nose, florid cheeks, scornful lips and the eyes of a cannibal. What he lacked in height he made up for in status and a lack of empathy towards any living thing.

'It's a bloody class issue,' sneered McCreary.

Jacobs eyed him coolly. 'If that were so, then they would have blocked your entry into the brotherhood. I rather think it has something to do with a certain project of yours.'

McCreary Constructions had recently won a contract to redevelop a Grade III listed building used by the Rotarians as a clubhouse.

'Arson or not, it were still unsafe,' mused McCreary.

'*Was* unsafe.' Jacobs spoke well and had the annoying habit of correcting the diction of others. He had few friends.

'Was unsafe. Wet and dry rot. Substandard RSJs. The lot.'

'So the fact that it burned down had nothing to do with the complex specifications issued by National Heritage?'

'Naw.'

'Nor their edict that you employ traditional building materials?'

'That's right.'

'You insult my intelligence, Stephen.'

McCreary looked down at his plate.

Jacobs stroked imaginary crumbs from the table with manicured fingers. 'On to more promising matters. The Handsworth redevelopment.'

'Ready to roll. Can you smooth it with the ways and means people?'

'As head of the ways and means committee, I think it might be arranged.'

McCreary refilled his glass and offered the bottle to Jacobs. He declined.

'Business park indeed,' chortled Stephen. 'The bloody idea's ludicrous.'

Jacobs winced inwardly at the profane language, but in their mutual interest he let it pass. 'The retail park industry is booming,' he offered. 'The nation is obsessed with building these vast out-of-town sites.'

Stephen rubbed his hands with glee. 'Don't I know it.'

'I imagine that they will ultimately become shantytowns, perhaps like those townships in Africa. Sheds full of starving computer software operatives and direct-mailing drones.'

'Not ours, though.'

'Indeed,' conceded the councillor.

'Did they really think Handsworth were going to become a boom town?'

'The market research says so. But then, market research will tell us anything we like.'

'Can you imagine the retail outlets we'd have? Curry Hut!'

Jacobs parried with: 'Single Mothers R Us.'

McCreary thought for a moment. His face brightened. 'Marks and Shell suit.' He exploded with laughter.

The councillor's lips rippled as he formulated a better notion. 'CrackDonald's.'

They both laughed at that one. Jacobs mentally stored the information for recycling at his next speaking engagement. 'Shall we call it a day, then?' he suggested.

'Aye. You're a right card, you are.'

'I hope not a knave,' replied Jacobs, raising a regal hand.

The waitress wilted visibly with relief and struggled back into her heels.

'CrackDonald's,' repeated McCreary, shaking his head. 'We'll do well on this.'

'I intend to.'

The waitress arrived and McCreary dropped a gold card on to his side plate. She took it and hobbled away. He rubbed his cigar into the ashtray and lowered his voice. 'By the by, we dealt with the last of them squatters.'

'Let's call a spade a spade. You mean the tenants?'

'Well, they were spades, most of 'em. Had to use the old hands-on approach, if you get my drift.' He puffed out his chest. 'One of the tricks you learn as a self-made man.'

Jacobs revealed tiny pointed teeth. 'Self-made? Doesn't that rather imply somebody badly put together through lack of instruction?'

McCreary dropped his serviette in the remains of his *tarte citron*, signed the receipt and pocketed the slip.

The councillor was already on his feet and shaking the creases from his suit.

'Can I give you a lift? The Jag's outside,' offered McCreary as they were helped into their coats like children.

'Thank you, no. I'll take a taxi.' Jacobs lived with his wife in a leafy part of Edgbaston where he could be sure of avoiding his constituents.

They came out on to the pavement. Spats of rain were flying about at random, and one landed on Jacob's forehead. He dabbed it away then busied himself with slipping on a pair of effeminate kid leather gloves.

'Doing anything interesting tonight?' McCreary asked.

'Oh, I should think so,' said Jacobs, fishing a cellular phone from his coat pocket.

'You old devil.'

The councillor stared straight through him.

'Well . . . I'd best be off,' said McCreary, embarrassed.

Before parting, they gave one another a firm and interesting handshake.

After failing to pluck his RAC card from the centre of the A406, Andy Crowe drove back to his flat. When he tried to phone Michelle again, he was told that she was out with clients. Translated, this meant she was getting pissed up with a slick of advertisers. On days like this, she would sleep it off in the office and then work on until eight or nine in the evening. Since he was due to pick up Rob Gillen, there was no chance of seeing her unless he didn't go to Birmingham.

He weighed his options and failed to reach a decision. If he managed to talk her round, then he would lose this rare opportunity with the Agency. If he went and did the gig, then the chances of salvaging the relationship would be smaller than a supermodel's breakfast. Perplexed by the dilemma, he went for his usual course of action: ringing promoters for work. It was a defence mechanism and also the worst part of a comedian's job. In practice it meant feeding numerous answering machines with increasingly curt and sour messages. Today, on his fifth call, he reached a real person.

'Dom, hi. Andy Crowe.'

'Hi, Andy.'

The tone suggested a slot machine of evasion was already grinding into action. He'd have to work fast.

'I'm off up north to do some gigs for the Agency. Wondered if you had time to put something in the book?'

'You with the Agency now?'

'Oh, yeah,' he said, feigning the bored manner of a Railtrack complaints clerk.

'Good for you, mate.'

'So. Have you got anything?'

Tumblers span and failed to hit the jackpot excuse. 'Look, I'm busy at the mo. Can you give us a bell when you get back?'

'Can't you do it before I go?'

'Well, I, uh . . . I haven't got my diary with me.'

He was prepared for this. The preferred method of rejecting unwanted acts was to invoke 'The Diary'. It was an object both mystical in its power and elusive in its whereabouts. The damn thing kept on getting misplaced or, as at the crucial moment in a movie, it was always juuustt out of reach. Having been spurned by the diary countless times, Andy had come up with a plan over Christmas.

'Dom? Did you get the present I sent you?'

'I dunno . . . I'm not sure.'

'Yes you did.' He raised his voice. 'And the reason I sent you a fucking diary was so you'd never have to give me this *bullshit* again.'

With that he slammed down the phone and left the house.

✶   ✶   ✶

By the time God arrived at Toddington services on the M1, he'd had a day of it. Following his revelation to the salesman, the man had dropped him at Chieveley. God hadn't minded, as there were many that found the prospect of travelling with a deity uncomfortable. He assumed it had something to do with guilt and fear. That or they thought he was psychotic. On that count he had no proof, as his memory wasn't all it could be. In fact he couldn't even remember when he'd started travelling round the motorways of Britain, only that it was meant to be. And of late, he had started to feel a sense of urgency about his mission.

Chieveley was cold and windswept, and after an hour he abandoned the slip road and went to the lorry park. Among the rigs was a large lorry containing a consignment of frozen foods. He knew the driver. God waved to his friend Bill and climbed into the cab, enjoying the warmth and the comforting odour of diesel.

'Brass monkeys out there today,' Bill said, unscrewing the cap on his Thermos.

'Let me guess. Tomato?'

Nodding, Bill poured the hot orange liquid into the plastic cup and handed it over.

God sighed as the heat warmed his hands.

'Where've you come from?' Bill asked.

'Only Bristol.'

'Not much of a ride.'

God shrugged. 'The driver was upset.'

'Maybe it's how you look?'

'Could be,' said God, savouring the taste of the soup. Bill's wife opened a mean can.

Bill took the remains of his mid-morning egg-and-bacon roll, cracked open the door and flung it out. The bread drew in a pair of screeching seagulls.

'Dave?'

'Yes, Bill?'

God didn't mind being called Dave. People were free to choose whatever name they wanted for him. In his time he had been the Almighty, the Creator, the Supreme Being, Lord, Shiva, Master, Buddha, Yahweh, Jesus and, of course, Father. But if Bill was comfortable with Dave, then Dave he would be, even if it didn't have quite the same ring to it.

'Where d'you want to be dropped?'

'Chiswick?'

Bill released the air-brake, put the rig into gear and rolled off.

God hated the Chiswick roundabout. The rest of the country could safety be circumnavigated exclusively by motorway, but in the capital he had to skirt the polluted northwestern suburbs. He much preferred odd-numbered days. On these, he avoided London by going round the M25. He loved its two-hundred-mile circumference, its plethora of signs and its eternal roadworks.

He was alone in this.

After being dropped there, a nurse took him up to the gyratory system, narrowly avoiding a collision with a speeding RAC vehicle. She let him off at Neasden Lane, and he was forced to walk the length of the Brent reservoir to the M1.

Three hours was a long time to wait at the big junction: there were already two people there, and by the unwritten law of hitchhiking they had prior claim on rides. One was a squaddie, the other a student. God sat on the crash barrier and learned that the corporal was heading to Luton and the student to Liverpool. The squaddie soon obtained a lift but the student was another matter: he was an unshaven youth who had dressed out of the dirty laundry basket. He wasn't helping matters by lobbing abuse at the cars as they thundered past.

'Word of advice,' offered God from the sidelines.

'What?'

'Smile.'

'Yer wha'?'

'People judge by appearances.'

'Like I give a fook what you say?'

'I'd like us to be on our way before dark.'

God was niggled. His feet were numb and his face raw with cold. He was considering updating his personal credo of acceptance and understanding to exclude students.

'If these wankers would stop then I'd be on me way. It's your fault, yer old dosser. You're puttin' 'em off.'

God rarely practised divine intervention, but considering he was freezing on the hard shoulder of the M1, he decided he had no choice. Rummaging inside his knapsack, he removed a blue-and-white scarf.

'Here. Give this a go.'

'Ta,' said the youth, wrapping it round his neck.

A few moments later a four-wheel-drive Commando Jeep taxied to a halt and picked up the student. God smiled as they sped away. The Oxford University scarf had done its work.

After that, he embarked on a rigorous routine of stamping his feet and shaking his arms to get the circulation back. He was still hopping from foot to foot when the saloon car stopped up ahead. He ran for it, slowing as he caught up with the vehicle. His gaze was drawn to a yellow rhombus in the rear window. Baby on Board. He tipped his eyes heavenward and made for the open door.

'Mother?'

'Is that you?' The voice was husky, distracted.

'If the *you* you're referring to is *me*, then yes,' said Councillor Jacobs.

The reception in the back of the taxi was poor. They were

trying to avoid traffic on the A38 by coming through Lady-wood. Rain was licking the pavements and making the traffic lights bright in the puddles.

There was a pause at the other end as the woman struggled with his surgically precise use of language. 'Neil?' she asked, finally.

'Of course. Are we all set for tonight?'

'Yes.' The woman shuffled into a sterner tone. 'And you had better be on your best behaviour, young man.'

The councillor murmured agreement and strained against his underpants.

'Have you booked the room?'

'Number twelve as usual, Mother.'

'What time will you get there?'

'I hope shortly before midnight.'

'Don't you be late – or there'll be trouble.'

'No, Mother,' replied the councillor sheepishly. 'Goodbye.'

He switched off the cellular phone and replaced it in his pocket.

The cab driver aligned their eyes in the rear-view mirror.

'Mums, eh? Nothing but trouble.'

Jacobs shone cannibal eyes at him. 'And what makes you think for one moment that that woman was any relation of mine?'

'Well, I . . .'

'Then hold your tongue and don't be so impertinent.'

CHAPTER FOUR

Man In a Car

———◆———

Andy's cigarette butt ricocheted off the wing mirror and burst into orange sparks on the road. A woman on the pavement opposite threw him a scowl as she passed by. A man in a car in mid-afternoon used to be cool, thought Andy. Used to be a grizzled, wisecracking detective tailing some squeeze to see if she's cheating on her husband. He pulled a Bogart face, then dropped it. Nowadays it's a child molester. On the other hand, I am a bit close to that convent school.

He was sitting in the car in a terraced street in Wembley Park, three miles north of his soon-to-be-ex-home. He had decided that since Michelle clearly wasn't speaking to him, he might as well go ahead and do the gig. If he returned that night as a conquering hero, then she would understand. If not, . . . well, he'd never been one for forward planning, so why start now? All he really had to do was drive the noxious Gillen to Birmingham, storm the gig, convert the infidels, slay the dragon and win back the girl. There were worse scenarios – most of them directed by Michael Winner.

The street was filled with an urgent buzzing as a swarm of uniformed teenage girls swirled past. Acutely aware of the child molestation issue, Andy slunk low in his seat and watched them through the fogged-up windows. Then he realised that having fogged-up windows was even worse, so he wound them down again. A pair in puffa jackets stopped to bum cigarettes off him, their mouths spasming with chewing gum as he dug out his Marlboros. They used his lighter with practised ease, blowing smoke rings as the nicotine kissed their pretty lungs. They couldn't have been much older than thirteen and they called him 'Mister'.

Andy did not feel like a mister.

The two swaggered away, legs scissoring in black tights, cartoonish, two Minnie Mice in high platform black trainers. He wondered if he ought to feel aroused, but when one of them gave him the finger, he decided that it wasn't going to happen. A bunch of older girls bundled past, dumping empty crisp packets, screeching with laughter, one of them pausing to blatantly hoist up her tights.

He was reminded of Michelle, who always placed her need for comfort above that of public decency. She'd burp if she felt like burping, and she'd tell someone to their face if they had food on their chin. She even once – after a long drunken rant about how much easier it was to be a bloke – went for a slash between two parked cars and was mortified when one of them drove off. The black tights were another connection. She had been wearing them, along with green boots and a holey jumper on the night they finally got it together.

Autumn term at the Trent Park site of Middlesex Poly. The isolated group of buildings was nestled in woodland, reachable only by a minibus service from the main road at Cockfosters. She was third-year English and drama, he second. Both had reputations for preying on the flesh of freshers and halls were their killing fields. However, like magnets of similar polarity they repelled. Of course their friends were certain they'd had sex at some point: it was a foregone conclusion, like summer following spring or computer salesmen having no fashion sense. Their supposed clandestine relationship was scrutinised with the reverence more often given to a pair of soap stars. True to their roles, they denied everything and remained courteous about one another except when drunk. Which was most of the time.

Their antagonism arose from an incident in Andy's first term. One night in the student bar, he and Michelle had gone through several beers and vodka chasers and had decided to continue back at her room in halls. There, she produced some weed and a bottle of Calvados she'd stolen from her father for a special occasion. They decided that a Thursday was a special occasion. By the time it was half drunk they were kissing and dry-humping. They smoked the draw and removed each other's clothes, but by two in the morning the roulette wheel of alcohol was spinning faster than the room and all bets were off.

Engineering students are not known for having a highly developed sense of humour. When Michelle awoke the next morning, she found her door wide open and a pair of targets scrawled on her exposed breasts in lipstick. Assuming Andy to be responsible for desecrating her mammaries, she sought him out (he was unconscious in a pool of his own vomit in the shower room) and screamed the place down. The engineering students were glad of the scapegoat and went back to doing things with inanimate objects with which they were more familiar. Soon afterwards Michelle left the halls of residence and she and Andy did not meet again properly until a disco the following year.

By then she had grown serious about her art and had cut her mane of dark ringlets to a gamine crop. Her body, if still not a temple, could nonetheless be considered a non-secular drop-in centre.

Andy had developed too. Female students regularly mistook his drunkenness and his air of bewilderment for depth. When he wasn't exploiting this device to bed them, he held court with hilarious improvised rants in the canteen. These were popular with all but the tutors, who commented that he was perverse not to bring such expression to class.

A band was on and Andy was being morose and poetic over a pint of Guinness at a table near the dance-floor.

'I preferred your other act.'

She was leaning over the rail that bordered the dance area. Her breasts, clad in a tight black leotard, were flattened against the chrome, her cleavage making a definite 'Y'.

'What other act?'

'In the canteen. It's funny.' She smiled, showing all her teeth.

'Someone has to draw attention from the food.'

Although he couldn't hear her laugh above the thudding bass he imagined it was a nice one. She wiped the perspiration from her neck, unwrapped the sweater from her waist and took a seat opposite him.

'Want a drink?' he asked.

She shook her head and produced a plastic bottle of water.

'What were you going on about? *Other* act?'

'Preferred it to this one. The wounded soldier. It doesn't suit you.' She took a sip of lukewarm water and watched his jaw tighten. 'I'm right, aren't I?'

'So why are you talking to me now?'

'Thought it was time to bury the hatchet.'

'You mean you've run out of people to shag as well?'

She pursed her lips, but her eyes were steady on him. Suddenly, she lifted the bottle to her neck and poured the liquid down her front. It soaked her breasts, causing her nipples to crinkle to hardness and Andy's trousers to swell.

'I thought I might try scraping the barrel,' she dead-panned.

'I'll get a barrel.'

'Ha, ha.'

'You know it wasn't me who . . .' Andy pointed to her breasts and drew invisible rings in the air.

'Yeah. I found out.'

'When?'

'Six months ago. Some party. You found out too?'

He nodded, then frowned. 'Now all I have to do is get the bastard that threw that dustbin through the engineering department window.'

'Well, if you do, I'd like to shake his hand.'

Andy held out his hand. She took it, smiling, and led him away.

They became an item the next day and inseparable for the rest of her time at college.

'Where the *sod* is he?' spat Andy, giving the terraced house the hard stare. Rob had said he'd be back at three and it was gone half past.

That had been only part of their phone conversation. Andy had listened with evaporating patience as Rob sprinted through his day's itinerary. This included meetings with a prominent TV company, something about filming and a voice-over. Michelle was right. He did hate Rob Gillen. He hated his act; his estuary drawl; his silk shirts; his long-legged strut; and his Rodinesque hands and feet.

He also hated the fact that he had his own television show.

Andy Crowe and Rob Gillen (né Richard, but there was already a Dick Gillen in Equity) first met at a comedy class when they started out as performers. Richard, already full of himself, heckled the tutor and never showed up again. Andy, always a diligent student, sat out the course and later came across him on their many open-mike nights together.

These shows were held in damp and shabby rooms in pubs and were attended by other turns, their friends and people who liked damp, shabby rooms in pubs. On stage, Richard was boisterous, invariably overran his allotted time and actively canvassed the audience to heckle him. He did this, he explained, for practice. It had the effect of making him impossible to follow: not because he was good but because he had 'turned' the crowd.

Still in his mid-twenties, Richard worked days as a salesman for a satellite television company and was therefore used to putting up with and selling crap. His material was unoriginal and undemanding, but what mattered more was that he showed no trace of nerves. This was a quality that had the other fledgling comedians scurrying to brand him with a nickname. They tried Gillen, Man of Steel, but it never stuck. However, when he became known by variations on his surname (Gilly, Gillsey), Andy knew he was on his way.

He, by contrast, continued to slug it out in the free spots, working hard at his craft and ruthlessly editing his jokes down to the pithiest one-liners. Sometimes there were no jokes at all, and he was essentially just another drunk in a pub shouting at strangers.

Although the London comedy scene was known as the 'Circuit', it resembled more a universe of planets orbiting at different speeds. Comics ranged far and wide and only came into conjunction at certain times of the year. It was, therefore, at least nine months before Andy and Richard worked together again on the same bill.

The North London pub was packed, and the condensation made runnels in the nicotine-stained walls. The dressing room was the pub kitchen and its sink the performers' toilet. Andy had pulled his act together and was getting paid work. The quality of his material shone through, and he'd become more comfortable on stage as a result. There was even a genuine element to the post-gig back-slapping by the other comics. Topping the bill that evening was the newly christened Rob

Gillen, who barged into the tiny kitchen during the interval and snapped off his new mobile.

'How's it going, Rob?' asked Andy, who had done well and was still basking in crowd love.

'Brilliant. I've got thirty gigs this month and I'm in with the Agency.'

'See you changed your name.'

'Yeah.'

'Dick suited you better.'

Rob mimed a man helpless with laughter.

'Did you catch my act?' asked Andy, fishing.

'Nah. I was doubling up. Only got here a couple of minutes ago.'

The conversation moved on to other things, which in comedic terms meant Rob trying out new material on him. He also managed to let slip that he had bedded two of the more attractive female comics and had decided that their on-stage feminist diatribes were a 'load of tosh'. He was then called to the stage and went through to tear the room apart. Andy watched for a bit but left before the end.

Nosing his car homewards through the late-night traffic on the Holloway Road, he admitted to himself that Rob's delivery was stronger than ever. Shame, he thought, that Gillen hadn't been around to hear his set. But as he discovered some months later, that wasn't entirely true.

CHAPTER FIVE

Keep Out of Reach of Children

————◆————

Danny One-Slice slumped back on the wooden slats and scooped sweat from under his breasts. He massaged it over his paunch then worked down, kneading the doughy flesh until his hand slipped underneath to cup his testicles. Clenching his buttocks, he raised and lowered himself on the white towel and rearranged his balls as if they were a still life. Puckering his lips, he launched a gob of phlegm on to the coals, where it fizzed and splattered like a fried egg on a griddle.

The other men in the sauna wrinkled their noses but thought better of complaining.

Despite the non-stop epilepsy of MTV blaring in the corner, it had been a good work-out. He had completed two circuits of all the machines bar the Stairmaster (which he didn't need as he ran up eleven flights at home). He had bench-pressed 120 kgs, worked his lats, abs and pecs until the muscles screamed for mercy, and then run for twenty minutes until the rubber treadmill was slippery with perspiration. After that, most of his flu symptoms abated, along with his feelings of antagonism towards Jason.

Discarding his luminous Bermuda shorts and navy blue vest, he showered, raked a wide-bladed comb through his hair and goatee, and settled down for his regular session in the sauna. He loved the heat and the mustiness of it and often told people that it reminded him of the Philippines. No one ever pointed out that the nearest he'd been to south-east Asia was a Thai restaurant in Sandwell.

With the prospect of Doug's job on the horizon, things were looking up. He placed a row of tiny aromatherapy bottles on the bench and gazed at the thermometer. It read 85 degrees. Having filled the wooden bucket from the tap in the shower room, he anointed it with droplets of Olbas, menthol and eucalyptus. Satisfied with the potion, he was about to splash it on to the coals when another body-builder rose and left the small wooden room. With a grunt, he drizzled the mixture on to the heater. Steam billowed and the pink bodies of the two remaining white men prickled with sweat. One of them was skinny-looking, more in need of a good fry-up than a gym: the other was Bob, an ex-boxer from Belfast who provided him with his steroids. Bob was in his late forties with white candy-floss hair and a body mottled and dimpled from old bouts. He was scanning the heat-crinkled pages of his *Racing Post* on the lower bench.

'How'd you get on with the Strombaject?' he asked.

'Not bad.'

'Only I was reading somewhere about your side effects.'

Danny dipped his hands into the bucket and sprinkled his thighs with water. 'Such as?'

'Think they said it was the liver.'

There was a pause. 'The liver isn't a muscle.'

Bob took this in. 'You're right there.'

'The pills are for muscles,' added Dan, making his point.

'All the same, you'll not be wanting to mix them. You want to make sure you drink a lot of water. Flush it through the system.'

'How do they go with Day Nurse?'

'Day Nurse?'

'And Night Nurse. I got this cold.'

The skinny man tuned in. As he focused on Danny, his eyes popped and he let out an involuntary gasp. Worrying his towel around his waist, he scampered out of the sauna.

'What's up with him?' murmured Bob.

'Anyway,' continued Dan, 'I've been mixing stuff all me life. It don't affect me.'

Bob folded his tinder-dry paper. 'Well, that's about it for me.' He wrinkled his bulbous nose.

'Jaysus, what's that smell?'

'Essential oils. Good for the skin.'

Bob was staring. 'None too good for yours by the looks of it.'

Danny rubbed his hands across his chest, sniffed and recoiled. 'What's this shit?'

'That'll be your toxins. I told you to watch it.'

As Bob sidled off, Danny gazed down at his body. His pores were oozing a rheumy liquid that smelled like a blend of Gruyère cheese and dead goat. He tried to rub it away and succeeded only in staining his towel yellow. He flung the cloth on to the coals and left it to smoulder.

Bursting out of the sauna, Danny locked the changing-room door, leaped into the shower and hosed himself down. After ten minutes of vigorous massage, he emerged and applied half a bottle of Aramis to his torso. This still didn't counteract the stink, so he showered again, grating a nail-brush over the worst-affected areas.

When he emerged, his skin was raw and blotchy where it had been in contact with the aftershave. He dressed quickly, ignoring the frantic banging on the door as other gym-users tried to get in. Next, he went through Bob's jacket for a suitable antidote and secured an impressive haul of pills. Slipping them into the side pocket of his sports bag, he wrenched open the door and shouldered a path out past the front desk.

The back garden of Doug's house was unlikely to win any prizes in the Britain in Bloom contest unless there was a category for weeds, mattresses and rotting junk. He had worked up a sweat carrying out the tightly baled guns and digging pits for them. He was smoothing rubble over a second hole when a thin voice wafted over his shoulder.

'Who died?'

It was his Greek landlord. A bald gnome of a man, Nicos Demesthenes had a face scored with deep lines and a voice as smooth as might be permitted on sixty unfiltered cigarettes a day.

'The cat,' replied Doug, hoping he hadn't been watched for too long and that he wouldn't have to do something drastic, like cuffing the landlord with the spade.

'We don' have no cat here.'

Doug rubbed a hand over his stubbly head. 'Not now we don't.'

'You had cat in room? You know I don' allow pets.'

'I know. You can't squeeze them for rent.'

'I was going to speak with you about that.'

'What?'

Nicos raised his hands in a gesture of woe that spoke of the centuries of tragedy his people had undergone. The ratty cardigan spoiled the effect. 'My rent,' he wailed. 'Where's my rent.'

'You'll get it.' Doug kicked a slab of old linoleum over the grave and set off back to the house. Nicos followed him along the downstairs corridor and up the stairs that reeked of cabbage and aged grease.

'I'm looking for my rent,' he said as he sucked on a dog-end.

'Well, let's look together, then.'

Doug instantly regretted saying this. The knives were lying partially wrapped up on his bed. Plus he couldn't recall if he'd put the Glock away or not.

'Maybe in your room?'

Doug barred the way. 'You're not coming in.'

'Is my house.'

Doug studied the man's shining pate. 'The Housing Act of 1983 states that the landlord must give due warning if he wishes to enter the room of a sitting tenant.'

'OK. I warn you now. I'm coming in.'

'What do you want, Nicos?'

'I see if you have made changes. To the decoration.'

'What decoration?' The main features of the room were its high walls, its cracked ceiling and its 1950s wooden furniture. If Nicos had decorated at all, the style could only be termed 'penurious simplicity'.

'Maybe you make improvements?' offered the landlord, suspiciously.

'The only improvement you could make to this place is with a wrecking ball.'

Nicos reached for the handle but Doug's hand was there. The feel of his papery paw was enough to make him flinch. With deliberation, Nicos steered his cigarette towards the fleshy part between Dough's thumb and fingers.

'Jesus. All right,' he spat, throwing the door open.

Demesthenes limped inside and Doug slammed the door. How was he ever going to become a master criminal if the bloody *landlord* walked in every time he had something going?

'See? No rent in here.'

Nicos didn't seem to notice the spread of knives laid out on the bed, the bin-liners and the gaffer tape. Doug remembered that he had put the Glock in the bedside cabinet. As he moved to position himself by the bed, Nicos started fiddling with the free-standing gas fire.

'This work OK?'

'Yeah, leaks nicely and makes it rain all down the windows.'

'Good,' replied Nicos, missing the point. He gazed at the fly-blown light shade above them, scanned the walls and ceiling and came to the wardrobe.

'There's a land in there, full of lions and witches, and it's rent-free,' Doug said.

The Greek opened the door and peered inside to see if this was true. 'No, only clothes.' He swung the door on its hinges, catching the light in the perished mirror. He stopped at Doug's reflection. It was sweeping the booty up in the bedspread.

'What you got there?' asked Nicos.

Doug pulled out his wallet and feathered through the notes. 'How much is the rent?'

'Four hundred sixty pounds,' said the landlord, not missing a beat.

'I haven't got it.'

He moved fast for an old man. Before Doug could challenge him, he'd pulled open the bundle and was examining the array of knives. Doug stood by helplessly as he perused the catch.

'Very nice,' Nicos said, selecting a long Bowie knife. 'You skin the cat?'

Doug vaguely remembered some excuse concerning a feline. God knows what they do with them in Greece. Suddenly, Nicos flung the knife at the door. The blade dug deep into the wood and made that sound you get when you twang a ruler on the edge of a desk.

'You give me all these,' said Nicos, waving a hand at the bed. 'And one hundred pounds.'

It wasn't a bad exchange: They hadn't cost him anything and he'd be square on the rent.

'All right,' sighed Doug.

Nicos nodded minutely. He threw the swag over his shoulder, went to the door and tugged the Bowie knife from it. 'This damage,' he said, scraping the blade across the panel, 'comes out of next month – OK?'

Jason walked the twin tanks of oxygen on to the trolley and tried to run them up the steel ramp into the back of the van. The load hurtled up a couple of feet then rolled down fast. Skipping backwards, he prevented the tanks from falling into the inspection pit by wedging his steel-toed boot under the left wheel. The second time he took a longer run-up. Reaching the point where his strength achieved equilibrium with the weight of the orange cylinders, he was surprised to find that gravity was the stronger force. On his third attempt, he managed it and sent the cylinders booming into the back of the Transit.

As he buckled them to the inner walls with leather straps, he thought about the job. It's got Danny involved so it needs muscle. Then there's me and the van and the oxyacetylene. Maybe it's a safe? Or a bank? Or perhaps we're gonna cut drugs out of a container at the airport? And how much dosh? Hundreds? Thousands? Millions? Or maybe it was something poxy like nicking cars, which only ever made him enough to piss away on a Saturday night.

He smelled cigar smoke. Dad was back. No sign of him, though. Jason wheeled the trolley to the rim of the van and was about to send it plummeting down when his father appeared in the bay. Joffe Senior was a man pickled in alcohol. His dyed-black hair was drawn up into a quiff and his drape suit screamed ageing teddy boy. He smoked a thin cheroot and his voice, when it came, was Wolverhampton.

'What's goin' on, Jason?'

'Helping out a mate.'

'Who?'

'Pete, up Aston way. He's buggered his Metro.'

'Can't he bring it in?'

Jason cupped his neck with a greasy paw. 'Think he wrapped it round a lamppost.'

'Bloody joy-rider, no doubt. Probably nicked the car in the first place.'

As he had never dealt with an entirely legitimate motor vehicle, Jason declined to comment on his father's moral stance. 'Have you looked out the front?' he asked.

' 'Course I pigging have, son. Why'd you close up the lot?'

A grin. 'Sold that Fiesta this morning.'

'The E-reg?'

Jason dug into his pocket and produced a wad of notes. 'Four-fifty for cash.'

Taking the proffered money, his father stroked the bills with his thumb. 'And the rest.'

With the tiniest morsel of remorse, Jason reached into the top pocket of his overalls and extracted another fifty.

'Keep going.'

Jason slid another few notes from his trousers, still leaving his father light by fifty pounds.

Danny shuddered as he steered the old woman to the chair. He hated this place and everything about it: the disinfectant smell, the sturdy pipes and tables, the functional flooring, and the regulations. He sensed caged eyes on him, at once envious of his freedom and yet brimming with a hidden superiority. He helped his mother to sit, then knelt to straighten her skirt. Her frail hands fluttered to her handbag.

He prised one of them away, gave it a reassuring squeeze

and stood by her. She smiled up at her son, then opened the clasp and delved inside. Extracting a lipstick and compact, she coloured in her lips. When she had done she put the cosmetics away and sat prim and tiny on the seat. Danny folded his arms respectfully over his crotch, as if already at the funeral.

A bell rang and the prisoners shuffled past. An old man with steel hair and skin the colour of peanut butter came and sat opposite them. His frame was large for a sexagenarian. His mouth formed a brave smile as his fingers mirrored his wife's on the glass.

'Hello, Sweetcakes. How's things?' he asked in a voice smoothed by time.

She leaned closer. 'Not so bad, Carlos.'

Danny tightened his lips. It was a lie. She was ill. She had a persistent cough from the damp flat and her arthritis had worsened to the point where he carried her to bed each evening. However, she'd forbidden Danny to tell his father that they had been dumped in the high-rise. It was her burden, she said, and she would bear it as her husband bore his sentence.

'Daniel?' She urged.

There was a gentle tug on his sleeve. His father was smiling up at him.

'You asleep, boy?' he asked as Dan pressed the phone to his ear.

'How you doing, Dad?'

'Fine. You OK?'

'About evens.'

'Still on the door at the club?'

Danny nodded.

'You want to watch yourself, Daniel.'

'You watch yourself. Lot of dangerous people in here.'

His father formed a fist. 'Better not start on me.'

Danny smiled at the gesture of defiance. It wasn't just old

man's pride; it was their bond. More importantly, it was a confirmation that justice had been done in their household – even if it hadn't been ratified by British law.

In the late 1960s, Danny's parents had escaped the Marcos regime and had made England their home. Carlos struggled to find menial jobs and supplemented his income with house-breaking. As soon as Danny was old enough, Carlos drummed into him that to survive you must accept life for what it is and take your due, even if that meant the occasional spell at Her Majesty's pleasure.

When Danny reached ten and his twin sisters were seven, Carlos got eighteen months for handling. A month later, Pepe arrived from Manila. News had reached their relatives in the Philippine capital and Carlos's brother had been dispatched to look after them – custom being that a family had to have a man and in Carlos's absence he would take over.

Uncle Pepe was a short, overweight, brutish man who smelled of spirits. His side of the clan had profited greatly under Ferdinand Marcos and he still acted as if he were a feudal baron. He wore a succession of loud suits and insisted that the family attend church on a regular basis; also that they contribute to the collection. His own concept of charity started at Ladbroke's and ended in the off-licence.

The children were always sent to bed early. Lying awake, Danny heard the rattling of the bed and the weeping coming from his mother's room. He bunched up his fists and gritted his teeth so hard that he developed migraines. His mother, Nina, had no one to turn to, as her family had perished back in the Philippines.

A sky-blue suit was purchased for Danny to wear on prison-visiting days. On these, Pepe drove the family to Long Lartin in his Ford Zephyr, drinking from his hip flask and warning Danny and his sisters to behave in front of their father. Then as now, Danny smiled through the visits, never speaking his mind, never letting down his mother, always burning with shame.

Six months into his father's sentence, Danny heard a thud in the bedroom next door and his mother's cry. Her bruises the next morning hardened his resolve to act. Already a bulky child, he knew he needed to add muscle. A friend's father had an unused set of bar-bells, which he borrowed and hid in his bedroom cupboard.

One Friday in the pub, Pepe had been chatting up the barmaid, an activity that had offended a group of young Handsworth men. He showed them his blade but was outnumbered and taken outside. When the police arrived he received not compassion but overt hostility. He returned to take it out on his brother's wife and family. Danny, a prepubescent ball of fury, stopped him in the lounge. Pepe parried his blows and beat him back into the kitchen, where Danny grabbed a knife and slashed the man across the chest.

His uncle survived, but Dan ran off that night and took the milk train to London. Three days later, he was arrested in Soho for dipping. On his return, Pepe deflected the suspicious fussing of the social workers and lied about his injury. Next visiting day, he had Nina and the family coached. However, Carlos, reading his son's face, held him back on the pretext of asking about his schooling. A weeping Danny explained all. Carlos swore his son to silence.

On his release, Danny's father returned to a celebration organised by his brother. The council block was festooned with banners and a band had been hired to play in the street. Family and neighbours partied long into the night and, once the guests had gone, Carlos kissed his children, made love to his wife and slit his brother's throat.

He surrendered immediately and was sentenced to life. Over the years, he had been shuffled from prison to prison and presently resided at Drake Hall in Staffordshire. It was the nearest he had been to Birmingham and his wife in nearly a decade.

'Be good to your mother,' said Carlos, drawing away from the table as the bell sounded.

'Do my best.'

'You be careful,' smiled the old man.

As he led his mother away, Danny felt his sorrow at his parents' predicament give way to growing excitement. This could, of course, he admitted privately, be due to the head-rush from the drugs. Once they were outside, he cracked open a fresh bottle of Night Nurse. Squinting at the label, he read the words 'Keep out of reach of children'.

Good advice, he thought. Little buggers.

CHAPTER SIX

The Dangers of Smoking

Andy sat sipping tea in Rob's kitchen. His gaze swept the room, taking in the sunflower walls, the Sabatier knives, the Le Creuset pans and Natasha and Ashley, respectively Rob's girlfriend and their one-year-old son. Natasha was empirically gorgeous: slender figure, blond hair, light blue eyes, snub nose and a large mouth. She looked, he decided, like one of those mums in the TV adverts that have never been within puking distance of a child in their lives. She even looked sexy in dungarees, for Christ's sake! Dungarees that — he couldn't help noticing — hung open at the sides to display her tanned tummy and a glimpse of white cotton panties. It also didn't help that her left breast was thrust into Ashley's tiny bud of a mouth. He had the urge to smoke and pulled out a fresh pack.

'Sorry, umm . . .' purred Natasha, waving a hand at the child.

'Oh . . . right.' He broke the cigarette in half as he tried to push it back into the packet.

'Come far?'

There were two responses to this.

'Couple of feet on a good day,' replied Andy, choosing the wrong one. She gave him a mother's look: one that implied he had irrevocably corrupted her child. 'Sorry. Force of habit. Couple of miles. Willesden.'

Willesden being a conversational cul-de-sac, they lapsed into silence.

Rob was in the living room trawling his post and playing back his messages. He had changed, noted Andy. He was bulkier round the waist and fatter about the face – something that didn't show up on *LiveWires*, the programme he hosted on Channel 4. And wasn't his hair receding? Must be a lot of pressure having a child about the place. Two if you included the baby. He looked again at Natasha. She had put her breast away and Ashley was asleep in her arms. She hadn't bothered to fasten the bib of her dungarees and the flap peeled from her chest like a strip of torn poster.

'Why'd you have a kid?' he asked.

She furrowed her smooth brow. 'Odd question.'

'I mean, did you wake up one morning and say, "Hey, we've had enough of sex and sleeping and having a clean house? Let's throw all that away and breed"?'

'You're trying out material,' she stated flatly.

Andy blushed. There had been a time when he used his natural wit. Nowadays he just seemed to scroll up the relevant file of comic observations.

'It's all right,' she added pleasantly. 'Rob does it all the time.'

'No change there, then,' he said, hoping to lure her in with the bait of Rob's past.

'Known him long?'

He permitted himself a smile. 'We started at the same time. Back when he was still Richard.'

'Oh, right. D'you do telly as well?'

'Yeah,' he lied, having only performed on a cable station with the budget of a homeless person's magazine.

'Might've seen you. What was your name again?'

'Andy Crowe.'

She wrinkled her pert nose. 'Didn't you play the Cave last year? In May?'

He didn't need to go into the diary where he logged every gig, payment and a rating out of ten for the performance. He recalled the show as a nine out of ten and remembered being cheered from the room as the new comic messiah. 'Yeah, that was me.'

'Oh, right. Yeah. Not bad, I suppose.'

Andy stood outside, puffing away. He hated non-smokers. They were sanctimonious and preachy and their clothes reeked of cotton and denim. He flicked his butt. Time they were moving if they were going to avoid the rush hour. A shiver went through him. In four hours, he would be proving himself to the audience, to the club-owners, to the Agency, to Rob and to Michelle: especially Michelle. He was about to go back inside when a drain at his feet gushed foamy liquid. 'He's only having a bloody bath!' he moaned.

More out of anger than need, he lit another cigarette. It occurred to him then that smoking had always been bound up with his and Michelle's relationship. It was more or less compulsory at college, unless you were one of those weirdo students who drank strange teas and practised yoga because you couldn't make friends.

The summer she graduated, Michelle landed a role in a fringe production heading for Edinburgh. They went up together and lived on chips, salty pies and drink. She received a ripple of favourable notices, causing the agents to crawl out from under their stones. The best offer came from one who promised her the West End within two years. She and Andy celebrated by climbing Calton Hill at midnight, intent on making love under the stars – or at least in view of a capital city drowned in posters.

He got as far as removing her jacket.

The first interruption came from a pair of lost American tourists from Wichita Falls who had managed the summit without the aid of any major lifting equipment.

Next time he got her shirt and shoes off.

A street performer on a unicycle, playing a flute. Andy ran after him, hurling small coins. That got applause from the Yanks.

The third time they were interrupted by a group of medical students drowning their sorrows after receiving the worst and briefest review ever to grace the early edition of a family newspaper ('Shite', *The Scotsman*).

They gave up on it after that. Michelle sparked up and promised Andy that if she hadn't made it in two years, then she would give up acting.

Important cigarette number one.

On their return, they moved into a tiny flat in Southgate while Andy completed his course. Michelle went for a plethora of castings: none of which were right for her, nor she for them. At that time she was still trying to obtain her Equity card by the unusual method of performing as opposed to stripping. Eventually, a minor theatre promoter forged the necessary contracts and her penury attained professional status. Following graduation, Andy made good and supported her in the way of all middle-class graduates with a useless degree: he took service industry jobs and swindled the dole.

As time went by it dawned on Michelle that her face didn't fit. The avaricious agent had secured her a couple of walk-on parts in the soaps, but she never got any of the castings. It was during one of these that another actress hinted she should have her nose done. She protested vehemently. There was nothing wrong with her nose. It wasn't large or hooked, merely a tad off-kilter as a result of a bicycle accident as a child.

Insecurity crept in and she began to study the minute variances in people's faces. There was, she noted, a big difference between, say, Sharon Stone and Sharon Stone with a wonky nose. The back pages of *The Stage* were full of them: Sean Connery with Dumbo's ears, Clint Eastwood as a bank manager, an ageing platinum blonde who was a dead ringer for Marilyn Monroe post-suicide. Not that she was any kind of a look-alike, but these sad theatricals really showed how low you could sink in the business, with the possible exception of becoming a juggler.

Things did not improve over the year and the nearest her agent got to the West End was when he needed her to act as his stunt wife for the première of an abysmal British comedy. Shortly after that came important cigarette number two.

It was Easter. Andy had saved up some money and had offered to take her to a hotel in Dartmouth for a week. She accepted gladly, having been channelling her energies of late by cutting down on drink, packing in smoking and crying a lot for no apparent reason.

He had recently had the car serviced and they sped along the M4 under a sky of vast white clouds. Having chewed the life out of a piece of gum, Michelle opened up the ashtray and extracted an item.

'What's this?'

He looked over. A cigarette butt.

'It's got lipstick on it.'

'So?'

She scrutinised it with the attention of a forensic scientist. 'I gave up fags a fortnight ago.'

'Except when you scrounged that one in the pub.'

'Andy, who's been in the car?'

'No one.'

'Come on.'

'I told you. No one.'

'So I'm imagining all this, then?'

'No, but . . . well, *I* didn't put it there.'

He tried to defend himself against the accusation of infidelity, but discovered that the court of human relations is a Napoleonic one. By Swindon they had sunk into prickly silence. They arrived at their hotel too late for dinner and fumed in their room with overpriced sandwiches.

Next day it was pouring with rain and they almost went home. Michelle went out and bought some fags and, on her return, bullied him into talking about their relationship. By nightfall they had run the topic into the ground, and the Mystery of the Lipstick Cigarette became their second taboo subject. The first was her blonde cousin whom Andy had once foolishly admitted to fancying like hell.

On the third day, the weather and her mood had cheered considerably, and they walked arm in arm along the beach like catalogue lovers. Crunching back along the pebbles, they stopped on the front to watch the Punch and Judy show.

'Weird,' she said, snuggling into him. 'This is a display of wife-battering and child abuse.'

'And crocodiles.'

'And crocodiles.'

'Someone should put a stop to it.' Andy pulled away from her, scampered round to the back of the tent and sneaked in under the canvas flaps. Moments later there was a violent commotion and puppets flew from the front of the tiny stage. The circle of children whooped with delight as his head emerged, grinning.

'That's the way to do it,' he said.

In retrospect, he traced a tectonic shift in their relationship to the cigarette mystery and was saddened never to have discovered the perpetrator. The truth of it was that the mechanic who had serviced his Polo had lent it out to his brother's wife.

She was training to be a marriage guidance counsellor.

*　　*　　*

Andy climbed the stairs to Rob's flat, scowling at the differences between it and his own place. Where were the cracked windows, the mismatched fittings, the breezes under the doors and around the vents? What *was* this with all the matching wallpapers and fabrics?

He went into the living room. There were fresh flowers in a brass vase on the smoked-glass dining table; bare boards; walls painted in lush flat colours; shelves stacked with videos. There was a top-of-the-range midi unit with its black plastic CD tongue extended. He could imagine Mr and Mrs Conran and all the little Ikeas dining happily in this room.

Rob's mobile lay on the table. He decided to try Michelle again, but as he put his hand to the phone, it skittered across the polished surface and clattered to the floor. He bent to the broken pieces and tried to fit them together. No good. Adopting the next-best strategy, he balanced the mobile near the edge of the glass so that the next person to touch it would upend it.

He went into the hall.

'Are you going to be much longer, Rob? I want to get going.'

Natasha poked her head out of a room to his left and shushed him. She was putting the baby to bed.

Rob cracked open the bathroom door. His hair was mussed and he looked ursine in his black towelling dressing gown. 'All right, Crowesy. Plenty of time.'

Andy made some mental calculations: if they didn't leave soon then they would have to take the M1, which meant not hitting Birmingham until around eight. Plus they had to find the venue. A nervous performer, he needed a good hour to pace the streets pre-gig, winding up his bravery like the spring in an old wristwatch.

He sank into the sofa in the living room. A framed black-

and-white photograph on the opposite wall depicted a seated naked woman with her arms resting on her knees. Her hair obscured her face but her pubic area was visible. It was lit from the ground and the hairs gleamed like wire wool.

Natasha padded through in fluffy grey socks.

He tried another shot at conversation. 'I thought Helmut Newton was meant to be sexist these days.'

As she looked over, he realised who the subject was.

'Rob took it actually. We like it.'

He screamed inwardly as she disappeared into the kitchen. If there were a wrong thing to be said at the wrong time he'd be there, feet poised and ready to cram into his mouth. Case in point – the day Michelle finally gave up on acting.

'That's it,' she spat, slamming the door behind her.

'What's it?' mumbled Andy, on his knees in front of the telly.

'I'm packing it in.'

He stuck a knife into the control housing under the screen and twisted it.

'Are you listening to me?'

Squinting at the static. 'Yeah.'

'What's wrong with the telly?'

'Remote's bust. Trying to tune it by hand.'

'Have you tried warming up the batteries?'

'And taking them out and swapping them round.'

'What about the old remote?'

'Tried it.'

'Then leave it alone.'

Andy jiggled the serrated part of the knife against the tiny screw head. The snow worsened and the volume trebled.

'I think I'm getting something.'

She tore the plug from the socket.

'I've spent the afternoon pretending to be a pot of yoghurt for some ponytailed public school tosser.'

Andy, to the blank screen: 'I wanted to watch that new comedy thing.'

'Watching telly's more important than my career, is it?'

'Didn't you just say you were giving it up?'

Bathing his face in cold water, he determined to listen in future. She had given him a good whack and the zip on her bag had caught him full in the face. His eye looked like a cue ball veined with red tendrils.

When they got to talking about it, he told her that of course he respected her decision but that she must be sure that it *was* her decision. And that just because he'd been doing crap jobs for a year instead of what he *really* wanted to do, that should in no way be a factor in her deciding to stop. She said no, actually, it wasn't. Then, pursing her lips, what did *he* want? Andy said he wasn't sure but this alternative comedy lark seemed to be blossoming on telly . . .

'Whatever,' she said.

He allowed a suitable grieving period for her acting career, and once the fortnight was up he persuaded her to go with him to the local comedy club. The acts were mediocre.

'You're easily better than this crap,' she said.

'You think so?'

'Remember the canteen at college? You were so funny.'

'I'm not sure . . .'

'Look, as long as you're not going to be a juggler—'

'I'm not a *complete* wanker.'

'Why don't you jot down some ideas and give it a go?' she suggested.

So Andy took the stuff he'd been working on for a month and tried it out.

The club was south of the river and he was given five minutes. The lights were far too bright and he was wearing his only suit.

'I came out as a comedian last month. Hardest thing was telling my parents. Dad told me to take my quips and banter and never lighten his house again. I was so angry I tried to run him over in my clown's car, but the door and the wheels fell off.'

In retrospect he thought the material too subtle for Crystal Palace. The audience had another word for it. Crap.

Natasha was at the chopping board in the kitchen. Andy leaned against the door frame.

'Is he going to be much longer? We *really* have to go.'

'Don't ask me.'

'I'm going in five minutes, with or without him.'

A baby alarm crackled into life on the counter beside her.

'Oo's a little bay-bee then,' said Rob in baby talk. 'Daddy has to go to work now. Hope Mummy's not doing anything naughty with Crowesy in the kitchen.'

Andy felt the heat in his cheeks.

Natasha dumped a handful of carrots into the food mixer.

' 'Cos we seen how Crowesy was looking at Mummy, didn't we? I think Crowesy wanted to lick Mummy's tits. And rip Mummy's clothes off and shag her on the kitchen table . . .'

Andy's mouth fell open in shock.

Natasha's shoulders heaved with laughter.

Rob came in with the baby alarm held to his mouth. He had shaved and his hair was combed back. He reeked of expensive aftershave. He was over six feet tall in his cowboy boots and he sported black 501s, a dark silk shirt and a knee-length leather coat.

He looked like the entertainments officer for the Nazi Party.

'Show time,' growled Rob Gillen.

CHAPTER SEVEN

Novotel Welcomes
International Drug Dealers

———◆———

Doug parked in the short-stay airport carpark near the
Novotel, opposite the terminal building. He went over to
the hotel and strode into its airy brick-pillared reception area.
The place was in a mid-afternoon slump and staff easily
outnumbered the customers. He was clean-shaven and had put
on a shirt, a tie and the charcoal-grey suit that he used for
court appearances. He carried a neat black briefcase which he
had stolen at Birmingham New Street station: despite it being
empty, he still enjoyed the sense of importance it lent him.

'Afternoon, sir. How may I help you?' The girl's smile was
broad and revealed a trace of lipstick on her teeth. She was
young and frizzy-haired and her name tag read 'Kimberley
Jones'.

'I'd like to book two conference suites with a connecting
door.'

'Certainly, sir. For when?'

'From tonight. My clients are arriving early tomorrow.'

'What facilities will you be requiring?' she asked auto-
matically.

'Meaning?'

'Fax modem? Photocopying?'

'Won't be necessary.'

'I'll just check availability for you.'

Her eyes darted to a screen and her polished nails rattled the keyboard like rain hitting a dustbin. Doug watched, finding the pretence laughable. They were both young enough to enjoy the same kinds of film and music and yet here they were pretending to be all adult and businesslike. Had they been in a pub, he'd have scrolled his eyes down her body and panted like a dog and she would have giggled.

'Will you and your clients be requiring breakfast in the room?'

'Nope.'

'I suppose they'll eat on the plane.'

He grunted assent. She was getting inquisitive. 'Do much travelling yourself?' he asked, rerouting the conversation.

'Not a lot. I was in Spain last summer. As a travel rep.' She crinkled up her nose. 'Didn't work out.' The rain slowed and she hit a full stop. 'We have two choices, sir. The Regency . . .'

Doug made to speak but swallowed the comment. He doubted many members of the royal family stayed here. One of the few objects in Heritage Britain without a 'By royal appointment' sticker was the Corby trouser press.

'. . . on the ground floor or the syndicate rooms on the sixth.'

'The syndicate sounds good.'

'It overlooks the runway. Will that be a problem?'

'Is it soundproofed?'

'All our rooms are soundproofed, sir.'

He nodded. Another plus.

'I'll get the porter to show you up.'

She rang a bell, moved to a series of pigeonholes and extracted a bulky plastic laminate with a set of keys attached to it. A youth appeared in a waistcoat the colour of his acne, and the two men travelled in respectful hotel silence to the sixth floor.

The room contained a long oval table and several chairs. There was an old overhead projector in one corner and a TV/video resting on a fake walnut unit. As the boy drew the blinds, Doug realised why facing the runway might be a problem for some. On take-off, the grey underbellies of the planes skimmed the ceiling. The noise leaked through the double glazing and made the water choppy in the glass jug on the table.

Ignoring the porter, who was showing off the TV as if it were a prize in a game show, Doug checked the interconnecting door and the shower and toilet. They too were linked to the other room, which was a mirror image of the first.

'These'll be fine,' he said, taking out his wallet.

While the porter straightened the chairs, he fanned out a hand of credit cards, wondering who'd be the lucky one to pay for all of this.

'What this bizniz, you say?'

It was an hour later and he was sitting in the rear of a BMW classic series seven. They had been twice round the Bullring and were heading off towards Aston. Beside him was Nelson, a Yardie known for his many mistresses and a propensity for slaughtering his opponents.

Doug was shit scared.

To his right sat a huge man he didn't know. This black giant reeked of stale sweat and his nylon sports clothing gave off enough static to power up the national grid. In the driving seat, another Yard man was toking a giant spliff. There was enough ganja smoke in the car interior to render the installation of the tinted windows pointless. Sensimillia seeds crackled and fell on to the driver's lap, causing him to weave across the lanes as he brushed them away.

'The business is a sweet deal,' offered Doug. 'I need you to front some cash and tomorrow you'll get back double your investment in coke.'

Nelson laughed, which he took as a good sign.

The second man joined in, making a whistling noise through the gaps in his teeth.

The driver passed the joint back to Nelson. It looked like a fat newspaper cigar.

Nelson: 'Me give up me cash? What sort a fresh bwoy you tink you got here?'

A pause. 'The kind who knows I can be trusted?'

Nelson blew smoke, then passed the joint to the unnamed man, who made a chillum with his fist.

'Fockin' Irish,' Nelson said. At least he was still grinning.

That he had only ever once been to the Emerald Isle wasn't something Doug wished to mention at this point. Yes, he had an Irish name and parentage, but that was about it. But if the Yardman wanted to see him as a downtrodden martyr or some kind of soul brother/rebellious freedom fighter, then that was fine by him. In fact, he would have sung three verses of 'Danny Boy', if it would have kept the man happy. It was well known in Birmingham criminal circles that Yardies were armed and volatile and that Nelson was their poster boy.

Nelson clicked his fingers. 'Gwan.'

'It's top-grade Colombian coming in from Schipol. Fifty grand's worth. I'm putting up twenty.'

His sphincter tightened as Nelson did his sums.

'You want thirty grand? Rass! You tink I got thirty grand?'

'This car alone is worth thirty gee's.'

'And you got twenty, Irish?'

'I'm getting it tonight.'

'Where from? The pussy in the wall?'

Doug joined in as they dissolved into hysterics. He wished he had been permitted to bring Danny along but Yardies were notoriously racist, and anyway Nelson had vetoed it. Plus there wouldn't have been room for him in the car: not with the other big guy.

The Jamaican was deadly earnest. 'You say top Colombian? How come I not know 'bout it?' Doug lowered his voice. 'I spent some time in Amsterdam a while back. Made my own connections. This is grade-A coke and you're guaranteed to double your bread.' He gave him a watery smile. 'You might get five or six times that if you convert it into rocks.'

That might do it. Tendering the crack conversion possibilities.

Leather squeaked as Nelson turned to him, his liquid yellow eyes burning into Doug's face. The Yardie raised a hand to his tongue and wetted his thumb and index finger. 'Gi''me taste.'

He'd known this was coming and as a precaution had taken a trip to The Hague a fortnight earlier to bring back a sample. He hadn't touched the stash, instead keeping it chilled in the mini-fridge in his bed-sit. It was one of the few places he knew Nicos would not dare explore. Producing a silver pillbox, he opened it so that Nelson could see the powder. The Yardie stuck his fingers into it like a child exploring jelly.

Cramming the cocaine into his cavernous nostrils, Nelson inhaled and swallowed back a pharmaceutical trickle. With the concentration of a connoisseur, he licked his fingers, daubed more of the drug around his gums, and then prised the case from Doug's hand.

Outside, the streetlamps had flickered on but the sodium made no impact on the sky. Through the car windows, Doug saw a windswept high street full of tatty shops, fast-food bars and squat municipal buildings. It was deserted save for a knot of kids strewing the pavement with food wrappers.

'When you need the bread?' asked Nelson.

Doug tried not to make his relief too evident. 'I'll have to see some of it now. So I can tell the guys you have it.'

Nelson reached into his pocket.

Doug flinched.

To his relief, the man produced not a gun but a thick roll of used twenties. He held the money under Doug's nose so he could smell it. 'Two gee's right there, *rass!*'

Oh, what the hell.

'Got any more on you?'

With a furrow deepening on his shining forehead, the gangsta produced two more rolls. Doug remained calm. 'OK. You'll need to bring thirty grand in total tomorrow.'

'Where we meet?'

'The Novotel at the airport. This guy is *very* nervous so you have to be cool. We're going to see him in Suite 603 at exactly six forty-five a.m. I've got the keys so I'll see you up there. Go straight up and be on time. Five minutes late and he won't deal.'

Nelson reached into his pocket again. This time he did bring out a gun. It was a nine-millimetre Glock 17 semi-automatic. Doug refrained from pointing and saying, 'Hey, I've got one of those.'

The Yardie held the cold metal to Doug's cheek and sucked on his teeth. 'You know we be carrying. No fuck-ups. Ayrie?'

Doug told his heart it could stop pounding any time it was ready.

Nelson put the weapon away.

The fat man turned and studied Doug's face. His mouth was open and his tongue lolled inside it like a pink gobstopper. He wondered if the man were going to hit him. Instead, the sportswear freak spoke up in a broad Black Country accent.

'Has it got a minibar?'

'W-what?'

'This hotel room?'

'Well, it's a conference room, so I'm not sure if . . .'

'How about them little shampoos?'

'In the bathroom? Sure.'

'I love hotels. Specially when you get them pillow choclits.'

Nelson glared at the man. 'Ya shut ya mout.'

'But . . .'

'Shurrup, Tone,' barked Nelson, his voice momentarily slipping back to its origins.

'Sorry, Nelse.'

'Dyam brodder.'

'I were only askin',' replied the hulk.

Ten minutes later, Doug stood shivering on a street corner. He hailed a cab, issued directions to the driver and collapsed on the seat. It was a while before he was calm enough to reach for his mobile: even then his fingers were so jittery that it took three attempts to dial the number.

'Take a vowel,' said Dan, adding in a whisper, 'A *vowel*, you tosser.' He was sitting in his track suit in his favourite chair at home. The seat was covered in tattered yellow upholstery and sank to the floor with his weight. *Countdown* was on and Danny One-Slice had not noticeably decreased his drug intake. The speed had dried up his nasal passages for an hour or so, but he was starting to sniff again. Having tired of the sickly taste of the Night and Day Nurse, he had counteracted it with a beakerful of rum and Coke. In his bedroom, the lucky dip of steroids and anti depressants lay discarded in his gym bag.

Danny listened to but did not watch the programme, being too engrossed in his task. To his left were a dozen black spray cans stacked in a cardboard tray; on his lap a roll of printed self-adhesive labels. Intermittently he would reach out, place a can between his knees and with exaggerated care attach the label to it. The tip of his tongue poked from the side of his mouth as he worked.

His mother Nina sat behind him at the dining table. She too was working on the project. Her tiny frame was wrapped in a crocheted shawl and her hands were immersed in a bowl of warm water. She was soaking labels from a different set of cans. These were pillar-box red and emblazoned with a complex list of chemicals and obscure warnings. Once she'd cleaned them, she put each can to one side to dry.

On the mock-teak stereo cabinet, Danny had fashioned a spraying booth from an old cardboard box. He had resprayed three dozen cans that afternoon, masking off the metal rims and the nozzle and covering each evenly with black paint. A matching black plastic lid completed the job.

'This OK, Daniel?' asked his mother, waving the last of the batch at him.

Dan smiled in acknowledgment, then stood up and snapped open a flat-pack box. He put a dozen cans inside it, packing them neatly.

'Tea?'

'That'd be great, Mum.'

She made to lift the bowl of water but her hands shook with the weight of it. Danny took it from her and she followed him through to the galley kitchen. While he poured away the cloudy liquid, she took glass mugs from the unit, filled the kettle and lit the gas with a match.

'Daddy's getting older, don't you think?'

'We all are, Mum.'

'Want something to eat?'

'No thanks.'

Her olive eyes looked at him quizzically.

'It's this flu,' he said, putting a hand to his throbbing nose.

'Feed it,' she said, reaching into the unit for a tin of

biscuits. She placed it on the Fablon-covered counter, levered it open and pressed a piece of shortcake to her lips. Saying nothing, she put it down and replaced the lid.

'How about a ham sangrich?' she asked.

Danny looked up at the cabinet. In the top corner was a fresh patch of crusted mould. He folded his arms and massaged his biceps.

'I'll go clear up in the lounge,' he said after a few moments, then passed through the plastic strip curtains.

As he gathered up the papers, something caught his eye. Plucking out a page of the Birmingham *Evening Mail*, his gaze fell on a photograph of the empty lot he had visited earlier in the day. In front of the site were two men in suits and hard hats shaking hands. The caption read: 'Cllr Jacobs and Stephen McCreary (left) at the new business resources site in Handsworth'.

Danny skimmed the article, then fetched a ruler. With the same precision he had used on his labelling, he severed the piece from the page. He folded it and took it to his bedroom, where he tucked it into the breast pocket of his dinner jacket.

A buzzing came from out in the hall. Dan went and hit the button on the intercom.

'Yo.'

A stream of crackling metallic diarrhoea. Dan pressed the button again and then left it. Whoever it was would find a way up. The council's only concession towards improving condi-tions in the block had been to install the intercom and security doors. Neither had worked properly since their inception.

Back in the lounge, he blew his nose heavily and settled down to wait for the cartoons. After ten minutes there was a thumping at the front door.

'Jeez . . . Fu . . . lift . . . broke,' gasped Jason.

Danny grinned. 'Good exercise, innit?' He barred the entrance, forcing Jason to remain out on the windswept balcony. 'You get the gear?'

Jason, still wheezing, raised a thumb.

'Better come in, then. Doug'll be giving us a shout soon.'

The youth trailed in behind him, reeling at the eclectic clash of colours in the lounge. Half the room was a brown-and-orange ogee pattern circa 1974; the other had been stripped to the plaster except where patches of Pear Tree Blossom and Rind had been applied from free tester pots.

'Hello there,' said Nina, emerging from the kitchen.

'Hello, Mrs. . . .' Jason trailed off and looked desperately at Danny as he realised he didn't know his surname.

'Shake my mum's hand,' commanded the colossal Filipino.

Jason did so. Nina fussed around him, imploring him to remove his puffa jacket and to be seated.

Jason held out the coat.

'What am I – the butler?' snorted Danny, tossing it over the back of a chair.

Jason indicated the aerosols in the boxes. 'What're they for?'

'Mind your own business.'

'Like some tea?' asked Nina.

'Three sugars,' replied Jason, adding a hurried 'please'. Once she had disappeared behind the curtain of coloured strips, he spoke up again. 'Come on, Dan. Fill us in, mate. What's Douggie up to?'

Danny drew the thin curtains to block out the view of the thunderhead clouds. Fat spats of rain were audible as they hit the glass. When he turned back, Jason had pulled out one of the cans and was studying it.

'Stud Spray?'

Dan snatched it off him, slammed it on the table. 'I said to leave it.'

'Didn't think you'd need that sort of—'

'Ain't for me, Muppet.'

The boy squinted at the graphic on the can. His gormless

face brightened. 'Hey. This is the one that they advertise in the back of *Fiesta*. S'posed to turn you into a babe magnet.'

'Yeah, right.' Danny rubbed a hand over his goatee.

'What you doing with all this lot, then?'

Jason's pleading expression demanded either an answer or a punch. Ordinarily, Dan would have chosen the latter, but he didn't want to upset his mum. He picked up the can. The gold lettering promised unlimited sexual success but no money back.

'This stuff is pheromones. They spray it on animals to get them hot. Made out of bull spunk or something.'

'Wicked.'

'Mum's earning extra cash. They send us a batch of the chemicals that the farmers use. We spray 'em black, switch the labels and a guy from Solihull collects every week.'

'An'you never tried it out?'

Danny looked at Jason as if he were something he had found in a tissue.

The phone rang as Nina emerged with the tea.

Danny talked quietly to Doug as his mother forced a sandwich on Jason.

'Seven-thirty. Corley,' Danny said, replacing the receiver.

'Where?'

'Service station. You and me are going in the Transit. You brought the van, right?'

' 'Course.'

'Let's go check it out, then.'

While Danny went to fetch his coat, Jason slipped one of the canisters into his pocket.

'So you'll bring your thirty K tomorrow?' enquired Doug.

Him and three Asians in the restaurant: the three brothers were all middle-ranking members of the Shera Punjab, a notorious gang that controlled a swathe of the Birmingham drug trade.

'How do we know you'll show up?' asked the middle brother.

'You can't lose out.' He was getting the hang of this dicing-with-death thing now. 'If I'm not there then you'll walk away. I'll have my twenty. You'll match it with your thirty grand.'

'Sounds like a rip-off,' snorted Nasir, the eldest at twenty-six.

'Fine. Don't come,' said Doug, rising.

The middle brother pushed him back into his seat. He was skinny with two commas of hair on his upper lip and a machete scar on his forearm.

Silence, except for a wet howl as a bus romped past.

Doug: 'Listen. I didn't want to say it but this guy, the dealer – he's connected.'

'What? He's, like, a made guy?' asked the youngest, who had seen GoodFellas over twenty-five times.

'Exactly. He's acting for a cartel. This shipment is what you might call their starter pack. Beginning of a new operation in the Midlands.'

'Why us?' asked Nasir.

'Because only I know the guy and he represents people who are very careful about who they deal with.' His fingers were crossed under the table.

The youngest nodded sagely and spouted a stream of Hindi to his brothers.

Doug got the gist. The Mob-run cartels and Yardies only liked to deal with their own. However, the Asians had engineered a worldwide reputation for handling smack. They had won over the Americans, who were now using them often in their operations. If, as he had hinted, the Shera Punjab believed he was making inroads there, then such an allegiance would be fruitful for both of them.

As he'd hoped, Nasir nodded his assent.

'The arrangements once more, please,' he said, bringing out a pen and a small neat notebook.

'OK. You bring thirty thousand to the Novotel tomorrow morning at exactly seven a.m. We meet in suite 604.' He waited while the man wrote it down. 'That's six-oh-*four*. Got it?'

'Got it.'

Well, thought Doug as he hit the street. I'd win an award from the Race Relations Board for the work I've put in today. If it were legal.

CHAPTER EIGHT

Delays Inevitable

———◆———

'Engaging,' said Rob.

'Do what?' asked Andy.

They were stuck on Western Avenue, having hit the traffic moments after leaving Wembley Park. It grew worse as they inched past Alperton Tube, and when they got back to Hanger Lane the Polo crept down the A40 slip like an old man on an icy slope.

'It's your adjective, innit?'

Andy grunted. Rob was referring to his description in the London listings magazine. 'What's yours now – accomplished?'

'Powerful. A master of mirth.'

'Not that you memorised it or anything.'

Rob fastened the buttons on his leather trench coat. He had refused to wear a sea belt on the grounds that he didn't like them. Andy thought it had more to do with his incipient beer gut.

'Your problem, Crowesy, is you're heading for trouble.'

'Tell me about it.'

'All right. We both started with promising young, right? I went on to sharp and challenging but you never made it above engaging.'

'I was reliably funny a couple of weeks ago.'

Rob howled. 'That means Pete hasn't caught your act in ages. Mind you, he only goes to the bigger gigs now anyway. Rest of the time he just juggles adjectives. No one notices.'

'What about the readers?'

'Like they count?' Gillen pressed his index fingers to his temples and slanted his eyes. 'You have much to learn, glasshoppa.'

Andy released the handbrake and moved all of two feet forwards.

'Tell you the worst one,' continued Rob. 'Very experienced. That's like saying you're an old whore who hasn't got it any more.'

'I'll look forward to that one. D'you know where this gig is?'

'Centre of Brum somewhere.'

'Done it before?'

'Hundreds of times.'

'Tough gig?'

'No. Sweet.'

'Do you know how to get there once we're in Birmingham?'

'More or less.'

'Agency said you had the details.'

'Contract's in here.' Rob kicked the sports bag that was resting between his feet.

'You don't want to leave it there. I had a problem with the car this morning.'

Rob plucked the bag from the floor and felt the underside of it. 'What's this shit?' he exclaimed.

'Rust, antifreeze, old fag-ends. Amusing bouquet, don't you think?'

Rob manoeuvred the bag into the back of the car and in so doing bashed the corner on Andy's head. He began to rub the bag across the rear seat.

'What are you doing, Rob?'

'Cleaning my bag off.'

'Oh, thanks!'

'Well, this car's a shitheap. Can't you get the heater on?'

Andy measured his next statement. 'The heater's buggered.'

'You mean we're going all the way to Birmingham and back with no heating? In sodding February?'

'Now you put it like that, it does seem a bit ridiculous.'

'What other way *were* you going to put it? Were you gonna wait until we sank into cryogenic suspension at Luton?'

'That's the criterion for going to Luton.'

'Crowe, you're a pillock. Why didn't you say something before we left?'

Andy demisted the windscreen with his sleeve. 'Because by the time you'd finished bathing in ass's milk, I was more bothered about getting there before Saturday.' A stream of red tail-lights blinked towards them as they again drew to a halt. 'Look, we're only at Greenford. If you want, you can get out and walk it to Northolt. Get the Tube back into town and go up by train.'

Rob stared ahead, his face clouded by the lowering sky.

'Nah. Can't be arsed. We're on the way now.'

'Right, then.'

Rob freed his mobile from the bag. He pressed keys, listened and shook the instrument.

'Sod! It's on the blink.'

'Oh dear,' said Andy, focusing hard on the central reservation.

Its iron-grille fence was thickly clotted with black pollution. Underneath it, diesel fumes had suffocated the grass. In the clear lanes opposite, a raft of vehicles sailed past.

'The happy traffic,' Andy muttered. 'Why am I always stuck in the sad traffic with all the sticker people? Baby on board . . . Celibates don't do it . . . Honk if you have a pulmonary embolism.'

No response from Rob. Andy worried his lower lip with his teeth. 'Can you grab my *A–Z*? It's in the glove compartment.'

Rob struggled to open the moulded fascia and finally dislodged a faded road map. One corner of it was soggy with antifreeze. He handed it over and Andy found the double page illustrating the capital. He scanned the green and red arteries.

'Well, either we carry on up the M40 or take the M25 to the M1. Both ways we're in for a long haul.'

'This'll clear soon. Don't worry about it.'

Andy hit the radio.

'. . . Nose to tail on Western Avenue all the way from Ivy Avenue. Solid up to the emergency roadworks at Junction Two. A contraflow system is in operation . . .'

He flipped to a music station. It was 4.40 by the dashboard clock.

They were still stuck an hour later, but this time in a fresh tailback on the M25. The weather was being temperamental. Thick, grainy clouds made the grey-green fields seem as if they lay behind muslin, and gusts of rain meant that Andy had to keep varying the speed of the wipers. They screeched like a donkey in labour. Their combined body heat had warmed the car to a bearable degree but the windows had fogged up again. Andy's attempts at clearing them had left greasy patterns on the glass.

'What I hate about Valentine's Day is you have to buy a present,' said Rob. 'I mean, you're forced to, otherwise she throws a wobbly. It's the old "You don't love me like you used to' crap." A pause. 'To which the answer should be, "No, it's a different kind of love now. The kind I fit in between other women and wanking in the shower".'

'This is material, isn't it?'

'What d'you reckon to it as an opener? It's topical.'

'Yes. It's topical,' Andy said.

They slid under the lozenge of a concrete bridge.

Rob: 'So, are you stretching your wings, then?'

'If you mean am I getting enough work, then yes. And this gig for the Agency should really help.'

Rob snapped his fingers irritably. 'No, I meant *it*. The flow, mining the seam, finding the vein, having the comedy god smile down on you.'

'I've had some stormers.'

'No you haven't.'

'Yes I have.'

'You haven't.'

'I'm not playing this,' said Andy.

'Crowesy, I'd of *heard* about it, wouldn't I? I'm talking about the gigs where you never want to get off. When you're flying, buzzing on raw energy. There was this one in . . .'

As Rob began to reminisce, the traffic moved on. Soon their speed hit thirty and Andy was able to engage fourth gear. As some of the tension drained from him, he decided he'd had enough of Rob's self-confessed brilliance for the moment. He would look for a conversational slip road. Next exit. Gossip.

'Hear about Peter Corfer?' he said, cutting in.

'No?'

'He's caught M.S.'

'What, that yuppie flu?'

'It's serious. He's losing the use of his limbs and he'll have to leave the business. Apparently, he's going back to Suffolk to be with his parents. He split up with Liz as well.'

'So he won't be running his club?'

'Shit, no. The guy's wasting away.'

Silence as they rounded a curve.

'Fuck,' said Rob. 'He had me down for a gig in April.'

As they approached the M1 link, the traffic tightened into a knot, and within seconds they were boxed in. An ominously long row of lorries stretched away in front of them. On the hard shoulder, a line of traffic cones threatened to swell into the outside lane. A yellow emergency speed limit banner proclaimed that they should keep to fifty miles an hour. They were doing two. Rob unzipped his bag, extracted a can of lager, popped the ring-pull.

'When we reach the end of this jam,' fumed Andy, 'I'll tell you what's going to happen . . .'

Rob slurped noisily at his beer.

'Absolutely nothing,' he continued. 'There won't be anything causing this.' He swiped a hand at the looming lorries 'We'll just go . . . ! They should make it worth my while! Give me a fifty-two car pile-up or something. Dead bodies, weeping relatives . . .'

'Is this material?' Rob asked.

'Of course it's not bloody material.'

'Should be. You've got something there.'

Andy worried a cigarette from his depleted packet and stared at the other comedian: 'Does everything have to be a rehearsal for a joke?'

Rob shrugged.

Andy figured this wasn't going to be the kind of journey where you sing songs or discuss interesting philosophical issues. The gig was due to start in three hours.

'Toddington, Toddington,' chanted Rob.

They were going at the Polo's top speed, which was sadly legal.

'We haven't got time to stop.'

' 'Course we have. The gig's not starting without us. Come on, I need a slash.'

Andy pulled into the slow lane and hit the indicator.

'Scratchwood. Toddington. Rothersthorpe. Watford Gap.'

'What's that? Your mantra?'

'All the service stations up to the M6. You'll get to know them once you start playing the bigger gigs out of town.'

They drew on to the forecourt and wove round the bays until they found a space. Holding their coats to their necks, they hurried to the toilets behind the fast-food unit. Rob performed a horse-like urination but Andy, standing next to him, was unable to go even when he tried the trick of imagining he was peeing on Rob's head.

Back at the car, Andy stuffed his hands into his armpits and stared at the clock. After five minutes, Rob appeared with a bulging plastic carrier bag.

'Beers and a Scotch egg. Keep us warm for the journey.'

'I'm driving. I can't drink.'

'Can if they don't catch you.'

Andy followed the exit signs, taking them round behind the petrol station.

'Of course, they don't have Scotch eggs in Scotland,' said Rob, tearing open the plastic wrapping with his teeth. Orange crumbs littered his lap. 'If they did, it'd be "Scottish egg".' Or by rights they should call it "Bits of manky old pork, flavouring . . . and an egg".'

'Not so catchy, though.'

'Hold up!' bellowed Rob.

Andy jumped on the brake. The seat belt bit into his chest and Rob sprayed manky pork, egg and flavouring all over the dashboard.

Andy spun round. They had come to a halt by the grass

verge. There were no cars or lorries in sight and nothing had hit them.

'What is it now?'

'That bloke's freezing. We ought to give him a lift.'

An ageing, rumpled man smiled and slid a callused hand up the warm bonnet of the car.

The Hitcher climbed in the back. Although Rob had been kind enough to offer the lift without consulting Andy, his generosity ended at giving up his seat.

'Where are you headed?' he asked, jovially.

'North.'

Andy wrenched the car into the middle lane. 'We're turning off at the M6.'

'The Watford Gap will be fine, thank you.'

'They've got one of those business card machines there,' said Rob. 'What kind of business would you want to start in a service station?'

'Stress councillor?' offered Andy. 'For families or business-men or' – he racked up his voice a notch – 'people trying *not to be late for their gig.*'

'You can drop me at Rothersthorpe if it's a problem,' said the Hitcher.

'It's all right. We're going your way anyway.'

'Trifle cold back here.'

'His heater doesn't work,' said Rob.

'Ah.'

All three lapsed into silence.

They headed out across open country, and a final glimmer of sun appeared among the clouds. The thin strip of orange shone brightly and threw colour on to the landscape like an old lady daubing on make-up. Featureless fields were smudged emerald and the trees blushered with pink and crimson. In the car, they wiped condensation from the windows as sunlight refracted in the water drops. The sun died on the rear windscreen like a glob of marmalade engulfed in bread.

It went dark.

As the headlights carved into the night, Andy relaxed his grip on the wheel. It seemed to him that in winter the day never got properly started. He spent too long alone in the flat, stumbling around in a perennial mist between October and March. Owing to the hours of the job, he'd become used to living for the consistency of night and sometimes felt like a vampire. Unfortunately the kind of vampire he identified with was the suffering post-modern type, rather than the glamorous, surrounded-by-Goth-babes, Christopher Lee kind.

The Hitcher handed something to Rob, who turned it over in his hands.

'You mentioned business cards.'

Rob held a small, embossed rectangle. In the centre was the single word **God**. Running along the bottom edge in tiny letters was the promise. 'Most events catered for'.

'Very good, yeah,' he said, passing it to Andy.

Andy glanced at it, then flicked nervous eyes from the road to his passenger's face in the mirror.

'So you're God, then?' asked Rob.

'Yes, and you?'

'Rob Gillen. And if you *were* him then you'd have heard of me.'

'I've been busy.'

'Doing what?'

God sat back and cupped his hands over his temples. Rob gave Andy an overdone scary face and pointed a finger over his shoulder.

'Travelling,' said God, after a while.

Rob threw up his hands. 'Oh, right, so God's a gypsy

selling immortal clothes-pegs. I suppose that the heather you get off stinky old women in railway stations really *is* lucky, then.'

'I hitchhike around the motorways.'

'Why?'

'I don't know,' answered God, meekly. 'All I know is I have to keep to the main trunk routes. I go up the M1 to Leeds, then across the Pennine way on the M62. I join the M6 at Warrington then travel south to the M5 at Junction Nine. From there it's down to the M4 at Bristol and then back to London. Sometimes for a break I spend some time at Taunton Deane on the M5.'

Rob said: 'I never knew that God was as boring as a train-spotter.'

'You take holidays in service stations?' queried Andy.

God kept up his enthusiasm. 'Yes. But I've been travelling in the zero formation for quite some time. What's so exciting is that tonight I start to move in a figure of eight – the Japanese symbol of infinity.'

'How do you get across London?'

'M4–M1 link on the M25. Or the North Circular Road.' God crinkled up his brow in thought. 'You look very much like a young man I saw there earlier today.'

'He *is* God,' said Andy, flatly.

'What's all this figure of eight stuff?' Rob asked.

'I'm going to start crossing over on the M6 each time I go round, passing near Coventry.'

'Nearest service station?'

God, effortlessly: 'Corley.'

'Name all the services from London to Manchester.'

'Scratchwood, Toddington, Newport Pagnell . . .'

'You forgot that one,' said Andy, giving Rob a poke in the shoulder.

God named them all.

'He knows his way around,' said Andy.

'Doesn't mean he's God. He might just be a well-travelled nutter,' commented Rob.

'Which God are you?' Andy asked. 'The Christian one?'

'Depends who I'm travelling with. To some I am Buddha, others Jehovah.'

'What about the Hindus?' chimed in Rob. 'They worship a cow. They wouldn't pick up Ermintrude, would they?'

'Hindus don't give lifts.'

'Always the smart answer,' Andy said.

Rob opened another beer. 'I'm an atheist. You don't exist, mate.'

God smiled. 'Maybe. Maybe not.'

'Enigmatic,' Andy said.

'Anyway, you don't look like God to me,' said Rob, disproving his last statement.

'You were exposed at school to some form of religious education?'

'Who wasn't?'

'Well, even the hardened atheist has some image of divinity.'

Andy broke in. 'But my idea of God is the old bloke with the white beard. You don't look like Santa.'

'Would you have stopped for me if I was dressed like Santa Claus?'

'Good point.'

'I resemble what each person would like to see in themselves.'

Andy and Rob craned their necks to look in the rear-view mirror. After a long moment they sat back and both stared ahead.

The noise of drumming rain halted as a concrete bridge darted overhead. The wipers flapped on until they were once more enveloped in water. The long silver worm of the central barrier snaked down into a deep gully. The traffic remained steady at sixty miles an hour. It was 7.23.

'Oy, God. Wanna Scotch egg?'

God declined and Rob demolished another as he burped through a fresh tin of lager. 'If you are God,' he said, 'then you'll have all the answers, won't you?'

'Try me.'

'Why one planet?'

'Don't be too sure about that.'

Rob and Andy made a siren-like camp noise.

Andy: 'My turn. You can't have done it in a week. Made the heavens and the earth, I mean. All those birds and fish and fowl. Either you had a whole team on it or it was a cowboy job . . . And you made man on the Saturday morning, if I remember rightly?'

'That's right.'

'Well, you did a shoddy job. What were you? Hung over?'

'Is this the "why do men have nipples question"?' God asked.

'I think he's doing material,' whispered Rob, theatrically.

God leaned between the headrests. 'What do you two do for a living?'

'We're comedians,' replied Andy.

Rob: 'Haven't you seen *LiveWires?* On Channel Four?'

'Never heard of it.'

'Ironic,' said Andy. 'You don't believe in God. He's never heard of you.'

'Yeah, well. Funny is money and he was stood in the rain,' muttered Rob.

Andy toasted a Marlboro and the tip glowed in the dark. Cars in the other lanes swooshed by in their mud skirts. Across the central reservation, a necklace of headlights paraded past.

'So what's it all about, then?' asked Andy. 'The meaning of life.'

'Good one,' Rob said.

'Yes, that is a good question,' said God, rubbing at a patch of condensation on the window.

'And?' they chimed together.

'And it'll have to be another time. We're coming up to Watford Gap, so if you wouldn't mind . . . ?'

Andy tugged the car across the lanes, failing to avoid a curtain of spray coming off the back of an articulated lorry.

CHAPTER NINE

Breakfast Served
Until You Get Here

———◆———

Danny and Jason were sitting watching the rain sluice against the windows of the Red Hen at Corley services. The restaurant was trying for a country feel, all barley tones, hanging sheaves of wheat and laminated picture menus. The boy was burning holes in a polystyrene drink carton. Danny, who was squashed between the chair and table like a hot dog in a bun, sneezed copiously into a wad of tissues.

'Sod this flu . . .'

Jason, holding his cigarette with surgical precision, severed the last plastic stalactite, separating the top from the bottom of the cup. He took a final drag, extinguished the butt in the gloop and swirled it round. Then he wiped his blond fringe from his eyes and held up his cheap watch.

'Gone seven, Dan. He should be here by now.'

Ignoring him, the Filipino reached down, unzipped his sports bag and drew out a palmful of pills. He placed them in a neat row in front of him and trailed thoughtful fingers through his goatee.

'Sustanon.'

Jason spun round nervously. 'Danny. Watch the gear. Can't do stuff here, guy.'

The giant moved his index finger along the line. 'Ananvar. Deca-Durabolin . . .' He paused and tugged at his gold earring. The next was a white tablet. He lifted it to eye level, scrutinised it and tossed it down his throat.

'Codeine,' he confirmed. 'And that one is . . . Primobolan.'

'What are they, Dan?'

'Steroids.'

Apart from the incident in the sauna, Danny hadn't noticed any adverse reactions to his use of steroids. Admittedly, his heart often beat faster than a Morse code operator trying to summon help, but he dismissed this – along with the insomnia – as being down to long-term amphetamine use. The water retention and the fierce crop of acne between his shoulder blades he attributed to the flu, and, OK, so there was more hair on his comb in the mornings. Age, he thought as he patted his crown. There was a thinness under the tightly woven curls that reminded him of a forest floor under a canopy of firs. Oh, and one more thing. His T-shirts were getting too tight. He'd asked his mother about it but when she denied shrinking them in the wash, he realised it was true: he was growing man-breasts. He wondered why no one had thought to mention it.

'They're dangerous, you know,' Jason said.

'Like I care what you say.'

Wisely, the boy left it alone. 'So where's Douggie?'

Danny chased a pill round his saucer as if it were a rogue pea. 'He'll be here. Don't sweat it.'

Back on the estate, Danny had inspected Jason's borrowed van with scepticism. It was an aged white Transit with the obligatory legend 'Also available in white' scrawled in dirt on the back. He checked the oxyacetylene by firing up the torch and then drove them out of Birmingham, up over Spaghetti

Junction and, as per Doug's instructions, on to Junction 4 of the M6. They turned round there and drove back to Corley, parking on the south side of the service area.

In the Red Hen, they refused to 'wait to be seated' and commandeered a booth by the window with a good view of the entrance. Dan declined food but Jason had the fish platter. This he managed to eat without once closing his mouth. Afterwards, Dan allowed him five minutes browsing in the shop. The allotted time came and went, and when Jason returned with a CD in a bag, Danny was about ready to enforce discipline. However, having promised Doug he'd keep a rein on his temper, he settled for gripping Jason's thigh under the table until the boy's leg went dead.

'What's the job then, Danny?' Jason asked now.

'I told you. Don't know. Wait for Doug.'

'Why do they call you One-Slice?'

Nothing.

'D'you cut people's throats?' Jason drew a finger across his neck, making a garroting noise. Getting only silence, he returned to his earlier line of enquiry. 'I reckon it's a bank. Maybe down in Coventry since we're here.'

Dan shrugged.

'Wonder how much we'll get? Could be millions.'

'Shurrup.'

The boy removed his purchase from its skinny bag. Under the shrink-wrap, the bold lettering on the CD case proclaimed it to be a definitive collection of Ibiza dance hits, despite it being the fifth in a series.

'Know what I'd do if I had the dosh?' said Jason. 'I'd start me own band.'

'What instrument d'you play?'

Jason threw Danny the insolent look he usually reserved for his father. 'You don't *need* to. All you do is programme the keyboard. Hey – guess what my band's going to be called?'

Danny's goatee shuffled disdainfully upwards. 'Nope.'

'Go on – guess.'

'The Dipshits?'

Jason leaned forward, waving the CD so it caught the light. 'Various Artists.'

'There's lots of things by various artists.'

'Exactly. So if my band were called Various Artists, then every time somebody asked for some crappy collection in HMV or Woolies, they'd get our latest release.' The boy sat back in triumph.

'You spend *time* coming up with this shit?'

'We'd always be top of the charts.'

Danny hooded his eyes and stretched his arms. Finding a yucca plant within reach, he bent it out of shape.

The restaurant was busy, with the harried waitresses landing at the tables like seagulls taking pickings from a trawler. Danny One-Slice kept his eyes on the entrance. People were rushing in out of the rain, stamping their feet and shaking moisture from their clothes. He sniffed and swallowed hard to clear his hearing. Perhaps Doug was already here. Maybe he'd misheard the instructions and his friend was sitting in the Granary on the other side of the motorway. No, Doug was late, that was all.

Doug was always late.

Because of it, Danny spent the greater part of his evenings pestered by anxious, gurning teenagers at the club. Always the same questions. 'Where's the *man*? Where's Douggie? Said he'd *be* here.' Dan, not giving a toss for anyone else's pharmaceutical requirements, apportioned each of them the same blank stare.

Sometimes Doug's lateness was infuriating – like one time when Doug left him in a squat in Aston for several hours. As it grew dark, Dan had become increasingly concerned about getting home to put his mum to bed. He eventually took out his frustration on a drum kit someone had set up in the basement. They never did get the cymbal out of the wall.

Other times it was convenient, such as the night when the West Midlands Serious Crime Squad busted the club. Having been off scoring, Doug showed up late with five hundred Doves. Danny had been entrusted with locking up, and when he let Doug into the empty premises, they harvested a massive haul of discarded stashes from the dance-floor.

' 'Course, I wouldn't buy a motor with the money. I can nick a motor any time. Goes against my principles.'

Danny tuned in. Jason was zipping up his puffa jacket.

'He ain't comin', is he?'

'He'll be here.'

'Bollocks. This is a wind-up.'

'You leave and you lose the van and anything we make out of tonight.'

Jason's lip came out as he slunk inside his coat.

'I'm having another coffee,' said Danny. 'You wanna coffee?'

The boy said nothing, so he summoned the waitress and demanded not a cappuccino, latte, decaff or pot, but a proper *mug* of coffee. He got it. He sipped it carefully as Jason tried and failed to harm the heat-resistant table-top with his lighter.

'He's taking the piss,' said Jason finally.

This time Dan let him stand without interruption. Doug had run inside from the rain and was approaching them, rubbing gleaming droplets of water from his scalp.

'All right, genius,' Danny said, high-fiving him.

'You can drop that now, Danny.'

Jason scowled and scuttled back into his seat.

Doug removed his army greatcoat and hung it on a pine stand. Underneath, he had changed back into jeans and a shapeless sweater. He took his place, hiked his sleeves up to his elbows and fished a ready-made roll-up from his tin.

'Did you get the gear?' he asked.

Danny gave him a solemn nod before pressing a fresh tissue to his nose.

'What's the job, then?' asked Jason.

Ignoring him, Doug took the menu and scanned the pictured meals. 'You eaten yet?'

Dan sneezed. 'Don't feel like it.'

A middle-aged waitress sailed to the jetty of the table, produced her tiny pad.

'Coke and . . . chips, please,' Doug said.

'We don't do chips on their own.'

He looked into her crinkle-cut eyes. 'I could go over and get them in Julie's Pantry. Then you'll lose my custom.'

Without blinking an eye, the waitress managed to convey that she neither cared nor wanted to get involved in a discussion. Her pen hovered over a pad held inches from her ample bosom.

Doug sighed. He didn't want any more fights. 'All right. I'll have cheeseburger, chips and beans.' He paused while she scrawled. 'Without the beans . . . or the cheeseburger.'

'See what I can do,' muttered the waitress, plucking the menu from Doug's hand and waddling off.

'I didn't come here to argue about chips,' snorted Jason.

Doug took in the boy's mop of lank blond hair, his burger-bun skin, his over-large lips and his sump-oil eyes. He continued to stare until Jason fidgeted and wilted.

'Has he been giving you grief?' he asked of Danny.

'Just say the word.'

'We need his van.'

'Yeah, but not him.'

'I am *here*, you know,' said Jason.

The waitress, who had been talking to a suit over by the till, returned with Doug's drink, a bowl of chips and the saccharin wish that he enjoy his meal. Doug said thank you, yes, he would, and sprayed his food with red stuff from the ketchup bottle.

'Fo,' he began, attempting to blow air over a hot chip he'd just put in his mouth. 'We're looking at twenty grand tops for as many minutes' work tonight.'

'Wicked,' said Jason. 'What is it? Bank? Safety deposit boxes or something?'

Doug tipped the bowl towards Danny, who took a chip and slathered it in sauce.

'Come on, Doug. Tell us.'

'Right now we're sitting about ten feet away from it.'

Jason looked round, wondering who'd be carrying that much cash this close to them. His face fell as the penny dropped. 'We're not doing over this place? A bloody snack bar? That's pathetic! And it's been done. In the beginning of *Pulp Fiction*.'

'That's a reason, is it?' countered Doug, calmly. 'Just because something's been done, then you can't do it again?' He counted on his fingers. 'Well, that puts out train robberies, banks, drug deals, stealing gold bullion with the aid of Minis . . .'

'All right,' fumed Jason. 'What, then?'

Doug tilted his head towards the thick plate-glass window. Beyond it was a square patch of acid-green sodden turf and, off to their right, a rain-slicked paved area. There, half illuminated by the fluorescent lights of the service station, was a small white tooth of a building. Two automatic bank teller machines were pressed into it like metal fillings.

'A cashpoint machine?' exploded Jason.

'Why not tell everybody,' deadpanned Doug.

Danny took this opportunity to reach across and clamp Jason's arm in a vice grip.

'You really should shut up. OK?'

With his bones on the verge of snapping, Jason took the advice.

Doug scooped ice from his Coke and dumped it in the ashtray.

'It's called a Carmody bank module. I've been through here a hundred times and it only hit me a month ago. I checked out Warwick and Hilton Park services, but this is one of the last of the old free-standing ones. The new ones are stuck right in the wall.' He cast his thumb towards the machine. 'This one should be a piece of piss.'

Danny's face folded into concentration. 'Isn't using a torch gonna draw a crowd?'

'I'm hoping we're not going to have to use it.'

'Then what's Spas Boy doing here, then?' asked Dan, folding his arms.

Jason glared at him. 'Who rattled your cage?'

Doug, losing it: 'That's enough, both of you. If you don't stop pissing about then we'll forget the whole thing and go home.'

Danny and Jason lowered their heads and studied their hands.

'The oxy is back-up in case we can't get it open with cutters. Take a look.'

Jason and Dan pressed their faces up against the window. Through the rain, they saw that the rear of the hut consisted of a metal roll-up shutter and on the wall beside it was a letterbox-shaped vertical metal slit.

'Way it works is this. The bank usually sends a team of two. One goes inside and the other one passes the money through. They refill it on average once every four days.'

'Why don't we wait and nick it off them when they turn up?' Jason asked.

'Because it's been *done*,' sneered Doug. 'Anyway, it's too risky. They're here at busy times, got all those alarms, carrying CS. All that shit.'

Danny smiled. 'Someone's been doing their homework.'

'That would be me.'

Jason: 'But aren't all the people in the restaurant gonna see us?'

'Was your school *special?* We're not doing it now. We're going to meet back here at midnight.' He ladled on some heavy emphasis. '—When there aren't many people around.'

'Oh.'

'This side of the service area is gonna be closed up. Only the Granary stays open over the bridge. We'll be in and out in twenty minutes.'

Danny opened his mouth to speak.

'Don't say it,' said Doug.

Danny thought for a bit. 'I was going to ask about alarm systems.'

'Modern alarms.'

A knowing smile passed between the two friends. They knew those yellow hexagonal metal boxes of old: they were often dummies or had faulty wiring, and could be peeled off a wall as easily as an old scab.

'How much did you say is in them machines?' queried Jason.

'About ten grand in each.'

'And we're not coming back till later?'

'That's right.'

'Bit of a shit plan, innit?'

Dan put his hands in strangling position and gave Doug an imploring look.

'Leave it, Dan.'

'We don't even know when it was last filled up,' continued the boy. 'Might be empty, for all we know. Even if it ain't – tons of people are gonna use it from now until midnight.'

'Point number one, Jason. It's raining and that'll cut down on numbers. Point number two. I've been timing the deliveries for the last fortnight. It was last filled up at four-thirty this afternoon.'

He grinned, showing all his teeth. 'Thanks for your input, though.'

'What about the money? It's traceable innit?'

'You use a cash card?'

'Do I bollocks. Readies only.'

'The notes aren't in consecutive numbers.'

Jason's attempt at pulling an impressed face looked like he was probing a mouth ulcer.

Doug: 'Right, we'll leave the van here. I'll drive you both back into town and pick you up at the club later on.'

'So the split is gonna be . . . ? Uh, we'll get about . . . ?' Jason tailed off, being unable to divide twenty thousand by three.

'We'll sort that out later,' announced Doug, slurping the last of his Coke. 'You want to take a slash before we go?'

'No. I'm all right.'

'It wasn't a question,' said Danny.

Jason took the hint and shuffled out of his seat.

Once he'd gone, Doug sparked a fresh roll-up. Around them, customers were leaving and the staff wiping down the tables. A particularly voracious coach party had left a mammoth pile of crockery.

'So is that the whole plan?' asked Danny.

'Bollocks it is. We'll talk later.'

CHAPTER TEN

Women: A User's Guide

———————•———————

'Do you reckon he *was* the Supreme Being, then?' asked Andy as they sped past the Rugby turn-off.

'Give over.'

'Mind you, it would've been handy. He could've fixed the heater.'

'Not even God could mend this shitheap,' muttered Rob, raising his left foot and putting it on his knee. He removed his cowboy boot and eased off the sock. His foot smelled of stale Bombay mix and hamster's cage.

The passenger reshuffle involved in dropping God at Watford Gap had brought the temperature inside the vehicle back to zero. As a result, Andy was driving as fast as he could in the hope that the engine would warm the interior. It took ten minutes for Rob's lager-laden breath and their combined body heat to fog up the windows. As the sodium motorway lights came to an end, they were thrust into dark countryside. The wind was buffeting the car and Andy had to concentrate hard on keeping a steady course.

'He never did tell us the meaning of life.'

Rob was rotating a finger between each toe in turn. 'Easy one, that.'

'Oh yeah?'

'Sex with as many babes as you can and as frequently as possible.'

'Thank you, Jack Nicholson. And for women?'

A grin. 'Same thing.'

'So your philosophy of life is basically shagging?'

'Yeah.'

'What about science? Art? Medicine?'

'Fucking. All those breakthroughs only happen so as some bloke can go, "Look at me. Look how clever I am. I've found a cure for typhoid. That's *got* to be worth a shag".'

'And art?'

'Birds with their kit off.'

'Medicine?'

'Everyone's shagged a nurse.'

'All right. I'll give you medicine.'

Rob massaged the ball of his foot. 'And why d'you think we're out here in the middle of Interbreedingshire in the cold and rain and shit?'

'Because we're going to work?'

'No, you prat. We're out to get laid.'

'I'm not.'

'Yes you are.'

'I'm *not*. If I'd wanted sex, I'd have turned this gig down.'

'Huh?'

'If I'd stayed in tonight, Michelle and I wouldn't have had a row and she wouldn't have chucked me and we'd probably be having sex right now.'

'Who's Michelle? Your dog?'

'No. She *was* my girlfriend.'

'When did you split up?'

'Last night,' replied Andy, realising that this was the first time Rob had shown any interest in him. 'See, the thing is—'

Rob held up a hand. 'Got to stop you there.'

'What?'

'Nothing. I just wanted to stop you. See, comedy is like sex. A gig is like meeting a top babe who fancies you. You both know she wants it but what you do is you act like you don't. You insult her a bit, let her think you don't care. Give her enough to get her interested and then let *her* do all the work.' His free hand rose in the air like that of a conductor, albeit one that was holding a sock instead of flourishing a baton. 'She'll give you the laughs, you play it cool. Drop in the odd one-liner and before you know it she'll do anything.' He shuffled the sock back on to his pale foot. 'Get the analogy?'

'Well, it's not rocket science.'

'And a bad gig's a lesbian.'

'Right,' replied Andy, uneasily.

'You're not going all PC on me, are you, Crowe?'

'Well, one of the basic tenets of what we do is—'

'Come on,' interrupted Rob with a thin sneer. 'You know the only thing we have to watch these days is the racism.'

The road was barely visible. Andy cut his speed and wound down his window. Beads of rain ceased their horizontal trudge across the glass and cold air rushed in to clear the windscreen. The headlights illuminated a tall blue sign. The Coventry turn-off. The trail of green cat's-eyes turned red as they veered off the M1. Andy glanced at the clock. Ten to eight. If he carried on at seventy then they would be in Birmingham by a quarter to nine. Find the club and he'd have ten minutes to run through his set on fast forward. It was tight, but they'd make it.

'What does Natasha think to your theories?' he asked.

'Dunno. Shut the sodding window, will you?'

Andy reeled in the pane, toasted a fresh cigarette and dragged deeply on it. The treetops on the horizon were a jagged row, as if cropped by pinking shears.

'Want to know when I get my best ideas?' Rob asked.

'Do tell. On stage?'

'Cheers, but no. On the muff.' He chuckled to himself. 'Kills two birds with one stone. Keeps Tash happy and I'm getting material. Mind you, she gets the right hump when I whip out the notebook so's I can jot the ideas down.'

Andy tried to form a picture of Rob performing cunnilingus and got a pig nosing for truffles.

'Is that it, then?' he asked. 'How you keep women happy?'

'Mostly, yeah.'

There was pride in his voice. Arrogant bastard, thought Andy. He thinks this whole conversation is about flattering him and his opinions. He was affronted. Rob may have been the more successful comedian, but to him they were still in the same year, like at school. Only difference being that Rob had made the first eleven and Andy was still coming in with sick notes.

And I've got to put up with this shit all night?

Sod that.

But then he began to consider the facts. They still had an hour of the drive, then the gig and later on the journey home. Furthermore, Rob was in prime position to put in a good word for him with the Agency. With this in mind, he determined on a course of action, which would make things easier. He'd flatter him. Get what he could out of the bastard. With a gulp, Andy bounced on a mental springboard and submerged himself in Rob Gillen's ego. He had the feeling it was mostly going to be shallow end.

'What's your dad's name, Jason?' Doug asked.

'Joffe. Russell Joffe.'

'And what's your surname, Jason?'

'Er, Joffe?'

The boy frowned and flicked hair off his face. There was a trick question in there somewhere.

Doug, Danny and Jason were outside in the carpark. The rain had ceased, only to be replaced by a biting wind. They stood by the Transit, stamping their feet and turning this way and that so as to avoid the worst of the glacial gusts.

Prior to their coming out, Doug had pointed out the lack of CCTV. The Red Hen restaurant had closed for the night and they had taken the opportunity of a closer scrutiny of the bank module. Danny reckoned he could easily bust the lock with the bolt-cutters.

'What's the problem?' asked Jason.

'The white van is good. I like the white van. Very anonymous,' Doug said. 'Sometimes I wonder why they don't stop *all* white vans, as there isn't a single one which isn't dodgy in some way or another. Anyway, that's beside the point.' He scrutinised Jason's podgy juvenile face. 'But since we're doing a bit more than smuggling a few crates of booze back from Calais, don't you reckon it would have been a bit better to have used a van that didn't have your Dad's fucking *name* on it?'

JOFFE'S MOTORS, REPAIRS IN A JIFFY was printed under the filth on the sides.

'Oh yeah,' said Jase.

'Shit. It was so dark on the estate I never saw it,' said Dan. With that he swatted Jason with one great paw, sending him flying to the tarmac.

The boy scrambled to his feet. Danny prepared another blow and he cowered away.

'Go to the petrol station,' said Doug, through gritted teeth, 'and get some spray paint to cover it up.'

'B-but it's me dad's van,' moaned the boy. 'He'll kill me.'

Danny One-Slice raised his hand.

'What colour shall I get?'

'Just cover it up, will you?'

Jason scuttled off to the Shell station.

'C'mon,' sighed Doug. 'Let's get back in the warm.'

'Lesson one. Care and maintenance of the female,' began Rob Gillen. 'First thing you have to know is that they have a million obsessions. Big three are hair, weight and little boxes.'

'Little boxes?'

'Don't ask me.'

'I guess it's all part of their feminine mystique.'

Rob missed the irony. 'They're always dying their hair, cutting it, washing it and playing with it, and who goes bald? Men do. Weight . . .'

'I know about the weight one.'

'Know about thin and fat mirrors?'

'I'll concede that Michelle has bent the laws of science on the fat mirror issue.'

Rob folded his fingers around the base of his skull. 'Angles is another good one. Watch a woman trying on shoes. She does that funny walk where she looks at them from every side like it's a diamond. They have to inspect every facet in case there's a flaw.'

Andy broke in. 'I always thought that Cinderella story was weird. Glass shoes. Poor choice of footwear, even if you are dancing with a prince.'

A grunt of assent from Rob. 'Cushions,' he said.

'Cushions?'

'Yeah. They don't exist in the male world. No bloke ever goes shopping for cushions. No man ever looks at a room and thinks: "What that couch could really do with is a great big bunch of cushions."'

'You have a point there.'

A fresh shoal of traffic appeared up ahead and Andy had to pummel the brake. Rob, who had still not bothered to fasten his seat belt, jerked forward and crumpled against the fascia. They slowed up, then began to chug along at twenty. Recovering, Rob propped his feet up on the glove compartment. Five past eight on the clock on the dash. Andy prayed that finding the venue wasn't going to be too difficult.

'What're the three magic words?' asked Rob.

'I love you?' offered Andy, feeling queasy about saying this in another man's presence.

'Nah. "You've lost weight." Works on all women bar cancer patients.'

'Ever heard of feminism, Rob?'

'Sure.'

'Women being equal and all that?'

'Yeah.'

'Just wanted to be sure.'

Rob thought for a moment. 'Listen, I've thought all that stuff through, right? I was saying to Tash a while ago that the women's movement has come on so much now that the point is we *can* take the piss. Ten years ago you couldn't say fuck all, but now they've got their equality. They're tough enough to take it.'

'Well, bless their little combat trousers,' Andy said.

'There's a line I do in my set that proves it. "Ever noticed that the women who carry rape alarms are the least likely to get raped?" Storms every time.'

'*Every* time?'

'Most times.'

'Rob, can I ask you a personal question?'

'Yeah.'

'You said earlier that we do gigs to get laid.'

'Right.'

'So I presume you're playing away?'

Rob grinned.

'Well, why? You've got Natasha at home.'

Andy felt the heat of his stare and glanced over. The tail-lights of the car in front illuminated Rob's eyes. They were hard in their sockets.

' 'Cos I can,' said Rob, flatly.

The traffic began to accelerate and a sign up ahead indicated that Coventry was close by. Andy dropped his gaze to the clock once more. Quarter past. Not good.

'One thing you *don't* want to forget about is presents,' said Rob, cracking open his third can of lager. 'Trouble is, there are things we remember and things we don't. We remember footie scores and the track listings of favourite records. We forget Mother's Day, birthdays and anniversaries. It's a male chromosome thing.'

'So we're missing the cushion chromosome?'

'Yup. Our DNA makes us interested in DIY. Hey, that's a good one.' Rob reached over for his bag and pulled out a crumpled Silvine notebook. Producing a pen, he jotted down the thought.

'What about today? Valentine's Day?' asked Andy, fishing.

'That's the one you *don't* want to forget,' chuckled Rob, as he capped his Biro.

'Doesn't Natasha mind you being out on the road tonight?'

'Did you see them flowers in our front room? I had 'em delivered this morning.'

'Arse!' said Andy.

Rob cackled, necked his beer. 'So, what's your problem with this Michelle, then?'

He took a breath and explained.

'Trouble is,' said Rob finally, 'lust has a sell-by date. Once it goes, there ain't nothing you can do to get it back. I reckon it fades after two years max. How long you two been together?'

'Six years.'

Not even a shrug. 'Thing is, it don't matter if you're with Claudia Schiffer, there still comes a point when she lies down and waggles her arse in the air and you're thinking, "Come off it, Claudia. Not that skinny old arse again." '

'Misogynist.'

'Cheers.'

'That's a bad thing, Rob.' Andy was as up on post-modern irony as the next hypocrite, but Rob's misogyny was wearing him down. It felt like a landfill site into which you could toss any opinion and never hear a word of protest.

'Look, Crowesy. Relationships are a bargain of silence. Who do you think she's thinking about when you're humping her? Odds on, it ain't you. We're the same with the old Frankenwank.'

'The what?'

'The fantasy cut and paste.'

They sped past the Coventry turn-off.

'Sorry, Rob, but I'm not going to reduce my relationship with Michelle down to your levels. OK, so she's thrown a wobbly, but she understands about the job.'

'Yeah, looks like it.'

'What do you suggest I do, then?'

Rob drained his can and dumped it at his feet. 'Phone her up soon as you can. Tell her you're coming home. Can't live without her, blah, blah, blah. Then do the gig anyway and make up some story about the car. Won't be hard. When you get home, keep on at her. All night. Don't let her sleep until she gives in. A few cups of coffee will stop you getting chucked out.'

'It's a bit more complicated than that.'

'Oh yeah?'

'I think she wants me to give up the stand-up.'

'What a bitch.'

Andy flushed. 'Don't talk about her like that.'

Dark clouds scudded fast across the sky, a scattering of stars behind them. Andy felt his hands tighten on the wheel.

There was now no chance of him having time to rehearse, and at this rate they were going to be late.

'I suppose your answer to everything is serial adultery?' he said, after a while.

'Here's a thing I heard. The mark of the true adulterer is he has superseded the urge to confess.'

'But everyone knows about your conquests.'

Rob's leather coat creaked. 'Can you stop up here? I need another slash.'

'There's no time.'

'There's plenty of time.'

'No.'

'Crowe. Corley's just up here.'

Rob reached out and shook the steering wheel. The car swerved crazily before Andy wrestled them back to the slow lane. A tanker blasted its horn and its full beam flooded the car.

'You arsehole!' spat Andy. 'Don't you *know* how dangerous that was?'

'I need a piss.'

Muttering curses, Andy hit the indicator and curved off the motorway.

The toilets were closed so they trudged across the bridge. Relieving himself under a framed print of a classic Bentley, Andy became aware of a presence at the next stall. The stranger smelled of patchouli oil, throwing him back to Glastonbury days and teenage girlfriends at night. In his peripheral vision he made out a tall man with a close-cropped scalp.

He washed his hands, wiped them on his jeans and went to the concourse to try to phone Michelle. The line was engaged. He hung up and waited. Over in the Granary, the members of a coach party were jostling their trays along the chrome runners. The server was a middle-aged woman ladling soup behind a plexiglass-paned counter. Further along, a girl with salmon-pink cheeks dished out fish pie.

His stomach rumbled. Eight twenty-one on his watch.

The man emerged from the toilets. Flanking him were a giant muscular black guy and a blond youth who reeked of paint. He wore grunge chic and looked to be in his early thirties. His skinhead cut made his features more prominent. The nose was long and the cheeks sunken by smoking or starvation. There was something familiar about him. Andy locked eyes with the stranger, whose gaze burned into him for a second before darting away. The trio left the building and the electric doors hissed shut, snapping the tail off the wind.

'Let's go.'

Rob, by his side now.

'I want to try Michelle again.'

The line was still busy.

'Never mind,' said Rob. 'Be plenty of babes at the gig. Let's get on.'

CHAPTER ELEVEN

The Judge, The Rasta,
Sarky Pig and Others

The rain made the cars shine as if showroom fresh. God, having picked up the lift at Trowell services near Nottingham, was dismayed to find that they were plodding along in the slow lane. Personally, he'd much rather be seeing the spindly T-shaped lights zip past, hearing the engine hum beneath him and tasting the thin metal of fear as they overtook the other vehicles. However, he accepted that there were worse things than travelling at forty-five miles an hour. Like going at forty-five in a caravan.

The interior of the aged Humber van had porthole-style windows and the fabric roof lining had long since perished. The engine noise, even at this low speed, was deafening. Sitting on bolted-down wooden benches was a group of young people all dressed in paramilitary uniform. It was like being a World War II bomber, awaiting a parachute drop into the unknown.

'Where are you going?' asked a bearded man opposite him.

'It's a long story,' muttered God. He was tiring of explanations and sprouting the seedlings of a migraine.

A placid expression grew above the scruffy beard. The

youth wore a rainbow-coloured jersey under his unbuttoned tunic and his hair was beaded into Rastafarian rat-tails. Seated next to him was a girl whose skin was as pale as alabaster. A severe fringe of chestnut-brown hair topped her oval face, and her eyes were green and almond-shaped. The others sported ragged military cast-offs and a communal blissed-out smile. God wondered if they were on drugs.

'Are we ready to do God's work?' came a stentorian tone from the front.

They chorused agreement.

'What's going on?' asked God.

'Say you love the army,' continued the voice, singsong.

'We all love the ar-my,' they responded in unison.

'Then give me ten.'

They began to chant: 'Thou shalt have no other Gods but me . . .'

As they whipped through the Commandments, God added another name to the list of people from whom he wouldn't accept rides. The Jesus Army – especially when they were on manoeuvres.

The house was too large for Councillor Jacobs and his wife, Stephanie. Set in several acres and backing on to woodland, the mansion had been built between the wars at the behest of a judge then famous for the severity of his sentences. The couple had taken one look at the gravel drive and gardens and had fallen in love with it. The councillor, who prized property above all, soon learned of the story attached to their new home.

Justice Perry and family had been happy there until the brother of a man he had sentenced to be hung came looking for revenge. Discovering the man in his scullery, the judge brained him with a length of pipe, which he kept under the bed for such eventualities. The miscreant was hospitalised and on his recovery subsequently appeared in front of one of Perry's colleagues on the bench. Perry ensured that the man received a long sentence.

The judge was a canny man. He had a detective do some research and discovered that the family of felons was of Irish origin and that there were five brothers in total. Certain that the rest would come after him, Perry armed himself with a shotgun and awaited the arrival of the middle child. He did not have to wait long.

One night, as the first chill of autumn fretted the leaves from the trees, the third brother stumbled through the ornamental pond and tested the doors on the veranda. Perry shot him through the glass.

After this, Perry made use of further connections and HM Customs arrested the fourth brother the instant he set foot on British soil. Of the fifth and final brother, little was known other than that he had left home for Canada at the age of sixteen.

Perry obsessed over the missing youth, certain he would return to wreak his revenge. He took to travelling to the courtroom in an unmarked police car and had his property guarded by fierce dogs. As the months passed, his relationship with his family deteriorated. His daughter left home for London and disappeared into the capital. His two sons were at boarding school and were suffering enough. His wife Beatrice remained stoic. Her family had lived high on the hog in the last days of the Raj and she refused to accede to intimidation.

One fine spring morning a parcel arrived at the gate. The postman, having long since refused to cross the drive owing to the family's Alsatians, rang the outer bell and called out to him.

'Sorry, Judge. You'll have to sign for this one.'

Perry scrunched across the gravel and indicated for the postman to place the parcel on the ground.

He did so. The first thing Justice Perry noticed was that the stamps were of Canadian origin.

'Open it,' he demanded.

The postman did as he was told. Inside the box were a noose, a piece of pipe and a single shotgun cartridge. He looked up, perplexed. 'What's all this?'

'A rather juvenile warning,' snorted the judge disdainfully.

'Oh, really,' said the postman, producing a knife. The last thing Justice Perry heard was the trace of a Canadian accent.

Visitors to Councillor Jacobs's home were subjected to this story whether they liked it or not. He had even gone so far as to purchase the judge's portrait from the council chambers and hang it over the fireplace. In the telling, embellishments had been added: the Irishmen were ogres, the police inept and, the *pièce de résistance*, the ghost of the judge stalked the house at night. This had the effect of dissuading friends and relatives from overstaying their welcome, which was his intention all along.

The taxi slowed at the gates and Jacobs used his remote to open them. The car deposited him at the front door and drove off spitting gravel at the rose beds. The garden was Stephanie's pride and joy. Jacobs was happy to leave her to the chaos of nature, his idea of the great outdoors being the potted palm in the atrium at the town hall. How else she passed her time was unknown to him as – in their brief moments together – he found his mind wandering to civic duties. He was often away on council-sponsored 'Awaydays' or attending functions at the lodge: in general, he liked to oil the wheels with the Masons, Rotarians and other white-collar criminals.

He unlocked the faux-Tudor door and strolled along the potpourri-scented corridor. As he made for the drinks cabinet in the living room, he noticed Stephanie sprawled in an armchair in front of the television.

'I didn't know you were in.'

'Where did you think I'd be?'

A crystal tumbler sat on a table at her side. It was empty save for a twist of lemon.

'I don't know,' replied Neil, pouring himself a fat finger of Glenfiddich.

The programme, a sitcom, featured a middle-class couple parading their lame problems for an undemanding public.

'Would you mind turning that off?'

'Yes, I would, actually.'

Jacobs studied his wife's face. She was what people referred to as a 'handsome woman' when they meant boyish, strong-featured or no longer pretty. She was taller than he and more substantial without having gone to fat. In some respects, he thought, still in her prime. She lolled idly, relaxed in slacks, loafers and an old gardening blouse. Her hair, long and luxuriantly ash-blond, was piled up on top of her head and fastened there with a butterfly grip. She was looking steadily at him through her television glasses, the screen reflecting a bright crescent off each lens.

'Are you following it?' he asked.

'Not really, no.'

He sipped his drink, his throat numbing with the warmth of the alcohol. 'How was your day?'

'Same old.'

He didn't pursue the line of questioning, deciding that if she were angry with him over some perceived misdemeanour then she could come out with it herself. 'I must be off soon.'

'Where to?'

'Some Rotarian thing.'

She removed her glasses. 'Have you eaten?'

'There'll be food there.'

She turned back to the television.

They rarely ate together any more save on Saturdays at a

local restaurant. There, with minor variations, they had the same meal and conversation about the week's events on each occasion.

Jacobs finished his drink and went upstairs to bathe and change. An hour or so later, he came down and popped his head back in the room. She was still there, watching the news. He went through to the kitchen. The farmhouse table had been set for two. Red paper serviettes were folded into the wineglasses and a single-stemmed rose stood in a thin vase. He held a hand in front of the eye-level glazed oven door. Still warm. A red casserole dish cowered inside.

He came back through.

'Darling, I'm awfully sorry. You'd prepared something.'

'Doesn't matter. Really.'

He went to the garage to fire up the Rover, looking forward to his night of passion.

God was having a rough time of it. Once he had let slip his identity, the faces of the youths jogged through a gamut of emotions: shock gave way to disbelief, followed by smug denial, piteous stares and patronising reassurances. It was quite a facial work-out. There were angry calls of 'Blasphemer', and from a voice in the corner the demand that he be expelled from the vehicle. Considering their present speed, he feared serious injury, perhaps a scuffed knee.

'If you are the Lord, then you'd have shown us a sign,' prompted a girl whose nose dripped like a tap with a loose washer.

'What kind of a sign?'

'How should we know? You're the all-powerful one,' said an overweight man who seemed a tad sarcastic to be a Christian. He had piggy eyes and lips so red he might have been wearing lipstick.

'Delays Possible,' answered God.

The girls looked to the bearded white Rastafarian for an explanation. God had learned that his name was Samuel and that he commanded respect from those in the rear of the van. God feared for all of them. Gullibility was etched into their faces and they looked to be easy prey for salesmen, fraudsters or Young Conservatives.

'That's a *motorway* sign,' said the sarky pig.

'Contraflow in Operation. Works Unit Only. Model Village. Historic Warwick.'

'I think what our friend here is trying to say,' interpreted Samuel, 'is that signs are meaningless. They are mere symbols and should not be held over the real truth. God's love.'

God mumbled under his breath. 'Welcome Break. Six Miles.'

'Are you defending him?' asked Sarky Pig in an effort to gain support.

Ooh, thought God. A theological pissing contest.

'That's a rather aggressive attitude,' said Sam.

'I'm not being aggressive,' replied Sarky Pig, aggressively.

Samuel shook his leonine mane. 'It's not a question of defending him. The man has a right to tell us who or what he believes he is. For all we know, he may *be* Our Lord. I mean – who's to say what form or vessel God would choose if he came back to earth? In the Old Testament . . .'

'Haven't you read Revelations?' broke in Sarky Pig. 'There will be mass destruction and the heavens shall be rent asunder. Or didn't you read that far? It's in the back, before you get to the pretty maps of Israel.'

'Yes, yes. Alpha and omega and all the angels appearing on the earth. You don't take that literally, do you?'

The girl with the wet nose stared at him. It hadn't occurred to her that the Bible was not a screenplay of things to come.

You only have to take a look at 'Chapter twenty-two, verse

eighteen,' continued Samuel. 'It threatens a plague on those who dare to add any words to the Bible. That's like saying you mustn't do any graffiti or I'll set the park-keeper on you. It's all a bit insecure, really, isn't it?'

'Have you lost your mind?' challenged Sarky Pig. 'We offer a lift to this devil and now you're questioning the good book?'

'Actually . . .' Samuel lowered his head. 'I've been questioning the book for a while. We do all this praying and preaching and all the time I'm asking myself – is this what Christianity is all about?'

The others looked at him quizzically.

Samuel raised his eyes and fanned a hand at God. 'You were about to throw him out. That's hardly Christian charity, is it?'

'He's a blasphemer,' bleated a Welsh voice in the dark.

Samuel came back with 'The world's full of blasphemers. Full of people who think they're God.'

'What's that supposed to mean?' ventured Sarky Pig in a tone that suggested the imminent divesting of jackets.

'Christianity's outdated. We think we're being modern, but we're still stuffy and dogmatic. This man here has answers. The key to what life's really all about. He travels around harming no one, living naturally and speaking his truth quietly. He's closer to the Christian ideal than any of us.'

'Uh?' murmured God, who had been busy relacing his boots.

'I want to come with you,' announced the bearded Rasta.

'Where?'

'To wherever you're going.'

'Birch services?'

'Sam? Are you really going to leave us?' asked the girl with the pudding-basin hair. She had a thing for him. When the white Rasta nodded, she burst into tears.

'Let him go,' said Sarky Pig. 'He's not fit to be in Jesus's army.'

'Will there be a court-martial?' God asked of the pale girl.
'I don't know.'

'Or maybe they'll shoot him for desertion,' he added,
tactlessly.

'Is that what you want, Samuel? To leave us?' came a
booming voice from the front seat.

'Yes. I'm discharging myself.'

'That's a sin you, know,' came the Welsh voice in the
dark.

Pig smiled haughtily. 'I never thought you were cut out for
this. You're not a real soldier for Christ – not like the rest of
us.'

'That's right,' answered Samuel in a voice that implied he
knew better.

There was a murmuring up front. The Humber van slowed
and came to rest on the hard shoulder. There was silence, save
for the sobbing of the almond-eyed girl. The Welshman
opened the rear doors to freezing mist. God rose and, still bent
double, thanked them for the ride and jumped down.

Surrounding him were black undulating hills. Lights were
embedded in the valleys like amber cast on velvet. Mist hung
wraith-like in the still air. God's footsteps sounded hollow as
he took his first few paces. It was going to be a bugger to hitch
from here.

Behind him, Samuel was saying his goodbyes. The pale girl
reached up and kissed him hard on the lips, her fringe moist in
the mist.

'I'm coming with you,' she said.

'So am I,' said the girl with the dripping nose, who
preferred the sisterhood of women to the community of
religion. Also she had run out of tampons and she knew
that the pale girl had some.

'Right, then. I'm coming too,' added the Welshman, who
secretly fancied the wet-nosed girl.

'But that only leaves me and Tim,' whined Sarky Pig. 'And he's only with us because he hasn't got any friends.'

'Would anyone like some tea?' asked Tim on cue. He held a Thermos and was quite well spoken.

'It's lapsang souchong.'

God watched the scene unfold with a growing sense of panic. 'Please get back in the van. You'll all freeze.'

'He is so unselfish that he cares not for his own condition,' bleated the pale girl, entirely for Samuel's benefit.

God hitched up his rucksack and walked off. Samuel followed with the others hustling behind him. God stopped. 'Look, we'll never get a lift. Not together.'

Back at the van, the remaining quartet watched the desertion with interest. God's movements and the followers shunting up behind him resembled a bizarre game of grand-mother's footsteps.

'Now come on,' said God, placing his hands on his hips. 'Go back, all of you.'

'We're coming with you,' said Samuel.

'You're not.'

Smiles from the flock. God hitched up his jacket and set off at a brisk trot. Soon he was jogging. He stole a glimpse over his shoulder. They were still behind him.

'Piss off, will you?'

Hearing the Rover crawl across gravel, Stephanie Jacobs switched off the television and peered through the curtains in the bay window. Once the tail-lights had blinked to nothing, she went to the phone on the stand in the hall. As she dialled, she noticed she still had black crescents of earth under her fingernails.

'*Evening Mail.*'

'Terry Warren, please. Extension 674.'

There was a pause as the connection was made. She stared at the front door, seeing shapes in the small squares of bubble glass set into it.

'Warren.'

'It's Mrs Jacobs. Our subject has left. I'll be over to pick you up at your office shortly.'

'Give us an hour or so. They've got me subbing.'

'Not for much longer, Mr Warren. And don't forget your camera.'

Without awaiting a reply, she replaced the phone and bounded upstairs.

CHAPTER TWELVE

Friendly Driver?

———◆———

The motorway banked round past the old Fort Dunlop building as they approached Birmingham. Andy's shoulder and right arm were soaked and freezing from keeping the window open.

'I'm *sure* I know that face,' he said, thinking back to the shaven-headed man at Corley services.

'Who?' Rob asked, pulling out a bottle of Rolling Rock.

Andy wasn't listening, being involved in morphing the face on to other comedians, friends and acquaintances. Rob levered off the bottle-top with an opener on his key-ring. Froth dribbled into the footwell.

'How many of those do you drink before a gig?'

'Enough.'

After a moment, Andy said, 'Well, we'd better find this place soon. I want to ring Michelle again.'

Rob hoisted out his mobile, which still refused to function. 'Let her worry,' he said.

'She isn't worried. She dumped *me*, remember?'

Rob's coat creaked as he scratched the nape of his neck. 'Tell you what, though. Bust-ups are brilliant material.'

Andy rolled his eyes. A grim row of tower blocks rose

behind the concrete slabs of a bridge. The sky looked like a filthy wrung-out rag. 'Which turn-off is it?' he asked.

'It's miles yet.'

'But we're coming up to the centre.'

'It's ages away.'

'Look, you're not a driver. Let's check the map.'

'I can remember the way.'

Andy doubted it. A tale from the previous summer's Edinburgh Festival had Rob Gillen drunk, drugged and lost in Portobello instead of on-stage at the Assembly Rooms. 'You said you had a contract from the Agency?'

'Somewhere.'

'Well, find it. There must be a map!' Andy rustled out another cigarette. The last thing he wanted was to undergo the male ritual of refusing to stop for directions. It was already half past eight.

Reluctantly, Rob tugged an A4 file out of his sports bag. 'I can't see.'

Andy flicked on the overhead light and reduced their speed. Yellow boards lashed to the crash barriers indicated that yet another contraflow was looming. Rob blew a low note on the neck of his beer as he fingered through his invoices, gig details and publicity material. He chortled, reminiscing over some previous triumph. Andy leaned across.

'Find the sodding details, Rob. We're coming to the main turn-off.'

Rob found a piece of paper branded with the heavy-set logo of the Agency. 'Birmingham. Rider. Fee. Hey, you're not down as support.'

'They only called me last night.'

'How much you getting?'

'Check to see if there's a fucking map, will you?'

Rob turned it over. A segment of the Birmingham *A–Z* was photocopied on the back. 'Looks like we come off at . . .

Junction Six. Where's that, then?' he asked, peering out at the loops and whirls of Spaghetti Junction.

'Take a wild guess.'

'We passed it?'

Andy didn't bother saying anything.

Sixty miles north-west of them at Knutsford services, a coach was beached in the parking area. Wrapped against the cold, the passengers floated away from it like a flotilla of lifeboats leaving a sinking ship. At first they were blown out of line by the wind, but they righted themselves and hove to the jetty of the service area.

Inside the coach, the driver slid out his copy of the *Mirror*. He'd read the sports and news pages and intended to use his break to complete the crossword. He noted grimly that a few of the old biddies had remained aboard so he wouldn't be able to surf the wavebands to escape the aural drool of Heart FM. He glanced at his watch. Another hour to Blackpool, then the long wait before driving the old bats back to Leicester. He gave out a sigh as he rearranged his spreading buttocks on the beaded orthopaedic seat.

Outside, the asthmatic engine fan blew hard but couldn't compete with the wind scything across the carpark. The body-work of the coach had scarred flanks as a result of a recent scrape with a listed building in Stratford. Its rear was mud-splattered and the rubber flaps were caked in soot-black road canker. Barely readable through the grime on its rear was the motto 'Friendly Driver'. Perhaps they couldn't spell 'Irritable Git'.

'What you wanna do is get a cat.'

'Do what?'

Andy had taken the next opportunity to leave the motorway and was burrowing south on the M5. He was struggling not to hyperventilate. This was the standard comedian's nightmare. Forget dying on stage or being naked in the street or having one's genitals ridiculed by a bevy of models – this was the big one. Being late. He begged a sip of Rob's beer and asked: 'Why would I want to get a cat?'

'They're like kids, see? Since Natasha had the boy, she's obsessed with him.'

'Is there a point to this?'

'Yeah. A kid or a pet draws fire.'

'Fire?'

'From the relationship.'

'Like a decoy, you mean?'

'Yeah. It's like having a barrage balloon. Maybe that's why kids have them at parties.'

'What?'

'Balloons.'

Andy wondered if saying nothing might discourage him.

'But I'll tell you something else. Baby pictures are the worst.'

Nope. No chance.

'No one wants to see forty pictures of some squalling sack of shit. Forty pictures of where the baby came *from* is another matter. Hey, what d'you reckon to this—'

Andy stared ahead, keeping his eyes out for the next turning.

'—idea I had? See, we all take videos and photos of the important things in life, right? Weddings, Christmases, birthdays. Never funerals. No one ever takes photos at a funeral.' He paused. 'Now let's have Mum, Dad and the kids with the deceased, aaandd *smile!*'

He concluded the routine by winding down his window and lobbing his beer bottle out into the slow lane. It shattered, leaving a glistening comet-trail of broken glass.

'Jesus, don't do that!' shouted Andy. 'You never know when . . .'

His words were drowned in the wail of the siren.

The coach driver revved the engine and the doors scissored open with an airy wheeze. The bulk of the passengers, most of them way beyond pensionable age, cooed like pigeons round breadcrumbs. As they clambered back on board, each one pulled an identical grimace and commented on the weather as if uttering responses at Mass. Tiring quickly of this, the driver pretended to examine his clipboard. The shrunken birds settled into their seats. He closed the doors, stood up and began to count the heads with his index finger, as if picking out a melody.

'Where are they?'

The twittering was inconclusive, so he scowled at them and slumped back in his seat.

The games area inside the services reeked of stale burgers. The carpet, though barely six months old, was already dotted with the blackened scabs of used chewing gum. The machines emitted a chorus of bleeps, buzzes and cascading tones. Crammed inside the ZombieDeath booth were two people whose trigger fingers pumped hard as they slaughtered the legions of the undead. Ironically, Mrs Lambridge and Mrs Chitterden weren't so far off being the undead themselves.

The motorway was silent, as if set for the first act of a play. Revolving coloured lights strobed blind streaks across Andy's vision. It seemed to take an age before the policeman reached the car. They watched the officer walk towards them, taking his time, noting the licence plate and the condition of the vehicle.

'Pigs,' sneered Rob.

'Shut up, will you?'

'D'you reckon they train them to walk that slow? Put the shits up us?'

'What do you mean *us*? It's my sodding car. It's me who'll get done.'

'For what?'

'They'll find something,' muttered Andy, dredging through advice from friends about what to do when dealing with the police. His arms were tingling like the last spluttering of a sparkler and his insides had turned to liquid. He'd had few brushes with the law, and those had mostly been in pre-student days. He had a grim thought: Your life doesn't flash before your eyes in the face of death. It happens when the police stop you.

The officer continued towards them. Before he reached the car, Andy reckoned he'd have time to smoke a cigarette, tidy up, maybe draw and shoot an entire animated film. Suddenly, a genetic memory kicked in and he knew exactly what to do.

'Stay in the car,' he hissed at Rob, then swung out and strode up to the policeman. 'How can I help, Officer?' he asked in the politest tone he could manage without actually morphing into a Radio 4 presenter.

'Is this a bottle bank?' asked the policeman.

No, it's a sodding motorway, thought Andy. 'Ah,' he said. 'Look, I'm sorry about my friend. He's a bit high-spirited.' He winced at the choice of phrase.

'Oh, yes? Like a drink, do we?'

Reading the subtext, Andy addressed the question with care. 'No, I haven't had a drink.' He threw Rob a scowl.

'Registration number, please?'

Andy told him.

'Do you have your licence on you?'

He did. It was scarred with six points – borderline offender.

The officer took it from him, studied it, then bent to his radio. He received a garbled reply and an irritated dimple appeared on his cheek. He circled the car, peering at it as if it were a complex chess puzzle. Andy prayed Rob would do as he was told and remain in his seat.

'Oi-oi. Haven't we done yet?'

No, of course he won't. What was I thinking?

Rob was out and leaning on the roof. The policeman turned to him.

'And your name is?'

'What's it to do with you?'

Andy pinched the skin on the bridge of his nose.

'Since you seem intent on littering the queen's highway and causing danger to other vehicles, I'd say quite a lot.'

'What's he on about, Andy?'

'Just tell him you're sorry, will you?'

Rob walked up to the policeman and patted him on the shoulder.

'Sorry, mate.'

The man winced at his lager breath.

But Rob hadn't finished. He turned to the police car and, mimicking the officer's cautious tone, said: 'Would you mind coming with me, please?' Without awaiting a reply, he walked over to their vehicle, followed by the dumbfounded officer. He tapped on the passenger window. A bearded, middle-aged sergeant buzzed it down and looked up him: his dour expression implied a lifetime of being disappointed in people.

'Whorrisit?' he demanded.

'This *your* car, is it, sir?'

The first policeman folded his arms.

'And what speed do we *think* we were doing, Damon Hill?'

The bearded officer nodded to his colleague, who unfolded his arms and touched his side-handled baton.

'Name,' the policeman stated.

'Rob Gillen.'

The second officer slid out of the car and towered above him. Andy watched the event as if it were a slo-mo replay.

'Having a bit of a joke, are we, laddie?'

Rob smiled facetiously.

'And what do we do for a living, then, *sir*?' asked the first officer.

'I'm a comedian,' grinned Rob, completely buggering up their next question.

Mrs Lambridge and Mrs Chitterden, having placed their names below 'Jamtag' on the winner of winners board, had availed themselves of the facilities and were rustling towards the exit.

'Splendid fun,' said Mrs Lambridge.

'Yes,' replied Mrs Chitterden.

Shouldering their bags, they waddled to the doors, which immediately hissed open. Mrs Lambridge fluttered a hand in the path of her friend. The ladies took a step backwards. The doors closed. They stepped forwards again. The doors reopened. They did a two-step on swollen ankles, chuckling as the doors opened and closed as if by magic.

'How on earth do they clean these things?' ventured Mrs Chitterden.

'Lord knows,' replied Mrs Lambridge.

When they got out into the parking area, there were now three coaches, two of them emblazoned with bright German commands. The ladies weren't happy: like the rest of the country, they had neither forgotten nor forgiven, their anger continually stoked by television documentaries.

'I wonder where the coach has got to,' returned Mrs Lambridge. 'He was supposed to wait. He was given orders.'

'Orders, yes.'

Mrs Lambridge placed a small square of plastic over her steel helmet of hair. 'I shall have words with his superior.'

Following a disjointed conversation with the German driver, they discovered that their vehicle was sandwiched between the new arrivals.

'Didn't you see me flashing the lights?' said their driver as they clambered aboard.

Mrs Lambridge sniffed the air.

'You was due back five minutes ago,' he added.

'You should have sent a search party,' said Mrs Lambridge.

'Search party,' echoed Mrs Chitterden.

'Take your seats and let's get on, eh?'

Mrs Lambridge launched her Parthian shot. 'I shall be taking your number.'

'Why, have I pulled?' cheeked the driver as he caught the eyes of a pair of flirtatious spinsters in the front seats. Wrestling the wheel in a tight circle, he made for the slip road.

Once on the M6 he straddled the middle lane, took up the Tannoy and announced that – traffic permitting – they would be on the front in Blackpool by half nine. Once he had finished, his elderly charges resumed their chatter.

'What's it tonight, then?' he asked of the spinsters. 'Bobby Crush? Ice dance at the Pleasure Beach?'

'Oh no,' they answered together.

'We're ever so excited,' said a crone with a face more lined than Clapham Junction. 'We're off to see Mr Roy "Chubby" Brown.'

CHAPTER THIRTEEN

Respraying The Town Red

———◆———

'Jason. *Jason?*'

His mother's voice bled through the walls of the boxroom. Jason didn't hear her as the Fun Lovin' Criminals were competing decibel for decibel with the hairdryer, which he had stolen it from her room and was standing in front of the mirror trying to decide whether his first robbery required a foppish fringe or a hard-man scooped-back ponytail.

Laura Joffe started up the steep stairs, her footsteps echoing on the bare boards. When knocking failed to rouse him, she put her hand to the handle of the bedroom door. At the same moment, Jason sprang it open from the other side. He was wearing a ratty claret-and-blue-striped dressing gown.

'What?'

'Dad's on the phone. Wants to know what you've done with the van.'

Jason dropped his shoulders in defeat, pushed past her and thundered downstairs to the hall.

'And your tea's ready.'

Ignoring her, he plucked the phone from its holster on the wall. Through the frosted-glass front door, pixillated cars and the low brick walls of the estate changed shape and colour like the faces of informants on *Crimewatch*.

'Where's me pigging van, Jason?'

'Tol' you. I borrowed it.'

'I said to have it back by six.'

'Sorry, Dad.'

'You've got it there, haven't you?'

'Er, yeah,' lied Jason. 'I'm off out in a bit. Want me to drop it by the lot?'

'Bloody better.'

Jason hung up. Wouldn't be a problem. Dad would be off down the pub soon, and anyway he'd have the Transit back by morning. As for having sprayed out his father's name – well, he could blame that on some of the local kids. Besides, it wouldn't matter anyway. By the end of the evening he'd be up by . . . By what? Seven, eight grand? Enough to get away from the crumblies and get his own place.

He jogged upstairs to find his mother fuming in the narrow passage. In one hand she held her hairdryer; in the other, its battered plastic case full of the various nozzles and attachments.

'Ask if you want to borrow it,' she warned. 'And your tea's out.'

'What is it?'

The smell of hot fat and oven chips crept up the stairwell.

'Chicken and chips.'

'What, Budgen's chips?'

His mother pressed her lips together.

'I hate Budgen's.'

'They're cheap.'

'So are McDonald's, and they taste better.'

He stamped into his bedroom, wincing as he caught his bare foot on a tack sticking out of the runner. Dad had promised to fit a new carpet over three months ago. Waiting for a bloke in a pub, he'd said. Jason's one ambition in life was to become a 'bloke in a pub': the sort of bloke who could get you anything so long as it was hookey. But that option hadn't been on the list of choices the careers advice officer gave him at school. Which was why he packed it in at fifteen.

Rustling through the clothes in his wardrobe, he selected a pale blue Tommy Hilfiger top and struggled into a pair of jeans with elephantine legs. He then crammed his feet into giant trainers. He looked like an oversized toddler in need of reins.

'Wicked.' He gazed at the mirror and flicked his hands in the air as if trying to shake off some strips of Sellotape.

He went to his puffa jacket and slid out the can of Stud Spray. Then he closed his eyes, raised an arm and laminated his armpit. He stuck his nose into it. Couldn't smell anything. Deciding that more was needed, he liberally doused his torso, using up half the can.

There was a scuffling at the door and a mop with a tongue sticking out of it snuffled into the room. At least he hoped it was a tongue. With all that hair you could hardly tell which end was which when it came to the family dog. Prince was an unimaginatively named terrier who spent the majority of his waking hours in old shoes and puddles. Unable to see where he was going or what he was doing, he caused much embarrassment to himself and his owners when it came to his choice of sexual partner.

'Come on, symbol,' said Jason, hoisting the mutt on to the bed.

The dog sat there, looking pathetic: its tongue poked out like salami out of a sandwich.

'Hey. Time the both of us got lucky.'

Then, with an evil glint in his eye, he sprayed the dog. He gave it better coverage than he did the bodywork on the cars in the lot.

*   *   *

Doug's silver Ford Mondeo was parked up in a back street. He had purchased the saloon car for its anonymity; a feature not prominent in the sales brochures, but one that had served him well during his many drug drops in the West Midlands. On the drive over to Jason's, the boy had teased him for keeping a baby carriage in the back. He'd explained that because of it the police had never stopped him, which shut the boy up for a bit.

They dropped Jason at his home, forcing a solemn promise out of him that he'd meet Dan by the club door at half eleven. Next, they went to Danny's high-rise flat so as he could put his mother to bed. After that they drove back to the town centre. It was nine o'clock, and Danny had a while to kill before he was due to start work.

The pub was formerly known as the Black Swan, but was now called El Cantina. Like most pubs it had not escaped the rigorous refurbishment of the mid-nineties, but being in Birmingham it had not succumbed to the ubiquitous Irish theme. Instead, the brewery had gone for mock-Ponderosa with exposed brick and plasterwork, bad-trip acid colours and stripped 'n' dipped woodwork. The blackboard menu was a bastard mix of Anglo-European and Mexican dishes, repeated in Santa Fe lettering on improbably distressed menus. This attempt at cloning a pub with a Tex-Mex restaurant satisfied neither clientèle, and as a result the place was empty. Good enough reason for Doug to have chosen it.

'Let's hear the rest of the plan,' said Danny as he furnished them with lagers. They tossed their segments of lime to one side. They looked stupid floating in a pint glass.

'All right. But only if you don't call me a genius until after.'

'OK.'

'Because it *is* a genius plan.'

Danny mimed zipping his lips.

Doug sparked a fresh roll-up. 'This is *way* bigger than the cashpoint job.'

Excited, Danny crammed his hands between his thighs to stop them escaping.

'We're funding the deal I've got going tomorrow morning.'

'What kind of deal?'

Doug snuffled his nostrils with his fingers. 'Charlie.'

In response, Danny blew his nose. By his side was an extra-strength family-sized box of Kleenex he'd purchased at the corner shop.

'Hey. That'd help clear me sinuses. Bit of marching powder. You got any on you?'

Doug shot him a dubious look. To his knowledge, Danny One-Slice had already chomped through four blues and a fistful of steroids and had drunk a pint of Night Nurse: qualification level for the all-drug Olympics.

'Maybe later,' he said.

Danny took a few deep gulps of beer. His Adam's apple volleyed up and down his neck.

Doug left his drink untouched. 'Remember when I lived in Amsterdam?'

The furrows in Danny's brow looked like rows of crawling worms.

Doug had spent a lot of time out in Holland, some of it inside. There, he had succumbed to the availability of cheap smack. When he ultimately returned to England, Dan had helped him to kick the habit. The Filipino's detox method was crude but effective and stood no chance of catching on in California.

'I've been in touch with an old contact of mine over there. Pieter. He's blagged a load of top-grade Charlie and he's bringing it over from The Hague. He's arranged for it to fly cargo from Schipol and he's sweetened the ground crews at both ends. He'll be here tomorrow morning. Early.'

Dan scratched his goatee. 'How much snow is he bringing?'

'Enough to turn Hurst Street into a ski run.'

'Bostin'.'

'And it's all kosher. I brought back a taster last month.'

'How much are we laying out?'

'Eighty grand.'

Danny's maths were a lot better than Jason's. 'Hold up. You said the hole in the wall's only gonna bring us twenty. We're sixty short.'

'That's where things get interesting.'

Doug took a long pull of his pint and put aside the glass. It left a wet crescent on the table.

'Six thirty tomorrow morning, you and I are meeting Pieter in a suite in the Novotel.'

'Where's that?'

'Right opposite the airport terminal. I booked it this afternoon. We've got two syndicate rooms on the sixth floor, 603 and 604. They've got a connecting door.'

'What do we need a room each for?'

'Our clients.'

'Clients.' Danny rolled the word around his tongue. It wasn't one he used often.

'You'll be on the door, Dan.'

'As ever.'

'Our twenty grand and a test bag of the coke goes in one room – 603. The rest of the stash will be in the suite next door. The folding and the coke are for Nelson so he'll put up the dosh.'

The giant raised a hand like a perplexed schoolboy. 'Have I missed something here?'

'Want me to go back?'

'No. Nelson? Yardie Nelson?'

'Yup.'

'Off his head, armed-and-dangerous-nutter Nelson?'

'That's the one.'

'Oh.'

'I talked to him earlier. He thinks we're putting together our twenty grand and thirty of his. Fifty K in all. He's due there at six forty-five.'

'With a couple of heavies.'

'I'm counting on it. I'll dish out samples, be cool, show them the take from the job. When they're ready, they'll hand over their thirty grand to Pieter, who's going to tell them that he'll count it and check for duff notes. With me?'

'Yeah.'

'Only he'll say he's rented out another room.'

Danny winced. 'Nelson ain't gonna let the guy walk off with his bread.'

'Sure he is. He's got me as collateral. Plus my twenty K and the sample bag. At that point, he's still on top.'

'Where's this mate of yours going with the money? Not down the arcade, I hope.'

'I'll come to that.'

Doug's face was stern. He had earlier taken some sulphate and the bones in his jaw were grinding away under the surface. Worry lines were etched deep across his forehead. 'Reason you're on the door is so you can make sure none of Nelson's mates decide to follow him.'

Dan pulled at the gold ring in his ear. 'But they've got guns.'

'We've got guns too. Yours is in the boot of the car.'

'Yeah?'

'Any time sir would care to pick it up . . . ?'

Danny smiled.

Doug drew two rectangles in the beer slops. 'But Pieter's gonna be in the suite next door. He's putting their money with the coke right on the table. Then he slips out into the corridor. As soon as you see him, you two go and hide in the linen cupboard.' He blotted a beery full stop. 'Show you where it is once we get there.'

'I'm lost again. You're in one room with Nelson, but the money and the coke are in the other?'

A nod: 'Then I take a slash,' said Doug. 'Only I slip through into the other room.'

Danny's face glowed with realisation. 'And then we all leg it with the thirty grand and the coke?'

'Not finished yet. I go to the door of the other suite – 604 – just in time to meet the guys from Shera Punjab.'

Danny sank the rest of his beer. 'The Punjabis?'

'Did I mention I did the same deal with Nasir and his brothers?'

'No.' Danny blew his nose again. Tissues were piling up around him, dampening and melting in the slops. 'You didn't.'

'I show them in, tell them to help themselves and say I'm off to fetch the dealer.'

'They gonna be all right about that?'

Doug, deadpan: 'I am leaving them alone with thirty grand and a suitcase full of top-grade cocaine.'

'Fair enough. What happens then?'

'Guess who's getting jumpy next door?'

Danny aped Jamaican patois. 'Yard *bwaays*.'

'The moment Nelson gets suspicious, he's going to bust through. Either he kicks down the bathroom door or he tries the connecting one.' Doug chuckled. 'I hope the bastard does because I'm leaving it unlocked for him.'

Danny sat and thought and pictured the carnage, but before he spoke he wanted to make sure he'd got it right. 'So, Nelson is gonna see three Asian guys with all the coke and *his* money.'

'Correct.'

'And Nasir and his brothers are gonna think it's the Yardies busting in on *their* deal?'

' 'S right.'

'And they'll all be carrying.'

Doug saluted him.

'It's gonna be a bloody massacre.'

Doug bowed his head gracefully.

'They'll wipe each other out.'

'That's what a massacre is, Dan.'

'What if they don't all die?'

'You and I are going back in there to mop up.' He saw Danny's face fall. 'Sorry, Dan, but there it is. We do have an incentive, though.'

'The coke and all the money?'

'The coke and all the money.'

Danny knitted his hands together, as if in prayer.

'That's why we did over the cop shop this morning,' added Doug. 'We don't really need the weapons for the cashpoint job.'

'Busy night.'

'Are you in, then?'

'What if I said no?'

'You never have so far.'

'Oh, all right, then,' said Danny, as if he'd been pestered into hoovering.

Doug held his glee inside. 'One more thing. If for any reason Nelson doesn't suss it right away, I booked a wake-up call in 603.'

'That's where Nelson is, right?'

'Yeah, but the call's in Nasir's name.'

'Oh, you *bastard*.'

Doug and Dan broke into peals of laughter and the giant almost demolished his chair. The barman looked over. Doug signalled that there was no trouble.

Dan shook his head, wiping tears from his eyes. 'There's gotta be holes in this, man.'

'You think of some while I get 'em in.'

'Get us a BMW as well.'

Doug raised an eyebrow.

'Bailey's, Malibu, Whisky.'

Doug returned with two pints and a tumbler of chocolate phlegm, and Danny began to question him further. It was an odd sort of pub quiz.

'What about the noise – guns and that?'

'The rooms are top-floor and right under the flight path. They've been soundproofed.'

'What about the hotel staff?'

'It's only suites on that side of the building. Plus, it's half six. The cleaners don't start till eight. We'll be out by seven fifteen.'

'What if those lazy Yardie bastards are late?'

'I'm gonna mobile Nelson. Make sure he's there on time.'

Danny threw back his drink. 'How about the Asians? What if they're not awake?'

'A race of newsagents?'

Dan smiled.

Doug sparked a fresh smoke. 'The timing on this is crucial, but we do have get-outs. If Nelson is late then we speed things up. Get Pieter out of the suite quick. If the Asians are early, you'll have to signal me – knock on the door or something.'

'What about if they come mob-handed?'

Doug explained that he had given instructions that neither gang come with more than two 'associates'. Also that he had thoroughly checked the hotel facilities, including the sauna, pool and possible getaway routes.

'Hopefully,' he concluded, 'we'll be long gone and the pigs will find a roomful of bullet-ridden Yardies and Punjabi gangstas. It should improve their clear-up rate considerably.'

Danny rustled fingers in his Brillo beard. 'Your name's on the register. You booked the rooms.'

'According to my American Express card I'm Mr Eldrich Dunt.'

'Don't leave home without it.'

'Well . . . don't leave home without someone else's card.' Danny grinned. 'Can I say it?'

'Go on, then.'

Danny aped Jason's Wolverhampton whine. 'Bit of a shit plan, innit?'

Doug punched him playfully on the shoulder. Dan didn't notice, so he offered a toast with their pints. 'To the bigtime. Finally.'

'Bigtime.'

They drank their drinks.

' 'Course,' said Doug, wiping froth from his lips, 'if world peace does break out between the Yardies and the Punjabis, I'll be ordering up a ton of *Daily Mail*.'

'Huh?'

'Shit paper.'

Danny nodded sagely, then: 'Said something about a toot?' Doug slid the silver pillbox over to him. 'You not coming?'

Doug shook his head. 'Later.'

Dan clacked across bare boards to a room marked Caballeros, and disappeared inside. Doug sat inert, thinking, listening to the muffled sneezes. He was still staring at his lap when Danny returned. The giant's face was lightly frosted in cocaine, as if he'd dipped his head in dew.

'Better?'

Danny sniffed, gave a flu-ey grin, handed back the pillbox.

'Right. Contingency plan. If there's trouble, we'll have a problem staying alive around here, so . . .'

Doug produced a slim folder and placed the airline tickets on the table. Dan noted the KLM logo.

'How many?'

'Three. Open-ended. Economy. Pieter has his return.'

'You, me and . . . ?'

'Your mum.'

Dan folded his arms. 'Thanks, but no way.'

'It won't come to that.'

'They say that on the telly. Then next thing you know, they're running through a hail of bullets.'

'That's *telly*, Dan.'

'Yeah, but it's based on real life.'

Doug didn't fancy getting into a discussion on media influences, so he informed Dan that it was going to be a busy night and he could do with a nap before events got under way. As they left, he suggested to his friend that he might like to wipe the Class A drugs off his face.

In another part of town, the George was having a themed Valentine's Night Special, which meant red satin ribbons on the bar, overpriced drinks and scraps in the ladies' toilets. Jason had decided he was catnip to the ladies.

'Baz. Baz! Here you go,' he shouted over the deafening beat as he passed a tray of lagers over the heads of a trio of underdressed girls. Baz's reply was inaudible as he hauled the drinks away.

Relieved of round duty, Jason began to focus on the women. The first was skinny with an oval face, hot cheeks and dark bunched-back hair. She reminded him of Olive Oyl in the old Popeye cartoons. The middle one was stocky with glittery fingernails. The third, who was sat on the far side of the red leatherette seat, drew his attention. Blond hair fell to slender shoulders where it fanned out in uneven chunks. A toothy mouth was smeared in lip-gloss and her eyelashes were so clogged with mascara that it looked as if spiders had taken up residence around her eyes. She wore a cropped lemon top exposing a bare tummy with a ring through the navel. Her breasts were the size of oranges. 'Tasty,' said Jason as he slipped in beside her and staked his claim with a territorial pint.

'All right?' he shouted. 'What's yer name then, Blondie?'

'Tine.'

'Jase. Wanna drink?'

She tapped her half-pint glass. 'I'm all right. Me mates might, though.'

Jason shot them a look. 'You don't want a drink, do you?'

'Vodka and black,' said the mousey one.

He threw her a sneer. 'I only just got back from the bar.'

'Why d'you ask, then?'

He thought about telling her to piss off and that he had no intention of buying her a drink (unless he drew a blank with Tine come closing time). Instead, he ignored her and turned back to the blonde. 'I seen you before. Model, ain't you?'

'No.'

'Must be life-size, then?'

That always broke the ice. Sure enough, her teeth appeared. 'What's got big eyes, great tits and likes to get shagged in a field?'

She reddened. 'I dunno.'

'Nor do I, but d'you wanna come on a picnic?'

She slapped him on the thigh and he knew he was in. The spray was working its magic. He took off his jacket so she could get a good whiff of it.

'So what d'you do, then? Where d'you live?'

Tine nudged her eyes to the Neanderthal cluster round the fruit machine. 'Shouldn't you be with your mates?'

Grinning at her. 'What mates?'

He had soon clipped the other two out of their space. He never bothered to ask whether Tine or her mates had boyfriends, nor did he care. When he did glance up, he reckoned that Olive Oyl was giving him the eye as well. This, thought Jason as the noise and pub bustle faded away, is gonna be a dead cert. He was unaware of the hostile glances of the men around him.

At the same moment, Laura Joffe was taking Prince for his usual evening walk (she always went out during the break in *News at Ten*). Wrapped in a heavy coat and scarf, she strolled patiently along as the dog snuffled and probed the street furniture. When she reached the common, she began to feel a straining at the leash. This was normal, as Prince liked to play. However, as she bent to release the dog from its lead, she heard a howling and a drumming of paws. It seemed to be coming from all directions at once.

CHAPTER FOURTEEN

Pulling The Chain

———— ◆ ————

The car bumped up the kerb and came to rest scant inches from a chain-link fence. Andy emerged and bent to lock his door.

'Are you coming or what?'

Rob stretched his legs and reached for his bag.

Fortunately, their meeting with the motorway police had resulted only in a caution. Andy waited for the police car to leave, then floored it to the next exit. This led them to the inner ring road, and from there Rob was able to direct them to the venue. Under the orange sodium lights, central Birmingham looked as if it were preserved in amber.

'Where's the gig, then?' urged Andy, his mood still as frosty as the temperature outside.

'Round the corner. On the left.'

He took off running. It was 9.25 and if he was lucky he'd be able to check in with the promoter and compère and be on-stage in five minutes. If not, his spot would've been given away and he'd face a livid booker and the long trawl home. Home to where? he wondered as he pumped the pavement. When it comes down to it, I'm here for what? The gig? The career break? Fine – but what's the point if I can't go home and share it with Miche?

As he rounded the corner, he found himself facing a two-storey squat brick building. Above the illuminated entrance was a row of blacked-out windows. Still legible on them were the words 'Billiard Hall'. Stragglers queued at the door. Andy shouldered past them and was stopped by a hand on his chest. The bouncer was only short but his CV was tattooed on his knuckles.

'Andy Crowe. I'm on first.'

The bouncer motioned to a flight of stairs leading up past poster-covered walls. Andy bounded up under the cheery gaze of a roll-call of famous comics. He wrenched round the elbow of the staircase, scrabbled to the top, took a sharp breath and prepared himself for the onslaught of heat and the surge of bodies.

The place was close to empty. A line of punters stood at the long bar and a further knot were clumped near the high, raised stage. There was seating for a hundred and fifty: a shelf ran the length of the walls at chest height, allowing for a hundred or so extra standing drinkers. The stage had a printed backdrop and was framed by banks of black speakers. He made a rough head count and came up with eighteen. He'd come to Birmingham for this?

'Bit of a pisser,' said Rob, shambling up beside him. 'Thought I'd pull in a few more'n this.'

Andy felt the adrenalin ooze out of him. He had been as tense as a wire for the last hour, thinking of all he had to prove. Eighteen? That was a definite cancellation for a club this size. Money-back time for the punters.

He followed Rob to a door beside the stage and they emerged into the bright, shadowless light of a tatty fluorescent corridor. Rob tossed his bag into a tiny room opposite, then strolled to a door at the end of the passage. He pushed it open. Inside was a cluttered office with greying computers squatting on beaten-up desks. Unopened letters slid glacier-like over coffee cups and full ashtrays. Bills and posters were tacked to the walls. In the centre of the room, an ageing long-hair with a pot belly and a grubby black T-shirt was scribbling with a marker on a wall chart.

'All right, you wanker?' bellowed Rob.

The man broke into a wide grin and the two of them bear-hugged like long-lost brothers. Once they had separated, Andy held out a tentative hand.

'I'm Andy Crowe. Tonight's support.'

The man jerked his head to one side like a pigeon. 'Andy 'oo?'

'C-crowe. Andy Crowe.'

The man looked to Rob for confirmation. When he received none, he eyed Andy with suspicion.

'Never heard of you. Open spot?'

Andy, well used to being a non-person after three years of circuit drudgery, submerged his ire.

'No, support. The Agency booked me in last night.'

The man's voice was insistent and charged with accusation. 'Loomis! I told 'em to book Andy Loomis.'

Andy realised that there had been a bit of a mistake.

For most comedians, a cancelled gig was a pit of frustration, an evening wasted, chances missed, money squandered. For Andy, it was a wonderful rush of relief. It was like losing his car in a carpark and then seeing his number plate between the concrete stanchions. It was Michelle coming on after a scare. It was his doctor's reassurance that the bowel problem he imagined to be cancer was 'nothing to worry about'. Pure elation, better even than the drug of performing.

'You'd better do it, then. But keep to a tight twenty.'

Andy stared at the long-haired promoter as if he'd pulled a knife on him.

'But there's no one here.'

The man flicked a nicotine-stained finger at the ceiling. Hanging beneath the broken polystyrene tiles was a CCTV screen. Visible through the static were waves of people entering the club.

'West Brom were playing a charity match,' he said by way of explanation. 'So we held back the start.'

Andy's bowels did a double back-flip and emitted what he realised was not mere gas. 'Where's the toilet?' he asked.

The promoter pointed back the way they had come. 'Eighty notes. That all right?'

Andy nodded and backed away as the two men fell to playing catch-up.

Edging along the corridor, he paused to crack open the stage door. Noise and heat hit him, along with chanting, then a glass being dropped and a cheer. The room was stuffed to the rafters with shining, sweating, beered-up faces.

He made it to the staff toilet in a second and a half.

Trousers round his ankles, Andy gulped in tight breaths. The Agency don't even know I'm here, he thought. I ought to just leave, tell Michelle I'm coming home. Yeah, that's what I'll do. There was a knock at the door. An unfamiliar voice wafted through. Brummie accent.

'How d'you want introducing? Shit comic?'

Given the choice of deciding whether this was a joke or an insult, Andy chose the latter. He figured it must be the compère. Probably a local boy.

'Just Andy Crowe, thanks.'

Footsteps faded and the stage door swung open. A blast of music was followed by the static of the house mike as the compère went on. Andy waited for the applause, counting the seconds as if for lightning after a thunder boom. He stopped at five as the compère's voice rose from the stage. A joke was fired off and landed in the first ranks of the crowd. Another, and comic shrapnel fanned out. It seemed as though the compère were setting his sights on another target. A woman. She caved under the attack. Where was the heavy artillery at the back? Holding fire? A lone soldier fired off a single shot. A hair-trigger heckle, wide of the mark. A salvo was fired back and the soldier was peeled from his friends and buried. The compère then laid out his full arsenal of sarcasm, cynicism, insults and filth. It took him a fraction over five minutes to snuff out their aggression and convert them to his cause.

Andy flushed the toilet, tucked in his T-shirt, checked his flies and shoelaces, and went to crack open the stage door. The compère was a scruffy youth in a tank top and jeans. He had a confident face, creased beyond its years. He was in the middle of a routine about masturbating in the bath. Andy's arms were numb and his legs were boneless to his thighs. His palms sweated, his chest pounded, and his breathing grew strained.

If I'm not on stage in fifteen seconds, he thought, I'm going to have a heart attack.

The compère elaborated on his routine, throwing in curlicues of comedy before hammering home the punch lines. Ten minutes. At last he moved to the side of the stage and, still talking, dragged the mike stand to the centre. He placed the microphone in the stand and exhorted the crowd to whoop and holler 'like an American audience'.

'And now, give it up, go mad, go crazy, give a big Birmingham welcome to . . . Andy Cow!!'

Twenty minutes later, in the street, Andy plugged a phone box with coins. It was strange hearing his own voice coming back at him. At least she hadn't erased the message.

'It's me. Pick up, will you, Miche . . . Come on. I know you're there.' The sweat was drying on his back. 'Okay, I'll try and call back later. Love you. Bye.'

The bouncer ignored him on his way back in. No one spoke to him or congratulated him or threatened to take him back outside again for a kicking. He negotiated with the cigarette machine for a packet of Marlboro Lites, snaked a path to the end of the heaving bar and plucked his pint from underneath the triangle made by the open flap. Then, head down and blinkered from the crowd, he crossed the room and went into the warren of empty rooms. The compère was perched on a stainless-steel work surface.

'Well done,' he said, his eyes on a scribbled sheet beside him.

Andy thought about it. Comedians rarely say what they mean, especially when passing comment on another's act. A congratulation can be silted up with envy or mere lip service from an inflated ego. An acknowledgment can be disguised toadying from a comic seeking a lift home. The compliment might have been laden with secret sarcasm – a trap to see if he'd believe it genuine.

'You should see me live,' he ventured.

The man cast him the briefest of smiles and returned to his notes.

Andy sipped his beer. It hadn't been all *that* bad. He'd survived. Got them laughing. True, it was shaky at the start, but once he'd thrown in his best closing material, he won their attention. All right, his stuff was a bit surreal and a bit intelligent, but hadn't it found a few new fans? He'd kept his cool and not speeded up or developed cotton-mouth. Hadn't even been heckled until near the end. Admittedly, he came off after fourteen minutes, but the promoter asked for short and tight. Rob Gillen burst into the room.

'All right, mate. Nice one,' he said – to the compère.

The scruffy youth reached out and shook Rob's out-stretched paw. 'Good to see you, Gillsey. Doing Edinburgh?'

'Nah. Not this year. You?'

'Three weeks. Assembly Rooms.'

Rob shrugged. 'Nice bit of gash out there tonight.'

The compère rolled his tongue around inside his cheek. 'Repeat performance of last time you was up, is it?'

Rob stage-winked. 'Could be.'

'Rob?' asked Andy.

'Yeah?'

'Any idea where that promoter is? I want to get my money.'

Rob cast a thumb at the door.

Andy spent the next quarter of an hour trying to locate the elusive hippie. OK, he reasoned as he searched the club, so I've come up here on a mistake, but it's still an Agency gig. If Pot Belly likes the act then he'll pass on the word. If so, the Agency will book me and I'll have a career and that'll mean reviews (no more 'engaging') and telly and no more gigs like this. I'll be able to support Michelle and get a mortgage and a proper dad's car and then one day when we're well off, we might even start thinking about kids. Where *is* that eighty quid?

He tried the bar, glimpsing Pot Belly as he sifted notes from the till. He trailed him to the office, where the promoter disappeared through a back door and reappeared downstairs with a cardboard 'Sold Out' sign. Andy stood by as the man spoke with the bouncer. When he tried to interrupt he was waved away with a 'Later'. Andy gave up. The man clearly had no intention of paying him until the end of the night. He was stuck in comedy hell.

He found a quiet place behind the speaker stacks as the compère took the stage for the second half. The heat and noise had doubled and the anticipation was palpable. However, even though the crowd was packed in like refugees, they were more receptive and their heckles were friendly. The compère rode their comments, milking them for a good ten minutes before centring the mike and running through Rob's impressive CV.

They needed little encouragement: Rob's reputation had been made on Channel 4's *LiveWires*, a show in which – despite most of its budget having been filtered away in overheads – he'd still managed to shine. The programme planners had had no faith in the series and had shunted its time slot from week to week. Andy, along with the rest of the circuit, shovelled scorn on the programme and watched every episode.

Rob came on to music. Loud heavy rock that psyched up the audience and underscored his importance as a performer. All in black, he strode across the stage like a knight surveying his domain. Once the music and applause had died out, he wrung out two minutes of laughs by gurning at them. Then in one deft movement he ripped the microphone from the stand and yelled.

'Isn't Valentine's Day *shit*?'

The crowd exploded with laughter.

Forty-five minutes later he left the stage, then returned and did another twenty. He drained the audience, saturating them with gags and observations and insults until their breath caught in their chests. They clapped so hard that Andy feared they would draw blood from their palms.

He slunk off into the bright backstage rooms and smoked and drank and waited. The compère breezed in for a moment but when Andy rose to speak, he disappeared again. He tried the office and, finding it empty, watched the punters leaving on the CCTV. He went back to the main room. The house lights were half up in an attempt to encourage the rest of the audience to disperse. The promoter wasn't visible and the staff, busy collecting and washing glasses, had not seen him. One of the barmen thought he might be doling out leaflets downstairs. Andy fought a path to street level but there was no sign of the man. Returning once more, he trawled empties until he found a full pint.

In the centre of the room, Rob and the compère were entertaining the remaining punters. Predominantly female, they looked like students. Andy had a pang for Michelle and swigged back his lager. Fuck Rob, he said to himself. I'm not waiting. Fuck this, fuck the promoters and fuck the fucking Agency too. He stormed back into the dressing room and grabbed his leather jacket. As he turned to the door, he found himself face to face with Rob Gillen.

'Ain't going, are you?' he slurred. 'I pulled us some gash.'

'What about our money?'

Rob produced two sealed brown envelopes and handed one over.

'And the promoter?' demanded Andy, sourly. 'I was waiting to ask him what he thought of my act.'

'He had to piss off home. Trouble with his kids or something.'

'Oh, for *Christ's sake!*'

Rob smiled, showing all his teeth. There were dark sweat patches under the arms of his silk shirt.

' 'S all right, mate. Me and him had a word about you earlier.'

'And?'

'Tell you later. We need your motor.'

CHAPTER FIFTEEN

23 Skidoo

Danny One-Slice, in his tuxedo, stood with arms folded, legs apart and brains frying in front of the twin portholes of the 23 Skidoo nightclub. In the years he had worked the door, the place had undergone numerous metamorphoses, changing its name with each fad or after visits by the Health and Safety officials. Although the queue snaked round the block, the DJ had issued instructions that no one be admitted. This was less an attempt to build excitement among the crowd than a desperate measure as he'd lost a contact lens. At present, he and the bar staff were scouring the dance-floor on their hands and knees.

Danny really wanted a spliff. The Anandrol and Sustanon had blended with the Charlie to give him palpitations, and the acne on his back had erupted: it felt as if his spine were developing a series of prehensile fins. Worse, his nose was running again, and scattering the ground with pink tissues was undermining his authority. He stood rigid with his collar chafing against his neck and his trousers prickling against his overdeveloped thighs. In addition, whilst changing into his tux, he had necked another bottle of Night Nurse: his mouth felt like the inside of a schoolboy's pocket.

As he revolved his shoulder blades inside his jacket, he

noticed something protruding from his top pocket. Removing it, he found the news item he had earlier clipped from the paper. There was the ruddy-faced construction engineer, Stephen McCreary, caught in that oh-so-smug handshake with that little git, Councillor Jacobs. In his dark suit and bright yellow helmet, the neat, tiny man looked like a match waiting to be struck.

Dan read on.

NEW BUSINESS IN HANDSWORTH

A new business park is set to revolutionise the industrial base of this old city suburb. Councillor Neil Jacobs stated that 'The redevelopment will be completed by the summer of 1999, providing much-needed office space and new shopping facilities. We're certain it's sure to bring Handsworth into the new millennium.'

He scrutinised the image, zooming in on the empty triangle of land between the two men – a barren plot that had once been the site of a 1930s council block: his and his mum's old home. The tenants had fought to stop its demolition and had lost. Tenants always lose.

The battle had begun five years previously when the council announced that there was some problem with the water tanks on the roof. Danny went up there with two of the environmental people and – after dangling them off the edge – learned that rather than being sent to stem any biological hazard, they had been ordered to find one: failing that, they had been told to make one up. Danny made sure they did not return.

A month later, workers arrived to dig up the forecourts

and the asphalt playing areas. 'Gas leak,' they announced, improbably attacking the ground with enormous JCBs. In six weeks, they had replaced the underground pipes with durable yellow plastic ones. These remained visible, as the men never bothered to fill in the holes. The depressions were soon awash with stagnant water and rubbish, and the estate became a danger area for young and old alike. Dan took to helping his mum with the shopping and ensuring she arrived safely at the bingo.

The war of attrition lasted a year. Streetlights went unrepaired and, as a result, break-ins and vandalism increased. Some of the tenants were rehoused and, when no new families were moved in, their properties were left boarded up. When a car was torched in daylight, the sense of community evaporated. The final straw was when the refuse collection service stopped coming.

Ordinarily, they emptied the steel wheelie bins at the bottom of the communal chutes each Thursday. When they didn't show, the overspill began to reek and stray dogs tore open the bin-bags. Many of the residents had known the war years and feared disease. One of them, putting her busybody skills to practical use, tracked down the firm of contract collectors and demanded an answer. Her discovery shocked the remaining tenants. They had been told that the place was empty and due for demolition.

A deputation went to the council offices where, after much fudging, an apology was made. According to a harassed minion, leaflets hadn't been sent out – administrative error, heads would roll. The plans, they were told, were available for viewing in a library some miles away.

The old redbrick building had been earmarked for closure and remained open only one afternoon a week. The information was pinned to a display board under a stairwell in a draughty hallway. There were the council's proposals, the new site specifications, an architect's fantasy drawing. This, with its slim modern lines and tree-lined avenues, suggested that either the artist was a fan of Jacques Tati's *Playtime* or he was on serious medication. The compulsory rehousing notices arrived on the estate the following week.

Dan fought the urge to scrumple up the article and instead made its edges razor-sharp with his thumbnails before tucking it back into his top pocket. A sign came from within the club. He moved aside the red velvet rope and began to weed out the unsuitable customers, which turned out to be most of them.

A 171 bus ploughing through light rain. Where is this? Brockley Rise. Seven of us at the stop, eating chips. 'There he is.' Coming from a school-mate. Who is it? Tel. He'd just downgraded it from Terry.

The boy leaps clear of the rear platform and runs off up a side road. The leader . . . Knowles, it was. He orders us to give chase while he and his mate go up the T-junction. They'll head him off by Honor Oak station.

'Classic pincer movement.' From his mate. He only ever read War Picture Library.

Running now, chips dumped, anorak zips flying. No, not anorak — a combat jacket, nicked that morning from Deptford market: too big. We get to the top of the road, four of us spreading out on the camber. Heart pounding. The thunderhead clouds part and winter sun daubs the chrome on the Morris Minors.

'Where's the grass?' Someone shouting.

'Thought you 'ad him?'

Splitting up. The sky sooty and lowering. A creak from a fence post opposite. Railway embankment behind, a steep cutting stuffed with brambles. The boy disappears into it. We attack the planks, serrated wood biting into my thighs as I twist over.

Slaloming down to the cinder tracks. A hundred yards away is the flaking wooden canopy at Honor Oak Station. Beyond, the twin dark tunnels. Above, sixty foot of blackened brick climbing to the road. Up there, two heads on the parapet, shouting.

Tel's on the track, balancing on the outside rail. In the distance, down where the stiff fingers of trees bunch into a brown fist, there are twin stars of waxy light. We're jeering at Tel now. Daring him to stay on. He jumps free before the train gets there.

A fast train. Pours into the tunnel. We're moving, as a pack. Get up on to the platform to meet Knowles. No sign of the boy. Suddenly, he sneaks out from under the white steps and disappears into the tunnel. Knowles points to me.

Musty air, diesel and rotting wood. Catching my feet on the sleepers as the arch grows large at the other end. A row of sodium lights visible at the rim — street lighting over at Forest Hill. Twilight here, and fresh rain. The embankment, an almost vertical scarp studded with spindly cedar and birch. Tracks dwindling into the gloom. The others calling, chanting, distant: 'Grass. Grass. Grasses die.'

I slip round and into the down tunnel, spidering my fingers along the wall. Pitch black. Brush cobwebs from my hair. It's newly spiked. Punk. A low shiver sings on the rails. Vibration slithers toward me. I hug the wall, flatten as the thunder approaches. It dissolves into a rain of screeching metal as spark showers come off the wheels. Carriages lumber past, slowing to a halt. Grime-encrusted windows. Through the fug of condensation inside, bowed heads: reading, smoking. Shit; you could smoke anywhere then.

The train waits and whines. There's a dual ping and it lurches forwards. Moaning off to Brockley.

'Where's the grass?' Knowles, bellowing into the tunnel. Pissed off.

There's an arch opposite, dark as soot, but my vision flowers in the dark. I cross the rails and there's the boy, the grass, tucked inside, every muscle clenched. I make out the line of his chin, his face, eyes lowered, waiting for exposure, humiliation, the beating. I open my mouth to speak.

'He's not here.' I shout.

I hold the boy in my gaze. Three, four seconds, then turning, go off and join my new mates.

Doug's eyes fluttered open as he came to on the candlewick bedspread. Beside him were a pair of scissors, a pile of banknote-sized pieces of paper and the semi-automatic weapon. The light bulb glowed green above him. A name on his lips.

'Andy Crowe.'

Chucking-out time in the George. The bell had gone for last orders and first fights and the youth of Birmingham were slopping out on to the streets. A group of drinkers gathered about the bar, finishing up and thinking about creating.

Jason was doing fine with Tine and Olive Oyl, who hadn't minded her rechristening. Even their mate was turning out to be a laugh. Using a standard ploy, he had forced them beyond their tolerance levels of drink, thus ensuring a degree of docility. He reckoned Tine was definitely up for it and, with a bit of luck, he might give her a bit of a seeing-to outside. Brilliant, that spray.

'Oy, wanker. Bit greedy, ain't you?'

Jason looked up to find he was surrounded by three men in their early twenties; two were white and one was Asian. The leader looked tasty enough; his ticket to the World of Violence being a scar that creased his forehead as if Baron Frankenstein had used him on a dry run. The second was fatter but a lot of it was muscle. Could be trouble there, he thought. The Asian, tall and dressed in tan leather, was a skinny sack of shit. Chances were he'd be carrying a blade. Best meet them head on.

'Fuck off.'

'Is he tellin' us to fook off?' queried the scar.

'He is,' said the second.

The scar made a grab for Olive Oyl. 'If there's fookin' to be done, we'd best tek these birds.' Jason had an idea there might be a scrap.

As he turned to see if his mates were still by the fruit machine, the blow caught him on the side of the head. His teeth were loosened and there was the metallic taste of blood as he crumpled to the boards. The stink of stale beer filled his nostrils and a shard of glass nipped him in the elbow.

Knowing not to stay down, he kicked out at the fat man's shin. This produced a howl. He clambered to his feet and lashed out. A grunt. Men falling backwards. He glimpsed a bright slash of colour as the girls made for the door. Scar grabbed him from behind and put him in a headlock. Pressure increased as he flailed. Fatty gave him a punch in the solar plexus.

I was right about him being hard, thought Jason as the wind was sucked out of him.

He doubled over but feigned his collapse for longer than necessary. Rising, he head-butted Scar. Everything went silver and silent for a moment as his world imploded. Then sound and light rushed back as if a projector had been turned on. The Asian came at him and Jason did his best to sidestep. He tumbled over a table, sending down a rain of empties. He fell again, doused in lager, anointed with ash, peppered with pub. Without thinking, he reached for an unbroken pint glass and lobbed it at his attackers. There was a shriek and the landlord, who had as usual kept his distance until the damage was complete, hoved into view.

Jason crumpled to the pavement like a wet rag. His friend Dean was waiting there to help him to his feet before the inevitable onslaught of sirens, ambulances and trouble proper.

'Where was you?' spat the boy.

'You seemed to be doing all right.'

'This look all right? There was *three* of them wankers.'

'Actually, we reckoned you brought it on yourself. Not sharing out the birds, like.'

The slim probability of getting off with all three women had not entered Jason's head. He wasn't good on maths.

'Piss off, Dean.'

'We're off for a Balti. You comin'?'

Jason grunted denial and tested his torso for damage. The right side of his face was swollen and there was blood on his elbow and forearm. The lager would keep his other injuries at bay. 'Nah, not hungry. You see where them birds went?'

'Nah.' They turned a corner and entered a canyon of high, ugly business buildings. Forced to button their jackets against the wind, their eyes watered and their teeth began to chatter involuntarily. One day they would dress properly for winter, but not yet.

'What about the Skidoo?' shivered Dean.

Jason stopped in his tracks. 'Sod it. See you later, aw right?'

He ran back, zigzagging through the redbrick streets. What was all that about? he wondered. Dean loves a scrap, would normally have pulled us out of there. What's he getting arsey with me for?

He arrived at the long queue. To his delight, Tine, Olive and her friend were huddled at the back. 'Hello again, ladies.'

Jason had imbibed enough beer to mistake their expressions of irritation for pleasure. He slid between them, threading Tine's and Olive's arms through his. 'Shall we?' he said, breaking ranks.

'What are you doing?' asked the third girl.

'I know the bouncer. Bloke called Danny.'

Tine's voice was mouse-quiet. 'That's not fair on the others.'

Jason snorted and strode on, ignoring the murmurs of dissent among the freezing punters.

'Back of the queue,' shouted a voice.

He took no heed and marched his charges up to the doors. Danny glared swords at him.

'What's happened to you? Police enquiry?'

'I fell out with some gentlemen of ill repute.'

Dan continued to stare without letting him pass.

'You gonna let us in, or what?'

Danny damped the urge to toss the prat to the back of the queue. Already the line of punters was beginning to unravel and fray. This was not keeping a low profile.

'Get in,' he hissed, grabbing Jason by the arm and shepherding the girls inside.

'Ma man,' said Jase.

Once inside, Danny kept hold of the boy as the girls went to dump their coats. 'Soon as Doug gets here we split, right?'

'Sure.'

'Better be. Off you go.' He gave the boy a gentle push to help him down the stairs.

Doug took another sip of coffee and turned off the gas heater. Condensation was streaming down the windows. Having packed all the necessary implements for the job into a neat black sports bag, he sat on the bed and permitted himself another quick nap.

Back then . . . Andy, in his parents' high-ceilinged flat in Forest Hill. The two of us lying on the floor staring up at the cracked ceiling rose, listening to his dad's Led Zeppelin albums. His parents were teachers. All those books piled high on the shelves; so different from my parents' place, where literature was confined to the Mirror *and the* Post. *Seeing my old bedroom now.*

What year was all this? Seventy-eight? Seventy-nine? . . . Can't stop the thought. A summer morning. Mum scooping me and Annie out of bed. Dad asleep. Mum's insistence that we dress in silence, telling me to stuff my best clothes into my case. Then a flurry of windows and wheels. A bus and a train, then another: this one bigger and fustier. Sandwiches on the hoof. That endless ferry journey. Mum cuddling Annie, staring at England's shoreline as it recede into the mist. She said it was the wind that made her cry.

Snapping back, Doug stood and checked his reflection in the age-spotted mirror. He was in his suit again, needing it for the meeting in the morning. He patted his pockets and did the usual checklist: car keys, passport, tickets, money, fags, gun. He picked up the bag, slipped out, and crept to the Mondeo, fired up the engine and drove to the end of the road. There was a kebab shop on the corner, spewing light out on to the pavement. As he waited at the junction, he glimpsed inside. Nicos the landlord was seated at one of the plastic tables.

The shop-owner was slicing the kebab meat with a long-handled machete.

Jason was giving it large. Tine and Olive Oyl were moving to the drum 'n' bass and gurning at him. Their friend was back on the subs bench – away in the chill-out lounge. It had been Jason decided, an ace beginning to the night.

Except that people kept bumping into him. Hard.

Another body caromed off him, treading on his foot and elbowing him in the ribs. A swathe of punters flooded the floor. Jason continued what he called dancing and what others might term flailing, but it seemed as though the punters were making a concerted effort to stop him. Gradually, Tine and

Olive were edged out of his space and, as a speed garage anthem raced into its pulsing beat, the lights went strobe and the kicking got serious. Jason lashed out, missing people as they pulled back in time to the beat. He received a boot to the thigh, then a dead leg. He fell to one knee. It crunched on the floor but he bounced straight back up.

'Come on then, you wankers!' he shouted.

They took him at his word. The floor became a heaving mass, like an army of maggots infesting a carcass.

Tine fought her way through to the rim of the dance-floor, pulling her crop-top back down over her breasts. The punters at the outer edge seemed oblivious of the trouble, but even as she raked her eyes around she sensed the ripples of paranoia. A plastic water bottle flew in the air and went spectrum in the lights. She groped to the wall and spotted a line of LEDs near the ground. She stumbled up the stairs, feeling the cool outside air separate the strands of her sweat-cloyed hair.

'Scrap on the floor,' she mewled at Danny's gargantuan back.

He turned to face her and, without registering emotion, shucked up his jacket and chin.

'Guy you came in with?'

She nodded.

'Little bastard.'

Danny carved a wake through the punters, making waves in the crowd and eddies among the blissed-out teenagers. Those that foolishly tried to jump him were dispatched with fluid grace. To his annoyance, Jason wasn't where he should have been — curled up in a bloody ball in the epicentre of the whirlpool. Dan grabbed the nearest raver and pulled him close to his face.

'Where'd the kid go?'

'Can't hear you, man.'

He tightened his grip.

'Some of them went after him,' croaked the clubber. 'In the bogs.'

Pushing him aside, he strode to the toilets. He hated the club lavatories and only ever used the staff facilities deep in the bowels of the building. Seeing the fluorescent male logo, he barged in and cleared the place of punters. He looked in the first stall. Empty.

A howl rose from the adjoining cubicle.

Wrestling the door from its hinges, he found two men squashed inside with their trousers around their ankles and their buttocks exposed. He grabbed them by the hair, marched them outside and lobbed them back into the crowd. Slamming the toilet door shut, he returned to the cubicle.

Jason, his face flushed with embarrassment, was fumbling to pull up his jeans.

Dan's goatee was raked at an amused angle. 'Never knew you was a sausage jockey?'

'I'm not.'

'Don't wanna hear about it. We're going.'

The Filipino looked away while Jason zipped up, then bullied him back across the dance-floor to the cloakroom, where he snapped his fingers for Jason's jacket.

'Thanks, Dan,' murmured the subdued Jase. 'Dunno what's happening tonight. I keep getting into rucks.'

Danny was handed the boy's coat and was about to pass it over when the can of Magic Stud Spray fell out of the pocket. He picked it up. 'You stole this from my mum's place.' Jason nodded. 'And you wonder why you got trouble?'

'I thought it was meant to pull the birds. I was doing all right.'

Dan bunched his fists. 'Yeah, but you got your side effects, boy. Pheromones attract the females but at the same time they make the men aggressive.'

'Never said that on the can.'

'Duh.'

'Shit,' said Jason, growing pale. 'That's why those guys . . .
It's the chemicals.'

A smile spread on Danny's face as he raised the can and
aimed it at Jason.

The boy shielded his face as Danny sprayed his entire body
with the thoroughness of a graffiti master. Once the can was
empty, he threw it aside. Then, with the back of his hand, he
swatted Jason to the floor. He had a sense that he was going to
be doing a lot of this tonight.

'Twat,' said Danny, straightening his sleeves.

Jason's mum arrived home in a state: her hair was messed, her
overcoat torn and her hands were shaking. There was no sign
of Prince. Russell was back from the pub, comatose in front of
the telly.

'Hell's bells. What happened to you?'

'Attacked by dogs,' she gasped.

'Not a full moon, is it?'

She stared through her husband. 'No, it's pigging not.'

'Where's Prince?'

'Under a bus, I hope.'

'What's that on your coat?'

She closed her eyes. The lower half of the long overcoat
was decorated in gleaming ropes, as if a family of snails had
used it as a funfair.

'Don't ask,' she said. 'Just don't ask. I'm going for a bath. A
long one.'

CHAPTER SIXTEEN

Some Helpful Notes
On Student Life

———◆———

The rear of the Polo was filled with writhing bodies, namely Rob and two students named Karen and Sophie. There was little space in the cramped, freezing vehicle and their booted feet kept kicking against the back of the front seats. The girl beside Andy was guiding him through the suburbs. She too was a student, although clearly not one of geography, as her directions consisted of pointing and stating 'That way', or 'Turn up here by the corner'.

Once they had left the club, Rob steered his brace of women to the car as if it were a holding pen. Andy, trailing behind with their sullen flatmate, demanded to know the promoter's opinion of his performance. In return, he received a hard stare and a nod at the breasts of the sulking girl. He took this to mean that she was supposed to be some kind of consolation prize. The sum total of their conversation so far had been her offer of directions and his non-committal response. She had a babyish face and short hair bleached white with peroxide. A small metal ring hung from her left eyebrow and she was wearing Third World sympathy chic – a shapeless grunge sweater, combat trousers and charity shop overcoat. Andy figured that Indian carpets and pictures of large aquatic mammals were going to feature strongly in their student digs.

In the back, Rob had the other two girls in a huddle.

'Ever heard of a double cream?' he asked innocently.

They shook their heads. Rob whispered first to one, then the other. This produced a lot of giggling. Karen, who had rust-coloured ringlets and a freckled face, looked to her friend for confirmation. Sophie, with waist-length dark hair and a mannish frame, nodded and began undoing Rob's belt. The pair then helped him to slide down his trousers and pants. Sophie released his cock and took the head of it in her mouth and, after a moment, Karen bent to join her at the shaft. A slow smile spread across Rob's face as his eyelids fluttered closed.

'Ah, showbiz,' he gurgled.

'Here on the left,' announced the bottle blonde.

Andy reduced his speed and searched for a space. The only one amidst an unbroken row of cars was a tight gap between the end of a skip and a monstrous Volvo. He came alongside and twisted his head over his shoulder in preparation for the reversing manoeuvre. Rob and Sophie's faces grinned back at him.

'Put your heads down. I can't see.'

Rob, winking: 'She already did that.'

'Just do it. And wipe the back windscreen, can you?'

'What with?'

Andy reached into the footwell and extracted a sodden mass of tissues. 'Here — try these.'

Sophie shrieked and Rob drew away from the oily black droplets.

'Piss off,' he spluttered.

'Use your hands, then.'

'Bollocks to that.'

Karen murmured something unintelligible. She was dozing off.

Andy spoke through his teeth. 'Will someone *please* wipe the fucking window?'

They did so, half-heartedly. Andy revved up and tried to get into the space but his angle was too steep. He tried again. This time the rear wheel mounted the kerb. On his third attempt, he eased in and began to wrench the wheel.

Rob and the girls chanted the hokey cokey. The sullen girl remained stiff in her seat.

Andy would remember the moment before as being filled with frustration and the clammy action of pummelling the steering wheel. The moment after was only silence, and then the flood of 'if onlys'. He ordered his passengers out. They stood in the street releasing humble sighs, creasing up their foreheads, paying their homage to the damage. Growing bored, Rob then hustled his charges away. The blonde waited a few more moments and followed them inside, leaving Andy alone.

He willed the injuries to appear less. In accidentally tapping the accelerator, he had reversed into the metal edge of the skip. He prayed that the bumper had absorbed the impact, but when he knelt to look, he saw it had buckled. Hard plastic protruded outward like broken bone out of flesh. The light housing had puckered and a single insolent bulb glowed among silver shards. The iron line of the skip had crimped a scar up to the hatchback door. He tried to open it and found it jammed.

Andy tried to rationalise this latest disaster. Maybe it was fixable? Perhaps it wasn't a write-off? Perhaps this was as low as he could go on this particular night? But then he remembered that his RAC card was lying in the middle of the North Circular Road.

He slammed his fist on the roof of the car. 'You piece of *crap.*'

'Want to come in or what?'

The blonde girl was standing in the doorway of a redbrick two-up, two-down.

With a defeated shrug, he walked round his tin sculpture and sloped into their home.

The living room was pure student. Decades of neglect had created a memorial to the spindliest furniture of the fifties. Peeling Anaglypta wallpaper was studded with student shrapnel – a hundred blobs of Blu-tack from previous juvenile attempts at home improvement. The seat of the sofa sank to the floor. It had undergone an inexpensive face-lift, its seats enhanced with cushions, its fabric draped in blankets. No Indian carpets, though.

As Andy folded into it, his fingers found crumbs of indeterminate history hidden in every nook. The room was lit by a desk lamp whose red bulb cast mauve shadows. There was a free-standing bar in the shape of a ship's prow on which stood a portable colour TV. The stone-clad fireplace contained a gas fire with fake glowing coals: only they didn't glow as the bulb had gone. He noted that on every surface there were rind-like crescents left by spillage from cups, plates and bowls. He felt quite at home.

'Want some tea or anything?' asked the girl.

'Coffee would be great. I could do with its devil magic right now.'

'Only got tea.'

'Tea, then.'

'Milk?'

'Please. And sugar. White sugar.'

She left the room and he smoked a cigarette, donating ash to the gunked-up red plastic pub ashtray. It wasn't long before she returned, certainly not long to make anything approaching a decent cup of tea. Placing the two steaming mugs on the carpet, she kicked off her trainers and joined him on the sofa. She sat cross-legged. Andy sipped the hot liquid, wincing at the temperature and taste.

'This has been the worst night of my life,' he said.

'You can't say that.'

'I just did.'

'But your life isn't over yet.'

'Comforting thought. What are you studying? Philosophy? Semantics? Pessimism?'

'None of the above.'

The ring in her eyebrow glinted dully.

'Doesn't that hurt?' he asked.

'Nope.' She leaned towards him. 'Go on, give it a tug.'

He touched it gingerly, testing it.

'Go on.'

He pulled it.

'Actually, that does hurt. I only had it done last week.'

He let go and sat back.

'D'you reckon your car's gonna be all right to drive?'

Andy released a sigh, too exhausted to want to talk about the wreck.

'You can crash here if you like.'

'Thanks.'

'I liked your jokes,' she said, adding, 'Karen says I've got a really weird sense of humour, but I thought you were really funny.'

He absorbed this for a moment. 'Well, it's refreshing to get a back-handed compliment. I was getting bored of all that unadulterated praise.'

'Come on. You must get it all the time.'

'Try never.'

'Why'd you do it, then?'

'I've been asking myself the same question. What are you — psychic?'

'No, I'm Rachel.'

She smiled and held out a thin hand. He took it lightly, afraid to shake it too hard lest it detach itself from her wrist. Is she giving me signals? he wondered. His thoughts spun like a tossed coin. What about Michelle? I can't . . . Flip. She's not answering my calls. Flip. I suppose that technically I'm a free man. Flip. Anyway, I'm imagining it. This girl isn't really interested – not unless she likes men with emotional baggage way over the permitted weight limit.

'What was yours?' she probed.

'My what?'

'Name?'

'Andy,' he said, deflated. He'd forgotten that just because someone liked your act, it didn't mean that they'd remember who you were. She was just making conversation. Smoothing the way while Rob completed his gynaecological examinations upstairs.

'Well, Andy, I think you're totally stressed out.'

'I still would have preferred a coffee.'

'Take your coat off.'

He did so. She clambered up behind him and placed her hands on his neck.

'God. You really are. Your shoulders are all hunched up.'

'Like I'm waiting for someone to hit me with a baseball bat?'

'Yeah, kind of.'

'That's normal.' He thought of adding 'because I live in Willesden' but didn't reckon it would get a laugh.

'Just relax.'

He tried to, unbuttoning his shirt so as she could slide her slender fingers around his neck and shoulders. She pulled at the skin, kneading it and warming it in her hands. She smelled of apricots. He gave in to it. She carried on long enough for him to want her to carry on doing it for ever: a shade under two minutes.

'Take your shirt and T-shirt off and lie on the floor.'

'Is this some weird cult thing?'

'Just do it.'

To make it more comfortable, she threw down a couple of the sofa cushions and covered them with a blanket. It was cool and dusty on the floor and he positioned himself as close to the fire as possible without his skin blistering. At eye level, the carpet was mined with small protuberances – dirt, dead flies, old peanuts.

'Flop your hands by your sides. Let them go loose.'

He complied, wondering what was coming next. Her sweater landed in a crumpled heap off to his left. 'Hey, you're not all naked up there, are you?'

No response.

'Are you?'

'Sssh.'

She knelt beside him and started to massage his back. He released a satisfied groan. Only actual sex could improve on this . . .

'God, that's good.' He said.

'You're all knotted up.'

'Got to leave the Boy Scouts something to practise on.' He relaxed into it. The feel of her hands and the hiss of the fire soon made his problems drift from their moorings.

The car came first: the damage was another few scars on a battle-hardened veteran of the roads. He knew a local mechanic who had recently told him that Volkswagens were reliable. Once he had stopped laughing, he accepted the man's offer of treating it as and when needed, just so long as they kept to a strict cash arrangement.

The gig? Well, it was done. Over. OK, so it needed ratification, but Rob Gillen was a strong link in the chain.

Plus, if he walked in now, he might choose to place Andy on the sexual adventurer roster. And that in itself meant more work. Sad, but true. A comedian's life is a solitary one and out on the road the rule is misogyny loves company.

Michelle? Michelle. Surely she wasn't going to throw it all away, was she? Admittedly, she'd become the policeman in their relationship, but they didn't get involved in domestics, did they? Andy winced. That didn't make any kind of sense. He had been on the verge of sleep. Ow. Now that was something sharp. 'What's going on up there?' he asked.

'Don't move or they won't go in properly.'

A pause.

'What won't go in properly?'

'The needles. I'm doing a course in acupuncture.'

His eyes shot open quicker than a camera lens. His right hand reflexively thrust itself backwards.

'I said not to move.'

'Run that by me again. Are you telling me you're using me as a human dartboard?'

'It's acupuncture. It's quite safe.'

'I don't want to quibble, but didn't you just say you were *doing* a course . . . ?'

'Yeah?'

'Which implies you haven't actually finished it.'

'Well, I've got the gist.'

'Gist?' he exploded. 'Of some voodoo art? You've probably just killed my twin brother!'

'That's a joke, right?'

'Yes, but this isn't. You could've asked before you turned me into a hedgehog. How many of those bloody things have you stuck in me?'

'Only five or six.'

Rachel, to her credit, remained calm as Andy rose from the floor yelping in pain.

'That's really going to hurt if you get up. The needles will move about in the muscles.'

'Ow, ow, ow. Take them out.'

'Stop moving and I will.'

Andy did his best to stay still, given that his spine was being lightly crucified. Rachel hovered around behind his back, trying to pluck out the darts.

'I was trying to help.' She pouted.

'You were doing medical experiments on me without my consent.'

'Anyone ever tell you you're prone to exaggeration?'

'Yes. My girlfriend,' he said, sourly.

Rachel slid the needles out one by one and placed them back into a velvet pouch. Andy collapsed on to the sofa and screamed.

'There's one missing,' noted Rachel.

'I know,' spat Andy as his eyes filled with tears. He reached behind and plucked the dart from the small of his back. There was blood on the tip. He threw it at the wall where it stuck easily into the lumpy wallpaper.

'Oh, *thanks*. They cost money, you know.'

He glowered at her and reached for his cigarettes. As he fumbled with his lighter, he dropped the cigarette and was unable to find it. He sat and willed the pain in his back to dissipate.

'There's one good thing,' Rachel said, gathering up her sweater.

'What?'

'Looks like you've lost interest in smoking.'

He stared at her with all his angst and tension flooding back. What, he thought, am I doing here with this maniac woman? 'Have you got a phone?' he asked.

'In the hall.'

He stepped into the freezing corridor where an old

Bakelite telephone sat on a pile of yellowing directories. The wallpaper had been torn off in patches and numbers were scrawled on the bare plaster. It was pitch dark upstairs. Andy took a deep breath, then a series of longer, slower ones, and then dialled his home number.

'H'lo?' said a sleepy voice.

'It's me. I've been trying to call all day.'

'I know.'

'You got my messages?'

Michelle yawned. 'Where are you?'

It occurred to him that 'with a blonde needle-wielding sadist' wouldn't go down too well.

'Outside Warwick services. Miche, we've got to talk.'

'OK.'

A breath of relief. 'I'm really sorry about this whole gig thing.'

'I do understand, Andy.'

The fire had gone from her voice. Tiredness, maybe. 'And I know this is about *us*, not just me. I was trying to get to your office all day and –'

She cut in. 'I know. And you know that I'd never try to stop you performing. It's just you're not *happy*.'

'You're telling me.'

There was a pause. She was rearranging herself in bed. He pictured her there, huddled up in the warm duvet. 'How did it go tonight?' she asked.

'Before I tell you about that, the car's trashed.'

'God. Are you all right?'

'I'm fine. Just a few bruises.'

'Is the car a write-off, then?'

'Not totally. It's the bumper and the rear lights. I drove it into a skip.'

She let that one sink in. 'You always hated skips.'

'I think it's still drivable. Listen, Miche; it was all a cock-up. They weren't even expecting me up here. The Agency had me mixed up with Andy Loomis.'

'Shit, Andy, I'm sorry.'

'And Gillen's a complete monster.'

'Yeah, you said you didn't like him.'

He knew that deadpan tone. They were getting along now. He smiled at the receiver. 'You know, if that guy had any real power, then women's career options would be scullery maid or whore.'

'There you go with your fantasies again.'

'Miche . . . Can I come home?'

Silence for a moment. 'I went out for a drink with Charlotte this evening. It was mainly so you couldn't get hold of me. I needed someone to tell me I was overreacting. But also . . . oh, I dunno . . .' A sigh. 'I'm entitled to be angry, you know?'

'I know.'

'I don't want it to end, Andy. We've invested a lot.'

'Nor do I.'

'Just get a bit of perspective, OK?'

' 'Kay.'

'It's your life, Andy.'

'Sadly, yes.'

'Come home soon,' she said. 'Love you.'

'Love you too.'

'Hey, bring us a crème egg, will you? No, wait. A Twix . . . no, a Booster.'

She was always like that with sweets. She wanted the chocolate rush, got the guilt, upped the biscuit quotient then ended up mainlining the good stuff anyway. She rang off, having chosen – as he'd expected – the original crème egg: mint flavour was the concession to health. Andy felt now as if a section of blueprint had been laid over him: as if everything fitted together again. He pushed open the lounge door.

'Where's the bog?'

Rachel was sipping her tea. Her sweater was back on and the sleeves covered her hands.

'Upstairs. Light's inside.'

As he reached the landing, he heard the phone go again. He found the toilet and fanned his hand around on the wall for the switch.

Rachel's voice drifted up from the hallway.

'No, it's Karen's place. I'm Rachel . . . Who? Yeah, he's here.'

Andy frowned in the dark.

'It's for you,' she called out as dispassionately as if he lived there.

His bowels turned to mush for the third time that evening. Who knows I'm here? His mouth dried to a thick paste and he could only manage a whisper as he took the receiver from her.

'Hello?'

'You *bastard*,' shrieked Michelle as she slammed down the phone.

Oh shit, he thought. Oh shit, shit, shit. Oh fucking, bollocky *shiiitt!* She must have been ringing back to change the confectionery order again. He called her again but she'd taken the phone off the hook. Despite the cold, he was sweating and his heart was doing three rounds against his ribs. He punched his fists against the walls. He knew what to do. Go. Drive home. Right now.

Thundering back upstairs, he bashed the landing switch. A floral shade gave off a weak pink light. He span to face the bedroom door and threw it open.

'Rob. We're going! Get your stu . . .'

His mouth fell open as he took in the tableau.

Both girls were naked. Karen lay spread-eagled on her back on the bed. Sophie was bent over her with her tongue buried deep in her vagina. Her hands flopped on Karen's breasts, tweaking at the nipples. Rob Gillen was wrapped around Sophie's back, his flabby stomach spilling over her as he pumped her from behind. Wiping strands of wet hair from his forehead, he gave Andy the thumbs-up.

'All right, Andy? Look – Sophie's choice.'

Andy made a gargling noise like a dental patient.

Karen was comatose and Sophie munched away like a sleepy ruminant. Rob hadn't even had the decency to break rhythm. Andy's eyes fell to the floor, spotting the mirror and the coke.

'Get dressed!' he shouted. 'We're leaving *right* now!'

CHAPTER SEVENTEEN

In These Dead Hours

———————◆———————

It was gone midnight at Corley. A damp wind blew asthmatically along the eggshell-blue tunnel bridging the lung-shaped buildings on either side of the motorway. Underneath, cars slewed past on the rain-slicked road. In the south building, the Red Hen was closed, as was the shop. Still visible behind its white metal grating were racks of garishly coloured sweets, tartan mugs, figurines of Tudor cottages, and the bin containing the Jim Reeves cassettes. On the north side, the games area was open for business so that weary drivers could exchange hurtling at ninety miles an hour in a metal box for sitting in another metal box and killing things.

Doug slid the Mondeo into a space on the outer rim of the north-side carpark. He and Dan emerged with their twin black canvas sports bags, Jason limping behind. The boy had been quiet on the drive. Not only had he just undergone his first homosexual experience, but Danny had also warned him that another error meant he'd be spending the night in Casualty. Doug found it all hilarious.

'So these pheromones attract the gays as well?'

'Uh-huh,' rumbled the flu-ridden giant. 'We've got labels for that market too. It's basically the same product.'

'You should be done under the Trades Descriptions Act,' muttered Jason.

'So should you,' retorted Danny.

'What you on about?'

'You aren't wearing your label – the one that says hundred per cent prat.'

Doug stopped at the kerb. 'Drop it. We've got work to do.'

The doors slid open and he led them up the stairs to the bridge.

Aside from a couple of stragglers and the Granary staff, the service area was deserted. Doug had spent several nights doing a time-and-motion study, noting carefully the length of the gap between the evening trade and the influx of nightbirds. It would be hours before the arrival of the truck drivers, leather-clad metal bands and sundry revellers: the kind of flotsam that clung to the place in these dead hours.

They crossed over and descended. Doug told them to wait by the exit and went to the toilets. Inside, he checked out the graph used to delineate the cleaning rota. During the night the job was done less frequently, and he guessed that whoever was responsible probably faked the time sheets. His theory was borne out when he glanced at his watch. According to the chart, the cleaner had cleaned the place two hours into the future.

Once they were outside, Jason went to the rear of the Transit and fished out the keys. Doug put his hand on the boy's arm before he had a chance to open up the rear doors.

'Hold on. We'll try with the bolt-cutters and the crowbar first. Don't want to use the torch unless we have to.'

Danny sneezed, sniffed, then placed a finger over one nostril and blew hard.

Jason gawped at the blob of fresh mucus on his trainer. 'Danny, you ponce!' he hissed. 'They're box-fresh Ree-boks.'

Dan only had to lift an eyebrow before Doug was between them.

'Just get the stuff out, Jason.'

The boy tugged open the doors. Danny slung the long metal tool over his shoulder and hooked the straps of his bag over the end of it. Looking incongruous in his tuxedo, he strode off towards the bank module.

Doug noticed that his suit had become sprinkled with crystalline droplets. In the perimeter lights, a fine rain was visible as a flowing curtain of orange needles. This was excellent. Rain would dampen any sounds they made. He followed the others over to the cash machines. The green screens indicated they were operational. He gave a silent nod to the others.

'One sec,' said Danny. He reached up, tore the hexagonal alarm box from the wall and severed the appropriate wires as easily as plucking threads from a jacket. He handed it to Jason, who tossed it into the children's play area.

'Go and put that in the bin,' said Doug.

Jason stared at him, his mouth hanging limply open. 'Aw, come on.'

'It's too obvious lying there. Stash it.'

Rolling his eyes, the boy did as he was told.

They moved to the rear of the small building. Doug motioned to the padlock, which was sticking out like a metal tongue from the base of the shutter. Danny gripped the chubby locking pin in the molars of the bolt-cutter. Flexing his biceps, he forced the handles together until there was a snap like a tooth breaking. Jason gave an excited thumbs-up, then crouched and pulled the padlock away. He slipped his hand into the gap and tugged upwards. Nothing.

'Crowbar,' said Doug, dentist-soft.

Jason slipped the forked end under the rim and lent it his weight. It moved only slightly. He strained, heaved and lifted his body in the air as he bore down on it. Doug left him to it and stepped out in front of the machine.

He raked his eyes across the empty carpark. A pair of headlamps flickered through spindly trees on the far side. He watched as they curved round the rim of the service area and slunk off towards the petrol station. Fine. All clear.

He returned to find Danny leaning on the bolt-cutters and watching Jason's desperate attempts to force the shutter. The dent Jason had created was negligible, like a minor crimp in a soup can.

'Dan. How about we save some time. You wanna do this?'

'Sure,' said the Filipino, lifting Jason away as easily as plucking a child from a slide.

Danny applied pressure on the bar with one mighty hand. There was a crack as the shutter sprang open. It rolled upwards fast and half of it was swallowed up in the housing.

'I loosened it up for you,' sulked the boy.

'Yeah, right,' Dan said.

'Shut up,' hissed Doug, tossing his bag inside.

They ducked down and clambered in. Doug produced a pencil torch and shone it round. In front were the bulky haunches of the cash machines. On the rear of the casings, twin-indented panels were bordered by long inset rectangles. The light illuminated thin black slits set into them. Keyholes. Doug shone the beam on Jason's face, grinning and gormless. Danny's was bathed in sweat.

'You all right, Dan?'

'Yeah. It's just this bloody flu. It's come back with a vengeance.'

'Not the drugs, then?'

'Nah.'

As he bent to the first metal plate, it occurred to Doug that he ought really to have had a word with Dan about side effects at some point. Long-term steroid abuse was well documented and studies showed that it led to heart disease, kidney damage and spontaneous acts of random, extreme violence. What the hell, he thought. Who am I to preach?

Producing a set of lock-picking tools from a slim wallet, he set to work.

'See, it's a bit like doing a motor, Jason. You feel for the tumblers, line them up and—'

A click as the hatch gave way. Doug swung it open. The green glow of the front panel was visible behind three-foot-high stacks of paper. Their eyes cascaded down the money.

'Bostin',' said Danny.

'Wicked,' added Jason. 'It's chocker.'

'Told you it was filled today.' Doug ran his index finger down one of the piles. The sound was more gratifying than the phut of a cork emerging from a bottle.

Jason reached out but, before his hand touched notes, it was wrapped in a dark manacle.

'Not yet,' mumbled Dan.

'Doesn't hurt,' whispered Jason.

'Look at your watch,' replied Danny, releasing his hand.

A frosting of glass and watch parts dusted the floor.

'Bugger.'

Dan grinned.

Doug unzipped his bag and removed six bales of clipped newspaper. 'Right. These are for replacing the stacks so it doesn't shut down.'

Jason: 'How d'you mean?'

'When it gets low, say to the last ton, the machine closes up so it can be refilled.' He shone the light on a pair of hooks deep in the guts of the machine. 'We want to leave some dosh inside so that the alarm isn't raised for a while. Makes sense, right?'

'Right,' said Jason.

'You've done your homework,' said Danny.

Doug thrust his hands inside and grabbed the top wedge of notes. Danny took over for the next few handfuls, but froze at a sudden whirring and a series of metallic clicks. Doug shot up a finger for silence.

Four electronic bleeps.

'Shit. Someone's using the machine,' he hissed. 'Stick some back in.'

Danny replenished the pile. There was another bleep and the machine rolled into action with ticking noises.

'Statement,' mouthed Doug.

He was on his haunches and Jason was cramped in the corner. Danny had a worse problem. Doug moaned inwardly as he saw the tremors waxing and waning across Dan's face. His neck muscles quivered, his mouth was stretched all out of shape and his eyes were closed tightly. Doug patted his pockets for something to smother the blow. Danny held his breath, his chest expanding like a balloon in the tiny space.

The noise of the cashpoint covered for them. At the moment Danny sneezed, it shuddered and coughed out thirty pounds. Danny had done his best to smother the explosion but was left with a cat's-cradle of mucus on his hands. Doug and Jase were covered in spittle.

The machine came to rest, the card was removed and footsteps shrank away.

Doug and Jason wiped the spray from their faces.

'Sorry, guys,' said Dan nasally.

'Piggin' hell, Dan,' said Jason. 'That's really disgusting.'

'You wanna make something of it?'

'Not here,' said Doug. 'Let's make our withdrawal and go.'

He inserted his skeleton set into the second machine, twisted it open and expertly flipped back the hatch. It too brimmed with notes.

The pile was soon transferred. First, Doug's bag was

stuffed to the brim, then Danny's identical case. A giddy sense of relief shivered through them.

'Right,' Doug announced. 'We're there.'

Jason: 'Jesus. Must be twenty grand in here.'

'That's what I said it'd be. Don't you ever listen?'

'When do we do the divvy-up?'

'Later. I'm going out first, then Danny. We'll put the tools back in the van then meet you in the Granary.'

'It's back over the bridge,' added Dan, as if he were talking to a cretin.

'I know where it is,' Jason snapped. 'And how come you two get to leave with the money? How do I know you won't leg it?'

'You don't,' said Dan.

Jason's face crinkled in preparation for an outburst. Before he could say a word, Doug held up something shiny.

'These are my car keys. Take them, then give them me back on the other side.'

Jason pocketed them.

'Right,' Doug continued. 'I want you to leave a bed of tenners and twenties at the bottom, then stack the newspaper on top. The machines will read it all as money. OK?'

' 'Kay.'

'Let's see you do it, then.'

With an exaggerated sigh, Jason took a wedge and placed it on top of the remaining cash.

'All right?'

Doug grunted. 'Don't forget to pull the shutter down after you.' Handing him the pencil torch, he then slid out. Emerging into drizzle, he spun through three hundred and sixty degrees.

'Clear,' he hissed.

Danny's huge back reversed out of the metal hut. In one hand he held his bag; in the other, the jemmy and cutters.

They strolled over to the Transit, deposited the tools inside and went into the main building.

Tramping across the bridge, Danny broke the silence.

'What now?'

'I dunno about you, but I could murder a breakfast.'

'Yeah. Full English. Eggs, bacon, beans – they might even have black pudding.'

'Sounds good to me.'

'Doug?'

'Yeah?'

'One thing – aside from you being a genius?'

'Go ahead.'

'Them keys you gave Jason? They're not yours, are they?'

Doug produced his car keys from a different pocket.

Danny's guffaw filled the tunnel, its echo spilling over the steps at either end.

Jason piled the notes into their corresponding slots, feeling like a spotty shelf-stacker in Asda. Worse: the way he'd been treated that evening, he was like the special-needs employee – the one they didn't even trust to stack shelves and who they forced into the carpark to collect the trolleys. Well, he decided, he wasn't going to be their trolley-boy. He was aching and sore and pissed off at how Doug and Dan treated him like a kid all the time.

Once he had finished replacing the stacks with newspaper, he parted each one an inch from the bottom and drew out the remaining few hundred pounds, stuffing the cash into his pockets.

'That'll bloody show 'em.'

He crawled under the shutter, pulled it shut and went into the service station.

CHAPTER EIGHTEEN

Hard Shoulder

Andy ploughed through the suburban streets, passing identical rotted porches, pebbledashed walls, double-glazed windows, rubbish-strewn gardens and concrete drives. On every parade, there were the same shops: hollow launderettes, gaunt old men's pubs and bright banners of the bookies'.

'Where the hell are we?' he growled.

'No idea,' said Rob, tugging his leather coat tightly around himself. He still hadn't bothered to fasten his seat belt.

'If you'd had a car I wouldn't be in this shit.'

'I can't drive.'

'I can understand that. You've got mugs like me as chauffeur.'

'I often take the train, as it goes,' offered Rob, helpfully.

'And then when you pull at a gig, I suppose you get the girl's *father* to drive you back to their place. Thanks for the lift, Mr Jones. Where do you want me to shag your daughter?'

'So that's what this is all about.'

Andy thought for a moment. Aside from his own personal problems, he was still appalled at Rob's valiant attempt to get into the porn hall of fame. 'Don't you think you were taking advantage there?'

'Didn't yours want a shag, then?'

'Shut up, Rob.'

'Thought not.'

'She was more interested in turning me into a pin-cushion.'

'Kinky.'

'Piss off, will you.'

He brought the car to a halt at a T-junction. Peering out, he saw a billboard-sized road sign, which indicated that if they took a left they would join the A38: from there it would be Spaghetti Junction, then the M6 and home.

In his haste to leave, Andy had managed to tear off the bumper. The right-hand rear light and indicator were smashed beyond repair, but at this time of night he reckoned he could drive back to London without being stopped again by the police. He comforted himself with the thought that the vehicle was still safe, if only by Italian or French standards.

He hauled the Polo on to the main road and they were soon deep in the trench of an underpass.

'So what was the sodding hurry, then?' queried Rob.

'I phoned home.'

'And?'

Orange light striped the dashboard as they went under a row of bridges.

'I told her I was at Warwick.'

'Sorted.'

'Except she called back and the blonde girl answered it.'

A moment's silence, then Rob Gillen threw back his head and laughed. 'That is a good one.' He pulled a pained expression as if he'd been kicked in the testicles. 'Ooh, that's a toughie.'

'Well, for once why don't you be sodding useful and try and *think* of something.'

'That which does not kill us makes us stronger.'

'No, that what doesn't kill me is hanging around for a

better chance. We're going to get back to London as fast as we can and then I'm going to start begging.'

'Don't want to do that.'

'Before you start, I'm after a *practical* solution. Nothing out of the Dudley Moore school of marriage guidance.'

'Women like to be kept on their toes. And anyway, she's got no proof of anything. In the end she's got to believe you or she can forget it.'

'Rob, has anyone ever told you you're a misogynist cunt?'

Andy shut up then as he tried to figure out whether he could use that term of abuse without being one himself.

The road widened into six lanes and rose up out of Birmingham city centre.

Rob was staring out at the sky. 'Blame it on me,' he said.

'What?'

'Mates' Law. Interchangeable blame. You tell her it's my fault.'

'Oh, I'll be doing that all right.'

'If she wants back-up she can call me and I'll confirm whatever story you like. Think of it as providing a service.'

'Doesn't Natasha see through all this bullshit?'

'Sometimes.'

'And she puts up with it?'

'There's the odd bit of tension.'

'Such as?'

'None of your business.'

'Oh, right. You won't talk to me but you're happy to slag *her* off in front of three hundred people a night.'

'Three hundred and fifty.'

Andy reached for a cigarette. As he lit up, Rob plucked it from his mouth and flicked it out of the window.

'What was that for?'

'Don't call me a cunt, all right? Cunt.'

Andy allowed his anger to slip down a gear as they came to

Spaghetti Junction. He threaded through the knot of flyovers as a fine rain freckled the windscreen. His back was aching and his mind was in turmoil, but he was strangely calm and removed from the whole situation. He decided this was due to shock and fear rather than the amateur piercing he'd received from Mistress Mosquito.

Once they were London-bound, he dug out the penultimate cigarette from his packet and clenched it between his teeth.

'You leave this one alone.'

'Look, Crowesy, those birds were in it for the crack.'

'They were so pissed they could hardly *walk*.'

'Get real. It was a laugh to them — something to tell their mates, remember their student days by.'

'Paralytic, loaded on coke and forced into lesbian acts?'

Rob grinned. 'Hey — great title for an Edinburgh show! You went to Edinburgh last year, didn't you?'

'Yeah. One man, one room, no reviews.'

Rob cackled, then lifted up his left leg, removed his cowboy boot and slipped an object out of his sock. He displayed his watch, which was undeniably expensive. He spun it round his finger and snapped it back on to his wrist.

'I always stash the watch. Some of these birds'll rob you blind given half a chance.'

He gave his breast pocket a cursory pat and immediately his face turned ashen. His hand shot inside his coat and ferreted around from side to side. 'I don't believe it. Those bitches have ripped off my sodding wallet.'

Andy did a poor job of suppressing his laughter. 'Oh, there is a God,' he said, adding, 'And we met him a few hours ago.'

'We've got to go back.'

'We don't know where they live.'

'That's my gig money. And last night's. There's over four hundred quid in there!'

'Have you checked all your pockets?' asked Andy in the most irritating tone he could muster.

'Turn back.'

'No.'

Rob grabbed the wheel. Andy fishtailed across the empty lanes, shouldering Rob's arm away as he regained control.

'I told you never to do that,' he yelled.

'Shit, Crowe. That's my money back there.'

'Tough. It's gone and there's sod-all you can do about it.'

This wasn't true. Rob commenced his tantrum by striking the passenger window with his elbow until it shattered. He drummed his feet on the sopping floor. He beat on the dashboard with his fists, and when that produced no discernible damage he kicked again and again with his heels until he had snapped off the lower lip of the glove compartment.

Andy, after a shocked gasp, drew to a halt on the hard shoulder. He said nothing, waiting until Rob had run out of steam. Slowly, his anger subsided and his head lolled on to his chest. Andy put the car in gear and came back up to speed.

'Right,' he began. 'Obviously you'll have to pay for the damage, but I've had it with you, Rob. I want to know one more thing and that's *it*. After that I don't want to hear another word. I don't want to hear about your women or your career or your opinions or anything.' Silence from Rob.

'And by the way . . .' He leaned towards the larger man. 'If they ever do a kind of reverse *This Is Your Life* with only people who *hate* you, put me down as a guest. OK?'

'Funny,' said Rob, flatly.

'Here's the question. What did that promoter say about my act? Is he going to talk to the Agency?'

Rob was sunk deep in his coat, frosted in nuggets of glass, a pile of them twinkling in his lap. Traffic was sparse with only the odd articulated lorry lumbering past.

'Well?'

Rob raked his hands down his face and yawned. 'Not much.'

'What?'

'He didn't reckon much to it. Nothing special.'

Andy went numb and stared ahead without focusing. The car seemed to be driving him. Before he could think of correcting their course, they shot past the M42 turn-off and picked up speed. His voice, when it came, was hollow, parched.

'I thought I did OK?'

'I'm telling you what he told me.'

'How long did you talk for?'

'About you? Not long.'

'He must've said more than that. What about the Agency?'

Rob faced him, one of his incisors glinting as he mustered the sneer. 'You're not on the list.'

'What list?'

'Well, it's not like it's written down, but it's a kind of sweepstake. Who'll do well, who won't.'

'Who is "we"?'

'The guys in the Agency, comics, us lot. It's all informal but it still counts. That's what makes the difference in the bookings.'

'So what's the verdict, then?'

Rob sniffed, and then sniffed harder as he realised that there was still cocaine clinging to the inner walls of his nostrils. 'It used to be you weren't ready, but now they don't want to know.'

'They what?'

'Not with all that stuff about you nicking material.'

'*What?!*'

Andy stamped on the brake and threw the car on to the hard shoulder once more. They squealed to a halt, leaving twin foot-long stripes of burnt rubber in their wake. Rob tumbled into the windscreen, tearing a gash in his temple as he struck the rear-view mirror. Although Andy was restrained by his seat belt, the wind still escaped from his lungs. He strained to breathe and tried to suck air into his mouth. He coughed hard and back it came. Slowly, he undid the latchplate on the belt and massaged his neck. There was moisture on his hands, blood leaking from the fresh acupuncture holes.

Rob lay crumpled against the dash.

'I told you to wear a belt,' said Andy.

Swirls of steam danced on the bonnet of the car. Beyond the curved metal crash barrier was a blackness so total that it seemed the world might end there. The engine cooled, ticking to silence. Rob let out a low moan and wiped a smear of blood from his head. It looked like chocolate. Andy's voice was cold and hard, drained of emotion. 'Run that by me again, Gillen.'

'Didn't you know?'

'No, I did *not* know. What is all this?'

'Rumours.'

'Not a rumour I've heard.'

'You wouldn't have.'

'Suppose you tell me.'

Rob did a half-shrug, wincing with the pain.

Andy slammed his fist on the horn.

Plagiarism was the final taboo on the comedy circuit. So sensitive was the comic community that the climate of fear echoed that of McCarthyite America in the 1950s. Any accusation meant a trial in your absence, an immediate verdict of guilt and sudden relegation to the status of undesirable: a comedic leper.

There were reasons for this. In reaction to the club scene of the seventies, the advent of alternative comedy had brought about a breed of writer/performer with his own comic vision. It was a triumph of eighties individualism, the rebirth of Renaissance man, style over content. By the nineties it had all bedded in and the clubs were filled with white male comedians doing stuff about dogs, drink, television ads and masturbation. The point being defended so keenly was that at least it was *their own* dog, booze, telly and wank material.

'Is it true?' Rob asked.

'Of course not,' raged Andy. 'And where do you get off asking me that when I know about what *you* did!'

'What are you on about?'

'That night in Archway a couple of years ago. You were closing. You said you never saw my act but a month later you did three minutes of it on telly.'

'Bollocks. Prove it.'

'I taped it,' Andy lied. 'And I've got other comics who'll back me up to say I was doing that material first.'

'So?'

'So.'

'You won't get far trying to smear me. Not with your rep, Crowe.'

'My *rep*? Who's been spreading this shit, anyway?'

'It's been around a long time.'

'I was buggered from the start. No wonder I can't get the gigs. It doesn't matter whether I'm any good or not . . . and *this* is why the Agency never shows any interest.'

Rob rubbed his chin. 'Andy, you ain't that good, mate.'

'Get out of my car.'

Rob looked over in surprise. Andy repeated the demand. When Rob didn't move, he got out, went round to the passenger door and flung it open.

'Out. Now.'

Before Rob could respond, Andy had pulled him out on to the road.

'Jesus, Crowe.'

Andy kicked him hard in the thigh. Rob howled and hobbled away.

'All right. Leave it out. It's down to me.'

'Well, that wasn't hard now, was it?'

Rob backed further away. 'I used some of your stuff.'

Andy took a pace forward.

'Go on.'

'I – I was green when the Agency picked me up. They were asking me to do half-hour sets and I didn't have the material. I saw you had that bit there and I'd been working on something similar but you had the gags. Had them down pat. I was only going to borrow it for that telly slot.' A note of pleading crept into his voice. 'I was going to pay you.'

Andy folded his arms tightly to his chest so as to stop them escaping.

'But I never saw you after that. A couple of comics mentioned you had a similar bit, but I sort of said you'd . . . well, that you'd had it off me.'

'Sort of?'

Even Rob winced at his culpability. 'Well, yeah. I was gigging a lot and the material bedded in. People assumed it was my stuff. So when they mentioned you had the same routine, I sort of stuck to my story.'

Andy dropped his arms and formed fists. He'd had it. Had it with playing nice, being subservient, letting himself be buffeted in the tide like driftwood, being English. He took another step forward. Rob held up his palms.

'Andy. Andy?'

'What?' Andy's face had twisted into a grimace.

'If you were that good I'd've come clean. We'd have been doing the bigger clubs together and at some point I'd've bought you a drink and told you what happened.'

'And how would you have put it, Gillen?'

'I dunno. Bit more subtly?'

'Not easy to be subtle when you're sabotaging my career, is it?'

'Yeah, well. I mentioned it now.'

'Now that you've trashed my career, helped ruin my relationship and bust my sodding car.'

'There is that, yeah.'

'You really are a twat, aren't you?' Andy took another step.

Rob backed up and the crash barrier bumped against his calves. 'Wait a minute,' he said, holding up his hands. 'You can think what you like about me, I don't give a toss. But you're too smart for this game, Andy. I can't write your sort of stuff. You know what a pressure it is to keep coming up with new bits. . . .' His breath steamed in the cold air as he warmed to his theme. 'Me, I can busk it, but you don't. You can't think on your feet. You get nervous and it all comes out like clever lines . . .'

'Make your point,' said Andy, his face set hard with tension.

'Look, mate. The punters never remember the material; it's the face. The way you are on stage.'

His voice softened. 'I'm sorry, Andy, but you haven't got it.'

'A chance would have been nice.'

Rob shook his head. 'You still don't get it. The Agency knows you've got good material. They know you're a trier. They don't care. It's business.'

'What am I supposed to do, then?'

'Carry on playing the pubs with the folkies. Treat it as a hobby.'

'Patronise me, why don't you.'

'I was trying to help.'

'What do you mean, folkies?'

'The pub scene's dead. Snuffed it years ago. Yeah, you got the new acts, but it's all middle-class kids into pretend thrills — like they are with football.'

This was new. Rob Gillen in intelligent comment shock.

'But for the rest of the sad acts kicking around it's comfortable. Easy. Nostalgia. Like I said, folk music.'

Andy took a deep breath. 'How about an apology?'

'Sorry, mate.'

Ignoring him, Andy walked away and up the hard shoulder. This was too much information. He stopped, sat on the metal rim of the crash barrier and looked round. The motorway stretched away, fading into the night in either direction. Rob remained standing by the car, waiting. Andy toasted his last cigarette without a coherent thought entering his head. Finally, he flicked the butt into the road and turned back.

Rob was leaning on the bonnet, tending to his wounds.

'Couple of things,' said Andy. 'It's not really been my day. I'm not going to go into detail because you wouldn't be interested anyway, but the woman I love has dumped me 'cos I *thought* I had to do a gig that mattered. And then it didn't matter anyway because you fucked it up for me from the start.'

'Yeah, but . . .'

'Don't say anything, Rob. Firstly, your lift quota is up. Travelling with you is like a winter break in hell. Only when you get there you find the rooms double-booked and you've got to sleep in molten lava with Mussolini. Am I getting through?'

'Crystal.'

'So there's a certain degree of antagonism here, right?'

'Right, yeah.'

'So what with you getting us stopped by the police and landing me with the scary piercing lady, I'd be well within my rights to punch your lights out.'

'You got a point.'

'But I don't feel like it. And it's not any sort of moral code or anything. I'm just tired and I want to get home.'

'Cheers, mate.'

'So that's what I'm going to do.'

Rob turned to the passenger door of the Polo.

'Rob?'

'Yeah?'

'I told you. You're not coming with me.'

Rob turned and stared, his face forming into a scowl. 'Come on. Give us a lift.'

'No.' Andy came towards him.

'You can't leave me here.'

'You could try apologising effusively for everything.'

'Look, I said I was sorry, you wanker. What more do you . . .'

Rob never got to finish his sentence as Andy had punched him full in the face. He fell back against the crash barrier and tumbled over on to wet grass.

Andy then strode round to his side of the car, got in and drove defiantly away. Or it would have been defiant if the vehicle had started first time.

CHAPTER NINETEEN

Now Fully Open

You what? You what? Youwhatyouwhatyou*what*??

The interior of the coach was a mass of sweating, burping, drunken bodies, and God wondered if this might not be a lift too far.

A few hours previously, on the other side of the Pennine Ridge, he had had trouble getting rid of the Jesus Army. The Beard, the girls and the lonely Welshman had all persisted in following him off into the mist. When they caught him up, he explained that it was his mission to hitchhike round the country and that it would prove impossible to do so when accompanied by them. Their faith faltered when he added that no one was going to stop for five people — not even other Christians. After a brief conference — most of it concerning the weather — the Beard waved at the van, which reversed back up towards them. They apologised, bade him farewell and promised to think of him in their prayers. God told them to multiply off.

This bunch was drunk, no doubt about that. Several cans and a couple of crates of lager had been passed out to greedy mouths. Some of them had even produced bottles of spirits and were downing them neat. One young man had consumed a vile concoction of differing beers and spirits and — to the delight of the others – had vomited out of the window. It left a long streak of bile on the glass.

The rest of the on-board entertainment was as puerile. They mooned, they chanted abuse at other cars, and they drew genitalia on the misted-up windows. One lout defecated into a polystyrene cup and passed it round for inspection. It was then flung from the coach, landing on the bonnet of a car belonging to an Asian family from Solihull. The husband commented that it was a change from having the shit thrown at their front door.

Having scooped up God at Keele in Staffordshire, the coach was ploughing south on the M6. As the lads sang on, he sat tight and tried to glean information about his new charges. They sounded as if they were from the South.

Three heads appeared above the parapet of the seat in front. Their glaring faces reminded God of vultures selecting carrion.

'You're a leech on society.'

'I'm sorry?' God queried.

The youth was barely eighteen and already a good twelve stone. He had sweated huge rings around the armpits of his shirt and his face was glazed with beer. 'Hitchhikers are taking the piss. This'd be sixteen bloody quid if you went National Express.'

'I don't have sixteen pounds.'

'Till you cash your dole money,' interrupted another youth, this one sparrow-thin with curly hair and mean gimlet eyes.

'I receive no benefits from the state.'

That shut them up for a moment. Another boy came stumbling along the aisle. He was stripped to the waist and held aloft a flaming bottle of brandy. A strip torn from his shirt was stuffed inside the neck of the bottle.

'I'm a fire-starter, twisted fire-starter,' he shouted.

A third youth, also overweight and wearing a rugby shirt, shouted out, 'Do belt up, Jocelyn. And the word is "arsonist!" '

'Where are you from?' God asked.

The fattest one announced the name of a minor British public school.

'We've been to the theatre in Chester,' chirped a wan youth in the window seat opposite. Then, as if to comment on the production, he threw up in his lap.

The Corley Travelodge is one of a string of moderately priced motels that have sprung up all over England in the last few years. The building is well ventilated and designed with function and comfort in mind. The rooms offer tea- and coffee-making facilities, *en suite* rooms, satellite TV and tiny toiletries for stealing. The motel itself – situated some way from the main service area – is in a convenient location for the travelling businessman: it is also handy for indulging in drug abuse, illicit dealings and extramarital sex.

Councillor Neil Jacobs was sitting on the bed of his ground-floor motel room. His Turnbull & Asser shirt was folded over the back of a chair with his tie draped over it. His jacket hung from a hanger in the spacious closet. His trousers were steaming in the Corby trouser press and his cuff links and watch rested in the empty ashtray. His socks were stuffed into his shoes, which were in perfect alignment under the desk. Removed in haste, his silk boxer shorts hung at a jaunty angle over the bedside lamp. A blissful smile spread across the councillor's face as he urinated freely into his oversized latex nappy. The warm liquid followed the curves of the material until it flowed out on to the rubber blanket beneath him. His lips trembled and his eyes sparkled with delight.

'Mummy! I wet myself.' He pouted.

'You naughty, naughty boy,' came a husky female voice from the *en suite*.

Sandra Pevsner was uncomfortable, which was really what the whole evening was about. At present, water retention was making it hard for her to compress herself into the green latex nurse's outfit. Framed in the bathroom mirror, she attempted to rub a handful of talcum powder under her breasts, an activity which involved trying to stretch the rubber garment with one hand while dusting with the other. Following her more unsuccessful attempts, the air in the cubicle was filled with motes of white powder.

'I'll be in in a moment,' she called out as, for the fourth time, the rubber snapped back and exploded talcum into her face. She frowned at her reflection. She looked like a clown in bondage.

'I wet myself. I'm a bad boy,' urged the councillor from the bedroom.

'Ruddy well hang on, will you?'

Sandra had had no idea that joining the dating agency would lead to this. She was a Birmingham housewife whose ex-husband had been a minor con artist. He had long since relocated abroad, choosing Australia as he'd heard that criminal types were welcome there and often encouraged to seek public office. Her two teenage children had stubbornly refused to pay rent or leave home: their idea of fun alternated between strip-mining the local mall of its sports clothing and lapsing into drug-induced comas in their bedroom. Visits by the police over the activities of her ex and her sons should have been enough to make Sandra swear off men altogether; but for her, hope sprang eternal. When social gatherings brought forth no fruit, she turned to LoveBugs.

Jacobs was a loyal customer of the dating agency, to the extent that he often mentioned the possibility of being given

free air miles. Being on his payroll, the owner was sympathetic
to Neil's special requirements and was happy to ignore the
inconvenient speed bump of the councillor's marriage.

Jacobs's first meeting with Sandra nine months previously
had proved propitious for them both. He house-wined and
dined her, listened politely to her complaints about her
children, and never once imposed himself on her in their
first three dates. On the fourth, he accepted her invitation for
coffee and informed her that she had found her sugar daddy –
so long as she would be 'Mummy'. When she requested
clarification, he suggested they meet at the Travelodge the
following Wednesday night. She spent a few days worrying,
but once she had accepted that her true feelings for him fell
somewhere between mere curiosity and ambivalence, she went.

Jacobs was overt about his needs. With pride, he opened a
large suitcase and displayed the blanket, the nappies, the bib
and bonnet and the rubber romper suit. Then, bringing out a
large unmarked plastic carrier bag, he presented her with the
nurse's uniform. She sank half a bottle of Bailey's, vacuum-
packed herself into the costume, and prepared for the worst.

It wasn't love by any normal definition of the word. Not a
natural actress, she at first found the role hard to cope with,
but as Neil explained, it was hardly Shakespeare.

It was more like Chaucer.

As directed, she bathed him, put him over her knee and
applied discipline. Raining blows, she rationalised furiously.
At least, she consoled herself, there was no danger of
pregnancy or transmittable disease, although she'd have to
watch out for nappy rash.

Jacobs was unfailingly polite and treated her in the way
men often do when denying a prostitute/client relationship:
he disguised the cash as gifts which were either left in the room
or delivered anonymously to her home. Sandra's standard of
living improved markedly.

Their encounters took place every ten days, and she soon began to savour the irony of it. Here, at last, she was being given the chance to discipline one of the men in her life – a task she relished on behalf of friends who told of being trapped in unsatisfactory marriages.

Although Neil never brought it up, she of course knew that he was the councillor for Edgbaston South. She prudently kept mum.

'Mummy. Mummy, I'm wet!' he bawled.

'I'm *coming*,' she replied haughtily as she slipped her bosom back into place. Wiping herself with a towel, she smeared the powder off her dress and re-entered the room. Jacobs was sitting on the bed with his little arms folded and his brow creased.

'I don't like your tone of voice.'

He would have sounded authoritarian had he not been sitting in a rubber nappy filled with his own piss.

'What tone?'

'That one. You're not doing this properly.'

'I am. We're only just starting.'

'Well, put some energy into it, then.'

Sandra buried the sigh as she scolded him. After a few strokes, he held up a hand – their agreed signal to stop the role-play.

'What is it now?'

'It's no good. We're going to have to start again. You aren't putting your mind to it.'

'I bloody well am.'

'Don't get angry with me, Sandra. It's you who's not doing it right.'

'What d'you mean?' she asked, wondering what was going on.

Jacobs sighed. 'Oh, I don't know. Why don't you try bathing me again? We can take it from there.'

'All right,' she said, lifting him up by the armpits.

As the yellow liquid drained down his pasty legs, Councillor Jacobs had an inkling of what had gone wrong. It had
been while she was slapping him. While he was writhing about
in the latex and inhaling that rubbery smell. He'd had the
strangest image. He saw them naked together, him on top of
her, Sandra moaning with pleasure.

They appeared to be engaged in furious copulation.

God had gathered an audience of the young, privately educated
drunks about him in the rear of the coach. In the low glow of
the interior lights, he had been telling them what he knew of
the world.

'The thing is,' he concluded, 'you're the product of an
anachronistic system that turns out emotionally stunted,
chauvinist bully-boys.'

'Yeah, you said that,' interrupted the curly-haired one with
the pygmy eyes. 'And that we should never be allowed to go
into banking or run the country.'

'Did I mention cricket?' asked God, shifting the subject.

'Yes,' sighed the fat boy. 'I prefer rugger anyway. I don't
want to be inadequate.'

'Good.'

'What was onanism again?' asked someone in the back.

'I know that one,' called out another. 'It's something to do
with arts policy and giving money to opera.'

God smiled.

'Well, I think he's talking rubbish. Let's bloody *have* him,'
announced Jocelyn the Fire-Starter.

God held up his hands. 'Wait. Haven't you listened to a
word I said about non-violence?'

Small Eyes: 'Yah, but you've been ragging us since we
passed Wolverhampton.'

'Who the bloody hell are you anyway?' demanded Jocelyn.

God told them.

Like most of his counterparts on the road, the coach driver avoided trouble. A while ago he had flipped the tape in his Walkman and was now bearing down on a caravan who'd had the audacity to seek out the middle lane. A finger suddenly poked at his shoulder.

'What is it?'

'We need to drop a passenger,' sneered Jocelyn.

'Ask your teacher.'

The boy turned to the front seat where a tweedy man lay dozing behind a book. Deathly pale, the teacher was prematurely middle-aged and wore an expression that suggested he'd seen hell and the wind had changed.

'Sir?'

The teacher looked up.

'We're dropping the hitchhiker at the next place we can. OK?'

The man nodded minutely and slunk back behind his hardback. Jocelyn passed on the message to the driver, who took the liberty of waiting until the boy was back in the aisle before wrenching the wheel and throwing him off balance.

Twenty minutes later, they pulled into a service area, hustled God to the front and deposited him on the tarmac. The doors hissed shut and they sailed away.

Picking himself up, God hunted around for his knapsack and stumbled towards the light. It was all going wrong tonight. Very wrong.

On entering the building, he inhaled the comforting breakfasty smells wafting from the Granary. He decided that first he needed to recuperate and get his bearings, and so he wandered through to the toilets. There, he chose a cubicle and slumped on the seat. In moments he had drifted off.

* * *

Andy was shuddering with shock and cold, but confusion was what brought him to a halt a short way up the motorway. There was a bridge a few yards up ahead and the ground was dry under its flat, angled concrete walls.

Should he go back and pick Rob up or drive on?

As he levered up the handbrake, he found that the first option had taken predominance.

Thrusting his hand into the compartment under the steering wheel, he found only an empty packet of cigarettes. As he tossed it through the broken passenger window, he reconsidered his decision. Rob had really buggered up the car. But then again, the man had no money and it might be miles to the next operational emergency phone. Even though Gillen was by nature cold-blooded, he still might catch hypothermia.

No, he's resourceful enough, Andy thought. He'll get a lift. He counted the seconds as he waited for the next car to pass. When nothing came, he swore, released the handbrake and put the car in reverse.

Backing up, he came to the wide bend near where he'd left Rob. He stopped again and got out. Lumps of perished lorry tyre were littered around like giant slugs. He called out Rob's name. Anger rose as it occurred to him that the man might be hiding. It'd be just like Rob to play one of his 'practical' jokes – those small cruelties that were at best impractical and at worst the product of a diseased mind.

'Gillen! I'm not playing hide-and-seek over the entire West Midlands.'

Nothing.

'Rooob.'

A breeze made rubbish skip along the road. An object bounced over and over, clacking as it came towards him. It was a small box with the regal Silk Cut logo emblazoned on it.

Andy picked it up, wormed his fingers inside and found that it contained one cigarette. It was damp but smokable.

He lit it, got back in his car and drove away.

Rob Gillen had, for the first time in many years, been taken by surprise. There was rarely any real threat of violence at his gigs, and if a punter seemed genuinely dangerous then the management always removed him. And when he did insult large sections of the boisterous crowd, there was always the back way and a waiting minicab.

Once Andy had driven away, he clambered to his feet. Stumped. Not being a driver, it was all a bit of a mystery to him. Sure, he knew the basic layout of the motorways, but how far was the next town? The next exit? A clump of articulated vehicles shot past on the opposite side. An Eddie Stobart, a milk lorry and a Norbert Dessendrengle. Better off over there, he thought. Must be the busy lane. I'll try hitching. He trotted across to the central reservation, slipped between the tall plastic posts, scampered to the other side.

Back where he had come from, it was the turn of six cars to pass by in quick succession. Rob rolled his eyes and turned away from the road. The fields were dark but there was a sprinkling of lights in the distance.

His boots were heavily clogged with mud. He had slipped twice, once in a puddle and once in something softer and smellier. This he blamed on Andy. He blamed everything on Andy: the crappy, freezing car, being stopped by the police, losing all his money, the beating. And it was an unprovoked beating. And the bastard had gone for his face, a face that didn't deserve to be freezing and bleeding and bruised and cut by the brambles he had just fallen into.

'No!' he said aloud, looking heavenward as if in *The Prisoner*. 'This is a Channel Four face.'

The sky was a flat nimbus of dark purple-grey; the ground

pitch black. A sliver of motorway was visible behind him. Something moved over to his left. More of them now, dark humps steaming against the horizon.

As they shuffled toward him, Rob's reflexes took over and he bolted back to the road, slipping and falling as girlish shrieks escaped from his throat.

CHAPTER TWENTY

Sausage, Beans, Bacon and Guns

Doug, Dan and Jason were tucking into their breakfasts in the smoking section of the Granary. Doug, having positioned himself so he had a panoramic view of the serving area, speared a plump, carcinogenic sausage.

'I hate England sometimes. All the rain and stupid people and . . . this place.'

Bean juice glistened on Jason's chin. 'What's wrong with it? It's got games machines.'

Doug didn't bother with that one. 'It's halfway between Heritage Britain and trying to be full-on American. It's trying to be so *comfortable*.'

'Not that comfortable,' offered Danny, who as usual was struggling to fit his bulk between the bolted-down seat and table. He had run out of tissues and had appropriated a handful of serviettes from the dispenser. These were piled beside his overflowing plate.

'Know what?' continued Doug. 'There's a whole bunch of things that get me about England.'

'Like?' prompted Dan.

'Like miles of delays on the roads when there's sod-all work being done on them. And speed bumps. You widen the roads to make it easy for the cars, then lay ramps of fucking tarmac to slow us up.' He fingered the plastic stirrer beside his cup of tea. 'And these bastards. Five million years of evolution and we're supposed to stick a plastic needle in our drinks. What else? Oh, yeah. Supermarkets. They're meant to be so quick and efficient, but everyone in the express lane goes and pays with a *credit card*. And I hate cashiers who put your loose change on *top* of the notes.'

'Yeah,' agreed Danny. 'You have to crumple it all up in your hand.'

'I hate CDs, because all the plastic bobbles break off. People who use a mobile phone just so's they can tell people where they are. Railtrack apologising – because they don't really give a shit. I mean, it's not like they come round your house all upset and say "Look, we're really sorry". They just bung it on a board. I hate people who do fun runs, 'cos running *isn't* fun and doing it dressed up as a woman is just *not* being a proper transvestite.' He sighed. 'I reckon we're the arsehole of Europe, and that's *including* Greece.'

He thrust another morsel into his mouth.

Danny was laughing so hard his stomach was making the table vibrate. 'Bostin', guy. You should be a comic.'

'I hate them. The alternatives.'

'*Bottom*'s good,' offered Jason.

Danny folded egg with his fork. 'Don't forget town councils.'

'Well, obviously,' said Doug, darkly. 'And the drones at the housing benefit. And probation officers, pigs, screws and wardens.'

Jason, unsure if this was meant to be funny, laughed all the same. They glared at him. Reddening, he searched for something else to say.

'What about the drug laws, Douggie? You've got to hate them.'

BIGTIME

Doug selected a mouthful of hash browns, swallowed them and sipped his tea.

'Why? That'd be totally counter productive to my operations. One of the world's most stable economies, drugs. What other business would let me pay no taxes or duty and have a guaranteed profit margin?'

'Well, er . . .'

'Go on. Name one.'

'Me dad's pretty flash with the books at the lot.'

'Smalltime,' replied Doug, with a wink to Danny.

'Doug?' Jason asked. 'Since we've done the job, how about giving us a line of Charlie?'

'No.'

'Aw, go on.'

Danny slid his fork under the table and jabbed it deep into the boy's thigh. Jason yelped but Dan cupped his hand over the boy's mouth.

'Are you gonna shut up?'

Jason, eyes welling with tears, shook his fringe in acknowledgment. Danny released his grip. Doug went back to his meal. 'Tell you what I do like. This. The traditional English breakfast.' He waved the bacon on his fork like a small flag. 'Never trust anyone who eats fruit at the start of the day. A good fry-up, that's what you want. Eggs and dead pigs and enough grease to cut through a stag-night hangover.'

Danny wanted to whoop and shout: not merely because he agreed with Doug, but because he desired release. The drugs were coming to the boil and his emotions were brimming over.

Jason prepared to remove the tines of the fork from his leg. Closing his eyes, he took a sharp breath and tugged. The metal slid out and clattered on to the wipe-clean tiles. He bit his lower lip and pressed a palm on to the wound.

'When are we doing the divvy-up?' he asked, his voice cracking.

Doug: 'Not yet.'

'But later tonight, right?'

'No.'

'But you said.'

'I didn't say anything.'

Jase was about to complain when he sensed the heat of Danny's palm on his neck, it had the effect of making his hairs bristle.

Doug placed his cutlery together and wiped each of his fingers in turn with the serviettes. After that, he took a roll-up from his tobacco tin, torched it and dropped the spent match in the crimped red ashtray. 'I need to invest it first.'

'Do what?'

'You'll get your cut in a couple of weeks.'

'*Weeks?*' screeched Jason.

Danny was about to belt him when he caught Doug's gaze and turned around.

A pair of motorway police officers had entered the Granary and were dawdling by the counter. One was a middle-aged man with a fat weather-beaten face and a bulbous nose; the other a short woman in her late twenties. She had a square, pleasant face and her chestnut hair was drawn back into her cap. They had removed their luminous tunics and had them draped over their arms. Each carried a tray. They looked intent on staying.

'Chill out,' urged Doug.

'Weeks?' repeated Jase in a whisper.

Danny put a finger to his lips as a grey-haired woman emerged and served out portions of soup from a tureen. The policeman slid his wallet out of his back pocket. The woman stopped him with a raised hand, offering to pay. They did the dance of the most generous with the man leading. She capitulated and he flipped through his wallet and came up

BIGTIME

empty. Refusing to be subsidised, he bade the WPC wait and left the restaurant.

'He's going over to the machines,' warned Dan.

'No hassle,' Doug said.

Jason's face bloomed pink. 'I reckon we ought to go. No sense in tempting fate, is there?'

Doug looked at him blankly. 'The machines have got enough in them so stop freaking out. What are you – paranoid?'

'No,' lied the boy.

'Unless there's a problem?' suggested Danny.

'No, no problem.' Jason half rose in his seat. 'But I . . . er . . . I told me dad I'd have the van back tonight. I'll shoot off, all right?'

'Thought you were worried about your cut,' Doug said.

'Oh . . . It'll wait.'

Danny pulled Jason back into his place. 'We leave when Doug says. OK?'

Jason tried a watery grin but the smile didn't reach the surface.

Doug spoke to him like a weary teacher with a dull pupil. 'There's no problem, Jason. We've got plenty of time to kill.'

'But the van . . . ?'

'We'll go once we've finished our tea.'

Jason drank his drink in one and held out the empty cup.

Danny was about to stuff the teacup in Jason's mouth when he noticed Doug's face growing rigid with tension.

'What's up?'

Doug spoke rapidly under his breath, the words bullet-hard. 'I know that guy and I think he knows me. Could be trouble. Stay here. I'll sort it.'

He rose, paced down the steps to the serving area and flattened himself against a wall of white trellis. A youngish tired-looking man in a leather jacket was paying for his meal at

235

the till. He was given his loose change on top of his notes. After shuffling it into his pocket, he took his receipt and picked up his tray. Doug waited for him to pass, then gripped the man by the elbow.

'Ow.'

'Hello, Andy,' Doug said softly.

Andy Crowe faced him. His face glowed with recognition. 'Doug? Douglas Mahoney.'

'Come and sit down.' Doug's manner was friendly, but at the same time he was exerting enough pressure so that if Andy didn't comply he would drop his tray. His pot of coffee rattled noisily.

'I saw you here earlier,' said Andy. 'I couldn't remember the face.'

'Come and join me and my mates.'

Andy allowed himself to be steered towards the giant Filipino and the worried youth. Jason forced a fake yawn. 'I'm really tired. Time for bed, I reckon.'

'Shut it,' Dan said as he assessed the new arrival. He noted that the man didn't have the smell of law about him, nor did he look like he'd be up to much in a fight.

Jason ignored Andy, being more concerned with biting his lip and clenching his fists in desperation.

Doug indicated to Andy that he should take the place opposite. The others moved their meals to accommodate him.

Andy felt as if he'd recently stepped off a long-haul flight. 'What's it been — twenty years?' he asked.

'About that, yeah.' Doug's gaze slid to the WPC at the counter. She was chatting amiably with the grey-haired waitress. Satisfied, he looked back. 'What comes around, eh?'

'Yeah. Suppose so.'

They stared at one another, bristling.

Finally, Andy reached for his cutlery. Danny took the knife from him.

'This is Danny,' Doug said.

'Does the Welcome Break do bouncers now?'

Jason said, 'If no one minds, I'm gonna have a slash.'

'No you're not,' said Dan, muffling another sneeze.

Andy, hemmed in by the tuxedoed doorman and the raised rail of the serving area, dropped his eyes to his plate. He picked up his fork and began to eat.

'So what are you doing these days?' Doug asked with exaggerated politeness.

'Stand-up,' replied Andy, awaiting the usual murmur of interest followed by the plethora of questions about famous comedians he would invariably *not* know personally. To his relief, nothing came from either Doug or Dan.

'D'you know them blokes out of *Bottom*?' asked Jase.

'No.'

'Actually, I think they've got a tape on sale in the shop. I'll just pop over and . . .'

'Shop's shut,' said Danny One-Slice.

Jason looked like a hyperactive child being denied toys or orange juice.

'Still living round Forest Hill?' Doug asked.

'No, North London.'

'Traitor.'

A brief sneer flared on Andy's face. He caught Doug's eyes for a second, then broke off and scoped the restaurant, taking in the mock-art prints, the wheatsheaf motif on the blinds, and the plastic greenery in the tubs. 'What brings you here, then?' he asked.

'I'm robbing the place,' replied Doug, matter-of-factly.

'That's a joke,' explained Jason, uneasily. 'Doug's a bit of a comedian.'

'Really,' said Andy, who had had quite enough comedy for one night.

Doug was chewing on the inside of his cheek in a way he

remembered from when they were kids. When he'd be figuring out the rules to a game or the instructions on an Airfix kit.

Danny shuffled in his seat, attuned to the tension. His eyes darted from Doug to Andy, his hands flexing, prepared.

Andy registered the changes in Doug. His silky brown hair was shorn to a skinhead scalp and his widow's peak made a clear Velcro 'V'. The wide span of his forehead was lined and his eyes were sunk in bony sockets. The nose and mouth were craggy promontories and stubble was wrapped round his chin like a scarf. He thought of his own fatigue and pinched the bridge of his nose.

Jason raised a pale hand.

Doug ignored it: 'So what's it like being a comic?'

'OK.'

'What'd you make a night?'

'Usually about a hundred quid.'

'I thought your mum and dad wanted you for university? They can't be too happy about you going round telling jokes?'

'It isn't easy freaking out liberal parents. You have to work at it.'

A trace element of a smile from Doug. 'A ton for a night. Not much, is it?'

Danny grunted. It wasn't that he was impressed, merely that he wanted to break the tension, get up, go outside, jump about in the rain. His skin seemed to be smothered in lard and his carotid artery was pulsing thickly. Not only was his damn nose still running but his hands were tingling all over and seemed to want to scuttle away.

'Doug?' whined Jason. 'Can we go?'

Andy continued, 'Take off petrol money and the journey time and the fact that a certain other comedian trashed my car, then I dunno why I bothered tonight.'

'What other comedian?' asked Doug.

'Rob Gillen,' sighed Andy, awaiting the inevitable ratification of Rob's growing cult status. To his joy there were blank faces all round.

Jason tugged at Doug's sleeve. 'Doug, we have to go.'

'Shut up, Jason.'

'What have you been doing all this time, then?' Andy asked.

'Like you give a shit.'

'It wasn't my fault.'

'No?'

'No, it wasn't.' Andy pushed his tray to one side, his face tightening in anger.

Doug's hand went to the inside pocket of his jacket.

Suddenly, there was movement in the serving area. The ruddy-faced policeman tore into the restaurant in an extreme state of agitation. He waved a fan of the newspaper notes and called out to the WPC.

'Someone's gone and done over the cash machines. Get on the radio.'

The WPC reached for the walkie-talkie on her belt.

'You twat,' bellowed Danny, grabbing Jason by the throat.

The boy attempted to gurgle an apology, but Danny One-Slice plucked him from his seat and tossed him clear across the room. He landed on a children's high chair, splintering it under his weight.

Andy threw his breakfast tray at Doug, following up with a punch to his ribs. Doug retaliated, moving in close and aiming body blows.

The officers heard the commotion and moved towards them. In a second, Danny had vaulted the rail and was facing them. Out of nowhere, a sawn-off shotgun had appeared in his hands.

'Hands off the radio,' he barked.

The woman froze but the man took a step forward, scrabbling for his canister of CS spray. Danny smashed the butt of the shotgun into the policeman's face, rendering him unconscious before he hit the floor. He cocked the weapon, aimed it at the woman officer, tore the radio from her belt and stamped it flat.

Doug pulled out the Glock and pushed it to Andy's temple.

'Don't move. Grass.'

CHAPTER TWENTY ONE

Flash, Bang, Wallop

Rob dashed back to the motorway, hared across the lanes and squeezed between the pillars that crested the central reservation. Once through, he sprinted to safety on the other side. His legs were shaking with the exertion and his heart beating like that of a cartoon animal in love. As he caught his breath, he inspected his body for damage. His face was bruised and his shirt torn from a scuffle with some brambles. He raked a hand through his hair, wincing as he touched a crusty, uneven lump on his temple.

'Bastard Crowe.' His leather trench coat was smeared in mud and dung and stank so much that he decided to remove it. However, as the wind bit into his chest and neck, he put it back on and tugged it tight. He glanced at his watch. Its hands were frozen at 1.24.

The road was a caramel streak under the canopy of the tall T-shaped lights. A car was coming towards him out of the night, its headlights ablaze.

For the drive, Stephanie Jacobs had changed into a practical grey trouser-suit and low black pumps. Her handbag rested at her side and her cashmere coat lay draped across the rear seat

of the BMW. Not by nature a vain woman, she had tonight
been unable to avoid her reflection in the rear-view mirror. It
was stage fright. Here she was about to take up a new role,
launching from the tired script of bored *hausfrau* to wronged
wife without rehearsal or direction. It was opening night and
she was dreading the performance.

Her passenger was a middle-aged man with a stout waist
and thinning morals. His creased mackintosh gave him the
look of a ball of crumpled-up paper: apt, since Terry Warren
was a journalist on the Birmingham *Evening Mail*. He was
turning the flashgun unit of a camera over and over in his soft
pink hands. It discharged another flash of white light. Had
they been in traffic, he would have caused speed-camera
whiplash and probably collisions.

'Do you *have* to do that?' asked Stephanie, tight-lipped.

'I've got to check it's working. Don't want to start
shooting, then find nothing's come out.'

'Well, we don't require any more photographs of the M6,
thank you very much.'

Terry put the unit to one side. Good stories dropped into
his lap about as often as he got laid these days. His post as
staff reporter was a mundane round of burglaries, muggings
and drunk drivers. He had often promised his colleagues that
if he had to trample through one more dead pensioner's flat
('For his last meal, Mr Arnold ate dog biscuits and tapioca!')
then he'd pack it all in.

The threat was a hollow one. Over the years, a promised
column had failed to materialise and he'd watched with grim
resignation as older, firmer friends jumped ship for better
prospects. Some of them reappeared on telly on the half-six
local bulletin; others went to London. Not Terry. He was
suspicious of the capital. This was mainly because his wife had
moved there when she abandoned him. What angered him
most about the separation was that she hadn't even had the

temerity to be unfaithful. She'd left him to be on her own, which was worse.

Terry gazed at Stephanie Jacobs's strong profile. Why had she chosen him? It can't be sexual, he reasoned. Not unless she likes her men like I like my coffee. Cold and bitter.

'Good Lord.'

Stephanie had seen the man waving his arms in the middle lane and was slowing up.

'Looks like a loony,' urged Terry.

'Are you a psychiatrist?'

'No.'

'Well, then.'

They were within a hundred yards of Rob Gillen.

'Where's his car?' Terry asked.

Stephanie touched the indicator and idled towards Rob, who had shuffled back to the crash barrier. 'You know what the emergency phones are like. He's probably had to walk a mile or so.' She peered out. 'He looks injured – and it's jolly cold out.'

Terry was about to make a fatuous comment about her being some kind of a Samaritan when he remembered that she *was* a Samaritan. Stephanie often worked their phone lines at night and had first made contact with him from their offices. When she'd outlined her request, he'd been glad that this prevented some luckless dosser from getting through. He knew this to be uncharitable, but what the hell? When had anyone shown him any kindness? That was until tonight. This was going to be the making of him.

Stephanie buzzed down the passenger window. Terry had no intention of talking to this maniac and was quite put out when the man leaned right into his face.

'Can you give us a lift?'

'What happened to your car?' Stephanie asked.

'I haven't got one. A mate dumped me out here.'

'Drive on,' said Terry, ignoring the journalistic first principle of chasing any potential story.

Stephanie: 'I'm not with you.'

'Long story. I was beaten up and dropped out here. I haven't got any money or any way of getting home.' Rob stamped his feet ostentatiously, hugging himself at the prospect of warmth.

'A friend put you out here?'

'Yeah.'

'And robbed you?'

'No, that was someone else.'

'I don't believe this,' said Terry. 'I think he's waiting here to pounce on unsuspecting road-users.'

Rob curled a cold lip. 'Oh, sure. On my own in the dead of night on a fucking freezing motorway!'

'One moment, please.'

The woman raised the window and spoke to her passenger. Rob watched the man gesticulate. The glass came down again and the woman leaned across.

'We'll take you as far as the next service station.'

Rob got in the back. The leather interior was soft and warm as a womb, and it was a minute or so before he realised how much he stank. Christ, he thought. What was the crop rotation in that field? Diarrhoea, fallow, then nappies? He wondered if he ought to try to explain, but quickly nipped the thought in the bud. Judging by the quality of the car these were rich people — and rich people never said 'Jesus, it stinks of *shit* in here'.

'Where you off to?' he asked.

'This man is a journalist. We're *en route* to catch my husband *in flagrante* with his current mistress.'

'Cool.'

'Why did you tell him that?' asked Terry.

'Why not?' Stephanie shrugged. Then added, 'He's a prominent Birmingham city councillor.'

'In more ways than one,' Rob said.

'And you?' she queried. 'Where are you trying to get to?'

'Back to London.'

'What brings you to our neck of the woods?'

'Up here doing a gig. Name's Rob Gillen.' He thrust a hand up over the front seat. No one took it. 'Might have seen me on telly?'

A pause while Stephanie and Terry studied his face in the mirror.

'No, I don't think so.'

'Children's presenter?' offered Terry.

Rob snarled at Terry's back. 'I'm a comic. *LiveWires*. Channel Four? I suppose you don't get it up here.'

'Oh, we get Four,' replied the journalist in a tone that implied he bracketed the channel's desirability with council tax and anthrax.

Stephanie piped up again. 'Do you know anyone in the cast of *Yes, Minister*? That was *such* a good programme.'

'All sitcoms are crap except the American stuff.'

'I'm beginning to see why this friend of yours dumped you.'

Rob searched for a comeback and failed. These two weren't on his level. He was tempted to be gratuitously rude, but although he'd never admit it to his mates (and especially not to other comedians, journalists or the promoters), she reminded him of his mum.

'Les Dawson was *very* funny,' said the reporter, peering out at the road through the viewfinder.

The camera was a standard SLR 35mm.

'You from the *Sunday Sport*?' asked Rob.

'*Evening Mail.*'

'What lens you using?'

'The normal attachment.'

' 'Course, you'll need a fast film. ASA 400, yeah?'

'Absolutely,' replied Terry Warren, aware that his few feathers were being ruffled.

'Well . . . that should be all right.'

'What's the problem?' enquired Stephanie.

'Nothing.'

She left a silence that it proved impossible not to fill.

'It's just that if you're shooting at night, you'll need a much faster film, say the new ASA 1000 Kodak GPZ. Plus if you're inside then you'll want a wide-angle lens. At least a twenty-eight-millimetre.' Rob leaned forward. 'It's a hobby of mine, as it goes. And he's no photographer.'

'All right. All right. I borrowed the gear off a bloke in the office,' grumbled Terry. 'I took the basic camera and the flash. I thought it'd do. I wanted to be sure I was getting the exclusive.'

'But that was *always* our understanding,' said Stephanie.

'You don't know them blokes in the office. They get a sniff of it and I'd have been flattened in the rush.'

Rob chimed in. 'Plus you probably thought you could sell the shots on to the *News of the Screws* or *the Sport* if they were kinky enough?'

Stephanie slowed the BMW, glowering at Terry until he wilted.

'Sorry, Mrs Jacobs.'

She faced the road. 'My only concern is that we obtain the incriminating photographs and that they are of a sufficient standard for your paper to print them.'

'You've always got blackmail,' added Rob, helpfully.

'This isn't about money, Mr Gillen.'

'It'll be fine,' said Terry, negating his point by setting off the flash once more.

Once their vision had returned to something near normal, Rob spoke up.

'I know someone who'll do a better job.'

'Let me hazard a guess,' said Terry, his nose crinkling at the stench coming from the back seat. 'You?'

'Pass the camera over.'

Terry hesitated but Stephanie snapped at him. Rob took the SLR and the flash unit and placed them on the back seat.

'Fifty per cent of anything we sell to the *Sport*?'

'Pardon me for saying so,' said Stephanie, 'but for a comedian, you have something of a venal attitude.'

'Cheers,' said Rob.

The BMW slid into the deserted parking area in front of the Travelodge adjacent to Corley services. A few of the lights in the motel were on. Terry was first to exit, owing not to keenness but because of a desire to vomit after inhaling the stench of Rob's clothing. Stephanie and Rob got out and Rob leaned against the wing of the car.

'What room's he in?' he asked.

'I'm not sure. I'd intended to bribe the night porter.'

'You've never stayed in a Travelodge, have you?'

She removed her spectacles and rubbed her eyes.

'They don't have staff,' Rob went on. 'Sure, someone's there in the day, but the place mostly runs itself. You'll probably find someone's got a key in the service station.'

'I see. So no records are kept of the clients?'

'Maybe on computer.'

She looked round the carpark, her gaze falling on a squat navy blue Rover some fifty yards off.

'That's my husband's car,' she said delightedly.

They approached it and Stephanie produced a spare set of keys, disabled the alarm and cracked open the driver's door. Inside on the passenger seat was a slim black briefcase. She drew it to her and spun the tumblers until they gave dual satisfying clicks. She began rummaging through the contents.

'What're you looking for?'

'He comes here on a regular basis. I found that out through his bank statements. I wondered if this might hold more clues.'

As she flicked through the papers it became clear that her husband was cautious in both his business and private affairs. When she emerged, her face was stormy.

'Damn it all. This should have been so simple.'

Terry Warren arrived beside them. His face was pale and there were spit bubbles round his mouth.

'Sorry. What's going on?'

Rob filled him in.

'I thought we knew the room number,' said Terry.

No one answered that one. Rob gazed at the low building.

'Your husband wants privacy, right?'

'I should think so.'

'Then chances are he's tucked away at the back. Let's take a look-see. There might be some curtains open.'

Without giving the others a chance to contradict him, he set off with the camera and slipped through a large holly bush at the corner of the new brick building. They followed as he clambered up over a grass mound at the gable end.

Descending, he came to a low wire fence, which marked the boundary of the property. It ran parallel to the back of the motel, allowing enough room for one person to pass between it and the building. Like most motels, this one had been built recently, and the ground was still packed with loose hard-core. Behind them were undulating fields.

They went single file, with Rob leading them past the first two windows. These were dark, the rooms either vacant or the occupants asleep. On the first floor, a ceiling shone blue from TV light. Rob discounted this on three grounds. One, men and their mistresses rarely snuggle down to watch telly after sex; two, he could hear the strains of the Open University theme; and three, in the window in front of him was a middle-aged man lying on a bed in a baby-blue bonnet and matching socks. He was facing away from the window, as was the stout woman in the lime green rubber nurse's uniform. She was applying talcum powder to the man's bottom.

'That wouldn't be him, would it?'

A gargling noise escaped from Stephanie's throat.

'That's him all right,' whispered Terry. 'I can see the headline. MANY NAPPY RETURNS.'

'That's terrible,' said Rob, raising the camera.

'You do better.'

'How about RUSKY BUSINESS?'

'Yeah, well . . . not bad, I suppose,' pouted the journalist.

'Will you get on with it?' hissed Stephanie.

Rob tried to focus the camera, leaning back as far as he could against the wire fence. 'It's no good. There's too much glare.'

'What do you mean?' she asked.

'With this speed of film, all I'll get will be the flash in the window. What we need is either to be right up close or—'

Stephanie threw a lump of hard-core through the pane.

'We lose the window,' finished Rob, releasing a barrage of shots.

Councillor Jacobs pushed Sandra Pevsner aside. 'What the hell is going on?'

'Hello, darling,' announced his wife, as if she had just bumped into him in Tesco's carpark.

'This is criminal damage,' he spluttered, indicating the shattered pane.

'Let's see those nice rubber pants,' called out Rob.

Terry Warren, galvanised into action for the first time in many years, bounded up on to the windowsill.

'Councillor Jacobs? Terry Warren from the *Evening Mail*. Might I have a word?'

'You certainly may not.' Jacobs turned and waddled into the *en suite* bathroom.

Terry went after him.

'Do you think this is appropriate behaviour for a council member, Mr Jacobs? For a Christian and a Rotarian? A potential Member of Parliament?'

'Probably is, actually,' noted Rob as he helped Stephanie up and over the sill.

Sandra Pevsner, in tears, was already pulling on her coat. She fumbled at the door but Stephanie was there first and had her hand on the frame.

'Does he pay you for this?'

'Only with gifts,' she blubbed. 'And we don't, you know, well, *do* it. Are you his wife?'

'Not for long.'

'He always said he was separated.'

'That can be arranged as well.'

'I'm so sorry,' cried Sandra, dissolving in tears. 'I never meant to hurt anyone.'

Stephanie's tone was firm, unyielding. 'This story will be appearing in the local paper and possibly the nationals as well. It will destroy my husband's career and expose our sham marriage, so if you know what's good for you, you'll lie low for a while.'

'Will the press be after me as well?'

'I think that's rather up to you, don't you?'

Sandra, her eyes clouded with mascara, could not meet Stephanie's gaze. 'I don't want anything to do with it.'

Mrs Jacobs nodded minutely. 'Well, now we know where we stand. Please be assured that the pictures will be used selectively.'

'I – I think I understand.'

'It's him I want ruined.'

She released the lock and Sandra slipped through and bolted off down the corridor. Seconds later the outer door buzzer went and her heels tapped away. Stephanie shut the door firmly.

Terry Warren had his tape recorder out and was pressing it up against the bathroom door. 'Councillor? When you said you wanted to see the NHS go private, did you specifically mean *your* privates?' He flattened his ear to the door. 'Christ. He's only having a bloody shower!'

Rob perched on the bed, trying to avoid the damper parts.

'Did you get the photographs?' asked Mrs Jacobs.

'Yup. Do you want more when he comes out?'

'These will be sufficient.'

Rob rewound the film, sprang open the back of the camera and handed it to her. 'I wouldn't get them developed at SupaSnaps.'

The sound of running water ceased and after a few moments Councillor Jacobs emerged wrapped in a towel.

'Anything to say about this, Councillor?' asked Terry.

'No comment,' replied Jacobs, plucking his silk pants from the bedside lamp. He disappeared back into the bathroom and came back for his shirt.

'You are a sick, sick man,' said his wife.

'He's a big baby,' threw in Rob.

Stephanie grabbed Neil's arm. 'Talk to me, damn you!'

Jacobs shrugged her away and buttoned up his shirt.

'I'm going to destroy your career and this damn marriage and I don't care what it costs.'

The councillor said nothing while he dressed. He buttoned his shirt to his smooth neck, fastened up his cuff links, then extracted his socks from his shoes and slipped his delicate feet into them. He removed his trousers from the press and pulled them on. He knotted his tie, laced his shoes and went for his jacket. The only omission to his daily routine was in neglecting to apply deodorant. Throughout, he paid no heed to the journalist's questions, the barracking of his wife or to Rob Gillen's lame jokes.

It was a masterclass in denial.

His final actions were to snap on his wristwatch, straighten his tie in the mirror and move to the door. Only then did he turn and face them.

'I am going directly to the offices of the *Evening Mail* to ensure that Mr Warren loses his job. Following that, some very unpleasant men will appear at his place of residence in order to do him harm.' Then, to his wife, 'You may of course have your divorce. But if you so much as breathe a word of this to anyone then it will not be you, but your parents who will suffer.'

He held out a finely boned hand to Rob.

'I shall have you tracked down as well. The camera, please.'

'There's no film in it.'

'Where is it?'

'Haven't got it, mate.'

'It stays with me,' said Stephanie, sternly.

Jacobs leaped at her, pushing, punching and grabbing hold of her handbag. Terry and Rob jumped after him but he swung his wife in their path. Terry fell to the bed, where the smell of urine made him retch once more.

Jacobs smacked Stephanie across the cheek and she collapsed against Rob. Terry lunged at the councillor, who kicked him in the balls. Jacobs pulled open the door, wedging it against his wife's body. He bent down to receive the bag. Rob got to it first and held it out of his reach. Jacobs clawed his hand into Rob's face. Rob howled, pulled away and cradled the handbag close as if it were a rugby ball. The councillor employed a trick he had learned at public school, raising a sharp knee and dead-legging Rob, who lost his balance. The contents of the bag spilled out. Tissues, a compact, eyeliner, a purse, a cascade of credit cards. Jacobs dug out the yellow cylinder of film, straightened up and slipped outside, slamming the door shut behind him.

There was silence as they assessed the damage.

Rob was first to speak. 'I bet that was crap about him having heavy friends.'

Terry shook his head.

Rob looked at Stephanie. 'I don't s'pose your husband watches much Channel Four, does he?'

CHAPTER TWENTY TWO

Small World, Big Trouble

Danny One-Slice covered Andy and the police officers with the shotgun as Doug went to the kitchens to corral the staff. Jason was lying dazed in the remains of the high chair. Doug emerged with four frightened people. He made a final sweep of the restaurant and, once he was satisfied that there were no stragglers, holstered the Glock. Finally, he took a seat in the non-smoking section and took a roll-up from his tin.

'Hell of a way to hold a reunion,' said Andy, clutching at his ribs. 'I thought there'd be bunting.'

'You never did know when to shut up, did you?' snorted Doug.

Andy held up his palms.

'What are we gonna do?' asked Danny.

Doug fired up and took a deep drag, massaging the smoke past his jaw and expelling it in a slow cloud. 'We're gonna have to stash these people somewhere. Give us enough time to get away.'

Dan nodded, sniffing back his flu.

'Jason!' Doug called.

The boy rose awkwardly, came forward and hovered next to him.

'You are one stupid twat, aren't you?'

'I . . . sorry, Doug.'

Doug lashed out with a foot, sweeping the boy's legs from underneath him. 'And now, to utterly compound your stupidity, you've told them my *name*.' He brought out the pistol once more, aiming it between Jason's eyes and stroking the steel in his hand. His finger trembled on the trigger. After a moment, he pulled it away and placed the gun on the table.

'You're not worth it. Last time I pick a driver from Henchmen 'R' Us. Get outside and sort out the jam sandwich.'

The boy nodded dumbly and sloped off. An idiotic grin began to form on his face as he realised that this command had two advantages. Firstly, he was out of range of the crazed Filipino. Secondly, he had been given permission to play with a police car.

'Oh, and Jase?' Doug called. 'Don't piss about out there.'

'Wasn't going to.'

'Yes you were. Let down the tyres and kill the radio, then get back in here.'

His lower lip sliding out, Jason left the Granary.

Danny eyed the captives lined up against the wooden trellis. The policewoman was kneeling beside her fellow officer and tending to his wounds. The night staff consisted of two rotund middle-aged waitresses, a lanky teenage kitchen porter and a porcine ageing chef in a grubby set of whites. Andy continued to knead his aching stomach. Thoughts of his ever getting home were evaporating fast.

Doug called from his seat: 'Chef? Have you got a walk-in-fridge?'

The white-haired, stocky man raised a finger in admonition. He had an eastern European accent.

'In my country—'

Doug put a halt to this by training the gun at him.

'Yes or no?'

'In back.'

'Dan, take 'em through and lock them all in it.'

Danny released another expansive sneeze and showered the staff. 'Sorry,' he said, using his free hand to dab at his sore nostrils.

'Leave Andy here,' added Doug.

Danny reached down and pulled the unconscious officer to his feet. He then gave him over to the chef and the kitchen porter, who wrapped the man's arms over their shoulders to support him. Dan herded them away to the kitchens.

Doug crooked a finger and Andy came over and stood by the table.

'I thought you'd be more scared – with all the guns and that.'

Andy shrugged. 'Once you've played to a couple of hundred pissed-up rugby fans in Loughborough, there's not a lot further to go with fear.'

'But you're scared really.'

'Bricking it.'

'Sit down, Andy. I'm not going to shoot you.'

He complied. 'So you weren't kidding when you said you were robbing the place.'

'I never joke about my work.'

It occurred to Andy that he too rarely joked about his profession, which had a certain irony to it.

'We have a problem,' Doug continued. 'You *know* me, Andy, so you'll have to come with us.'

'Any other options?'

'No.'

Andy considered this. 'I'm out of fags. Can I ponce a rollie?'

Doug slid the tin across and Andy began to construct a cigarette. Despite the pain, fear and shock, he was still feeling the onset of tiredness. The soporific mood music and soft lighting weren't helping any. He finished making the roll-up and reached for Doug's lighter.

'Why did you grass me up, Andy?'

'Good to see you weren't holding a grudge.'

Doug looked heavenward. 'Doesn't anyone ever give a straight answer to a question?'

'Jesus, Doug, we were only . . . what? Twelve, thirteen?'

'So?'

'You want to watch more daytime telly. Let it go is what they tell you in the chat shows.'

'Why did you grass me up?'

Andy blew smoke. 'The police told me that neither of us would get done so long as I said who was responsible.'

'And you believed them?'

'Considering my knowledge of police interrogation methods back then was based on *Kojak*, then yeah. And my parents were there as well. Adding no pressure at all. Look, how could we have known that the Army & Navy store was looking to make an example?'

'But I was the one who got charged. You should've kept your mouth shut.'

Andy held his gaze. 'Well, life wasn't exactly easy after that. I got a *lot* of shit at school. Your new mates made sure of that.'

'You asked for it.'

'Yeah, right,' replied Andy with sarcasm. 'You really changed that year.'

'Growing up.'

'What about when you went away? In the summer?'

'It was hardly Disneyland.'

'Didn't you go back to Ireland or something?'

'Try kidnapped.'

'Really?'

'Mum took me and my sister back to Galway 'cos of Dad. Her family were a bunch of farmers. The bog-stupid kind. We had all sorts of fun. Tractor-racing. Witch-burning. Spot the cousin. Dad followed us out there. Demanded to see us. They kept me and Annie well tucked away. When my mum had finished talking to him, the brothers beat the crap out of my dad. They were like a pack of dogs . . . without the table manners.'

'Jesus, Doug, I'm sorry,' said Andy quietly.

'No you're not.'

Andy made to speak but no words came out.

'The old man wouldn't let it go. He went to the Garda and established that he had a right to be in town, if not on the property. That was before all those restraining orders and shit.'

'Right,' agreed Andy, impressed by Doug's legal knowledge.

'He took a room in a B&B and hung about. The brothers warned him off coming near us but he found ways.'

Andy listened as Doug explained how he had sneaked out of the house at night; of the anticipation as he stole through wet dew under a starlit sky. How he followed the cliff path, hearing the spray and the booming of the waves as he made for clandestine meetings with his father. He had pined over the loss of his best friend that summer and the absence permitted his imagination free rein. The truth, unrolling now like a hidden canvas, was unlike the sketches he'd created in his mind.

'So one night, the eldest brother catches me on the way back in. I got a hiding and a promise of more to come. I stopped talking and eating and after a couple of days Mum cracked. Said I could either stay with them or take my chances with Dad.'

'So you came back to Lewisham?'

'Yeah.'

Andy's side of the story was far less exciting. During that

sullen summer, he'd cycled to Doug's house every day, leaning his bike against the wall and waiting there, sometimes for the whole afternoon. Doug's return was a disappointment. One day, late in August, he arrived to find the windows flung open like a child's advent calendar. There was no one in. He bumped into Doug the next day outside William Hill's. He had been placing a bet for his father.

Once back at school, Doug joined an older crowd: boys who smoked and spat and dared each other to perpetrate ever more risky crimes. Andy tagged along despite their obvious dislike of him. After a while, Doug – still needing to impress – devised a simple scam and roped Andy in as his partner.

The thefts occurred in the larger department stores around south-east London. Doug's choice of goods ranged from small objects to sweaters, trousers and raincoats. The first two items of clothing were easy enough to shift on to the market traders, but the raincoats were expensive and identifiable by their brand names. Doug's solution was simple. Instead of fencing them, Andy would take them back and obtain a refund. All he'd have to do was say that his mother had bought the article in question as a gift but that it was the wrong size.

He got caught on the second attempt. He had always been a poor liar, and his overt nervousness and lame excuse of losing the receipt drew the attention of the staff, then the security guards and ultimately the management. Trapped in a stock-room, he admitted the theft. His parents were summoned and Doug was picked up for questioning that evening.

Jason had been having fun with his activity centre. The police Range Rover held all sorts of things to press and play with, such as the speed gun and the dashboard-mounted video camera. Then there were the breathalyser bags, which he scattered to the wind. Resisting the urge for a test drive, he took the radio apart and slashed the seats, two of the tyres and, out of sheer bloody-mindedness, the spare on the hatchback.

He came back inside at the same time as Danny emerged from the kitchens. The Filipino was chewing on a chicken drumstick and his shotgun was tucked under his arm like a baton. He looked like Colonel Sanders going to war.

'You should've said you had guns. I could've had a go,' whined the boy.

Dan tossed the bone aside. 'Yeah, that's what we need. The Travis Bickle of Birmingham.'

'Who?'

Danny ignored him and instead sniffed hard to clear his sinuses. His vision went out of focus. Shaking his head, he rotated a finger in his right ear in the hope it'd pop like it did after swimming. It didn't. He smacked the side of his head, swallowed, stared and raised the shotgun in alarm.

'Dan. *Dan.* What're you doing?'

When his sight cleared, Danny found that, instead of threatening a dragon with fiery green scales, he was standing in front of a display of pots of *confitures* and yoghurts, heavily bordered by parsley and fake greenery. He wiped a handful of sweat from his brow.

'This bloody flu!' he said.

Doug joined them, his gun pressed to Andy's side.

'All set, then?'

The four of them went out and marvelled at the damage Jason had inflicted on the police car.

'There goes his no-claims,' said Andy.

They crossed to the Mondeo. Doug unlocked it and ordered Dan into the back.

The giant shook his head.

'I'm not going in the back. I get car-sick.'

'Sodding hell, Danny.' Doug scratched an irritated hand over his rough scalp. 'Just get in the back and keep the gun on Andy.'

'What, he's going in the front?'

'Sure.'

'You want me to get car-sick *and* sit with the prat?'

'Cheers, Dan,' said Jase, skipping out of reach.

Andy: 'I don't mind staying if it's a problem.'

'Shut up,' said Doug.

'Can I go in the front?' Jason asked.

Doug and Danny together: 'No *way*.'

Doug rubbed his scalp even harder. 'For God's sake, why don't all *three* of you go in the back? Take the baby carriage out and put Andy in between you. That's what *professional* criminals would do.'

Danny and Jason glared at one another.

'I'll stay here then, shall I?' offered Andy.

Danny pointedly slid into the front passenger seat and folded his huge arms.

Doug banged his bag of money on the bonnet and bent to the window. 'Danny, please get in the back.'

'I'll drive,' said Dan, sliding across to the driver's seat.

Doug gave in and motioned to Andy to get in the passenger side. He did so. Doug clambered in behind with Jason and handed the car keys to Dan.

The engine started without any fuss at all.

Danny: 'Where to?'

'Head for the next turn-off. We'll come back on ourselves from there.'

They never made it as far as the motorway.

Andy, having correctly surmised that once they reached their destination he would become surplus to requirements, decided to act. His only hope, he figured, lay in preventing their escape. Therefore, as Dan spluttered the windscreen with another tumultuous sneeze, he grabbed the wheel and wrenched it to the right.

They caromed off the police car, shattering its left wing and punting it through ninety degrees into the base of a lamppost. Danny regained control but it was too late and they slewed towards an RAC membership trailer in the forecourt. All four of them were thrust forward as the car ploughed into it.

Andy had a second to enjoy his revenge on the RAC before Danny elbowed him in the face.

He awoke staring at shimmering lights. As his vision cleared, he realised that it was the neon reflection of the Shell petrol station in a puddle. Also, he had been dragged from the car and was on the ground with Danny standing over him. His foot was raised.

'Hold it,' barked Doug, nursing a bloodied nose and clinging on to his bagful of money. 'We'll take his car.'

Andy was raised from the tarmac and propped against the damaged Mondeo. Through a puffed-up eye, he made out Jason trying to kick free the wheel arch of their getaway car. The coupling on the RAC trailer had punctured it, rendering the vehicle immobile.

Doug's voice, full of anger and tension: 'Where is it?'

Andy turned to him. 'What?'

'Your car. Where's your sodding motor?'

He pointed a limp arm in the direction of his aged Polo. Three pairs of eyes turned to the vehicle. Two pairs of eyes swivelled back to Doug.

'Forget it. We'll go in Jason's van.'

* * *

Mrs Lambridge and Mrs Chitterden had had a wonderful time in Blackpool. Roy 'Chubby' Brown had done over an hour and a half on stage, and some members of their party had laughed so much that they had had little 'accidents'. Their driver, who'd been sampling the nearest pubs during the show, sped back down the M6 at a fair lick. The only thing marring Mrs Lambridge's enjoyment of her night out was resting on her lap.

'I don't understand it,' she exclaimed as she rustled Mrs Chitterden out of a doze. 'I generally find that people are fond of fish paste.'

'Fish paste,' murmured Mrs Chitterden.

Mrs Lambridge's head drew back in annoyance as her delicate fingers probed inside her canvas bag. They came out clutching a tinfoil package. It had been her turn to make the sandwiches for the others and, not having much money, she had made the two jars of fish paste and salmon spread stretch to twenty rounds.

Sadly, her companions had opted for chips in a cone from Harry Ramsden's. Despite her exertions there were no takers, and she had had to make do with a nice long brood. This had no discernible effect as everyone had drifted off before the services at Charnock Richard.

'We shall have to eat them presently. They won't keep.'

'Where are we?' asked Mrs C, rolling her rheumy eyes.

Mrs Lambridge popped a triangle of food into her mouth and peered past the hessian orange curtainettes. They appeared to be coming off the motorway. The coach grumbled to a halt and the doors hissed open. The driver's voice wafted over the greasy plastic antimacassars on the seat tops.

'What did he say?' asked Mrs Chitterden.

'He says we're stopping for fifteen minutes.'

Although Mrs Lambridge had entirely concocted this statement, this made it no less true to her.

'Shall we go in?' she asked.

She rose and she and her friend gathered their belongings. Neither she nor Mrs Chitterden ever left anything in the coach, as they trusted no one these days – especially surly coach drivers. As they hustled to the front, a handful of other ladies followed like ducklings after their mother.

Moments later, the driver, who had only stopped for a quick pee in the bushes, clambered back on board and drove off.

Crossing the cold and rainy tarmac, the ladies were pleased when a large coloured gentleman stood aside for them as they came into the warm.

'I fancy some soup,' said a gnomish woman wearing her best lilac hair.

'They won't be open,' exclaimed another.

They huddled in the serving area, paper-thin hands scrabbling for plastic trays and placing them on the shining chrome runners. A couple went over to the beverage area to tut at the prices. Mrs Lambridge and Mrs Chitterden studied the array of watery scrambled eggs and coagulated beans at the breakfast counter.

'It isn't really "traditional", you know,' said Mrs Chitterden. 'Far from it.'

'Breakfast. Lovely,' said another lady, joining them.

'It ought to be kedgeree and kippers, by rights.'

'I spent all day on those sandwiches,' said Mrs Lambridge in a small, strangled voice.

'Shop,' announced Mrs Chitterden brightly.

CHAPTER TWENTY THREE

This Chapter Contains
Scenes of Senseless Violence . . .
Now Read On

———◆———

In the hotel room, Terry Warren had been comforting Mrs Jacobs, whose resolve had dissolved the moment her husband left the room. He brought an extra blanket out of the cupboard, wrapped her in it and made tea, which he spiked with a good dose of whisky from a hip flask he carried for medicinal purposes. She soon took directly to the bottle and did not rebuff his advances. He decided he'd try using shock as a seduction tool from now on.

As soon as Rob saw her in tears, he begged some change from Terry on the pretext of phoning his girlfriend from the service station. This was more a way of escaping a roomful of emotion than any genuine concern for Natasha.

On leaving the motel, he was very surprised to see Andy lying face down in the carpark, surrounded by wrecked vehicles. He melted into the shadows and watched as a huge bouncer in a tuxedo plucked him from the ground and dragged him back into the Granary.

He scurried to the nearest corner and watched as a group

of pensioners passed by and went inside. He pumped his fists. That bloody Crowe, he thought. He left me for dead out there. Time he got what's coming.

He stole another glance. There were four of them. As the bouncer stepped aside for the oldies, Andy turned with his back to him. Element of surprise, thought Rob. He let out a howl and charged the automatic doors.

They shushed open and Gillen flew at Andy. Groggy and disorientated, he groaned as the fists pummelled his shoulders and promptly collapsed with Rob spread-eagled on top of him.

'Bastard! Bastard, bastard, bastard.'

Andy flung a fist behind his head. It connected with bone and produced a gratifying yelp. He rolled away and swung a kick at his assailant. It missed, striking Jason on the ankle. The boy hopped from foot to foot.

'Ow,' he bawled. 'That's twice someone's kicked me in the bloody leg.'

Danny made it a hat trick.

Rob came back at Andy, flailing madly.

Danny tried to prise them apart but his vision was blurry and they seemed to slip through his grasp like eels. The fight assumed playground proportions as Andy and Rob batted at one another.

Doug barked a sharp order and Danny stopped the fight. He did this by raising the shotgun and blasting a hole in the false ceiling. White chunks of tile rained down and half the fluorescent lights blew out.

'I said,' spat Doug, covered in polystyrene snow, 'throw 'em out the door. What did you think I said?'

Danny furrowed his brow. 'Use the gun, but not on the floor?' he suggested sheepishly.

'Not even close. What's up with you, Dan?'

Danny wiggled a fat finger in his ear. 'Flu. And I think I'm gonna have to kick the 'roids.'

'Well, that's something,' Doug said with hooded eyes.

'Bastard,' blurted out Rob, his eyes stinging with cordite.

Danny cracked open the shotgun, slipped in another cartridge and jerked the barrel from person to person. Everyone went quiet, waiting to see what he'd do next. His vision had begun to swim in clear syrup, and sprites of silver pollen were exploding in the air around him. Doug started to talk to Jason, only the words weren't there. Now Doug was holding up his pistol and both the comedian and the stinky guy in black were getting to their feet. Danny swallowed to bring himself back to the surface. A bubble popped and his head became searing hot: so hot that he thought his brain might froth out of his ears. His dress-shirt clung to his gargantuan back with sweat and his woollen trousers were prickly against his tree-trunk legs. He tugged at the gusset to let the air circulate round his balls. It made no difference.

'. . . two get inside,' Doug said.

Dan's hearing had returned. 'Jason. Gimme your blade.'

'I haven't got a blade.'

A nod of the shotgun in Jason's direction. 'What did you slash the copper's seats with, then? A comb?'

Jason gave him the blade.

It was a retractable Stanley knife. Danny bent and severed the legs of his trousers around the broadest points of his thighs. Reaching the stitching on either side, he tore away the material until he was standing proud in his new jagged shorts. He resembled a well-attired castaway. Kicking off the ends of his trousers, he scratched contentedly at his calves and thighs with his fingernails.

'That better?' asked Doug, unsmiling.

Dan nodded.

'Then can we all *please* get inside?' Doug stared at them in disbelief. His job appeared to have metamorphosed from armed criminal to that of tour guide to a particularly dim party of foreign visitors.

Rob Gillen went in first, dabbing at fresh blood where Andy had opened up his head wound. Andy followed and then Jason, who sidled up to the queue of pensioners.

'What's going on, young man?' asked Mrs Lambridge.

Jason's grunt was that of a Saturday employee.

Doug held up the gun so they could all see it. 'Ladies. *Ladies*. We won't keep you long, but for now I'll have to ask you all to go through and take a seat in the restaurant. Thank you.'

'Shop,' trilled Mrs Chitterden, who was still facing the breakfast counter.

'Danny, Jason, take them all over to the back and pull down the blinds. I need a couple of minutes to figure out what we're going to do, all right?'

Shepherding the wayward pensioners proved difficult, and Danny and Jason tried not to swear as they shooed and cajoled them to their places. Andy and Rob went to one of the tables and sat pointedly with their backs to one another. Doug poured himself a coffee, took a seat near the till and worried his knuckles into his eyes.

This wasn't even supposed to be the hard part of the plan.

Danny's shotgun blast had had another effect. God, who had been asleep in the toilets, woke up. Smacking his lips, he emerged from the cubicle, inspected his bruises in the mirror and splashed his face with water. He stared at himself. His hair was grey and matted, his cheeks sunken, his eyes red-rimmed. He sensed the onset of another headache. He decided he would beg some aspirin from the counter staff. Plus, he was hungry.

Emerging on to the concourse, he realised it was still dark.

The Granary smelled odd, different somehow. Blue smoke hung in the air. Had someone burnt the toast? That would be most unlike Victor, the Romanian night chef. God began to salivate. Victor would surely offer him a meal.

He entered the restaurant, slipped between the steel counters and went through to the kitchens. Deserted. Even the dish-washing machine wasn't grinding and spluttering as normal. Victor must be out the back, smoking one of his harsh cigarettes. But where was the kitchen porter? And cheery Noreen and Lily? As he meandered about, he sensed a dull knocking.

Question was — was it real or was it in his head? God rubbed his eyebrows and leaned against the cool, tiled wall. He was becoming more confused these days: his diary notes confirming it as they fluctuated wildly between a neat script and near-illegibility.

The sound was louder near the walk-in fridge. He went to it and pressed on the heavy iron handle to release the locking mechanism. A breath of cold air escaped and the door swung open. Victor stood there with frost in his stubble and chilly tears in his eyes. He threw his arms wide and hugged God so hard he almost took the stuffing out of him. He pulled away, keeping one horny hand on God's shoulder. He pressed a finger to his lips.

'Ceausescu's men have returned. We must plan another coup.'

Before God could decipher this, a policewoman appeared. She was shivering in her white blouse, having donated her tunic to one of the waitresses.

'Are they still out there?' she asked.

'Who?'

'The armed men.'

'Armed men? I . . . I didn't see anyone.'

The WPC stepped out and scanned the kitchen. 'Can't take any chances. Is there a back way out?'

'Through emergency doors,' said Victor, already helping the policeman to his feet.

The kitchen porter indicated a long, tiled passageway, with a pair of black double doors at the end. Stacked boxes of cleaning products lined the route, making it difficult to manoeuvre the unconscious policeman to the exit. The WPC led the way and applied silent pressure to the bar. It gave, the door swung open and one by one they slipped out into the night. She shut the doors behind her.

'Where to?' asked Lily.

'Just a moment.'

The WPC crept to the corner and took in the damage in the carpark. The Range Rover was wrapped round a lamppost. To get to the car she'd have to cross the entrance and be visible from inside. She decided not to chance it. Instead, she loped round the building until she came to the restaurant window. Ducking, she peered in through the gap between the frame and the bottom of the blinds.

A blond youth and the coffee-coloured giant with the shotgun were gesticulating to a group of elderly women. There were two other men in leather jackets who looked dodgy enough. Impossible to tell how many were gang members and how many were civilians. She thought to radio for help, then quashed that as she remembered that the bouncer had destroyed their two-ways. She returned to the staff. They were huddled against the outer wall of the kitchens.

'We'll go to the petrol station. I'll get help from there.'

They traipsed across the lorry park to the neon apron of the filling station. An Asian adolescent was asleep at his post and didn't move as the group of refugees approached. The policewoman tapped on the hatch. The youth stirred. She tapped louder on the thick glass and demanded he open up. The youth refused until she had passed her ID through on the

metal tray. He inspected it and shuffled across to the doors
with his bunch of keys.

Once inside, Victor located the first-aid box and they
bandaged the policeman's head. The youth told them they
could all have coffees so long as they left the money in the jar.
The WPC rang the central control room at Leek Wootton
and told them that the situation demanded immediate
response. She was informed that an Armed Response Unit
was on its way and that she should stay on-line to await
instructions.

'I've seen God,' said a dazed Rob Gillen.

'What?' queried Danny.

Rob pointed over to the service area. 'God.'

Everyone looked, seeing nothing but trellis, plastic foliage
and a board announcing coffee at £2.60 a pot.

'Shocking,' said Mrs Chitterden.

'He's trying to scare the oldies,' said Jason.

'Less of the old, young man,' said Mrs Lambridge. Her
hearing, though selective when visited by relatives, was quite
attuned to rude youngsters.

'You'll be seeing Him soon enough,' said Danny, directing
his comment at Rob Gillen. He had taken an instant dislike to
the stocky comic. He focused on Rob's podgy cheeks and
small mouth. The man had the look of a snitch or a Mary. 'I
know you,' he said, taking in the leather trench coat, the fancy
cowboy boots and the torn silk shirt. 'You're a country and
western singer, right?'

'Close,' said Rob. 'Except for the country . . . and the
western. I'm on *LiveWires*.'

'What's that? A sex chat-line?'

'No, it's a TV show.'

'He's the guy I told you about earlier,' said Andy, flatly.

Forty watts of inspiration illuminated Jason's face. 'Oh yeah, I know you. I seen that programme. You're the presenter bloke.'

'Compère.'

'Here, I've got one for you.'

They listened as Jason fumbled his way through an interminable story involving two nuns – no, *one* nun, some puppies, a doctor, a camel and clingfilm. The punch line – such as it was – received puzzled stares. Jason, thinking he had missed something out, started the whole thing again until Danny stopped him with a sharp prod to the breastbone.

Doug came over. He had a fresh cigarette in his mouth and the smoke zigzagged in the air as he inspected his lieutenant and their captives.

'Right, Danny. Like I said, we'll take Jason's van. I reckon the oldies are too blind to ID us properly.'

'What about the comics?' Danny asked.

'Bring 'em for now. I want us out of here. Let's go.'

Back to square one, thought Andy.

'We ought to be leaving presently,' said Mrs Lambridge as she tapped her twig-like wrist. 'Else the coach driver will worry.'

Their driver was careering up the M69 with no idea that any of his charges were missing.

'Presently,' echoed Mrs Chitterden.

'Stay exactly where you are for the next five minutes,' snarled Doug, training the gun on the pensioners.

'My nephew has one of those,' said the lady with the lilac hair.

'I don't think that's a water pistol,' whispered another.

Doug grabbed the bags and strode off. Danny and Jason pushed Andy and Rob towards the exit.

Doug crossed to the bridge stairs and took them three at a

time. Reaching the top, he stopped as he heard a stentorian boom from below.

'What the *hell* is going on here?'

He gazed round the clammy walls of the bridge and then looked back down the stairs. Jason was on the bottom step but the others weren't in sight. He unsheathed the gun and began to descend, dreading the next complication.

It was a David and Goliath situation. A diminutive middle-aged man in a pin-striped suit was standing in the doorway ordering Danny to surrender his weapon. The man had pink cheeks and thinning hair and sported a pair of effeminate black leather driving gloves. He appeared not to be armed.

Doug wondered why Danny had not already punched this man's lights out.

On leaving the motel, Neil Jacobs had climbed into his Rover, placed the key in the ignition and paused to assess his position. First of all, he had threatened a journalist in front of witnesses. It had been a bluff . . . and yet? Yet McCreary might easily be co-opted into employing another henchman. It wouldn't come to that. The editor of the *Mail* was a personal friend. Warren would be out on his ear before the first edition reached the newsagents'.

He tapped open the yellow film cartridge on the dashboard and unravelled its contents. Stretching the mauve film until it was taut, he then rustled it into the glove compartment, where it curled into a celluloid nest. It was their word against his. He thought of Sandra and his bowels tightened. What if she did confess all to the papers? Cuss and tell? He raked his eyes across the tarmac. Her Ford Fiesta was gone. He lay down across the seats. No sense in going home yet, if at all.

Stretched out there with his hands behind his head, he missed his wife and the journalist, who sped off back to

Edgbaston to consummate their union. What if he were to be hauled over the coals? he asked himself. Stephanie would have her divorce and doubtless the house as well. Never mind. He had enough salted away, and his accountant was so good with the figures that he'd often suggested he use a glamorous assistant. No doubt he'd be able to conjure his portfolio into the ether before the decree nisi. But then, of course, there was the press. The tabloids. The feeding frenzy. Well, it would abate. Always did. Protocol would demand his resignation from his council seat, but he could build directorships and consultancies piecemeal.

Another idea germinated. With a good press agent he could turn this around. He'd find some shrink who could describe his condition as an affliction. Make him the victim rather than the aggressor. Call it – what? – Abusive Regressive Syndrome? He could even chair a few support groups or, even better, start a charity. He smiled at that one. Charity. A godsend for the businessman: funded by fools and run by the morally unimpeachable. *Carte blanche* to rake in the money and skim off the proceeds in running costs and overheads.

Jacobs had watched the birth of the National Lottery and been utterly flabbergasted at the gullibility of the public. The desperation of the poor and elderly to chuck it all back to the rich had made him proud to be British. He told anyone who would listen that it was as if the populace were intent on wiping away the permissive age and getting back to basics, class-wise. Indeed, there were lottery watchdogs and the ombudsmen, but when it came to it, the people had spoken. They were selflessly giving their all to rebuild our national heritage from the top down.

Granted, thought Jacobs, he wasn't a prime candidate for donations, but once he had started up the operation, he'd be eligible for a nice fat grant. Cheered by this reasoned approach to his crisis, he smacked his lips. What he needed more than anything right now was a decent cup of tea.

Doug's patience was thinner than road-kill. When Danny did nothing about this new irritant, he got things moving by squeezing off a shot. It shattered the fibreglass head of a blind charity boy by the door. The councillor looked over in surprise and shock.

'Who the fuck are you?' demanded Doug.

Rob answered, 'He's a perve. All right, Rubber Boy?'

Jacobs did not dignify that with a response.

The babble in Danny's brain had scudded away like spent rain-clouds. Furthermore, his nose had stopped dripping and his hearing had improved markedly. Keeping the shotgun trained on the man, he reached into his breast pocket and plucked out the newspaper article. With careful fingers, he unfolded it and held the photograph up to the councillor's face.

'Councillor Jacobs?'

'What of it?'

Not a good answer. Danny pressed the twin barrels of the shotgun to Jacobs's nose. 'I'd like to talk to you, if that's all right?'

If possible, Jacobs turned paler.

'Danny, will you leave it alone,' shouted Doug.

'This asshole put me and Mum in the bloody flat in the sink estate.'

Jacobs winced at the scatological nature of Danny's comment.

'Danny! We are *leaving*.'

Dan's years as a bouncer made the decision for him. 'Look, I'll take this outside. Only be a couple of secs, then we'll be off home.'

Doug threw up his hands as Danny dragged his captive out

by the scruff of his neck and tossed him to the ground in the carpark.

'Lasalles. The old estate.'

'I-It was c-condemned. Structurally unsafe.'

'Bullshit,' said Danny. 'You forced that to happen. You ordered holes dug; you let the streetlights go. You stopped the rubbish people coming.'

'I had n-nothing to do with it.'

Danny had the councillor's left arm in a vice grip. In seconds it went numb, as if the councillor had been sleeping on it all night.

'A-all right, yes.'

Dan scratched his goatee. 'You're putting up this business park. What's the point of that?'

'T-the surveys indicate substantial p-profits can be made from renting out retail units . . .'

Danny tightened his grip. 'You don't care about the families you evicted.'

'It was compulsory purchase – I had nothing to do . . .'

Danny was having none of this and dragged the protesting councillor over to the petrol station.

Inside the shop, the Asian adolescent, the night staff and the policewoman watched their approach with horror. The unstoppable bulk of the bouncer steamed in the freezing air, and the tiny man hung off him like some grotesque appendage. The WPC had had the presence of mind to order everyone down and quickly told the youth to throw her the keys. She locked the door with seconds to spare and slipped her handcuffs through the handles before joining the others in the staff rest room.

Danny marched up to the doors and tried them. He bellowed at the adolescent, who sat open-mouthed, frozen to his seat. Dan bounced the councillor off the glass, then walked him to the grille. He leaned in so his mouth was close to the sliding metal tray.

'Turn on pump number six, will you?'

The youth mimed incomprehension.

'Number six,' articulated Danny slowly and loudly. 'The unleaded one.' Be friendly to the environment, he thought.

The boy looked for advice as the WPC frantically signalled in the negative. He turned back.

'You haven't got a car.'

'There's no law says I've got to have a car. I'm filling up me lighter.' He grinned.

'I can't . . .'

'Turn the pump on.'

Danny emphasised his point by cocking the shotgun and aiming it at the youth.

He switched on the pump.

'A-A-anything else?'

Dan made great play of standing on tiptoe and studying the racks. 'Give us two Twixes . . . a packet of Rizla reds, and . . . one of them Bic lighters.'

'I thought you had a lighter?'

Danny pretended not to hear this.

The youth complied, refused payment and disappeared behind the pillow-sized packets of crisps. Danny took the provisions, bit the end off one of the chocolate wrappers, stuck one bar in his mouth like a cigar and stuffed the others in his breast pocket. He then dragged his captive to the pump, where he unholstered the petrol gun and snapped the green tube behind him like a whip.

He smiled broadly at Jacobs, who immediately voided his bladder. This time the councillor gained no pleasure from it whatsoever.

*   *   *

'What's he doing?' asked Jason.

Doug had ushered his captives through to the back of the restaurant and had half rolled up one of the blinds. Danny was holding the screeching man by the hand as he doused him in petrol.

'You don't want to know,' said Andy.

Danny squeezed off the handle at twelve pounds and three pence and reholstered it. 'Admit that you did it and tell me why.'

The councillor moaned. 'D-did what?'

'Screwed us all out of our homes.'

'You w-wouldn't dare . . .'

'Is there something not clear here? You're covered in petrol and I'm holding a shotgun.'

'W-we had to get the residents out so we could demolish and develop the property.'

'Who is "we"?'

'A consortium. M-McCreary, me and others. But you were all rehoused.'

'In a time-share with the slums of Brazil.'

Councillor Jacobs shivered with cold and fear and threw up a vol-au-vent.

'That's not very nice,' said Dan, who stepped back so his shoes wouldn't get splashed.

Jacobs looked up, pleading.

'You try living there,' continued Danny. 'We're at the bottom of the shit list and that's down to you. There was nothing wrong with the old estate, was there?'

'N-no.'

'So what's the game?'

'The business park is part of the Handsworth redevelopment.'

Danny took out the plastic lighter and rolled his thumb minutely over the metal tumbler. Fear widened the councillor's eyes.

'Please. Listen. Oh, L-lord.' The words tumbled out. 'As a councillor I can't be seen to be in league with the developers so McCreary and the consortium have bought it. I'm a s-sleeping partner. B-but we . . . We're not planning on completing the project.'

'No business park?'

Jacobs shook his head. 'McCreary's making only a minimum outlay on the foundations; the-then one of the other investors is going into receivership. It's all planned. T-to unbalance the whole project.'

'What's the point of that?'

'I-It's complex, but b-basically, I'll buy back the land for the council at a vast price. All profit for us. My con-connection is hidden too deep . . .'

Danny stared at him in shock. 'You can do that?'

'Happens all the time.'

'But that's . . .' Dan was lost for words.

'H-how it works.'

'You don't really give a toss about people, do you? It's all shovelling money about — mostly in your direction.' He plucked a handful of paper serviettes, from his pocket twisted them into a tight taper and lit it with his new lighter. He held it close to the councillor, who flung his arms over his face. 'You're a right bastard, you.'

'Yes, I'm sorry. Please don't kill me.'

'I should, though, shouldn't I?'

'Please, I beg of you.'

Teasing him, Danny swung the burning tissue around the man as if it were a sparkler. Jacobs moaned and yelped and quivered and began to cry. Danny One-Slice looked at the crouching, snivelling figure and tried to summon up feelings of pity. He managed only revulsion. This was the way the world was. Nothing much he could do about it in the end.

He turned away and faced the service station. There was a searing sensation in his left hand. Cursing, he dropped the last knot of tissue paper as it burnt his fingers. Muttering to himself, he began to trudge back towards the Granary. He stuck his fingers in his mouth and sucked away the pain.

Between the blinds he could see Doug and Jason waving at him. He waved back cheerily. It looked like they were pointing, trying to tell him something. Then he noticed the flare of bright orange reflected in the window of the restaurant. He turned round and saw a human Molotov cocktail.

'Oh, bugger it,' he said.

The flames touched the petrol and raced up Jacobs's body. They covered him like liquid serpents as the councillor ran blindly back and forth. Inside the kiosk, the Asian youth was frantically trying to mime the burning man away from the petrol station. Danny started back and, grabbing a small fire extinguisher from beside a pump, chased after the councillor. Jacobs was quick on his feet; he'd give him that. He went left, right, round the pumps, and skittered towards a patch of damp grass, where he flopped to a charred heap on the kerbside. Danny trotted up and sprayed the contents of the extinguisher over him.

Unfortunately, Neil Jacobs had died of shock before his corpse hit the ground.

CHAPTER TWENTY FOUR

Great To Be Here In
(Insert Name Of Town)

The WPC peered out over the racks of sweets. The bouncer/
castaway had gone and there seemed to be no danger of the
petrol station igniting. Ensuring that the others remained on
the floor, she checked on the progress of the Armed Response
Unit. She was told that their ETA was another five to ten
minutes. Apparently, they had been delayed by two events:
one, a shoot-out in a central Birmingham nightclub, two, a
report of an elderly Greek man who had been apprehended
carrying more knives than a Samurai warrior: he had held the
team off for twenty minutes with a strange battle-cry that
sounded like the word 'rent'.

Danny One-Slice entered to horrified faces. 'Sorry,' he
said.
　Doug was livid. 'What was all *that* about?'
　'Sort of old business, really,' said the colossus, shuffling
embarrassedly from foot to foot.
　'That doesn't help us at all.'
　Danny made for the breakfast counter. Doug would have

followed him had he not needed to keep the Glock trained on Andy and Rob.

'What you doing, Dan?'

'I'm a bit peckish.'

'Danny, we're *going*.'

Doug gritted his teeth. There was commotion as the ladies began to talk among themselves.

'*Now*, Danny.'

Behind him, Jason was staring sightlessly into space. After witnessing a real death with gore and screaming and stuff, he wanted to switch off the game and chill out to the static hiss as he shut down the machine. As Doug and Danny argued on, his reflex for self-preservation kicked in. Liquid fear surged through him as he bolted across the restaurant, ran out of the Granary, up the stairs and charged across the bridge.

Danny immediately gave chase. Aided by adrenalin, steroids, Night Nurse, speed and a lack of restrictive trouser, he bounded after him, thundering along the tunnel above the silent motorway.

Jason risked a look back over his shoulder only to find that the giant was gaining ground. His enormous leg muscles rippled with energy, and he held the shotgun aloft like a caveman's club. There were flecks of foamy spittle in his beard. He whooped and hollered, his voice booming in the long tunnel.

'You've got this coming, boy.'

Jason hared it down the stairs, past the Red Hen and out into the carpark. He reached the Transit and scrabbled at the door. Tugging at the handle, he found it locked. He scampered round the other side and tried again. The passenger door flew open and he scrambled across to the driver's seat. He reached for the ignition. No keys. He hit his pockets as if they were on fire, then, in despair, looked up.

Danny was silhouetted in the glow of the service station

entrance. His legs were planted apart. He had the shotgun in one hand and – dangling off the little finger of the other – the keys to the Transit.

Jason's face fell.

Danny dropped the keys and cocked the sawn-off shotgun.

Jason ducked as the windscreen shattered into a million pieces. The glass shower seemed to last an age, then the rear doors blew out and snapped back on their hinges. Cold air was sucked inside. Jason poured out of the van, landing on his palms on the shining asphalt.

'Paybacks,' announced Dan, grabbing him by the jacket. He bounced Jason off the side of the van with each complaint. 'First off, you stole me mum's magic spray.'

Thump.

'You come into the 23 Skidoo like you own the place. That really . . .'

Thump.

'Pisses.'

Thump.

'Me.'

Thump.

'Off.'

Danny swapped hands. 'You're a twat.'

Whump.

'You didn't put the money back in the cash machine like Doug told you to.'

Crump.

Jason hoped the list was finite. The bridge of his nose was broken and he had cracked a few ribs. Not keen on becoming a human pancake, he determined to act. With a reserve burst of energy, he stiffened as Dan prepared for his next lunge. This time, Jason placed his feet and hands on the van on contact and pushed back with all his might. Danny grunted, released his grip and shuffled backwards.

It was enough. Jason wriggled out of his grasp and zigzagged away. With blood pouring from his nose on to his shirt, he careered across the carpark, remembering to keep well away from the petrol station.

The bouncer gave chase as he made for a slippery grass bank at the boundary of the services. Jason hurtled up it and cleared the low wooden fence in one jump. Without pause, he ploughed on across the harsh stubble.

Danny's head hurt and his heart was trying to break free of his chest. Slowing to a halt at the perimeter fence, he saw the boy's shape bobbing up and down against the night sky.

His first instinct was to blast off a shot, but sense prevailed. Let him suffer out there, he thought. After all, he and Doug had the money. When it came to the split, Jason could beg for it as far as he was concerned. He plucked a pebble from the ground and threw it as hard as he could in the boy's direction.

He was rewarded with a yelp as Jason's silhouette dropped to the ground.

He turned back towards the service station, and the grin fell from his face. A series of flashing lights sped past down on the motorway; sirens screeching. Gripping the shotgun, he raced into the building and tore across the bridge.

Down on the other side, Doug was at the Granary entrance with the Glock in his hand. ARVs were shuffling into the carpark and the blinds of the restaurant were awash with blue light. As the heavy vehicles growled to a halt, doors were slammed, orders shouted, weapons cocked. From above came the persistent heartbeat of helicopter blades. As the chopper's searchlight stroked the restaurant, strips of white light blazed in through the windows. After a moment, the beam sloped away and went to probe the darker recesses of the carpark.

It was the whole circus.

Doug's face was taut with tension. 'Great, Danny. We're fucked now. What was all that shit with Jason? You should've let him go.'

'He was going for the Transit.'

'You had the keys.'

'I know.'

'So?'

A pause. 'If we're still taking the van, it's gonna be a bit chilly now.'

Doug's skull shone ice blue. 'We can't even get over the bridge, you pillock. We're bloody stuck here now.'

Angry with himself for having upset their plans, the giant Filipino aimed at the automatic doors and squeezed off a shot. The glass burst outwards and rained on the demolished RAC trailer.

There was silence as a pile of leaflets offering rescue and recovery fluttered in the air.

Then came the response. Spitting bullets took the arm off the charity boy, hit the 'Breakfast Offers' board and destroyed a toy car used for giving rides to children. It bleated a few strangulated tones.

'Bollocks,' Danny said as he reloaded the shotgun.

'Well, at least they know we mean business,' said Doug. 'Let's get back inside.'

They approached their captives. Doug waved his gun in the air.

'This is the bloody bargain bin of hostages. Half a dozen oldies and a couple of duff comedians. Not a lot to work with, is it?'

'*Television* comedian,' corrected Rob, as he chewed on a sandwich Mrs Lambridge had given him. Andy shot him a withering sneer.

Weighing heavily on Andy's mind was the possibility that

he might never see Michelle again. But if he did get home alive, he had constructed a list of things he'd like to tell her.

Firstly, he had realised that a comedy career meant hanging around with people like Rob Gillen for the rest of his life, and that wasn't something he was prepared to do. Second, his obsessing over the Agency had been a waste of time and energy. He wasn't going to be allowed to take part in the feast, nor even sit at the children's table. He was comic *non-grata*. Third, he had allowed the corrosion of selfishness to eat away at their relationship unchecked for far too long, and he wanted to chip away the barnacles.

As he sat eyeing his various nemeses, he decided that nothing was going to stop him from getting back to Michelle – not Doug, nor the Filipino, and especially not Rob bloody Gillen.

Danny stood guard as Doug went through to the kitchens. He re-emerged with a dirty chef's apron and, pulling a black woolen balaclava from his suit pocket, he rolled it over his head and held out the apron like a surrender flag. He issued instructions to Danny to keep them covered and marched out.

The helicopter returned, its spotlight beam scissoring the night.

'Excuse me, young man.' Mrs Lambridge had taken a couple of uneasy steps and was level with Danny's barrel chest. She had appointed herself leader by virtue of being the first to speak. 'Mightn't we be allowed some tea?'

Dan scratched his itchy thighs. He was sitting on one of tables with one foot dangling and the other up on the back of a chair. The shotgun rested across his lap, and the sacks of money were bunched up next to him.

'Tea?' repeated Mrs Lambridge.

Mrs Chitterden and the others took up the chant.

Rob smiled, but did not meet Andy's gaze.

Danny eyed them suspiciously and remained mute.

Mrs Chitterden rose and shuffled towards him.

'I need the powder room.'

'Sit down.'

She looked at him uncomprehendingly.

'Sit her back down, would you?' asked Danny, with a nod to Andy.

He steered the elderly woman to her seat. 'I'm afraid you'll have to wait. The man is armed, you see.'

Mrs Chitterden's eyes were as big as saucers behind her large glasses. 'Are you the waiter?'

'No, I'm a comedian.'

'Chameleon?'

'No, com-ed-ian,' he said, raising his voice.

This brought a ripple of interest from the gang.

'We're rather fond of the comedy,' said one.

'We've been to Blackpool,' confirmed another.

'Very amusing man,' said a third.

Having tuned in his comedy antennae, Rob was on the verge of speaking when Doug strode back in.

'Right, Dan, I've told them we're armed and we've got several hostages and they're backing off. I've got to make the meet by half six which gives us' – he glanced at his watch – 'about two and a half hours to sort this all out.'

'I should like some tea,' said Mrs Lambridge.

'Tea, yes,' added Mrs Chitterden.

'Tea's off,' said Doug.

Bristling, Mrs Lambridge folded her arms beneath her considerable bosom. 'There must be tea. It's twenty-four-hour.'

Doug brought out his gun. 'You know what this is?'

'I may be old but I'm not stupid, Mr . . . ?'

'Doug.'

'Mr Douglas. My late husband was in the army . . .'

'Territorials,' corrected Mrs Chitterden.

'Yes, but he was competent with a rifle,' said Mrs Lambridge, pursing her lips. 'When we were on the farm in Sussex —'

'Danny, please shut them up. I can't even think in here. It's like holding the *Antiques Roadshow* hostage.'

Doug walked off.

'Ladies,' said Danny. He had to repeat himself to be heard over another outbreak of bickering.

'Ladies. Please.'

'*Could* we get something to drink?' pleaded Mrs Chitterden.

'I'm spitting feathers,' said a wiry gnome-woman from Skipton. She was known for speaking her mind, even after she had lost it.

'You keep quiet.' Dan frowned. 'And I'll see what I can do.'

Doug was over by the salad bar. 'Danny,' he said in a tone that had reached the end of its tether and fallen off, 'Dan, if you give them *tea* then they'll all be wanting the bogs all night. Just shut them the fuck up, will you?'

'Dreadful language,' stage-whispered Mrs Lambridge.

'That's it.' Doug stormed over with the gun raised. 'Right — who's first?' He pointed the Glock at Mrs Lambridge, then at Mrs Chitterden, jerking his gaze from one elderly lady to the next as he swung it further round to reach Rob and Andy. 'You're comedians — entertain them.'

'Do what?' Rob asked.

'Tell them some jokes.'

'I don't do jokes. It's more observational stuff.'

Doug pressed the gun barrel into Rob's neck. 'Do it. Both of you.'

Rob choked. 'I can't go on first. I'm the headliner. Andy should open.'

Andy raised his eyes heavenward. 'A gun to his head and he's still quibbling over billing.'

Rob gave him a watery grin. 'That's showbiz.'

Doug pressed the barrel deeper into his skin. Rob held up his hands.

'All right, I'll do it. Andy, come and introduce me.'

Andy padded to the centre of the raised smoking section of the restaurant. He stood there for a moment, staring at the floor, getting himself together. He looked up, taking in the expectant faces. He glimpsed Danny with the shotgun, then Doug, who was holding out his palms, his eyebrows raised.

'Get on with it,' Doug barked.

Andy's tone was flat and resigned. 'Ladies and gentlemen. Hostages and criminals. Please welcome – Rob Gillen.'

He moved away to allow Rob to take centre-carpet.

'Is that it?' Rob asked.

'I'm not good at improvising in siege conditions.'

'You could've at least built me up a bit.'

'Have they started?' asked Mrs Lambridge.

'Rob – it's a service station, not the London Palladium.'

'Is *this* the waiter?' asked Mrs Chitterden, pointing a quivering finger at Rob.

'No, I am *not* the waiter,' said Rob.

'Oh.'

Suddenly, as if a light switch had been thrown, Rob went into performer mode. 'I think you've been overdoing the Ovaltine, love. Was that a heckle or your last will and testament?'

'What's he on about?' asked Mrs Lambridge.

Rob grinned like a shark. 'Hey – what is all this heckling? Do I come to the nursing home and interrupt *you* while you're drooling . . . ? No? Well, shut up, then. And who called me a waiter? Do I look like someone who can't even get a part in *The Bill* . . . ?'

No response. He let out a sigh.

'OK. Acting jokes too subtle.' He mimed crossing something out on his palm. 'Isn't Valentine's Day crap, eh? You buy a card for your lover or your wife – or both . . . And it has to be exactly the right one, doesn't it? It can't be the funny one or she'll think you're trivialising the re-*lation*-ship . . . It can't be too soppy because then she thinks you're treating her like a *girly* instead of a modern feminist. Has to basically imply you worship her but you wouldn't *dare* put her on a pedestal. Me? I do. I put women on a pedestal, 'cos you can see up their skirt from there . . . 'course, the Valentine's cards you really have to avoid are those *huuugge* ones *above* the top shelf in the newsagents'. The faded ones with the bunnies on them that have been around since rationing.'

The brickwork glowed red in police light.

'They're so big they were used as air-raid shelters in the war . . . So old the message inside is "I wish to go courting. Please inform your chaperone . . ." '

A whirring of helicopter blades.

'Who buys them anyway? Giants in love? Other big bunnies? People who hate their postman and want to give him a hernia delivering it . . . ?'

The crackle of a police radio.

'And you don't have to sign a Valentine's card. Hey, did you ever worry about poor old St Valentine? Every single letter he gets, he's scratching his head and he's going: "Who's this from, then?" '

Light glinted. Mrs Lambridge was folding the piece of tinfoil which had been used to wrap her sandwiches.

'I always give my girlfriend the *designer* card. The fancy one that's smug and clever and says "We're emotionally mature adults exchanging a nicely designed image on embossed card". And what does she say? "*I wanted de nice soppy one wiv de weally big bunnies*" ' He threw up his hands, then leered. 'Still, what can you do? She's only fourteen . . .'

His eyes hopped across the room, looking for sympathy, understanding, a laugh. Nothing. He collapsed at the nearest table. 'Tough crowd,' he said.

Danny raised the shotgun. 'Your turn.'

Andy pointed to himself.

'Yeah. You.'

Dan turned to Doug, got a nod.

'Have a good one,' said Rob, all thumbs-up and relaxed now.

Andy stood up, took a deep breath and began to speak.

'Well, I don't usually do hostage crises, although I have done funerals – mostly my own. My neighbour's always drilling. Every day it's drilling, drilling, drilling. So last week I borrowed an industrial Kango hammer, put it right up against the dividing wall and as soon as he started drilling I went BRAAAAPP. . . . Made a mess of his dental surgery.' A smile from one of the ladies.

'. . . I went to a bookshop. Asked the assistant if she could tell me where the self-help section was. She said no.'

A titter from Mrs Lambridge.

'. . . I bought an electric typewriter but I still prefer my old acoustic. . . .'

'Drilling,' said Mrs Chitterden.

'. . . Today I had a premonition and déjà vu at the same time and they cancelled one another out . . .'

A dimple appeared in Danny's cheek.

'I once went out with a girl who worked in a flower shop by day and a chocolate factory at night. Only lasted a month. I ran out of ideas for presents . . . I once overthrew a bouncy castle with one spear . . . Suffered when I was young. My parents sent my inner child to boarding school . . . My school had no funding. One year I was in a production of *Joseph and His Not Bad Blanket* . . . The next year it was *Cat* . . .'

'That'll do,' said Dan.

'. . . I was burgled once and the thieves stole my paying-in book. Before I had a chance to tell the bank, they'd paid in over three hundred pounds . . .'

'Hold it,' said Dan, raising the shotgun.

Andy sat down to a ripple of applause.

Rob leaned over. 'You'll do great on the day-room circuit.'

'He's rather amusing,' said Mrs Chitterden.

'Not as funny as Chubby,' said the woman from Skipton, who prided herself on her critical faculties.

Rob turned to them, incredulous. 'Chubby? You've been to see Roy "Chubby" Brown?'

A chorus of yesses.

'B-but he's the most offensive . . . a sexist dinosaur.'

'Coming from you that should be a compliment,' muttered Andy.

'He was very good,' said the gnome woman as she inserted a pin in her hair.

'The room was packed,' said another.

'Weren't you offended?' asked Andy

'It's only a laugh,' said Mrs Lambridge. 'It's not *real*.'

Andy and Rob made fish mouths.

Mrs Lambridge leaned towards them, fake pearls clattering against the pair of glasses hung round her neck.

'Oh, we know it's awfully rude but it's all in good fun. Rather like one of those roller whatnots.'

'Coasters. Rollercoasters,' said Mrs Chitterden.

'But you're not *supposed* to like him,' said Rob.

Mrs Lambridge eyed him steadily. 'We didn't mind *your* showing off, young man.'

'But I'm being . . . ironic.'

'Yes, dear,' said Mrs Chitterden. 'I'm sure you are.'

'Funny,' said Mrs Lambridge with an air of finality, 'is funny. And that's all there is to it.'

CHAPTER TWENTY FIVE

World Domination O.N.O.

Doug paid scant attention while Andy did his act, being too preoccupied with his own problems of escape. The Ford Mondeo was trashed and the Transit unreachable across the bridge: this left the limited options of either demanding a getaway car or using the hostages as a human shield while they commandeered another vehicle. The pensioners were too shrunken and unstable to provide cover, so it would have to be the comedians. Better yet, he reasoned, he could form a phalanx by pulling out a couple of chilled Granary employees from the fridge. With that thought, he gave the nod to Dan and strode through to the kitchens.

Something was wrong. He raked the room with the gun, then went to the steel door of the walk-in fridge, raised his weapon and punched the handle. Inside were racks of meat and plenty of provisions but a distinct lack of police officers and staff.

He spun round to face the corridor that led to the emergency exit. One of the doors hung ajar, its bar loose and the lower bolt trailing on the ground. His first instinct was to release a volley of shots in frustration. He swallowed the urge until it dissipated.

Lowering the pistol, he flattened himself against the wall

and slid sideways until he reached the battered door. As soon as the breeze blew it shut he secured it. He found a broom and wedged the handle through the rungs so it couldn't be opened from the other side.

He retreated to the kitchen and clambered up on to the central metal table. Draping his legs over the end, he lay on his back and rested the Glock on his stomach. Above him on the greasy ceiling were twin fluorescent strip lights. Dotted about in their ridged plastic housing were myriad black specks. Dead flies. Doug stared at the lights then squeezed his eyes shut. Green lozenges skated in the darkness behind his eyelids.

'Doug!'

Danny was bellowing from out in the restaurant. As he swung off the table, a blow to his forearm made him drop the gun, which clattered across the linoleum. His assailant swung another punch but he parried it and rammed his fist hard into the man's stomach.

The comedian dropped to the floor as if he had been tickled by a cattle prod.

Realising the gravity of his situation, Rob Gillen had sunk into depression. Not only had he performed the worst gig of his career to a bunch of octogenarian Chubby Brown fans, but also he was in the grip of a pair of thugs who might at any moment cut short his comedy career with a bullet. Admittedly, that had its attractions: posthumous fame, videos, cassettes, celebrity tributes and cult status, to name but a few. But he wanted to be around to see his reputation soar, not plugged full of holes in a place where they couldn't even make a teapot that poured without spilling. He couldn't believe it was happening: not after all the years of graft. Mind you, if he did survive, it was going to be the greatest story. The big

anecdote: the one he'd dine out on in years to come and
expand on to sycophantic radio presenters.

He determined that his escape would be of the Willis/
Bond variety, achieved with panache, violence and a great put-
down afterwards. He steeled himself, biding his time, pre-
paring his muscles, glancing at Andy over with the biddies.
The lumbering Filipino was watching him, watching them. He
waited for the moment to strike. Waiting for . . . just the right
. . . moment.

As Rob ran shrieking towards the kitchen with his arms
akimbo, Danny rose and tracked alongside him. The bouncer
kept the sawn-off trained on the others.

'Doug!'

'Got it,' replied Doug, as he felled him.

Rob tried to pull himself across the floor but Doug was kicking
him hard. He howled as the bones cracked inside his body.

'Where did you think *you* were going?'

'Let me out. I want to go,' moaned Rob, as if he were being
kept behind at school.

'We all want to get out. What makes you so special?'

Rob, not feeling special at all, groaned as Doug stamped
hard on his shoulder blades and then trod on his left arm with
all his weight. Doug felt no compassion whatsoever towards
Rob. He had lied to the hefty comedian. He *had* seen his
television programme.

Rob screamed and blacked out. When he came to, his
peripheral vision was cloudy like milk. He bucked and kicked
and tried to clamber to his feet, but when he tried to get
leverage with his hand, the pain hit him. The nerves shorted
out and an electric arc of agony scorched from his elbow to his
neck. His eyes sprouted tears and his stomach threw partially
digested food into his throat.

Somehow, he remained conscious. Through watery lenses, he scoped the kitchen. Twin metal sinks. Dishwasher. Tray of condiments. Jar of acid-yellow mustard. Catering pack of cheap instant Chicoffee. Towel dispenser. Twin emergency doors. Hardly *The Generation Game*. Hold on. The doors were matt black with grubby steel patches at shoulder height. A line of light glimmered in the crack between them. It looked warm and flattering, pink like stage light. He took a tentative step forward.

'Where are you off to now?'

The gun barrel creased his cheek.

Brian Savage, commander of the Armed Response Unit, had his men on stand-by awaiting instructions. Armed officers had ringed the building, and the movements inside were being recorded with heat-sensitive imaging cameras and on sound tape. However, before he could intervene, police procedure demanded that a trained hostage negotiator must first be summoned to say his piece. The one assigned to their unit was ten miles away in Knowle.

Tom Mason was a whiz with crackhead criminals and berserk gun-wielding husbands, but tonight his wife was away and her mother had refused to baby-sit the kids on such short notice. At present he was attempting to dialogue with her, an undertaking that was proving difficult from the other side of the letterbox. Behind him in the car, his six- and seven-year-old children, Samantha and Stuart, were dozing in their jim-jams. A police driver was waiting to speed him straight over to Corley.

Savage removed his black baseball cap and primped his salt-and-pepper hair back to life. Privately he hoped that Tom wouldn't show as, despite his many years of achievement, he still longed to sort things out in the way of his hero – the

Duke. To Brian, a veteran of the West Midlands police, sensitive policing meant an extra layer of mattress between suspect and baton. Problem was – how many of those trapped inside were the perpetrators and how many were civilians? Savage had concentrated operations on the kitchen exit, leaving forensics to continue searching the vehicles in the carpark.

On the south side, the bolt-cutters and oxyacetylene torch had been found inside Jason's father's Transit. It and the automatic cash tills had been ringed with blue-and-white-striped tape and thoroughly dabbed for prints. It hadn't taken long for the forensic scientists to uncover Jason's lame aerosol job, and a pair of squad cars had been dispatched: one to the lot and one to the Joffe home.

The motorway police had barricaded the M6 with cones and roadblocks for several hundred yards either side of the service area. Awaiting an estimate as to the duration of the siege, they were poised to inform the Highways Agency of the situation. The resultant build-up of container vehicles resembled a French lorry blockade, but without the violence.

Two ambulances had arrived from the Cov/Warwick and one from the George Elliott hospital They were waiting in a safe area behind the petrol station. There, sand had been poured across the forecourt and all the pumps had been turned off.

God and the policeman had had their wounds dressed and the other escapees were being treated for shock.

Victor the chef was sneering at the sandwiches in the cooler cabinet in the shop.

The remains of Councillor Jacobs's body had been wrapped in a tight black plastic body-bag.

He would have wanted it that way.

* * *

Doug stood over Rob with the gun barrel drilling into the back of his neck. Tears cascaded down Rob's face and dripped off his chin. He hadn't cried like this since the fifth form when Joanna Frye had left him for Gavin Taylor. She had lost her virginity to him and he'd sworn that one day he'd get his revenge on nasty girls.

'You OK in there?' shouted Danny from the door.

'Situation under control.'

Dan scuttled off back to the restaurant, where he found Andy holding one of the sports bags containing the money. He raised the shotgun. 'Put it down.'

'I wanted a word.'

'That's your word. Put it back.'

Andy held out the bag by its handle. 'I've been thinking. Why don't you take this?'

'Down, I said.'

Andy's tone was even. 'Look, Doug's busy in the kitchen. There's a chance you could make it over the bridge with the money. I'll make a diversion if you like.'

Danny tore the bag from his hand.

'Or maybe not.'

Dan plonked the bag on a nearby table.

'Still. It was worth a try,' added Andy, to no one in particular.

The ladies had not moved from their seats, and a couple were chewing on their sandwiches. Danny frowned and scratched at his crotch. He was thirsty and the roustabout in his head was spinning his brain like they were in one of those revolving sofas on the waltzer.

Andy spoke up again. 'Thing is, these situations always turn out badly. Usually end up in a hail of bullets.'

Danny grunted. He'd mentioned this to Doug earlier, but wasn't going to offer that information.

'So I was thinking about damage limitation. It's not getting any better in here. Maybe you should give up before anyone gets . . . hurt.' Andy finished his sentence from the ground, Danny having just swatted him with a giant hand.

The Filipino rose, took the bag he had swiped from Andy over to the ladies' and swapped it back for the original one.

Rob's big chance. Through the stage door was the stand, its ancient metal feet planted on the dusty stage. Underneath were patches of old gaffer tape, remnants of older battles fought. Light glinted off the steel shaft making it look like a sword unsheathed. Around it was a coiled black snake of power.

The lights shone brighter than the star leading to Jerusalem.

Any moment now, he thought, the herald would make the crowd cheer and shout and build a crescendo of excitement. He would wait, protected in the dark, hidden like a jewel until the last possible second. And then he would enter with sleeves rolled and colours ablaze. And he would conquer.

Doug pistol-whipped him. Rob's dislocated arm collapsed and he fell to the disinfected floor. Sprawling, he saw his chance and lashed out with a muddied cowboy boot. It caught Doug on the shin.

A thump and a curse as the man tripped and fell.

Rob rose and made for the light. A deafening explosion. Brickwork rained on him. He scrambled forward and thrust out his good arm. There was an object in his way. Mike stand? No, something wooden. He wrenched it free and suddenly there was an agonising white pain. His trousers filled with liquid and he tumbled into the light.

Rifles were primed for action. As Rob emerged, Savage barked the order to aim and cover. It was too late. One of his men let off a round, catching Gillen as he fell. Doug immediately fired from inside the kitchen until his clip was empty. He shattered headlights, burst tyres and punched holes in the bodywork of the ARVs. The return blast splintered the emergency doors and its force pushed them closed. Bullets ventilated a box of cleaning fluids, which leaked bleach and detergent.

Once the shooting had finished, the officer who had fired was suspended from duty. Sitting sulking in an armoured van, he rationalised his mistake. Was it the tension? A faulty weapon? Or was it that his victim seemed familiar? Perhaps a gut reaction to sighting a known felon?

Or was it that the bloke looked like someone off the telly?

CHAPTER TWENTY SIX

The Night They Fried
Danny One-Slice

———◆———

'We're being held hostage,' whispered the gnome-like pensioner to her companion.

'Are we on an aeroplane?' asked her friend, who had been dozing.

'No, not on a plane.'

She formed an 'O' with her rouged lips.

From his position on the floor, Andy had counted Doug's shots and had guessed he would need to reload. He nudged Mrs Lambridge on the ankle.

'Excuse me, but can you make a distraction?'

'Sorry, dear?'

'Make a noise? Move around or something?'

'What's that?' asked Mrs Chitterden, who was always keen to become a conspirator.

'Could you make a fuss? Imagine it's pension day. Someone queue-jumped you in the post office.'

Mrs Lambridge gave Andy a big stage wink.

Danny had backed off to the serving area and was straining his ears for signs of life in the kitchens. He called out to Doug, and on receiving no answer, sensed a rush of paranoia. What if he was alone now? What would he do? He leaned on the chrome serving runners and blew his nose into the last of the pile of serviettes. There were oval rings of sweat under the arms of his tux and he didn't smell too good. He was dying to take a shower and change into a fresh T-shirt, track suit bottoms and flip-flops: lie back in his favourite chair with a cool rum and Coke.

He was not best pleased therefore when the gaggle of ladies lined up along the top of the steps like Zulu warriors.

'Tea,' they chanted.

He raised his arms in resignation. 'How many more times do I have to tell you? There's no tea. Go sit down.'

The ladies split into two groups, Mrs Lambridge leading three of them forward, the Skipton woman urging the other trio back to their seats.

Andy, who had been huddled at the back among the coats and bags, sprinted out and hurdled the serving counter. Danny hauled the shotgun in his direction, then thought better of it and trained it on the ladies. He walked backwards, clawing the air with his free hand.

'You get back here.'

Andy threw a tray of midget coffee percolators at him. They bounced off and clattered to the floor, eliciting a cry of surprise from the pensioners.

As Doug emerged from the kitchens, Dan threw the shotgun to him. Doug caught the weapon, cocked it and stabled the ladies up in the raised section.

Danny tore off his tuxedo jacket and turned to Andy, who promptly tipped the tea urn at him. It plummeted to the floor and boiling-hot liquid flooded out. The silver top spun round and round in decreasing circles, emitting a grating sound that rose in pitch until Danny stepped on it. As he did so, he missed his footing, slid backwards in the steaming pool and toppled over.

The ladies moaned at the loss of their potential beverage.

Andy moved along behind the breakfast counter, eyeing the colossus through the plexiglass shields. Danny rose and faced him. Andy stopped dead. They skipped to the left and to the right, trying to anticipate one another's next move. Andy dropped his gaze to the food containers and tried to lever out one containing baked beans. Failing to budge it, he threw a handful of warm beans at Dan. The behemoth wiped juice from his face, took a step forward and went down again in the teaslick.

Andy squatted on his haunches, put his back to the unit and braced his legs on the wall. Straightening his knees, he freed the counter, rocked it so it was beyond its balancing point and tipped it over. The metal unit fell on Danny's chest and a slurry of meat, egg and beans coagulated against the plexiglas an inch from his face.

The giant gripped the counter and levered it aside. He got to his feet, lifted the whole thing off the ground and hurled it through space. It landed in the chilled food cabinet among the mineral waters, yoghurts and limp parsley.

'Shit,' said Andy.

Danny grinned at him.

Andy hared it into the kitchens.

Dan caught up with him by the ovens. Andy, wedged between the hobs, spun the dial on the fat-frier and pulled out the wire chip basket. It dripped oily grease but had long since cooled. He threw it at Danny anyway. In panic, he jumped up on to the griddle, skipped across the hobs and landed on the floor. Behind him, the fat slowly started to bubble.

The two danced round the room. Danny was first to tire of this and took hold of the end of the long worktable. Manoeuvring it from side to side, he got Andy trapped against the sinks. He had him now. Pulling back, he was ready to slam it against Andy, truncating him at the waist.

But at the last moment, Andy dropped and crawled as fast as he could under the table and out between Danny's legs. Dan bent to get him and banged his forehead on its metal rim.

Andy got to his feet beside a pile of twenty-five litre drums of cooking oil. Hauling out the nearest, he heaved it at the giant's back. It bounced off him like rice. Danny One-Slice grabbed him by the throat.

'You're trouble, you.'

Andy made a Germanic noise, flung out a hand and found he was clinging to the towel roll.

'Gonna dry me to death?'

Andy flailed hopelessly. His other hand grasped the nearest object.

The spatula did negligible damage to the 'roid-raged Filipino.

Andy tried again, this time his fingers finding sand. He dug his hand into it and seasoned his attacker. Suddenly he was free and choking back his breath.

Danny was crumpled on his knees, head in hands. He opened his mouth wide and emitted a series of sneezes vociferous enough to register on the Richter scale.

The restaurant echoed to the sound of half a dozen ladies chiming '*Gesundheit*'.

Andy checked out the drum of pepper.

Danny kneaded knuckles the size of pigs' trotters into his eyes.

'That'll only make it worse,' warned Andy.

But he knew it wouldn't be over until the man was unconscious or dead. He went for a steel carving knife that was attached to a magnetic strip on the wall. When he held up the shining blade he knew he couldn't use it. He cast it aside and looked at the bullet-ridden emergency exit doors. Needles of light shone through the holes. He turned to face his assailant. Danny had opened one fluid red-rimmed eye and was lumbering towards him.

Andy made for the walk-in fridge. From inside it he grabbed a deep metal tray containing several slabs of breaded plaice. He tipped the fish to the floor and stood rigid behind the door. When Danny arrived, he hoofed the door at him. The Filipino caught it, absorbed the force and swung it back so hard that the handle dug a two-inch crater in the wall. The door missed Andy by a whisker.

Terror spasmed his muscles but an auxiliary power unit seemed to kick in. He rammed the metal tray on to Danny's head and manoeuvred past him into the small tiled room containing the fridge-freezers. Fighting against the vacuum suction, he tore open the nearest one and started tossing food at the colossal cyclops.

Prawns flew out, then stiff steaks, frozen peas, carrots. They showered the kitchen floor as if the freezer were possessed by a bulimic poltergeist. Danny, still protecting his eyes, was beaten back by the force of the attack. Some of the bags broke open on impact and frozen veg skittered across the linoleum. Andy dug in deeper and found what he was looking for. A frozen shank of lamb. He ran at Danny and dealt him a vicious blow to the neck.

Doug needed to firm up his position and decided that his best course of action had to be threatening behaviour. He took the smallest and weakest pensioner by the elbow. 'If anyone tries anything, I'll kill her.' No reaction. 'Did you hear me? I said I'll kill you.'

'Yes, well, I suppose I've had my time.'

'Rose!' tutted her friend, who had taken her tablets and was more awake now.

'Oh, come on,' said Rose. 'It's been a good innings.'

'Shut *up*,' barked Doug.

'You can't imagine it,' added Mrs Lambridge, who wasn't one to be ignored for long. 'My husband died eight years ago. He used to work for the coal board but they dismissed him at fifty-seven . . . Reorganisation, they said . . . Precious little compensation but Henry assured me everything would be all right.'

'The point of this is?'

'Well, we're all widows here and . . . well, to be honest, life hasn't a great deal to offer us. What with the arthritis and my hip operation, which – I might add – has been round the corner for donkey's years. Money's terribly scarce and it's taken months to save for tonight's trip.' Murmurs of agreement all round. 'I suppose what I'm saying, young man, is that we don't feel particularly threatened.'

'There are worse things,' said another.

'This awful *weather*.'

'This time of year . . . before the spring,' said Mrs Chitterden.

'Mrs Lambridge,' Rose piped up. 'You have plenty to live for.'

'I don't think . . .'

'You have *cats*.'

Mrs Lambridge smiled at the thought of Trinder and Karno curled up at home.

'I have nothing,' continued Rose, clutching her handbag to her chest. 'Which is why I carry my particulars with me at all times so as I might be identified. Look.' She rifled inside her bag and produced a dark navy rectangle. 'My passport.'

At this her friend smiled in triumph.

'There. I *knew* we were going on an aeroplane.'

*   *   *

Andy recalled a time when you did amazing things: somewhere around the age of ten, when every child seems to have the gift of defying gravity. In those days he'd think nothing of performing a standing somersault, punting in an impossible header or tackling the highest branches of an oak tree. Look at that! he'd shout to his mum after a particularly fine wheelie. Did you see *that*? Her reaction was usually muted, a dismissive 'that's nice' or a brief smile like winter sun between clouds. This, he knew, was how people were going to react to the way in which he dispatched Danny One-Slice.

Jumping up on the draining board, he kicked over piles of plates as his pursuer came lumbering after him like a 'B'-movie monster. 'Sodding hell. Don't you ever stop?'

Danny let out a cackle, which mutated into another furious sneeze.

Andy jumped and landed awkwardly on a mop handle that lay astride a bucket. The handle snapped in two: the jagged wooden end spun in the air, arced across the kitchen and struck Danny right between the eyes. Stunned, he lost his balance, skidding on a scattering of bullet-hard frozen peas. Andy punted the mop bucket across the icy floor. It ploughed through wisps of white steam and rammed into the giant's shins. Danny bucked, twisted in the air and fell head first into the chip-frier.

It pinged.

Biting his lip in empathy, Andy approached the steaming hulk. Not dead, not dead, he thought. The muscles in Danny's broad back had already begun to slacken. His body slid to the floor and came to rest in a kneeling position. His fried head collapsed on to his chest.

He had a chip in his mouth.

Andy bent and studied him. Ropes of hot fat were dripping off his slippery, shining face. His eyes were closed and his cheeks, nose and lips were glazed with oil. He didn't appear to be burned or blistered, merely asleep. Sweat was oozing out of him and the back of his shirt was soaked.

Danny's fists, earlier such lethal weapons, rested tightly in his lap. Andy watched as they bloomed into lazy fat fingers. His chest rose and fell minutely. Andy stood, studying him. He looked like a caramelised Buddha. He must be in shock, thought Andy: or trauma, or whatever they call it now. Whatever the medical term was, he was out of the picture.

Then Andy, too, slid from the frame.

He came to on the restaurant floor with no concept of how much time had passed. Around him, the harsh lighting was cruel on the parchment faces of the ladies. They were propped sleepily at the tables. He checked his body for injuries. There were welts and bruises and a sizable lump on the back on his head, but otherwise nothing appeared to be broken. Then, like a fallen child receiving the ratification for his pain by a grown-up, it came back in great gulps. The back of his skull felt like someone had taken a blowtorch to it.

'You awake?'

Doug's voice, somewhere behind him. His legs came into focus.

'Sadly, yes.'

'You killed Danny.'

'He's still breathing.'

'You a doctor?'

'No.'

'Shut up, then.'

'Tetchy.'

Doug's Zippo flicked open. His cigarette hand appeared, its fingers stained the umber of old pub.

'What happened to Rob?'

'Police shot at him. They do that, you know.'

'Cynic.'

The gun waved in his eyes. 'Get up, Andy.'

He clambered on to the seat. It took a while adjusting to the light. His eyes were like two balloons someone was trying to force underwater. His head throbbed as if he'd been for a quick drink with Gazza. His ribs, thighs and stomach ached dully, but the pain in his neck kept him lucid. He tried to massage away the hurt. All that acupuncture had done him *no* good.

'There's no point in you carrying on with this,' Andy said.

Doug leaned on his elbows and looked him in the eyes. 'You always were a pessimist.'

'Well, under the circumstances . . .'

'I'll get out. Don't you worry.'

Andy tried to get comfortable in his seat, slumping into it. 'What happened with you, Doug?'

'How d'you mean?'

'Your life. Turning out like this.'

'If I need a social worker, I'll ask for one.'

'Well, there's a clue.'

Doug glared at him. 'You're gonna help me out of this.'

Andy closed his eyes. When he opened them again, a freshly rolled cigarette had been placed in front of him. He took and toasted it. The petrol smell of the Zippo nearly made him retch as he thought of the cremated man at the filling station. He sucked smoke into his lungs and the nicotine buzz helped some. Doug was still studying him. The stubble on his skull was a sprinkling of iron filings, the veins on his temples the green of tarnished copper.

'What?' Andy asked.

Doug released a whisper of smoke. 'It's payback time. You owe me.'

✻   ✻   ✻

Outside, a car had arrived and a frustrated Tom Mason poured from it. Commander Savage was there to meet him with a brisk salute.

'Here's the situation. We have one man dead, ID unknown at present. One man down and six elderly females being held inside. Four staff and two officers escaped with the aid of a hitchhiker whose identity we've also been unable to ascertain. The WPC who sounded the alarm says it's all down to a job gone wrong on the teller machines. The man injured has bullet wounds and a dislocated shoulder.'

He stopped speaking. An insistent high-pitched voice wafted towards them.

'Dad.'

It was Stuart Mason, Tom's son. Samantha was in the back of the car with a woman police officer, but he had clambered out and was on his way over.

'What,' fumed Savage, 'the hell is that child doing here?'

Tom Mason took his time. 'I couldn't get a sitter.'

'Do what?'

'Look, let's just get on with it, shall we? I'm here now.'

'You can't have children running about. This is a highly volatile hostage situation,' barked Savage.

Tom rubbed his chin. 'Yes, well, I realise we don't have a play area or baby-changing facilities here, but you try telling that to my mother-in-law.'

'Dad, can I play with the sirens?'

Tom bent to his son. 'No, Stuart. Now go sit in the car with your sister.'

Stuart, who was pushing seven and a quarter, was led away. Tom faced Commander Savage again.

His face looked as if it were attempting to contain some kind of nuclear meltdown.

'So,' Tom continued as casually as possible, 'is the injured man one of the perps?'

'It's probable.'

'I'll talk to him first, then.'

'He's gone. Airlifted to the Cov/Warwick.'

Mason bristled. His authority overrode Savage's at this juncture, and the commander did not have the right to stretcher off a potential source of information. 'What about the others inside?'

'We're picking up what we can but it sounds like a right bun-fight in there. Quiet now, though.'

Savage's radio burst into life as the helicopter pilot reported that he had landed for refuelling. The commander handed his megaphone to Mason, who was already being helped into his Kevlar jacket.

'Do your worst,' he said.

Tom Mason took a few paces, nearly jumping out of his skin when a police siren bleated.

'Stuart!' he shouted through the megaphone. 'I told you to leave that alone.'

CHAPTER TWENTY SEVEN

Here's What You
Would Have Won

———◆———

'You might be wondering what this is all in aid of,' said Doug.

'No.'

'All right, then.'

Andy, sighing: 'Tell me.'

They were still in their places in the Granary. The ladies had all but nodded off. Doug gave a crafty smile.

'We took twenty K from the cash machines and I need to get it to the airport by six thirty latest.'

'You'll be able to get a fuck of a lot of duty-free with that.'

'I'm not going *to* the airport. The deal's being done near there.'

'Why do I get the feeling I'm involved?'

'You'll see.'

'But you're hemmed in by armed police.'

'Not true.' Doug removed the balaclava helmet from his suit pocket and dropped it on the table.

'Unknown criminals are hemmed in by police.'

'I'm not with you there.'

Doug leaned on his elbows and steepled his fingers. The

Glock was still visible in the waistband of his trousers. 'What are you after Andy? Out of life, I mean?'

'Good question.'

'Well?'

Andy's mouth was dry and he wished now that he hadn't tipped over the tea urn.

Doug spoke first. 'You want the audience to love you? Is that it?'

Andy stared ahead without focusing. He hadn't realised that psychoanalysis by an old friend turned criminal was on the agenda. 'Part of it,' he agreed grudgingly. 'It's a driving job, really. Eight hours of hell on the road and twenty minutes of love if you're lucky.'

'What about fame and fortune?'

'There's that too.'

'So you wanna make it big?'

'Yeah, of course.'

Doug seemed pleased by this. 'See, Andy, I'm fed up spending my life pressed up against the window. Looking on from the sidelines. This is my chance. I'm getting a mound of Charlie and setting the two biggest drug gangs in Birmingham against one another. I'm gonna set myself up. Be a player.'

'Is that after you do the five years for armed robbery?'

'Not in the brochure, mate. Give us your car keys.'

'You'll never make it.'

Doug slammed his hand on the table. Some of the ladies twittered awake. 'Give me the fucking keys.'

Andy did so. 'It's the old Polo I pointed out earlier. Look for a heap of rust with a shattered window, no rear bumper and bodywork screaming "failed MOT".'

Doug took off his jacket and pushed the balaclava across to Andy. 'Take off your coat.'

'Why?'

'Do it.'

Andy slipped out of his leather jacket. Doug put it on and transferred the contents of his pockets into it. 'Now you put mine on.'

'What?'

'You're going out there to surrender – but as me. You'll say nothing, right? They'll be busy dealing with you while the nice ambulancemen and the police come in and rescue me and the ladies.'

Andy raised a finger to object but slowly lowered it. 'Nice plan.'

Doug smiled. It was about time that someone recognised his plotting skills. He got to his feet and handed over the shotgun. 'And you're to take this. Make it look authentic.'

Andy held it. 'I don't suppose it's . . .'

'Loaded? No. But this one is.' He patted the Glock. 'You owe me, Andy.'

Their eyes met.

Doug dropping him as a friend had been a turning point in Andy's childhood. From cosseted pre-adolescent, he became a pariah at school and in the streets. Withdrawn and sullen, he'd only had himself to rely on for company and did not bloom again until college. Here was Doug offering him – what? Redemption for those missed years? Did that matter any more? Somehow it did. After all, hadn't history just repeated itself through Gillen's machinations?

Tonight seemed like the culmination of a storm that had been brewing for years. He'd been sitting watching it and shrugging off the lightning in his life as harmless. And yet all the time the air was cooling and the sky turning as black as soot. And now the rain had come.

'I'll do it on one condition,' Andy said. 'If you get out of here, don't go through with this drug deal.'

Doug, sarcastically: 'Oh, sure. All right, then.'

'You've got the money from the cashpoint. You should use it. Start again.'

'As what? I've got a record and no qualifications.'

'Security guard?'

'Piss off.'

'Look, Doug. You know what I'm saying. Just think about it, all right?'

Doug shrugged his shoulders.

'That's as good as I'm going to get, isn't it?'

A nod.

Andy took a deep breath. 'Come on, then, let's get the ladies to the door. As soon as the police get hold of me, you'll want to bundle out.'

They went over and helped the pensioners to their feet.

'Have we landed?' asked Rose's friend.

Andy gathered up their bags for them. He put their compliance down to tiredness, although Mrs Lambridge still had a twinkle in her eye. They moved in a slow crocodile past the patisserie.

'Doug, give yourself a chance,' said Andy.

Doug rolled his eyes and gripped the bags of cash to his chest.

A megaphone boomed into life. 'Come out, you bad men,' said a child's voice. Then there was static and a deeper fuzzy tone. It seemed annoyed. 'This is Tom Mason acting on behalf of the West Midlands . . . leave that alone, Stu. I'm here to negotiate a compro . . .' There were small sounds of squabbling and then a wail.

Doug and Andy looked at one another in amazement.

'They get younger all the time,' said Doug.

The ladies clung on to them as they waded through the tea and spilt foodstuffs. Hanging off the ceiling and spinning on one wire was a placard offering the Early Riser breakfast at £4.65.

'Shocking,' tutted Mrs Chitterden.

Doug got to the doors. 'I'm coming out,' he yelled. 'Don't fire.'

Outside, Tom Mason, who was soothing his son after smacking him on the legs, looked up in surprise.

'You're not that good,' sneered Commander Savage.

Andy rolled the balaclava over his head.

Doug came into his sightline. 'Hold the shotgun by the barrel, otherwise they'll take a pop at you. Move very slowly and do *exactly* what those bastards tell you, OK?'

Andy nodded.

'Good luck, mate.' Doug offered a hand.

They shook. Andy leaned towards him and started to speak but Doug's brow creased and he knew he hadn't been understood. He made to roll up the balaclava but Doug pressed a hand on his shoulder.

'Get out there,' he urged.

Andy's head felt hot under the tight woollen helmet. He gazed back at the scared old women, the ruined restaurant and the blue flashing lights strobing the walls. There was Doug's face, full of anticipation and . . . something else. Hope.

Holding the shotgun at arm's length, he shuffled forward. A cold breeze blew in through the shattered automatic doors and made the hairs on the back of his hands stand up. He stepped into the light, hearing the applause of cocked rifles; seeing the lumbering vehicles, and the shapes of men with the glimmer of infrared at their shoulders. Red spots of light clustered at his chest. He took a faltering pace past the ruined plastic toy car and the beheaded blind charity boy.

The doors slid open, grating as they grazed the shattered glass. His first step out on to tarmac was unsteady, like a drunk leaving a lock-in. The thought occurred to him that service stations were never going to seem quite the same.

Jason was lost. The first field he crossed stank of rotting cabbage and the second had recently been doused in foul-smelling fertiliser. He had slipped several times and his trousers were clinging to his legs like wet sails. He shivered. The service station and the motorway had long ago disappeared from view, and he had lost sight of the lights of Coventry.

He took a few squelching paces, and freezing water seeped in over his ankles. The ground was marshy here. Rather than wade deeper, he made a wide detour and came over a ridge. Below were farmyard buildings. He approached them, clambering over a five-bar gate into a cow field. The sleeping beasts awoke and began to low and bay gently. One after another they rustled to their feet and followed him. Soon the herd had him surrounded. He tried to recall what Danny had told him about the chemical components of the pheromone spray. When the bull shattered the gate, he suddenly remembered.

Behind the eye-slits of the mask, Andy was transfixed in the aurora of light. Savage tore the megaphone from Tom Mason's hands and ordered him to drop his weapon. Andy did so. As directed, he sank to his knees and lay on his stomach with his arms and legs spread wide. His hands were wrenched up behind his back, cuffed and restrained by two officers. The balaclava was pulled from his head and he was lifted to his feet. He was dragged across the carpark and flung into the rear of an armoured van.

'How many of you?'

Andy said nothing. His interrogator was a harried man in a

Kevlar jacket. He looked as if he hadn't slept for about a decade.

'How many hostages?' urged the man.

'The old ladies? About half a dozen. Plus there's another bloke,' added Andy, thinking to include Doug as planned.

'What about the one who came out of the kitchen exit?'

'Is he all right?'

'He'll live. Is he one of yours?'

Tempting. Get Rob in a bit more trouble. 'No, he was a hostage too.'

'How many more inside?'

'There's one in the kitchen. Can you see he gets medical attention?'

The man would have continued to ask questions, but was interrupted by a knock on the van door.

A WPC leaned inside and whispered something. The man cursed and reached down to a black case at his feet. Andy feared that this might be some kind of torturer's portmanteau.

The man produced a Barbie doll and handed it to the WPC.

After that, he retired and Andy was left alone. He heard shouting and running but no one was thrown in with him so he reckoned Doug was still in with a chance. The air sang with sirens and pulsed with light.

On leaving Andy, Tom Mason bought his offspring's silence with the promise of McDonald's, then went to help the ambulance crew shepherd the ladies away from the Granary.

'You'll have to be treated for shock,' he announced.

'Will there be tea?' asked one.

'Yes, there'll be tea.'

A begrudging smile spread over Mrs Lambridge's face. 'There's tea,' she said to Mrs Chitterden.

'Tea,' replied her friend.

The Armed Response Unit flooded the building under the captaincy of Commander Savage.

On entering, they raked their weapons in a wide arc as they secured each area of the restaurant and kitchens. Danny was still comatose where Andy had left him. The fat had hardened on his face, making him resemble an enormous opaque jelly baby. It took six men to stretcher him to the waiting air-ambulance.

As the police came to meet them, Doug urged the ladies forwards. 'They're a bit confused,' he shouted above the commotion. 'We were in here for hours.'

'And you are?' asked one of the police.

'Andrew Crowe. I was trapped in there with them.'

The procession was moving towards the waiting ambulances. Doug had been given a blanket and told he'd be interviewed in full later. He played confused, trying to be helpful whilst keeping a tight rein on the two bags.

They proceeded through a line of spindly trees to the lorry park, and Doug saw his chance.

He gave the nearest pensioner a shove, and she toppled amid shocked gasps. As Mason and one of the ambulancemen bent to help her, Doug stepped backwards, shrugged off his blanket and wrapped the loot in it. He dropped to his knees and spotted the Polo over by the rim of the carpark. Police attention was focused in the other direction, so he skirted round through the bordering trees. Keeping low, he ran to the car, opened the driver's door and hunkered down in the rear seat.

The vehicle stank of petrol, coolant and stale cigarettes, and a bitter wind blew in through the shattered window. Doug listened, wondering if and when they would notice his absence and whether they would again search the cars. Thoughts multiplied as he assessed his chances. Variables: the grannies, the staff, the policewoman who had been there at the start – she'd easily figure out that he and Andy had done a swap. Or would she? Danny had loomed large in the events. Plus, of course, Andy might grass him up again. This wasn't safe. He'd be spotted the moment someone flashed a torch in the car.

He got out and unlocked the hatchback. It was jammed, but gave suddenly with a wrench of metal. Doug ducked, his heart making sledgehammer blows in his chest. Commotion still, but all of it a hundred yards away at the service entrance. He stole a glance from behind the rear wheel. The special ops team had stood down and a pair of them held steaming cups of coffee. He climbed inside the boot, covered himself with the blanket and lowered the lid until only a pencil-thin line of sky was visible. Curling into a foetal position, he rested his head on the money and listened.

The ambulances began to leave, their sirens wailing plaintively back along the motorway. Then came the rattling of chains, the whine of a winch. They were towing away the crashed vehicles. There was nothing in the Mondeo, which could be traced to his bed-sit. No link to his true identity. He checked the pockets of Andy's jacket, making sure he had transferred his passport and plane tickets. They were there. What wasn't was his mobile.

It was ages before the armoured police vans rolled away with the squad cars. All the time, voices shouted orders and people moved around checking and rechecking the service station premises. They were marking out their next paper migraine: taking photos and amassing information – all of which would have to be converted into a mammoth pile of reports. Despite the cold, Doug felt himself drift towards sleep. Each time the dreams drew near, he dug his nails into his shins to keep awake.

The first chirruping of birdsong. How much time had
elapsed? It was past six. Doug cracked open the boot.
Whispers of mist hung low on the ground. He climbed
out, scoped the carpark, and stretched his cramped limbs.
Seemed clear. Hustling the bags into the passenger seat, he got
into the car and took a proper look. Silence save for the
fluttering of police tape in the breeze. He strained to hear
sounds on the motorway. Soon there was a low rumble and
headlights appeared behind him. A long line of articulated
lorries began to wheeze towards the coach park. They had
opened up the road.

He gunned the engine, which started on his fifth attempt.
He went slowly past the service area, which was manned by a
pair of bored-looking beat officers, and slid down on to the
M6.

Following his prepared route, he came back on himself at
the next junction. He didn't speed, being unable to in Andy's
car. He cursed himself for having forgotten his mobile. He
might have called Nelson and delayed him. Or cancelled the
meeting. Improvised something. It was gone six thirty and the
morning traffic was clogging up fast. He headed for the M42,
looking for the airport spur.

He pulled into the airport car park a few minutes past
seven. The sky had lightened and planes boomed overhead,
their vibrations rattling the lampposts. He looked up at the
tall scarp of the Novotel building. Was Pieter up there now? It
didn't seem as though a gun battle was in progress behind the
dull rows of tinted windows, so he decided to proceed.

He pulled out the bags. Something was wrong. There were
three cases. He opened the first to find a file of papers,
handbills, a broken mobile and an old Scotch egg wrapper.
Not his. He placed the other two on the seat and unzipped
them both. He stuck his hand inside and pulled out a
reassuring fistful of notes. He dug deeper and touched a

triangular metal object. What was this? Another gun? There was hardly any money in there. Just the top layer, and an odour.

Fish paste.

And lavender.

Doug stared and shuffled through the bags to the bottom. A thin, rueful smile slowly formed on his face. Ten minutes later he had stacked the wads of bills inside Andy's jacket and was hurrying to the departure terminal.

In a kitchen in Humberstone near Leicester, Mrs Lambridge was counting out twenty-pound notes on her kitchen table as Trinder rubbed up against her legs. She wrote down the sum in shaky Biro on the back of an old beige envelope, then used some elastic bands she had saved to tie them into bundles. She then phoned Mrs Chitterden. The line was engaged. She tried again, making the connection on her third attempt.

'Were you trying to telephone me?' she asked.

'Yes,' said Mrs Chitterden. 'I appear to have some money in my bag.'

'A little under four thousand pounds?'

'Three thousand, seven hundred and eighty,' said Mrs Chitterden.

There was a pause.

'It's the oddest thing,' she continued, 'but I can't for the life of me remember doing the lottery of late. Certainly not winning.'

Mrs Lambridge remembered the brief chat she'd had with Andy at Corley. He had told her that she reminded him of his gran — a woman with selective deafness and a mind as a sharp as a hatpin.

When he then outlined the plan, she assured him neither she nor Mrs Chitterden would tell.

'Very good, dear,' said Mrs Lambridge. 'How about a visit to Osborne House in the spring?'

'What a lovely idea,' replied her friend.

God's head had been dressed and he had patches of gauze on his bruises. Despite his confused state of mind, neither the police nor the ambulancemen could coerce him into going to hospital. Once the WPC had explained to Commander Savage that he was quite the hero for freeing them all, he was allowed to go off on his own. He went for a walk, clambering over into a nearby field and watching the sky until dawn broke.

When it was light he returned and strolled to his usual hitching place on the verge by the slip road. An articulated lorry wheezed to a halt but he turned down the offer of a ride. He did the same to a second truck and a third. It wasn't until a car stopped that he approached the driver.

'Hello,' said the woman. 'Where are you off to, then?'

'South, I think.'

She was thin and in her mid-thirties and wore her hair in a short brown bob. 'Jump in, then.'

The car was warm and smelled nice and the radio was soft in the background.

'What's your name?' she asked as they wove across the lanes.

'I'm not sure,' he said, thinking *I am not God.*

'Well, we'll have to call you something.'

He shrugged. 'What's yours?'

'Pamela.'

'I like that.' He turned round and saw a bulky case on the back seat. 'What's that for?'

'I'm a vet.' She smiled again, then told him of her work. She explained that she lived in Tottenham but that she had been visiting relatives in the Midlands.

He loved her voice. As he listened, he sensed a delicious tingling sensation all over as if he were being stroked. *I am not God*, he thought. Shortly, as they were laughing over some piece of nonsense, she suggested he be named after the next car that overtook them.

It was a Rover.

'I am not God,' he said joyously. 'I am *dog*.'

And with that, he wound down the window, stuck out his head and barked as his hair blew in the breeze.

CHAPTER TWENTY EIGHT

Restart

Rob Gillen had a dislocated shoulder, a bullet wound in his arm and a missing right testicle. In hospital the bullet was removed and bagged for evidence and his wounds were sutured, cleaned and dressed. He was wheeled into a ward for observation but did not regain consciousness that day. Although his pupils responded to stimuli, it was feared he had gone into deep trauma. Later tests proved that, apart from a high blood/alcohol level, he had a clean bill of health. His identity remained a mystery until a nurse came on for the evening shift and recognised him as 'Whatsis-name . . . that fella off the telly'.

When he finally awoke he was not best pleased to discover that his manhood had been decimated. The surgeon explained that he was lucky the bullet had missed the femoral artery or he'd have bled to death. Rob said he'd have preferred to have bled to death and told him to piss off. He told everyone to piss off, except for the attractive colleen who had earlier identified him. If truth were told, Rob was really very upset.

Andy spent the following day in sparsely furnished cells and interrogation rooms. In the latter he encountered a number of detectives whose attitude veered between the pedantic, the patronising and the overtly hostile. He recounted the events of the previous night with precision, except for exaggerating the calibre of his performance to the pensioners.

Although he emphasised that he'd been forced to do the switch at gunpoint, the detectives nagged at his connection with Doug. In their minds, their mutual history and his willingness to be a conspirator were suspect. Despite his repeated denials, they were also convinced that Andy knew of the whereabouts of the stolen money. He stuck to his story that Doug had taken it with him when he left.

At midday, the body of Pieter Muller was discovered in Suite 604 at the Novotel. He had been shot in the head by a nine-millimetre Uzi, a trademark Yardie weapon. No drugs were found on the premises. Ms Kimberley Jones (who found the body) said in her statement that a shaven-headed man had booked the two syndicate rooms the afternoon before. It wasn't until halfway through her shift that she remembered she had forgotten to book the wake-up call. She left it as long as her embarrassment permitted and then phoned up to the room. After twenty minutes without a reply, she went up and found the Dutchman spread-eagled across the conference table with his brains spattered on the blinds. She swore she would never work in the hotel trade again.

Andy's Polo was found in the short-stay carpark adjoining the hotel. His keys were in it and Rob's bag lay on the back seat. There was no sign of the stolen money. The vehicle was dusted for prints and towed to a police pound: no attempt was made to repair the heater or to mend the shattered passenger window.

*　　*　　*

It was not looking good. Andy had no knowledge of the legal process, a factor the police used to their advantage in omitting to offer him the services of a solicitor. Each time he went over his story, it added to the circumstantial evidence. The charges were aiding and abetting; possession of a firearm; criminal damage; and – in lieu of any other suspects – the theft of the money. His case was not helped when the WPC positively ID'd him late that morning.

'Suppose we'd better get you a brief,' said DI Harbury, as he led him back to the cells. He was a man long on intolerance and short on patience.

'You mean a lawyer?'

'I mean a solicitor.'

'I haven't even got an agent.'

The detective's face folded into a sneer. 'You can use the duty solicitor if you want.'

'Do I still get my phone call?'

A nod.

'Can I call anyone?'

'Within reason.'

'Long distance?'

'If necessary.'

'How about the Pope? He does absolution.' The detective stared at him. 'Never mind.'

'You a Catholic, then?'

'No.'

'So why would you want to call the Pope?'

'Forget it. Bad joke. Can I have my call, please?'

DI Harbury marched him along a corridor. Grubby fingermarks adorned its grey-green walls and clambered around the board to which the phone was screwed. He rang Michelle at work and was as usual snubbed by her PA. He hung up.

'She's in a meeting.'

'The Pope isn't female.'

'Not the Pope. My girlfriend. Can I leave a quick message at home?'

'If it's quick.'

Andy left the number of the police station and an urgent précis of what had happened.

Danny One-Slice, after being airlifted to the trauma centre in Birmingham, was rushed to the burns unit. Miraculously, his sight and hearing were undamaged and the surgeon thought it likely he would make a full recovery provided his ox-like constitution survived the rapid detox. This would be ministered under sedation. Medical opinion held that he would need to remain there for months and that he wouldn't be fit to stand trial for the foreseeable future. This was in part due to the skin grafts, which would need time to take and heal, but there was another reason. They had taken several pints of dark molasses-like liquid out of him and were having a whale of a time figuring out just what the hell was in his bloodstream.

Councillor Jacobs's identity was ascertained through dental records. His wife Stephanie was contacted and made a pilgrimage to the morgue to identify the body. Afterwards she contacted Terry Warren at the Birmingham *Evening Mail* to ask of him that he respect the dead and ignore the events of the previous night (including the sex). Terry, who had been frantically writing up the more perverse aspects of the story, assured her that he would. He promptly went to his editor and begged that they go with the more lurid story. After bawling him out for not sticking around to cover the hostage crisis, Terry received a promise that they would see what they could

do. Friday's edition ran with 'Hero Councillor killed in Corley
Massacre'.

The duty solicitor was ill with flu that day. His replacement
was a young man named Steven Kinane, who wore a sharp suit
and a loud tie and who had something of a personal grievance
against the West Midlands Regional Crime Squad. He
immediately claimed that Andy's statement was made under
duress and demanded that the charges be reduced. His client,
he explained, had done all he could to help them with their
enquiries and had no idea of the whereabouts of said contents
of the automatic cash tills. The criminal damage charge was
laughable and all they really had him on was the aiding and
abetting. Andy liked him a lot.

DI Harbury ground his molars as the lawyer harangued the
police for their inefficiency. Somehow the Birmingham Six got
in there: Andy, watching their reactions, suspected that the six
were mentioned a lot when the shit needing stirring. Kinane
was relentless, and by late afternoon Andy had the sense that
the police were losing interest in him as a master criminal.
After much consultation, he was released on bail and a court
appearance was set for one month's time. It had been dark for
some hours by the time they left the police station.

He readily accepted Steven's offer of a celebratory drink
and they went to the nearest pub. It was one belonging to a
brewery chain that liked to ape the spit 'n' sawdust feel
without the sawdust. He downed his first pint then went to
feed the pay-phone in the corner. He had to shout to be heard.

'What was all that about the police?' Michelle asked, her
voice primed with suspicion. 'Are you lying to me, Andy?'

'If I was lying, then why would I still be up here in
Birmingham?'

'Guilt?'

He raised his eyebrows at the wall. She was good with the comebacks. 'Wasn't it on the news?'

'What?'

'The hostage thing.'

'What?'

'At Corley? I was one of the hostages.'

'That was you?' Shock in her voice.

'Yes. I tried to call you . . . hang on.' He slipped in another coin. 'From the police station.'

'My PA didn't tell me that.'

'Miche, if nothing else, can you please downsize that bitch?'

'Were you arrested?'

'Yes. It's a long story.'

'How about starting with that woman on the phone?'

He bared his teeth. 'She was a needle freak.'

'A junkie?'

'Close. Amateur acupuncture. Rob dragged me to this student place so he could audition for *Confessions of a Window Cleaner Part Two.*'

'And you?'

'Nothing happened.' Bad answer, he thought instantly.

'I'm hanging up.'

'Michelle, wait.' He suddenly wished he were in one of those American courts where he could demand that the phrase be 'stricken from the record'. But then he'd have to be a judge. And black. She said something but he couldn't hear. There was a blisteringly loud track on the multi-CD and the pub's in-house metal merchants were sawing at their air guitars like Tourette's sufferers. He pressed the receiver closer.

'Is your car all right?' she asked.

'Buggered.'

'You'd better find a room, then.'

'Yeah, maybe,' said Andy, thinking, But it's only nine o'clock.

There was a pause during which he found it impossible to discern her mood.

'Look, Andy, I'll tell you what – why don't I . . .'

The pips went.

'Miche, I haven't got any more . . .'

The line went dead.

'. . . change,' he added pointlessly. He went back and joined Steven Kinane for another pint. He tried to call again when there was a lull in the decibel storm but the answering machine was on. Steven updated him on Rob's condition, and once they finished wincing they got to talking about comedy. Kinane – surprise, surprise – was fascinated by the job. Andy wasn't up for talking shop and only managed a terse twenty minute diatribe. He was finding it hard to concentrate, and numbness was creeping over him: not nice drunk-numb either, just incredibly tired. 'Do you know where they're holding my car?' he asked.

'Should be in the pound. Want me to try and get it back?'

Steve was still full of energy, hungry and hustling.

Andy cracked open a fresh pack of Marlboro Lites.

'Why the hell not.'

They spent an hour on paperwork before the official deigned to sign the release form. Threading through an automotive graveyard, they navigated dented wrecks and circled deep potholes until they found the Polo sunk in a water-filled rut. A mechanic was inspecting the underbelly of a Saab with a wire-encased bulb.

'Scuse me?' called out Andy. 'Any chance you could give us a hand getting my car out?'

The mechanic emerged and dipped his hands in a tub of

Swarfega. He had sandy hair and a youthful face. 'Which one is it?' he asked, kneading grease from his blackened hands.

'The dead Polo.'

'Came in this morning, right?'

Steven made his farewells while the mechanic looked the car over. 'Keep in touch,' he said.

'Have to. Court, remember?'

'Right. Got my card?'

Andy patted the pocket of Doug's suit jacket and thought of his own missing leather one. Michelle had bought it for him last birthday and he'd been welded to it ever since. He was starting to feel very sad.

'Get home safe,' said Kinane as he walked off.

Andy nodded through a description of how crap his car was from the mechanic. The man offered to have a look at the heater and lights and mentioned he'd got a spare passenger door lying around somewhere. Uncertain as to whether he'd just met the only true altruist in the world or whether he should offer him money, Andy offered him money. All his wages from the gig.

'Do what you can, all right?'

The blackened face brightened. 'Cheers, mate. You can go sit in the office if you like.'

Andy went there and sat and smoked. Heart FM did nothing to warm the room.

The minicab drew up at the same time as the first revving of his engine. A Granada's headlights played across filthy windowpanes and stroked a model on a calendar.

'Andy? You in there?'

He rose and ran, smashing his hip against a table in his hurry to get to the door.

'Miche? What are you . . . ?'

She was there on the other side of the link fence in her ankle-length winter coat and high boots.

He hobbled across and tried to kiss her through the rungs. Conceding that this was no way to conduct a reunion, she paid the driver and came round to join him.

'How the hell did you get here?' he asked, incredulously.

She tapped her head with a woollen finger. 'It's called initiative. I took the train from Euston. On the way up I mobiled that pub you were in and checked out the address. You really *are* going to have to learn about 1471.'

He pulled a vinegar face.

'Then I got a cab from New Street. When you weren't in the pub I called the police station and found out where the car pound was. Da-naa!' She flung her mittened hands wide.

'You're brilliant. All that, just to find me.'

'What else is there to do on a Friday night?'

'Well, there's *Friends* and *Frasier*.'

'Damn. Forgot to tape them.'

He noted that she was wearing his favourite colour of lipstick. Scarlet, freshly applied. He took her in his arms, gripped her tight and kissed her, alternating big and slobbery with slow and grinding.

'God, I missed you,' he said, stroking her hair.

'Never.'

'Am I forgiven, then?'

She gave it to him deadpan.

'Well, I'm not paying for the full-page ad.'

The sky had shaded from azure to eggshell. It was half seven in the morning and the M40 was never going to get any clearer than this. During the night, he'd told her the whole story.

'So, what were you hoping to do by swapping the money over?'

'I wanted the old ladies to get enough of it so Doug wouldn't be able to do his deal. They didn't object.'

'And Doug?'

'Didn't want him getting killed by some drug lord.'

'But you could have refused to help him. The SWAT team would've busted in sooner or later.'

'He had a gun.'

'So did you. He gave you the shotgun.'

'Wasn't loaded.'

She frowned and gazed upwards, working it out. 'You said Danny fired his third shot at the doors and then reloaded.'

'OK, Columbo. It was loaded. But I wasn't going to risk a Mexican stand-off. Did I tell you he shot Rob in the brains?'

'Jesus, no! Is he dead?'

'No, but he's missing a bollock.'

She bit her tongue.

'Hey, let's go out tonight,' Andy suggested. 'Belated Valentine's?'

'You've got a gig, haven't you?'

'Sod that.'

She smiled. 'Really?'

'Yeah. Might take up something less dangerous, like snake-breeding.'

'Not in our flat.'

He put his hand on her thigh and she snuggled into him as they came into London. The sun had burnt the mist off the road and the sky was turning into a cold spring blue. Diesel fumes warmed the air as the city came to life. They rose up on to the Westway, where the light glinted gold off the tower blocks. Michelle rummaged through her bag and found a pair of cheap sunglasses with bright plastic rims. She put them on.

'There's nothing like the drive home, is there?' said Andy. 'This feels like a whole new start.'

He smiled at her and, squinting, lowered the driver's visor.
It came off in his hand.

Danny took a sip of water from the tumbler at his side and
dropped his bandaged arm back to the blanket. Strange, all
this whiteness wrapped around his coffee body – like he'd
been mummified alive. Least he was alive. How long had it
been since the events of that night? Days? Weeks? Could even
be months. Hospital was a lot like prison: regimented, no
clocks and the food was dire.

A tiny hand crawled over his, mou   kles and
squeezing the fingers.

'How you feeling today?'

'Not so bad, Mum.'

Nina patted his hand. The police   ed her
across to the bed and got her settled in th   ual. He
would soon be popping in with a cup of tea from the machine
in the corridor.

'Did you get down to Geriatrics like I told you?'

She pursed her lips. 'You going to nag at me all day,
Daniel?'

Danny let his hand slide to the scabbed-up area on his chin
where his goatee had been.

'You did t   yeah?'

'They assigned me a socialist wor   e flat
is just too bad.' Nina leant in closer, her ey   s she
whispered, 'And Daniel, she says that you   be *top*
of the housing list. Daddy is so pleased.

He turned his face to her, smiling an   moon.
Hers clouded over momentarily.

'Oh, I forget. This came for you.'

She handed him a large brown envelope. The stamps and
postmark were Dutch. He peeled back the gummed edge.

Inside was a postcard of the Amstel in spring. Danny dug in deeper and slipped out a long, ornate paper rectangle. It was an international money order made out in his name for nine thousand pounds sterling.